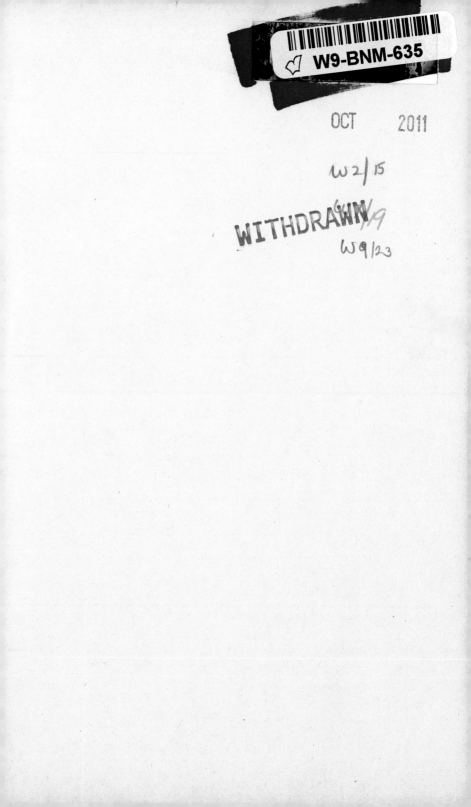

"Inventive and incisive, Bunn's fiction never disappoints. And he's scored again with *Book of Dreams*. Don't miss this one."

—Jerry B. Jenkins, *New York Times* bestselling author
of the Left Behind series

"*Book of Dreams* is wonderful. Davis Bunn has created a literary delight that underscores the power of God's word. A page-turner with an inspiring supernatural element. I could not put this down."

—Anne Graham Lotz, bestselling author of *Just Give Me Jesus*

"*Book of Dreams* is an exceptional story. The concept itself is re-markably fresh, with a genuinely unique design. There are very few inspirational-style concepts that have the potential to cross over and become major mainstream hits. In my opinion, *Book of Dreams* is at the top of this list. Exciting, relevant, and accessible. A remarkable story, one that will linger long after the book is put down."

—Norman Stone, producer/director of *Shadowlands*

"*Book of Dreams* is a fascinating read. A totally new concept, which makes it a rare achievement. The story really makes you think. The theme is both very challenging and mesmerizing. A first-rate effort."

—Hy Smith, former executive vice president,
United International Pictures

BOOK

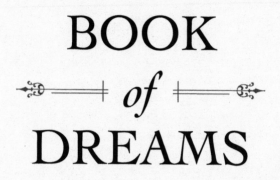

of

DREAMS

BOOKS BY DAVIS BUNN

Lion of Babylon

The Black Madonna

Gold of Kings

All Through the Night

My Soul to Keep

Heartland

Imposter

The Book of Hours

The Great Divide

Winner Take All

The Lazarus Trap

Tidings of Comfort and Joy

Acts of Faith Series (with Janette Oke)

The Centurion's Wife

The Hidden Flame

The Damascus Way

BOOK

of

DREAMS

A Novel

DAVIS BUNN

HOWARD BOOKS
A DIVISION OF SIMON & SCHUSTER, INC.

NEW YORK   NASHVILLE   LONDON   TORONTO   SYDNEY   NEW DELHI

Howard Books
A Division of Simon & Schuster, Inc.
1230 Avenue of the Americas
New York, NY 10020

First Howard Books trade paperback edition October 2011

HOWARD and colophon are trademarks of Simon & Schuster, Inc.

For information about special discounts for bulk purchases, please contact Simon & Schuster Special Sales at 1-866-506-1949 or business@ simonandschuster.com.

The Simon & Schuster Speakers Bureau can bring authors to your live event. For more information or to book an event contact the Simon & Schuster Speakers Bureau at 1-866-248-3049 or visit our website at www.simonspeakers.com.

Designed by Jaime Putorti

Manufactured in the United States of America

10   9   8   7   6   5   4   3   2   1

Library of Congress Control Number: 2010041810

ISBN 978-1-4165-5670-1
ISBN 978-1-4516-1055-0 (ebook)

This book is dedicated to:
Allen Arnold,
whose vision and enthusiasm inspire us all

BOOK

of

DREAMS

1

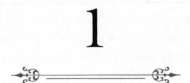

Teddy Wainwright was a very happy man. Not many people had the chance to reinvent themselves at the ripe old age of sixty-three. He finished typing his resignation, hit the Send button, and gave a satisfied sigh. Shirley would be so proud of him.

His young aide set the photographs of Teddy's wife and daughters into the last crate. "That's the lot, sir."

"Thank you again for your help." Teddy slipped his aide a letter. He had been up until almost dawn, working and reworking the words. There was so much to pack into a few paragraphs. The envelope bore his wife's name. Nothing more. "Here, put this on top."

"No problem, sir." His aide set the envelope in the box and fitted on the lid. "I'd just like to say again how sorry I am you're going."

"That makes two of us." His secretary of nineteen years walked through his open door and waved the multiple copies of his formal resignation. "This is so hot it must be radioactive."

Teddy Wainwright signed each letter in turn. "This is also a long time coming."

"Your daughter's on the phone."

"Put her through." He reached over his desk and shook his aide's hand. "I wish you every success in your new position."

"I could come with you, sir. Matter of fact, I'd like to."

"You're better off here." Teddy had rewarded the young man's loyalty by promoting him to a junior vice presidency. "The legislation required to formally start the financial oversight commission is months off. Until then, I'll be cooling my heels in Washington. Which is why I haven't even invited my secretary to join me. Yet."

"I'm a patient guy. You should know that by now."

"If or when things get going, I'll give you a call, see if you're still interested." Teddy lifted the receiver, waved his former aide through the door, and said to his elder child, "Perfect timing."

"You really did it?"

"The letters are winging their way to the board and the papers as we speak."

"Mom must be so thrilled."

Teddy Wainwright turned and stared at the spot where his wife's photograph had sat since he had become president of the Centurion Bank seven years earlier. His throat was so tight he found himself unable to respond.

His daughter asked, "When are you giving the speech?"

Teddy checked his watch, though there was no need. He had been counting the minutes for a month. Longer. "Five hours."

"I called because I wanted you to know Sis and I are here together and we'll be praying for you."

He had to clear his throat twice before he could say, "Thank you, honey. That means the world."

"Go out there and knock 'em dead."

"I intend to."

"They've had this coming for a long time."

"Too long."

She hesitated a long moment, then said softly, "I'm so proud of you, Daddy."

Teddy Wainwright told his daughter good-bye, then pressed the phone to his heart. He held it there long enough for the receiver to emit the beeping alarm, telling him to cut the connection. His secretary reentered his office and saw him sitting there, staring out the window. "Everything all right?"

"Everything is fine." He set the receiver down in the cradle and wiped his eyes. "Everything is just great."

"The garage just called to say your car is waiting downstairs. I checked with the airport and your plane is inbound. And your wife is on line three."

Teddy Wainwright rose from his chair, plucked his suit jacket from the back of his door, and slipped it on. "Tell Shirley I'll call her from the car."

His secretary handed him a plastic file. "Your speech."

"Thank you."

"I hope you know what you're doing."

"I do."

"The banks won't like this. It's one thing for some politician or journalist to take aim. But when one of their own turns on them, it's war."

Teddy Wainwright heard both her years of experience and her very real fear. But all he felt was the same sensation as the previous evening, kneeling on the floor of his home office. The strength he had known at that point, the conviction, the certainty. He slipped the speech into his briefcase. "I should have done this years ago."

She did not say anything more, just stepped away from his office door. They had said all the farewells that were necessary, shared the meals and the hugs and the tears. His departure was anticlimactic.

Teddy crossed the foyer shared by the bank's five senior executives and the boardroom. All the doors were shut. His so-called friends had turned their collective back on him. The other two secretaries refused to meet his gaze. When Teddy reached the elevators, his secretary was still standing in the doorway to his former office, a strong, intelligent woman who had watched his back for years. Worried for him.

Like everyone else on Wall Street, the bank's executives used so many limos that they had their own parking area just beyond the handicapped zone in the basement garage's first level. Teddy did not recognize the driver, but this was nothing new. The man was pale-skinned and lean, with clean hands and a well-pressed suit. He held Teddy's door, then slipped behind the wheel and said, "We're headed to Teterboro Airport, Mr. Wainwright?"

"That's correct."

"You want me to call ahead, make sure your plane's ready?"

"That won't be necessary. Would you mind rolling up the divider? I need to make a call."

"No problem, sir. There's coffee in the thermos."

"Thank you." Teddy pulled his phone from his jacket, but before he could punch in his home number, the phone rang. Teddy checked the readout and recognized the senator's office. "Wainwright."

"Good morning, Mr. Wainwright, this is Allison, in Senator Richard's office?"

"Yes, Allison." Teddy recalled a pert young woman who managed to turn every sentence into a question. "What can I do for you?"

"The press has been showing a *huge* interest in your talk, so the senator was wondering, could we shift your testimony forward an hour so your comments can make the evening news?"

"Let me check my schedule." He opened his briefcase and scanned the typed page his secretary had slipped into the folder with his speech. "I'm due to arrive at Reagan National at two thirty."

"The senator will be *so* pleased. Can I ask, do you prefer to be addressed as Theodore?"

"Teddy is fine."

"Thank you. One more thing, Mr. Wainwright, could we

please make sure you'll hold your opening remarks to fifteen minutes? This is *so* important, since the committee members will want their responses to make the newscast—"

"Fifteen minutes will be more than adequate."

Terry cut the connection and cradled the phone between his hands. He had spoken several times before the US Senate's Banking Committee. But on previous occasions he had always been part of a team. His last time seated before the curved dais had been the worst, when the Wall Street banks had come hat in hand to the federal government, begging for a bailout. One they did not deserve. Everything Teddy had spoken into the microphone had fallen from his mouth like dead weight. A ton of lies strung together with desperation and urgency.

Well, not this time.

He phoned his wife. When Shirley answered, he said, "I had the sweetest call from our daughter."

"She and her sister have their entire prayer group coming over. They're going to watch you on C-SPAN."

Sunlight played between the New York high-rises, dappling his side window. He and his older daughter had fought a series of increasingly bitter disputes throughout her teenage years. Then the year she graduated from university, Shirley had brought their daughter to faith. And everything had changed. At least for her.

Teddy had held out for a good deal longer.

Until nine months and three days ago, to be exact.

His wife went on, "I'm supposed to already be over there. But I wanted to speak with you first." Shirley had been living in a state of perpetual joy ever since he had agreed to pray with her. But Shirley did not sound happy now. She sounded frightened. "Are you sure this is what you want to do?"

The previous nine months should have been the happiest of his own life as well, at least on the surface. Teddy did not merely believe that his burdens had been lifted, he *knew* this. He was *convicted* by the reality of his freedom.

And that was where the problem lay.

Teddy Wainwright was a victim of his own success. He had lived a life of unbounded ambition and greed. He was a skilled manipulator and a man accustomed to wielding almost unlimited financial power.

Now he had been saved from himself and his misdeeds. But this freedom came at a price. The eyes of his soul had been opened. Coming face-to-face with his true nature, in the one mirror he could not ignore, was a dreadful experience.

Teddy realized Shirley was still waiting for his response. "This is not only what I want. It's what God wants too."

Shirley was a solid woman. Strong and beautiful, both inside and out. "The years I've prayed, hoping someday you might speak those words."

Teddy pressed a fist to his chest, trying to push the emotions back inside. "I'm sorry it took me so long."

They shared a moment's silence, then Shirley said, "What about all the things you used to describe the opposition? 'Vindictive, murderous, determined to crush anyone who stands in their path.' Those were your words, not mine."

Teddy knew she was hoping for a soothing word, a promise of assurance. But he was not going to lie. Not today. "I had a remarkable experience last night."

"You certainly were late coming to bed."

"I like the quiet hours when the world is asleep. God seems a lot closer then."

"Hold on just a moment, please." Shirley set down the phone. Teddy thought he heard her sob. He bit down hard on his own emotions. If he started now he might not be able to stop. Besides, the limo driver kept glancing at him in the rearview mirror. Shirley picked up the phone, sniffed loudly, and said, "All right, darling. I'm back."

"I finished my speech and was sitting there with the Bible open in my lap. And it felt like God entered the room."

Her voice was unsteady as she replied, "Maybe he did."

"I've had some amazing moments recently. But nothing like this."

"God spoke to you?"

Teddy stared out the window, and recalled the overwhelming sense of *presence*. The unquestionable sense of eternity. "Not in words, no. But the message was very clear just the same."

"What did he tell you?"

Teddy took a long breath. "I have to do this, Shirley."

She wanted to argue. Teddy felt her tension and fear radiate over the phone. But all she said was, "Will you be coming back tonight?"

The need for total honesty restricted his response. "As soon as I am able."

"I love you, darling."

Once again Teddy cradled the phone tight to his chest, and ended the conversation with a prayer of thanks.

The limo gained speed as it pulled onto the freeway. Teddy fanned the speech across his lap. Six pages in all. Double-spaced, printed in an oversize font so he could look up at the senators and then find his place easily. Each page took just over two minutes to read. He had a great deal more that he intended to say. But the specific details would come out during questioning. Teddy knew his remarks would have much more impact if it appeared that the senators' questioning drew him out. He intended to use the questions, however they were phrased, to make sure these revelations emerged.

One passage in particular caught his eye:

It is not enough that the banks' misadventures brought the world's economies to the brink of disaster. Wall Street is not satisfied with all the distress they have created for our economy and political system. The leaders of our nation's

*largest banks are intent upon repeating the same dire mis-
takes all over again.*

Teddy had been redrafting that paragraph the previous evening
when the divine force had filled the room. Now the limo's tires
zinged and rumbled as it accelerated through traffic. Rushing
him toward a new destiny. Teddy felt the same undeniable presence return.

He had faced a series of choices that he now saw stretched
back to that first night when he had gotten down on his knees.
Each one had carried a genuine threat to the way he had previously viewed his life, stripping away one lie after another. And at
the same time, each choice had drawn him a bit closer to yesterday's experience. He had not realized that at the time, of course.
All he had known was a sense of divine rightness, of reknitting
the nation's financial fabric and restoring some of what he had
himself helped destroy. Teddy read:

> *I have accepted the position of chairman of the new finan-
> cial oversight commission precisely because this insanity
> must be stopped. The banks intend to neuter this commis-
> sion before it is fully formed. I know this for a fact. Their
> aim is to render the commission powerless. The American
> people demand new financial oversight. The banks have
> resigned themselves to this. So now they have shifted tac-
> tics. Their Washington lackeys are peddling influence and
> spending money, pressuring Congress to transform the
> commission into mere window dressing. This cannot be al-
> lowed to happen.*

The sound of honking horns drew Teddy's gaze from the page.
He realized the limo was slowing and maneuvering out of the
fast lane. He tapped the intercom button and asked, "What's the
matter?"

"The engine just cut out, sir." As the driver spoke, it happened again. This time Teddy felt as much as heard it. The motor went silent, coughed, then picked up again. The limo was so heavy that its forward momentum softened the jerks. "It was going fine until . . . There it goes again."

The motor fluttered, surged, then died a third time. The driver turned on the flasher and steered toward the curb. He tucked the car into a bus stop. He rolled down the glass divider and said, "I'll ring central and have them send you another car . . ." The driver studied his cell phone's readout. Then he turned around and said, "Mr., ah . . ."

"Wainwright."

"Sure. Could you check and see if your phone has a signal?"

Teddy opened his phone. "Apparently not."

"We must be sitting in a dead zone." The driver turned the key. The engine clicked but did not fire. He shook his head and opened the car door. Instantly the limo was filled with the roar of midday traffic. "I'll just walk around the corner to where I can phone this in, Mr. Wainwright. Shouldn't be long."

Teddy did not speak. There was nothing to be said. The car door shut, leaving him isolated. But not alone.

The sensation was far stronger now. Although it was unlike anything Teddy had ever experienced, he had no question what was happening. There was simply no room for doubt.

A young woman appeared by the same corner the driver had just rounded. She was very attractive though quite small, and carried herself with an air of fresh innocence. Teddy sat and watched her open the rear door and slide into the seat beside him. She had a pixie's face and round, gray eyes, clear and seemingly without guile. "A limo. Wow. I guess you must be someone really important."

Her hand emerged from the pocket of her raincoat, holding something that might have been a silver pen. When the image had come to him the previous evening, Teddy had faced a dark wraith, little more than a twisting shadow.

Teddy stared at the woman, and for a fleeting instant found

himself seeing her true form. He realized the image had been absolutely true.

His mind locked on to the verse from Second Corinthians that he'd been reading the previous evening when the room filled with that undeniable force. Just like now. "So we fix our eyes not on what is seen, but on what is unseen, since what is seen is temporary, but what is unseen is eternal."

As the young woman reached toward him, Teddy said, "I've been expecting you."

2

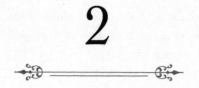

FRIDAY

Friday morning, Elena unlocked her office's front door and stepped into the reception area. She shut the door on the rumbling bus traffic and the early-morning sunshine. The receptionist Elena shared with her five colleagues had not yet arrived. Elena checked her image in the antique mirror opposite the desk. The mirror had only been hung the previous week. It was silver backed and six feet tall and veined like a crone's face. The mirror was positioned so the receptionist could survey the entire waiting room from behind her desk. It showed a distinguished-looking woman in a fawn-colored suit, with long, auburn hair and a timeless gaze. Elena was going to have to discipline herself to avoid looking in that direction, for the action was a futile gesture. After nine years as a practicing clinical psychologist, Elena did not need to inspect her reflection to know her professional mask was in place. And there was nothing she could do about the vacuum that lay beneath.

The world knew Elena Burroughs as a foremost authority on dreams. For three years and counting, her book had topped the bestseller lists around the globe. *The Book of Dreams* had sold eighteen million copies and been published in three dozen languages. Her rare public appearances were sold-out events.

For Elena, that one glance in the mirror was enough to reveal the lie.

She loathed the adulation that surrounded her infrequent lectures. She no longer did any publicity or televised events. She hated herself too much afterward.

Elena climbed the carpeted staircase to her office on the British first floor. The entire building still smelled faintly of fresh paint. When the university had begun renovating their offices the previous autumn, Elena had inserted herself forcefully into the process. One of her defining traits was impatience with anything that did not move at a pace to match her own. And if a single word described the University of Oxford's approach to any change, it was *glacial.*

Elena persuaded a reluctant university to give her the sum planned for the renovations. She then doubled it with funds of her own. What she really wanted was an office to match those she had often seen in the United States. Modern and discreet and elegant in a properly subdued fashion. She knew anything the university did was going to wind up looking like a newer version of the stodgy interior they replaced. And the only way she could get what she wanted was to give it to everyone. From the receptionist to the newest associate in the fourth-floor garret. Even the elevator was new, a sleek tube that moved silently between the floors.

Her grateful associates all took the renovations as a sign of her having recovered from the tragedy that had dominated her life for five long years. Elena saw no need to correct them.

Elena used the ninety minutes before her first patient to catch up on her paperwork. Gradually the building around her began to hum with activity. She smelled fresh-brewed coffee and heard friendly banter in the reception area downstairs. At five minutes to nine, Elena checked her computerized calendar for the day and frowned. She rose from her desk and walked back downstairs.

The main entrance opened into a brief hallway leading to the reception area and Fiona Floate's kingdom. Fiona was the lone secretary for the entire building, and the only one they needed. Her new roost was an ergonomic chair behind a long elm counter, one shade darker than the maple floors. A Japanese vase held a spray of tulips and baby's breath. The florist had a standing order to provide three matching displays every Monday, for the reception desk and Elena and the other female clinician. Elena assumed her male colleagues could buy flowers for themselves. The two women had never thanked Elena. Elena considered their silence a perfect example of British understatement.

Elena waited while Fiona directed an arriving patient into the redesigned waiting area. Only two of the offices had antechambers, Elena's and the director's. Patients for the other counselors waited in the public area opposite Fiona's desk. When they were alone, Elena leaned over the counter and said, "My nine o'clock."

"Mmmm." Fiona did not check her computer. She did not need to. Ever.

"What happened to Richard?" Her regular appointment was a postdoc student with an almost crushing burden of self-loathing.

"Quite ill, actually. Physical ailment, for a change. I slotted this in yesterday."

"I did not see a last name for my appointment."

"A good thing, that, since I wasn't given one."

"Is she a student?"

"Not that I am aware."

Oxford's system permitted the clinicians to accept patients from outside the university. This was necessary, as treatment of patients did not simply end upon graduation. Since her fame began spreading, however, Elena had stopped accepting new patients from beyond the university perimeter. The risk of being confronted with another rabid fan was just too great.

Fiona answered her unspoken question. "Miriam referred this patient. She asked that Sandra be slotted in. Immediately."

This was news. "Miriam phoned?"

"Yes, Elena. Miriam phoned."

"When?"

"Yesterday evening after you left."

"Why didn't she try my mobile?"

"Do you know, I didn't ask." Fiona was clearly enjoying this. "One might assume it was because she didn't want to speak with you. Perhaps in order not to be pestered with questions for which Miriam didn't have answers."

"Oh, thank you so very much."

"My pleasure. Will there be anything else?"

Elena returned to her office. She was in the process of phoning her closest friend when the outer door opened.

The university counseling offices were located in what once had been a private residence on Broad Street, an avenue bisecting the central city. Elena's office occupied a formal parlor. The room had been divided into a small antechamber and a larger office that looked over the building's rear garden. Elena had fitted sliding double doors between the antechamber and her office. Through the open doors she observed a man in a navy suit enter and survey her waiting area. He then crossed the room, nodded once to her, and scanned the office. Then he retreated to the outer door.

More than two dozen heads of state had formerly studied at Oxford. The current student body included family members from the sultan of Brunei, three former US presidents, the prime minister of Israel, the kings of Saudi Arabia and Jordan, and leaders of nine other nations.

Elena knew a professional bodyguard when she saw one.

Elena rose to her feet as the woman entered. She was perhaps a decade older than Elena's thirty-five years. She carried herself with the casual elegance of someone who had handled both money and power for so long, they formed a second skin. She was dressed in a beige cashmere cloud and pearls.

The bodyguard slid the double doors shut, sealing the two of them inside.

Elena spoke the name on her computer screen. "Sandra?"

"That is correct." The woman's accent was unmistakable. Northeastern United States, perhaps Canada.

"I am Dr. Burroughs."

"You are American as well?"

"I am. Won't you have a seat?"

"Thank you." The woman carried herself without the nerves of most first-time patients. She chose the rosewood Louis XIV chair drawn up to the other side of Elena's desk and said, "You came highly recommended."

Elena knew the woman expected her to ask how she knew Miriam, or what the woman's last name was. Instead, Elena resumed her seat and waited.

The elegant woman asked, "Are you recording, Dr. Burroughs?"

Elena lifted the top of a Georgian silver box that rested on the desk next to the telephone. Hidden inside were a set of four electronic controls. "This first button is the general alarm. It rings at both the receptionist desk and inside my director's office. All of the offices have one. The second button cuts off my phone. I press it, and the light on my phone goes from green to red, see? The third locks the doors leading to the outer office—"

"Please don't touch that button."

"Very well. I will leave the doors unlocked as per your request." Elena held to the monotone she used with her most fractured patients. "See? The light remains green."

"The fourth button?"

"That cuts on my recorder. I have a digital system installed in my top right drawer. The light turns green when the recorder is on. Would you like to see it?"

"That won't be necessary."

"Please, I would prefer that—"

"No thank you."

"Very well."

The woman opposite her did not relax as Elena might have expected. Instead, a faint tremor ran through her slender frame. Only then did Elena realize how much control the woman imposed upon herself. The woman said, "Thank you for your candor."

Elena did not speak.

The woman's hands did a skittish dance from the chair arms to her lap and back again. "I am having dreams."

Elena waited.

"Nightmares, actually. Worse than that."

Elena nodded once and remained silent.

"They are so vivid I find myself unable to leave them behind. They shade my entire existence. They shatter my days as well as my nights."

Elena watched the woman age as she spoke. "How long have you been having these dreams?"

"Twenty-six days."

Elena blinked. Nightmares generally did not show a clearly pronounced arrival. She had never heard of such a thing before. Even if they did arrive suddenly, patients were unable to date them so precisely. "They come every night?"

"*It,*" the woman corrected. "One dream. Always the same. And yes, it attacks every night. Many times."

"You have had this dream more than once in the same night?"

"The first doctor I approached prescribed a very strong sleeping pill." The woman shuddered at the memory. "All the drug did was hold me down, where the nightmare could claw at me. Six times."

"You're sure it was six?"

"Of course I'm sure. Why, what does that mean?"

Elena shook her head. Such precision was unheard of.

The woman continued, "For the first time in my married life,

I am sleeping in a separate room from my husband. My screams kept shredding his nights. And Lawrence . . ."

Elena understood the woman's hesitation. "Let's pretend that this isn't the first time we're talking. Let's pretend that we have been friends for years. And as a friend, I will treat your problem with the utmost seriousness and care. I will not try to smother your symptoms with drugs. I want one thing, and one thing only. To help you."

Generally Elena waited a few sessions to be so open with a new patient. She needed to ensure that the patient was indeed someone who sought help. And would respond to such a direct approach. Oftentimes those who most needed help were also terrified of the prospect. In such cases, a direct invitation would only slow down the opening process.

But Elena sensed that this woman was different. It was more than her intelligence, or her desperately concealed need. These symptoms suggested a completely new issue, one that confounded the standard dream doctrine. They invited a new approach. Elena went on, "Let's pretend that you can tell me everything. It's clear that you want to. And I want to hear. And nothing, not a single solitary thing, will ever escape this room. Including who your husband is. And what he does. And why your dreams terrify you both."

The woman responded by coming apart. She folded so fast, she almost managed to hide the deep creases that marred her lovely features. She began weeping convulsively.

Elena was up and moving and there to catch the woman as she slid off her chair and landed on her knees.

3

Elena called the hospital, then arranged for Fiona to reschedule her next two appointments. They took the
woman's Mercedes limo to the John Radcliffe, the university
teaching hospital. A receptionist directed them through the
crowded waiting room, down a long hallway, and into an empty
MRI chamber. Elena's new patient treated this rare immediate
treatment as merely par for the course.

Elena stayed in the control room while her new patient underwent a brain scan. One of the woman's bodyguards remained
in the hallway, the other stood against the wall behind Elena.
Though the two young technicians performing the scan said
nothing, Elena could sense that the bodyguard's presence
spooked them both.

While the woman was deep inside the machine, the doctor
slipped into the room. His name was Robards, and he had been
the best friend of Elena's former husband. Elena thought he had
aged considerably since their last meeting. She supposed they
all had.

The doctor's aloof greeting reminded Elena of her husband,
who had abhorred any show of affection around the hospital.

Robards swept up the woman's chart, studied it a moment, and said, "I see you've failed to enter her name."

"That is correct."

He glanced at Elena, then at the bodyguard, and went back to the file. "What precisely are we looking for?"

"I wish I knew."

"Symptoms?"

"Severe nightmares. Traumatic stress. Related issues."

"Any severe pain?"

"None other than what might be put down to interrupted sleep cycles."

"Seizures?"

"None. Right now I am simply hoping to eliminate the worst."

He set down the folder and leaned over the largest of the three screens; he studied it a moment, then asked, "Anything so far?"

The chief technician replied, "No evident anomalies that I have detected."

Robards straightened. "I'm due in surgery. Shouldn't be long. I'll have a look at your mystery woman's results when I'm done."

"Thank you, Reggie. For everything."

When he reached the door, he offered Elena a terse smile. "At least she brought you out here again. I suppose I should be grateful for that favor."

While they waited for the results, Elena held the woman's hand. "Will you tell me your name?"

The radiology waiting room was one of three open-ended chambers that fronted the tea counter. To their left was the sitting area for lab tests. Beyond that was a nursery shared with the pediatrics wing. The children's play area was sealed, but the din still echoed through all three rooms. The noise isolated the two women.

The woman studied Elena for a long moment, then replied, "Sandra Harwood."

"It is nice to meet you, Sandra. I am Elena."

"My husband asked me not to tell you who I was." She turned away. "Lawrence will be livid."

One of Sandra's bodyguards stood by the exit, across the room from where they sat. The other had returned to the limo. Elena said, "My husband was a biochemist doing research here at the Radcliffe. I have not been back since I cleaned out his office."

"He died?"

"Five years ago. I miss him terribly."

That brought Sandra's nerves closer to the surface. "I don't know what I would do without Lawrence. Wither on the vine, no doubt."

The words might have been plucked from Elena's own shrunken heart. "Is your husband ill?"

"Lawrence is extremely healthy for his age. He has a regular checkup. There are a couple of minor issues, but nothing that could be considered threatening."

Speaking those words caused Sandra's eyes to well up. Which was hardly a surprise, given the nightmare she had related to Elena. That knowledge, and the hold Sandra kept on her hand, pressured Elena to say, "This week marks the point at which I have been a widow the same amount of time that I was married. My husband was eleven years older than me. He was a celebrated biochemist looking into rare blood types at Duke, where I did my clinical training. I followed him here. Jason loved everything about Oxford. After he died, I had every intention of returning home. But I never did. I suppose I hoped that by remaining here I might hold on to a bit of his passion. Jason was passionate about everything. Life, love, Oxford." She took a breath that should have come far easier after all that time. "Me."

Elena had told this new patient far too much of herself and did not care. The memories were a boisterous mob. She had half hoped that returning to Jason's professional abode would not hurt quite so bad after five years. She should have known better. Yet the shared information served a purpose. Elena valued how Sandra Harwood had confessed her name. She reciprocated by sharing secrets of her own.

Their conversation was halted by the arrival of two of Jason's former colleagues, who had obviously been alerted to Elena's presence by the radiologist. Elena endured their warmth as she would a visit to the dentist. She did not need their recollections and their sorrow to miss Jason.

The radiologist arrived while the two biologists were still waxing on about the vacuum Jason had left behind. Robards shooed them away, then addressed his words to Elena. Evidently he was still very uncomfortable dealing with an unnamed patient. "The preliminary results indicate a complete all-clear. I've detected nothing that even raises the hint of trouble. Completely normal in all respects. A well-functioning and healthy brain."

Sandra had remained seated throughout. "I am indeed grateful, Doctor."

Elena added her own thanks, then ushered Sandra Harwood over to where the bodyguard waited. She made an appointment to see the woman after the weekend break and refused Sandra's offer of a ride back to her office. Elena's time with the woman had come to an end. The medical examination and Elena's confession of personal details had established a rapport. Sandra Harwood now saw Elena as a source of clarity in a frightening time. Anything further ran the risk of establishing an emotional dependency.

Elena waved the woman and her limo into the Friday sunlight, hoping she would never need to learn what it meant to travel with four inches of bulletproof glass between herself and the world. She climbed into a waiting taxi and allowed herself a final glance back at the window that had once belonged to Jason's office.

Clinical psychologists were not supposed to use terms such as *soul mate*. Nor were they permitted to ever suggest that emotional wounds were a permanent fixture. Or that a life would always remain hollowed by loss. Elena grimly hoped that perhaps one day she would stop waking up in the middle of the night, furious with Jason over how he had abandoned her.

The closer the taxi drew to Oxford city center and her office, the larger her other concern loomed.

Elena had no idea what the woman's problem might be. Or how she should go about treating her. None whatsoever.

4

SATURDAY

Elena did not sleep well. This was hardly a surprise. Sleep had long been a reluctant friend, one who appeared and vanished with whimsical regularity. What was different about this night was that Elena did not care.

Saturday morning she took the train into London, and then the tube from Paddington Station to Notting Hill. Elena walked through the market, pausing to buy flowers and a jar of figs preserved in ginger and honey. Miriam's house was a half mile farther on, a detached Victorian that crowned a steep side-street. Miriam had a photograph in her entryway taken a century before, when the lane had been shaded by elms so vast they formed a green tunnel. The few trees that remained were now surrounded by metal fences, placed there to keep vehicles from shouldering them aside in their desperate search for parking space. Yet the lane still held the charm of a bygone era. The sidewalks were empty save for the sunlight and a late-spring breeze. The market's clamor swiftly faded. Elena climbed the stairs and shifted her purse and packages so she could pull the old-fashioned bell-knob.

Miriam Al-Quais opened the door, saying, "Ah. You've come. I hoped you might."

"You knew I would." Elena kissed the proffered cheek. The act brought back the fondest memories of her childhood. The cool skin, the fragrance of crushed rose petals. "How are you?"

"What a question to ask someone of my years. Come in, my dear. Such lovely flowers. And figs. Shame on you. You will make an old woman fat."

Miriam Al-Quais led her back through a house of soft shadows, sunlit alcoves, and faint flavors drawn from Elena's earliest recollections. Miriam was her mother's dearest friend and Elena's own godmother. Elena's grandparents had sent their daughter off to England for a year of finishing school. The only bright spot to that dismal period, spent inside a drafty old monstrosity of a Jacobean manor, had been the school counselor. Miriam and Elena's mother had remained friends ever since.

Miriam's name, Al-Quais, was as famous as it was ancient. Al-Quais was one of the few Christian lineages that had survived the birth of Islam. Her family had once been residents of Tyre, the most famous port within the Phoenician trading empire. According to family lore, they had been converted to Christianity during the apostle Paul's first missionary journey. Miriam had populated Elena's childhood with such marvelous tales, always related as irrefutable fact.

Miriam Al-Quais carried herself with severe gravity. She was a smallish woman with hennaed hair bundled tightly against the back of her head. At eighty-one, her features remained even and remarkably unlined. Her eyes were her most astonishing feature, two dark and burning coals. They probed deeply and invited an intimacy that Miriam seldom returned.

Miriam had always maintained a certain aloof distance from Elena. Her affection for the younger woman had rarely been stated. Yet Miriam's imprint upon her life ran deep. Miriam had been a clinical psychologist for over forty years. Miriam had been the reason why Elena became a clinician. When Elena had accompanied her husband to England, Miriam had come out of retirement to sponsor Elena's passage through the British examination and licensing process. Miriam had been a very strict supervisor and treated their sessions as training times. She discussed at length potential differences between the British and American psyches. She lectured more than she listened. And Elena counted herself among the most fortunate of students.

Elena entered the kitchen and performed the ritual begun during her earliest training sessions. She made tea and served it in the sterling silver service and the Wedgwood china. They sat on Miriam's rear sunporch. The furniture was wicker with quilted padding.

Elena asked, "How much do you know of my new patient?"

"Nothing whatsoever. I was called by a trusted friend, a Harley Street physician. The friend asked for a referral. I do not even know the patient's name."

"Why did you phone the appointment through yourself?" Normally the patient, or the patient's primary-care physician, would make the initial connection.

Miriam sipped her tea. The china was so fragile that Elena could see the arthritic curl to Miriam's fingers through the cup. "My friend stressed the urgency. I thought my initiating contact would accelerate the process."

"So you have no idea who my patient is."

"I just said that."

There was no insult in repeating the question, and both women knew this. Elena was formally establishing the confidence required to consult with another clinician about a patient. "In that case, I need to ask your advice. The patient is female, in apparently excellent health, aged in her early fifties. Well educated, poised, intelligent. Accompanied by two bodyguards who certainly appeared to know their business."

Sunlight dappled the room. The house sat on a hillside overlooking the London sprawl. In the distance, Hyde Park spread out like an oval green carpet. Miriam sat opposite her. She had not so much aged as moved beyond the reach of time.

"The patient has been suffering from nightmares for twenty-six days. Actually, that is incorrect. She has experienced a repetition of one single nightmare. And as the dream has recurred every night since it began, I can only assume it is now twenty-seven days and counting."

Elena told her everything she knew of the dream.

Sandra Harwood had not called it a dream at all. She had called it an experience, as vivid as any waking moment. Which only made the event all the more grueling.

The dream had remained constant over the nights and the weeks. The only alteration had been its frequency. Some nights it only attacked her once. Other nights it came as many as six times. Every assault, except the night she had been held down by a sleeping pill, ended with her standing or kneeling beside her bed, screaming with terror.

Each time, the dream began with the sound of cheering.

Sandra Harwood stared out over huge crowds. Enormous. She stood upon a stage and waved to a throng one degree off berserk.

There were television cameras everywhere. Blank glass eyes that followed her every move. And balloons. And bunting. And signs. And colors and hats and horns.

The indoor stadium was packed. Sandra Harwood shared the stage with a half dozen others.

She was the center of attention, and yet she was not. She waved to people she couldn't really see. She smiled, exhilarated with the energy and the power that pulsated through the auditorium.

She was more excited than she had ever been in her entire life. The streamers and the confetti fell like multicolored snow. The auditorium appeared filled with a billion fractured rainbows.

At the center of the stage, a man stood behind the podium. He spoke into the microphones. She could not clearly see the man at the podium because of the confetti, but she knew him. In fact, Sandra considered him a very dear friend. The man at the podium gestured toward her. Only then did Sandra realize she stood beside her husband. Lawrence Harwood had one arm around her waist. With the other he waved to the crowd. She did not need to look at him to know he was as excited as she.

Then she felt the eyes.

This other man stood behind the curtains at the stage's far side. He was not really visible. But he was there. He was partly shadow and partly human. He was a living wraith.

She knew the wraith was watching her. He smiled at her, and instantly her exhilaration vanished. She became flooded with a cold and helpless dread.

The man at the podium, her dear friend, called out her husband's name.

The crowd screamed louder still.

Sandra realized it was all wrong. She tried to tell them to stop. She begged her friend not to name her husband. She shrieked for her husband not to step forward. But the noise was too great. And her husband was blind to the risk and danger that now consumed her.

The streamers and the bunting and the confetti all turned to ash. The crowd's clamor became ghoulish. The lights went dark. All but one.

The light is focused upon the podium.

Her husband is there.

In his coffin.

Elena finished relating Sandra's experience with "It is not just that the dream itself or its exact repetitive nature defies standard analysis. The patient does not show any of the expected symptoms. She is well adjusted. Emotionally stable. She claims to have experienced no extraordinary trauma. She appears to love her husband very much. She states that their marriage is sound. They have two children. Both are in their late twenties. Married.

One grandchild, an infant. There have been no recent arguments or unusual stresses. She describes her childhood as normal, and the relationship with her parents remains good."

Miriam said, "And you believe her."

"I have no reason not to. She appears too desperate to mask a possible causal factor with lies. She is frantic with worry. And yet, beneath the quite evident fatigue and fear, she appears to be exactly what she claims. A well-adjusted mature woman with a highly fulfilling life."

"And you like her."

Elena set down her cup. It was not an unfair question. A clinical distance was important in arriving at valid analysis. Some patients, especially those with psychopathic tendencies, used emotional affection as a means of domination. "She is utterly terrified. She has lost control of her life. These experiences have wounded her. I feel for her. Yes. Very deeply."

"And yet, here you are, a world authority on dream interpretation. Facing a patient whose dilemma defies your analytical abilities."

Elena studied the older woman. "Are you suggesting I pass this patient on to another clinician?"

"My dear young friend, perish the thought. I am simply seeking to clarify for you the facts surrounding your situation. You, the expert, are baffled by a patient whose symptoms are unexplainable."

"Completely." But it was not merely the patient who was confused. Miriam's observations did not make sense. "You're saying I am too reliant upon my training and studies?"

Miriam smiled in a very curious manner. Her lips did not move. But her eyes tightened in genuine pleasure. "There comes a point where we must risk everything, our heritage and our training and our future direction, upon a course for which there is no standard definition."

"I'm sorry, I don't follow—"

"We have come very far, you and I. From a young child

whose questing mind and open heart called to an old woman and lit her days. Even then, I wondered if perhaps you were the one."

Elena no longer recognized the woman seated opposite her. "We were discussing a patient."

"No, my dear. I'm sorry. But you are incorrect. We are speaking about the future. And the distant past. And how they might indeed be intertwined." Miriam rose from her chair. "Wait here, please."

Miriam was gone for perhaps half an hour. Elena heard the occasional sound from the upper floors. She did not mind the solitude. Miriam's home was one of the few places where Elena felt utterly able to release her deepest tensions and relax. The home invited the inspection of secrets, particularly on such rare spring days. The sunlight created a gleaming patina over the city. Even the distant towers held a mystic quality. London became a haven where the divide between past and present was dissolved. Here was a sanctuary where a woman might permit her inner child to emerge and dream safely once again. Where knights on shining steeds appeared at the moment of direst need, to protect the defenseless from dark forces. Where pennants waved gaily from the king's tower, and peace was a force in the land. Where hearts could heal, and hope was a constant friend.

When Miriam returned, her face was scrubbed clean of makeup. Elena had the sudden impression that her friend had been weeping.

5

Elena asked, "Is everything all right?"

"Everything is fine." Miriam seated herself and placed a case upon the table between them. "I have carried this for seventy-two years. It was given to me by my great-grandmother. She died the following year. I was nine."

A lance of genuine fear pierced Elena's heart. "Are you unwell?"

"My health is not the issue." Miriam traced a finger across the case's surface. "Take careful note of what I just said. I have *carried* this. As in, bearing a burden. It was entrusted to me, and now I am offering it to you. It does not mean that you will be able to *use* it. I have never known any benefit. Only the responsibility."

"What is it?"

Miriam had become the immutable, timeless wise woman. "This is yours to accept or reject. My great-grandmother did not offer me any such choice. She commanded, and I obeyed. But times change. So I am making this request of you."

"How could I refuse you anything?"

Miriam did not so much smile as offer an enigma. "If you

agree to take it, your responsibility will remain until you select another individual and pass it along."

Elena studied the woman with her seamless features and ancient's gaze. For some reason, her voice shook slightly as she replied, "My answer stays the same. I could not possibly say anything but yes to you."

Miriam rose and walked around the table. She placed a hand upon Elena's cheek. Such displays of affection were rare between them. Elena's graduation. Her wedding day. Jason's funeral. Miriam's hand traced downward and settled upon Elena's shoulder. "Open it."

The packet was silk velvet, about the size of a briefcase, and not quite square. The cover was held in place with three cords. Elena fingered them and decided the cords were in fact woven gold. The ties were green gemstones, each the size of Elena's thumbnail.

"Emeralds," Miriam explained. "The coverlet was a gift from a grateful recipient to my great-grandmother."

"Recipient of what?"

"An excellent question. Perhaps one day you will know the answer for yourself."

Elena opened the flap and withdrew a book of sorts. The front and back covers were two intricately carved planks of petrified olive wood. The hinges appeared to be white jade. Elena set the book in her lap and ran a hand over the cover. The wood was smooth as glass. She wondered how many hands had done just what she was doing now.

She opened the cover, revealing a page containing just four letters, woven together like the cords that sealed the packet.

"The script is Aramaic," Miriam said.

Elena discovered her own voice had become as unsteady as her hands. "What does it say?"

"*Abba*. The Aramaic word for Father."

Elena ran her fingers over the page. The sheet was very soft, yet thick and uneven. When she pressed down, the pages gave slightly, as substantial as a blanket.

"Vellum," Miriam said. "Made from antelope hide. This book is a replica of a much older version. There are four such replicas, each older than the last. This particular replica is four hundred and thirty-one years old. Each is an exact duplication of the original, down to the type of vellum used to make the pages and the book's cover and the hinges."

Miriam walked back over and settled into her seat. She went on, "In the very early days of Christianity, most of the population of new believers could neither read nor write. Symbols were fashioned that they could understand. Carvings of favorite Bible stories, such as Jonah and the whale. The cross of our Lord Jesus. Symbols worn as jewelry, such as the sign of the fish. And paintings, known as icons. These were carried from place to place by pastors and missionaries. Stories were told from the Scriptures that related to these images. And over time, many of them became linked to miracles. Spontaneous healings. Visions. Hearing the voice of God. Entire cities coming to faith in a spontaneous outflowing of the Holy Spirit. The stories are myriad. It became accepted throughout Christendom that any miracle associated with one such image was linked to *all* true copies. Why? Because the image itself was not the source."

Elena traced the letters on the page. "And this?"

"The original document formed three scrolls. Or so the legends claim. In the fifth century, the first book was supposedly fashioned from those scrolls. By that point, such bindings had become a common means of preserving the most precious scroll manuscripts."

Elena repeated, "The fifth century."

Miriam nodded. "So my great-grandmother told me. The original now rests in a safety deposit box with the other duplicates."

"How old were the scrolls?"

"They dated from the second century." Miriam smiled. "That is, if you believe in legends."

"What am I supposed to do with this? I mean, other than keep it safe."

"The tradition is simple enough. Study one page until it speaks to you."

"Speaks," Elena echoed. "Speaks how?"

"How should I answer that, since it never spoke to me at all?" Miriam's tone seemed to mock her own words. "Either you will find the answer for yourself or you will not."

Elena's professional abilities were based upon a carefully honed objectivity. She had been trained to hold patients and issues alike at arm's length. And yet here, in this moment, she felt an almost giddy desire to dive straight in. Elena stared at her friend. She had the sudden sensation of unseen faces crowding in behind Miriam, smiling at her. "When do I move to the next page?"

"The common way of referring to them is *plates*. And to answer your question, if one plate does not speak, what can you expect from the next but more of the same?" Miriam studied the book in Elena's hands. Elena had the distinct impression that her friend was not sorry to let it go. "That was the answer my great-grandmother gave me. Out of respect for her memory, I have never turned the page."

6

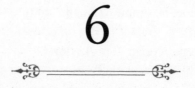

SUNDAY

Elena greeted the Sunday dawn seated on the bench she had often shared with her husband. Her home was on Boars Hill, the highest mount in Oxfordshire. Jason had set the bench in their rear garden where two sugar maples rose to frame the city below. The leaves were just appearing now, a green as fresh and sharp as the morning chill. The maples had been Jason's favorite. Their leaves went through an astonishing change of color, turning so dark as to appear black in the afternoon shadows of high summer, then brandishing an almost comic autumn color. Each season was so vital to these trees, Jason explained, that they needed to shout the changes in the only voice they had. Elena set her coffee mug on the grass beside her bench and wished the memories did not carry such a woeful edge.

The book sat on the bench next to her. Elena had studied the first plate for over an hour the previous night. The image had danced behind her eyelids all night.

Other than that, she had sensed nothing.

In the strengthening daylight Elena stared at the cover and recalled how, as she had prepared to depart the previous day, she had asked Miriam how long it would take for the book to speak to her.

"Days. Weeks. Months. Years. Perhaps never." Miriam had smiled. "You must understand. Time held a vastly different meaning to those who studied this book before you."

Elena settled the book in her lap. Using one finger, she traced the olive wood's whorling design. The petrified wood had been darkened over the centuries. The rings were little more than ink stains upon a shadow background. Elena felt the same compounded energy she had known the previous night. She wondered if there really was such a thing as telemetry, where an inanimate object absorbed the energy of those who handled it and transmitted this force to someone sensitive enough to be aware of the impossible.

She opened the cover. The first plate was yellowed with age and stained with other fingers that had traced the single word, the cursive Aramaic letters fashioning the name *Abba*. Aramaic had been the language of Jesus, the common tongue spoken throughout Judea. The word's most common translation was Pa, or Papa, or Daddy. It was the way Jesus had referred to his heavenly Father, with loving familiarity. In doing so, Jesus had gone against the traditions of the epoch, when Jehovah was considered so distant from his Judean followers that the holy Name could only be spoken once each year, by the temple's high priest, who entered the innermost sanctum and whispered the word to an empty chamber.

Elena turned the page. This was as far as Miriam had ever come. Elena wondered how her friend must have felt. A bearer of secrets two thousand years old, passing the book on to another, never having come to understand the true significance of what she held.

Elena decided she would probably find out eventually.

Her initial eagerness had worn off. The one emotion she could identify just now was a sense of concern. Just exactly what had she let herself in for? Was she to spend the rest of her life responsible for a collection of books and empty legends? Had anyone other than her oldest friend spoken of these things, Elena would have dismissed the tale as the dust of past centuries.

Nothing more than a collection of mysteries from an era before modern medicine and clinical analysis. Merely an instrument of secret hysteria.

Elena lifted her gaze. Boars Hill was a steep incline that rose just beyond Oxford's ring road. At this time of day, the university spires appeared close enough to touch. The dome of the Sheldonian, the medieval hall used for all formal convocations, gleamed like a crown of Cotswold stone.

She returned her gaze to the plate. The previous day, Miriam had walked her down the lane, as though seeking to shelter Elena as long as possible from whatever was yet to come. Miriam had explained that the plates contained the Lord's Prayer. One phrase per plate.

Unlike on the book's introductory page, the words on the next page were not written with ink. Instead, the letters appeared to be fashioned from pure gold. Elena thought they had been beaten into the surface of the vellum, but she could not be certain. Though the vellum was yellowed, there were no stains upon this page. Elena wondered if anyone had ever dared touch it. In four hundred and thirty-one years.

Our Father, who art in heaven.

The four letters of the introductory page had filled every square inch. A shout of ink and age. *Abba.* The letters had been surrounded by accent marks and hyphens.

This plate was very different indeed.

The previous evening, Elena had thought the golden letters had formed a flower. They had appeared to her like a tulip at the brink of unfolding, the tips not yet curved open.

Now, however, in the strengthening dawn, she realized that her initial impression had been wrong.

The words did not form a flower. But rather a flame.

Our Father, who art in heaven.

The words seemed to find shelter in the morning breeze, as though chanted by the leaves overhead. As though the birds sang them in time to Elena's own heart.

She had spoken the words her entire life. But in this moment of a new dawn, it seemed as though she was discovering a new meaning. A new *power*. Elena realized the artist had fashioned the script in order to drive home a specific point.

Elena felt her heart begin to sing these words, *Our Father, who art in heaven.* She felt herself filled with passion and hope and longing, strong as an eternal flame. Held to earth by the candle shaped by the Maker's own hand, a human form intended to burn incandescently with longing. Seeking ever to leave the source of its burning passion and rise up to the Maker.

The words were no longer ancient but utterly new. Utterly *now*. So great was the burning desire, she found herself whispering the words. She spoke in English, a tongue unknown at the time that this page had been fashioned. She whispered the words along with the two thousand years of followers who had gone before her, guided into prayer by the holy Teacher himself.

And in that instant, everything changed.

It was not so much a realization as a vision. And yet not so much a vision as a door.

There was no sound, and yet the images that swept through her mind and heart seemed to carry with them the song of ages past. Elena fell onto her knees, the book spilling to the grass beside her.

7

MONDAY

The city of Oxford was a living contrast. The inner city was dominated by the university and its thirty thousand students. Ringing this core, however, was some of the worst urban sprawl in England. The factories to the city's northeast produced one-third of all the country's motor vehicles. Most inhabitants of this outer city loathed the university and everything it stood for.

The Oxford city council bitterly resented the university and its privileged status. The university had been granted a quasi-independent status some eight hundred years earlier. This had been strengthened in the sixteenth century, after the university granted the royal family shelter during the Cromwellian civil war. Since the city council could not touch the university, they snipped at the edges. The traffic system was abysmal. Parking was nonexistent. Even the most senior don was forced to pay the university-area rate of five dollars an hour. Which was why most dons, no matter how elderly and no matter how bad the weather, endured public transport or cycled to work.

Because Elena's clinic was open to patients from the city at large, however, their building was granted one parking permit. For her part in renovating their offices, Elena's grateful col-

leagues had given this to her. She had once been offered thirty
thousand dollars for the slip of paper attached to her wind-
shield.

For the first time in years, Elena was late to the office that
Monday. Elena locked her car and hurried down St. Giles, only
to discover her first appointment was already waiting. Sandra
Harwood's limo was pulled up in front of the office, a bodyguard
standing sentry by the front door. Elena waited for the bodyguard to open Sandra's door and said, "I am so very sorry."

"Max will need to check your room before I can come up."

"Of course." Elena watched the bodyguard seal her patient
back inside the bulletproof limo, then said, "Come with me."

Fiona greeted her. "I invited them inside but that man refused."

"It's okay." She hurried up the stairs, unlocked her office
door, and repeated to the bodyguard, "I apologize for making
you wait."

"No problem, ma'am. We just wanted to be sure we got here
on time." The bodyguard gave both rooms a quick sweep, then
said, "I'll just go escort Ms. Harwood."

Elena followed him back downstairs and stationed herself by
the outer door. As Sandra entered, Fiona asked, "Would you care
for a coffee?"

"Please. White, one Sweet'N Low if you have it."

Elena lifted two fingers to Fiona and said to Sandra, "Won't
you come up?"

Once back inside her office, Elena said, "I can't tell you—"

Sandra waved her apology aside. "Do you have anything for
me?"

Elena waited while Fiona brought in the two coffees and
asked, "Should I offer one to the gentleman?"

"You can," Sandra replied. "I doubt he will accept."

Elena said, "Shut the doors, please." When Fiona had sealed
them in, Elena asked, "How have you been?"

Sandra tasted the coffee, grimaced. "The same."

"Is there something the matter with the coffee?"

"The coffee is not the problem. I had another attack just before dawn. It always takes a while for the nausea to pass."

"The dreams have persisted, then."

"Persist is too light a word. They brutalize me. Last night it attacked four times."

Elena decided to forgo the protection of her desk. She did this occasionally to emphasize some approaching transition. Other times she wanted to present dreaded news with a compassion that required closeness. This time was different, however.

She settled her coffee on the edge of the desk next to Sandra's. She pulled over a second chair. Seated herself. Tasted her coffee again and confessed, "The reason I was late was that I did not fall asleep until dawn. I was so far gone I fit the alarm clock into my dream."

Sandra did not respond. The woman clearly found nothing remarkable in a sleepless night. Up close the woman's tension was much more evident. Despite her faultless makeup and perfect hair, the strain was etching itself deeply into her features. Tight crow's-feet extended from her eyes and her mouth.

Elena said, "I couldn't sleep because I was struggling to decide how I should speak with you today."

That brought the woman around.

Elena went on, "Dream analysis is one of the most controversial issues within psychoanalysis."

Sandra replied, "I know all that. I've read your book."

Elena covered her wince by settling her cup back on the saucer. As she did so, she was struck by a sudden image. Elena found herself recalling the day Miriam had urged her to write the book. She had forgotten entirely that the idea had originally come from the old woman, which was hardly a surprise, given Elena's state of mind at the time.

That particular day, Miriam's sunlit porch had overlooked a frozen world. It had been early January, seven months after Jason's death, and Elena had been struggling futilely to reknit her world. Miriam had urged her to renew a personal interest, one shared with almost no one. Within the realms of clinical psychology there were many who scoffed at dream analysis. Elena had wanted to make it the basis for her doctoral thesis, but her adviser had rejected the proposal out of hand. He had then described dream analysis as one step removed from medieval mystics.

That frozen January day, Miriam had said a study of dreams was precisely what Elena needed. A personal passion brought to the light of day, one she had not ever shared with her departed husband. A new reason to heal and enter a future without Jason.

Elena realized Sandra was watching her. She stammered, "I-I was remembering something I have not thought of in years."

"Does it have to do with my nightmare?"

"I don't know . . . perhaps." She took a long breath and searched for the thread of what she had intended to say. "Dreams often reveal very deep issues that the conscious mind seeks not only to avoid, but to actually flee from. Yet the unconscious mind realizes that this repressed emotion and memory must be confronted. It expels the putrid mess with the same steady insistence with which the body forces out pus from an untreated wound. Either the wound is cleared, or the individual will suffer from an increasingly serious infection. This is as true with mental and emotional wounds as with the physical. If the individual refuses to accept this need, and represses the issue, then fragments are often released in the dream state."

"But this is not what is happening here," Sandra declared. "I am not repressing anything."

Elena had often heard such claims. Normally she treated them as just another indication of repression and denial. But this time, she said, "I agree. I do not think this is the case with you."

Sandra visibly relaxed. She tasted the words: "Thank you. That means a great deal."

Elena went on, "Repressed emotions and memories will often follow certain patterns within the dream state. These patterns are hotly debated. Some analysts follow upon the work of the psychiatrist Carl Jung. They believe that the patterns are based upon what are known as archetypes, structures that are universal to all of mankind, as though they were part of our genetic code. Others, including the father of modern psychiatry, Freud, suggest that most repressed images have to do with a more fundamental and physical-based pattern."

The woman seated next to her listened with a singular intensity. "If you don't think I am repressing an issue, why are you telling me this?"

"Because what I am about to say," Elena replied, "is so unprofessional, I need to preface it with something that establishes my credentials."

The woman was a true professional at masking her emotions. The only sign of what she held back was a slight quiver to her voice. "Tell me everything."

Elena said, "Your husband is the American ambassador to Great Britain."

Sandra Harwood shook her head. Not in denial. But in impatient rejection. "You could have discovered this any number of ways."

Elena said, "Next week, the Vice President of the United States will announce that he is not going to be the President's running mate in the upcoming elections."

The woman's professional facade weakened. "How do you know this?"

"For the moment, I need you to set such questions aside. If what I say is of use, we can discuss them at a later time." Elena carefully framed the words she had practiced and debated through much of the night. She was no clearer on whether it was right to say them as she had been at dawn. "I do not intend to hide anything from you. But how this has come to me is less important than whether or not it helps you deal with your nightly trauma."

Sandra Harwood studied her a long moment, then nodded once. "I can accept that."

Elena took a long breath. "Your husband is going to be offered the position of vice president. He has already been approached. You know this. The President will call your husband with the formal invitation tomorrow afternoon."

Sandra Harwood struggled to maintain control. "He has dreamed of this moment. For years. We both have."

Elena hesitated.

"What is it?"

"I had the impression," Elena replied, "that I was shown these things as a means of establishing authenticity."

Sandra Harwood's gaze widened. "You were *shown*."

"That is correct."

"To establish *truth*."

"I have no way of knowing this for certain. But that is what I think."

Elena was waiting for the inevitable question, the truth of *what*. Instead, Sandra Harwood leaned back in her chair. Tears erupted from her eyes. "You don't know, you can't understand, how good it is to know I'm not going crazy."

"You are not insane."

"Or suffering from a tumor. Or early-onset Alzheimer's. Or . . ." The elegant woman searched her purse for a handkerchief. "I've been so afraid."

Elena waited. There was nothing to be gained by saying the woman had every right to be afraid.

Just not for the reason she had thought.

◆

Elena rose from her seat and walked to the rear window. She could not leave the room without alerting the bodyguard. But she needed Sandra Harwood to be utterly composed before she continued. Alert. Ready. Or rather, as ready as anyone could be.

The rear garden was surrounded by a high stone wall. Rose bushes that had been planted while Victoria was still queen clenched the Cotswold stone and sent out another generation of buds and green shoots. A pair of stone benches rested beneath English willows. In the distance, the steeples of five colleges poked into a china-blue sky. The most distant was New College, called such because it was the youngest of the three colleges founded in the twelfth century.

Somewhere around the year one thousand, the city's monasteries had been approached by wealthy Cotswold merchants who sought teachers for their sons. At the time, neither the church nor the king wished for the landed gentry to gain the ability to read and write, for their ignorance permitted those in power to rewrite the laws at will. The bravest monasteries defied the pope's orders and admitted students to learn Latin, Scriptures, and mathematics. Elena stared out the window and reflected on how there were worse places on earth to call home.

Behind her, Sandra asked, "Is there anything else?"

Elena took that as her cue. She returned to her chair and said, "Your husband has a heart condition."

She absorbed the shock well. "This was supposed to be a secret."

"It's not."

"How did you . . ." She stopped. "I'm sorry."

"There's no need to apologize. I will tell you everything. Just not now."

"You don't have any connection to the political establishment?"

"Not here, and not in the US. And anything that I say to you remains utterly confidential."

"Lawrence has been checked out by the best. They say his condition is under control."

BOOK *of* DREAMS 45

"It is," Elena agreed. "So long as he does not take on an inhuman level of stress. Such as on the national campaign trail."

"You mean, it could kill him?"

"I mean," Elena corrected, "there are people who want him to take this position so that he will die."

Sandra whispered, "The wraith I saw off to one side of the stage."

Elena said, "The man you identified as your husband's opponent has a different candidate in mind. Someone the President does not want to run alongside. They see your husband's health issue as the perfect means to put their candidate in place."

Sandra's gaze had distanced. Her entire upper body rocked slowly. Back and forth. "They intend to install their candidate as a last-minute replacement. When no one else is available. They want to steal—"

Abruptly Sandra rose from the chair. "I must go. I don't know how—"

Elena interrupted, "There is more."

"M-more?"

"This is not the only reason why your husband has been put forward. But telling you the rest is important only if your husband refuses the vice presidency." Elena rose to stand beside the ambassador's wife. "And grants you both a future. Then you and I must speak again."

"Y-you'll tell me how you know . . ."

Elena nodded. "I will tell you everything."

8

WEDNESDAY

Miriam said, "You look very nice, my dear."

"Thank you."

"Are you going somewhere special?"

"Yes."

Miriam smiled at Elena's terseness. "Down these stairs. Show this gentleman your card."

The bank's security desk flanked the entrance to the vault and the safety deposit boxes beyond. The guard accepted the document Miriam had obtained from the bank's vice president, stating that the safety deposit box was now transferred to Elena's ownership. He checked Elena's new key card against the computer records. Then he inspected the women's passports and asked Elena to sign the register.

They followed the guard through the barred entrance. A series of curtained alcoves adorned the hall leading to the vault. The box that Miriam had transferred to Elena was about three feet square. The guard slipped Elena's new card through the reader, then his own. When the door clicked open, he asked, "You need any help?"

Miriam replied, "We're fine, thank you."

When the guard departed, Miriam drew a cart over and helped Elena slide out the metal drawer. Elena then pushed the box into one of the alcoves. Miriam sealed the curtain, then opened the drawer to reveal four packages, all wrapped in plastic and vacuum sealed. Each was the same size as the book sitting on Elena's coffee table.

Elena asked, "Which is the original?"

"The one on top."

Through the clear plastic sheet she saw what appeared to be a blackened blanket. "What is that?"

"Waxed vellum. How long it has been in place, I have no idea. There is a seal on the other side."

Elena inspected her friend. "You sound so . . . I don't know. Detached."

"I am still growing used to the idea that you had a vision."

"Or something."

"It is so good to know I have chosen rightly. You have no idea what a burden has been lifted from my heart."

"I hope you're right. About the choice, I mean."

"I know what you mean. My dear, I am certainly capable of making a wrong choice. I should know. My life is littered with them. But God does not."

Elena traced one finger across the plastic surface. "When did you seal them?"

"Thirty years ago. More."

"Can I open it?"

"My dear, you can do whatever you want. These are yours now."

"You don't have a list of rules?"

"I have nothing except a few terse sentences imparted by my great-grandmother. I have always assumed that part of selecting an heir is being certain they will hold these books in trust."

Elena found Miriam's calm assurance vaguely unsettling. "I wish I was as certain as you sound."

"I know."

"I have so many questions."

"I'm sure you do. If I recall, your pastor is a very good man."

"One of the finest I have ever known."

"Well, then. If you trust him with the state of your soul, I would suggest you trust him with this as well."

"Should I tell him about . . ." She waved a hand at the sealed tomes.

"My dear, you may tell whomever you want whatever you feel is correct. On that point my great-grandmother was perfectly clear. She made a habit of explaining the trust bestowed upon her to everyone she worked with." Miriam slipped the cover back in place. "Shall we go?"

Elena followed her back into the vault and helped her slide in the drawer. "I feel like there ought to be some rite of initiation. A vow of some kind."

"All that is between you and God," Miriam said. She closed the door with a click, then stood there, her hand resting on the steel. "Do you know, I believe I can see my great-grandmother smiling down at me."

Elena's taxi pulled into the stone gates with the lamps burning real gas flames. Elena wore her finest outfit. She had purchased the blue midlength cocktail dress and matching pashmina shawl when her book first hit the bestseller list. At the time, she had thought such matters were important. By the time she had finished her one and only international tour, Elena had learned that when the public's appetite was whetted, they would devour her regardless of how she dressed.

The previous afternoon, Fiona had entered Elena's office as her last patient departed and announced that Elena had an important phone call. When Elena answered, an officious lady identified herself as the ambassador's personal aide. She wanted to know why the embassy had not heard back from Elena regarding the ambassador's invitation.

When Elena responded that she had never heard anything from the American ambassador in her life, and nothing from his wife since Monday, the aide had turned contrite and said that Ambassador Harwood was hosting an event at his private residence the next evening, and was so hoping she might be able to come.

A white-gloved marine guard waved her taxi driver to a halt. The young man opened a door and asked, "Good evening, ma'am. May I see your invitation, please?"

"Certainly." But a sudden case of nerves left her fumbling with the catch to her purse.

If the marine noticed, he gave no sign. Finally she passed over the embossed envelope couriered to her that afternoon. The marine unfolded the sheet, then asked, "Can I please see some ID, Dr. Burroughs?"

"Of course." The ambassador's aide had told her to expect this as well.

"Everything is good here, ma'am." He handed back the papers, straightened, and offered his white-gloved hand. When she alighted from the taxi, he gave her a crisp salute. "Enjoy your evening, Dr. Burroughs."

The ambassador's residence was in a leafy alcove at the border of Saint John's Wood, west of central London. The house was very grand, but to Elena's eye almost everything was in dire need of updating. Another pair of marines stood at attention by the front doors. Elena joined the formal greeting line moving slowly through the front portico.

The marble-tiled alcove had a peaked roof and gilded chandelier. Sandra Harwood stood beside a tall man of aging Hollywood good looks, just like the photograph Elena had found on the embassy website. To the ambassador's right stood a portly woman with a grandmother's smile, and beside her stood a man even wider than his wife. Elena recognized the secretary of state from his numerous television appearances.

When Elena arrived at the head of the line, Sandra Harwood greeted her with professional cordiality. She granted Elena the same amount of time that she had the dozens of others who had come before. She made some apologetic joke about misplaced invitations, and said she hoped Elena had not been put to much trouble by the last-minute notification. Elena did not even hear her own reply.

Sandra then turned and said to her husband, "My dear, I'd like to introduce Dr. Elena Burroughs."

In person Lawrence Harwood possessed a solid gravitas, a stern authority, and genuine comfort with power. "My wife rarely speaks so highly of someone as she does of you, Dr. Burroughs."

"Thank you, Mr. Ambassador."

"Could I ask you to kindly turn slightly to your left? Our embassy photographer would like to capture the moment." He moved in closer, smiled for the flash, then turned her back around in a smooth motion he had undoubtedly practiced a million times before. "It's not every evening we have the honor of hosting the author of a national bestseller, that's for certain."

"*International* bestseller." His wife smiled, already shaking the next hand in line. "How many languages has your book been translated into now?"

"I've lost count."

"Well, I look forward to speaking with you later. Can I introduce you to Secretary and Mrs. Roddins?"

Elena exchanged greetings with the visiting couple, then allowed herself to be launched into the party. She entered the main ballroom, accepted a glass of champagne, and wondered what she was doing there.

The reception was an elegant affair, but also quite impersonal. The ambassador, his wife, and the visiting Washington couple circulated through the room. Yet neither Sandra Harwood nor her husband ever glanced in Elena's direction.

Almost an hour passed. A visiting ensemble of Juilliard students played Baroque sonatas. Various people glanced Elena's way, took in her solitary stance, and dismissed her as being of no consequence. Elena positioned herself by a marble pillar. From her vantage point she could observe the room, the smiling faces, the diplomatic chatter, the power. She did not resent this. She simply did not belong and did not care. She checked her watch and decided to give the ambassador's wife another half hour.

It took only ten minutes. A slender British gentleman with the lean features of a long-distance runner and the markings of a silver fox came over. "Dr. Elena Burroughs?"

"That's right."

"Nigel Harries. How do you do."

"Are you military?"

Gray eyes with a dagger's piercing quality inspected her. "I was, at one time. Long ago. More recently with MI5. I assume you know what that is."

"Yes." British intelligence was split into several divisions. The two most important civilian branches were MI5, which was responsible for internal security, and MI6, for international. "Did the ambassador's wife send you?"

"Absolutely not. The lady you mention has no connection to me or my current organization. None whatsoever." He had a military officer's manner of diction. Each word carved in units as precise as bullets. "Do I make myself clear?"

"Perfectly. What is your current position?"

"Ah. A good question, that. I'm the head of a private security outfit. I thought you might be interested to know that your office has been bugged."

"When?"

Elena was a professional observer. She could tell the gentleman was intensely pleased with her response. She did not waste time with either outrage or surprise. She did not ask the unnecessary. As in how he knew about the bugging. Nigel Harries replied, "Your office was clean yesterday. It was bugged when we checked again this morning."

"Which means the listeners did not hear my last conversation with the ambassador's wife."

This time, the gentleman's humor actually surfaced. "As I told you, Dr. Burroughs, I have no information on that count. None whatsoever."

"Of course."

"However, it may be a good idea if you were to inform your receptionist that a change has been made to tomorrow's schedule, one you forgot to inform her about."

"For what time?"

"Would nine tomorrow morning be convenient?"

She thought through the next day's appointments and decided. "I can make that work."

"Excellent. Our mutual acquaintances will be most pleased. You may be surprised by the direction of this next discussion."

Elena glanced around the ballroom. The undercurrents of power were more visible now. "She will be speaking for the listeners and not for me."

The man's gaze tightened in approval. He bowed slightly. "I regret to inform you that there will be a break-in tonight, in the office building next to yours. A gentleman will stop by in the morning. He will offer your receptionist a pamphlet from Strand Securities. I suggest you give us a call."

9

THURSDAY

The next morning Elena rose earlier than usual. She logged into the counseling service's system, inspected her schedule, and made three calls. The first was to her pastor, asking if she might stop by that morning. Her first patient that morning was Sandra Harwood. Elena felt she had no choice other than to accept that the security man's warning was valid. She moved her next two patients to later that afternoon, in an attempt to maintain professional confidentiality. Elena then left home and drove to her church.

The receptionist informed her that the vicar was running late, so Elena walked next door to the church-run café. She ordered a coffee and took it to a table that granted her a view of the church's front door.

Saint Aldates was a modest structure situated on the side of Oxford's central district opposite her offices. From the outside, Saint Aldates looked like just another city church, its grimy stone facade interrupted by a lone stained-glass window. The entrance fronted a small plaza shared with the café and Pembroke College. Across the street rose the spires of Christ Church, perhaps the most imposing of all the university's colleges.

Oxford's college system was developed during the early medieval era, when the growing number of students forced the monks to formalize the structure. The university still held to many of the edicts laid down almost a thousand years earlier. Students enrolled at one of the colleges. The university maintained the administrative umbrella. The university was responsible for final exams and for granting degrees. Most lectures were university-wide. But tutorials, the personal system of instruction for which Oxford was known throughout the world, was handled through the colleges.

Christ Church had been her husband's favorite college, a vast repository of lore and fable. Isaac Newton's apartment was just visible through the café window, a peaked corner of the college's front wall, which itself was designed to look like a mythical fortress. The Anglican cathedral of Oxford was built into the rear of the main quadrangle. According to legend, the chapel floor contained marble tiles laid down when the site was home to a Roman temple. One of the rear quadrangles contained the tree where a certain young girl named Alice played with the college kitten, while her uncle taught mathematics and wrote a tale about his favorite niece entering a realm named Wonderland. Elena finished her coffee and reflected on how this was what she most loved about the city and the university—the past neither died nor faded away, but rather lived in parallel to the contemporary.

Elena watched the pastor hurry down the side passage and enter the church. Brian Farringdon held to an air of perpetual youth, which was remarkable given everything he had endured. Elena stopped by the counter for a second cup of coffee and entered the church to find him standing by the reception desk, checking his messages. Brian smiled a welcome and said, "The only thing finer than a stranger bearing gifts is a friend."

Elena handed over the coffee and asked, "Can I have five minutes?"

"I can even give you ten. Come on back."

Three years earlier, Brian Farringdon had lost his wife to cancer. He was left with their son to raise, a boy aged eleven.

Elena normally did not do grief counseling. But she could hardly have refused the man who had buried Jason and helped her through her own dark hour. Brian had been her patient for six months. Soon after he stopped coming, his son had entered puberty with a savage fury directed against his father, the world, and God. Elena had counseled the two of them for another year.

The interior of Saint Aldates was something of a shock to newcomers. Twenty years earlier the church had been gutted. The sanctuary was now a modernist semicircle, framed by glowing Cotswold stone and redwood pillars. A glass wall separated the sanctuary from the classrooms and the stairs leading to the church offices.

The church worship had undergone a similar drastic change. Saint Aldates was a leader in what was known as the Vineyard movement. The movement had originated in Toronto, after a staid and stodgy church was struck by revival. Over the three years that the revival continued, pastors visited from all over the world, including a number from England. Impatient with the turgid Anglican system, desperate to stem the tide of secularism, they had returned from the revival hoping to light a new spiritual fire.

Nowhere on earth had the Vineyard movement found such a reception as within the sedate Anglican churches of England, Scotland, and Wales. A growing number of these churches now split their services in two. The first service maintained the standard Sunday-morning rituals, and were attended by a mostly gray-haired community whose numbers grew ever smaller. Saturday evenings and Sunday afternoons were an entirely different matter. These services were riotous, with loud music and louder singing. The Spirit was invoked on a constant basis. The services lasted as long as the people wanted to remain. Which was often until midnight and beyond.

Elena followed Brian into the vicar's office and waited until he settled into his chair and peeled the lid off his coffee to say, "I have a problem."

"In that case, you better shut the door."

Elena knew all about holding to overtight schedules. She covered her recent events in succinct bites. She said nothing about the book. Not because she intended to keep it from him. But the book was not crucial to the moment. It would need to wait for a time when she was not shouldering herself into the pastor's overcrowded day.

Even so, when she finished, Brian sat sipping from his cup for a time, then lifted the phone and said, "Tell the others to start the meeting without me."

When he hung up, Elena said, "I can come back."

He waved that aside and went back to sipping from his cup.

"Really. It already feels better just to have told somebody," she added.

Brian continued to stare out the side window. His office overlooked the square's lone tree. "To recap what you just told me. You were approached by a wealthy and powerful American lady. She was having dreams that defied normal analysis. You arranged for an inspection at the Radcliffe. The lady is in good health. You feared there was nothing you could do for her. You prayed for guidance. God answered in a very clear and vivid manner. You passed on the message to the lady. Everything that came to you in your prayer time has now been confirmed in reality."

"That's it in a nutshell."

Brian looked at her for the first time. "God really rocked your boat, did he?"

The smile came with difficulty. "It feels like I've been struck by a personal tsunami."

"Good. Very good indeed. I'm happy for you. It's high time something drew you from your comfortable little shell."

"Excuse me, that's not—"

"When I first started coming to see you after losing Anne, do you remember the first thing you said to me?"

"That I was not an expert in grief counseling."

"And do you recall my response?"

"I . . ."

"I said that was good, because I wasn't interested in grief, I was interested in moving on. And that's exactly what you need to do, Elena. You had a good life with Jason. He was one of the finest men it has ever been my honor to know. But he is gone now. He dwells with the Father. And I am certain, absolutely positive, that Jason would tell you the very same thing as I do now. Wake up. Life is calling. God is here. Waiting for you to open your heart to a new dawn."

And suddenly she was crying. The pressure clenched her chest and squeezed out the tears. She had no choice but to release the sobs and search for breath. Brian opened a lower drawer and set a box of tissues on the desk. And he waited.

When she could draw a steady breath, she said, "I'm sorry."

"There's no need to apologize."

"I never cry."

"I get that a lot." He went back to studying the tree beyond his window. "Most of the time when people come for counseling I have to sit here and bite my tongue. But I am going to treat you as a friend and an equal. People can become comfortable with anything. Including loss and pain. They build it into their personality. It frames their life. It becomes hard to give up. Because beyond this lies the unknown."

It didn't help that she had said the same words a hundred times and more. Elena reached for another tissue. "I miss him so much I don't let myself acknowledge it very often."

"You think losing Anne hasn't torn at my nights? But what is even worse, and I hope you're paying attention, because this is very important. What is worse is accepting that God can heal even my shredded soul. Because this opens me to the prospect of a full life *beyond* my loss. Why? Because it is a life without my true love, the woman I never thought I could survive without."

Elena needed another long moment to recover from that one. "I must look a total wreck."

"I seriously doubt your patients will notice. My visitors rarely did."

His brusque tone offered her the only grip she could find on control. She glanced at her watch. "I have to be going."

"Let me ask you one final question. How often have you sat there in a service and prayed for the Spirit to move in your life?"

"I don't—"

"How often have you lifted your hands to heaven and said, 'Come, Holy Spirit, come'?"

She blinked away the last tears. Brian was watching her now with a gaze she could only describe as fierce.

"I will take your silence to mean you've said the words at least a few times. And look what's happened. God answered your prayers."

"Don't you have any doubts about what's happened to me?"

"No, Elena. I don't. Not one whit. You are not hysterical. You are not seeking to use your experience for your own aggrandizement. Your experience follows a pattern laid down by Scriptures. If God were looking for someone to give earthly interpretation to a divine vision, I could not think of anyone better."

She forced herself to her feet. "Thank you for your time."

Brian reached for a pen and paper. "There's a friend of mine I think you should speak with. He did his doctorate here on the Old Testament and still holds a post as professor at New College. These days he spends most of his time in Rome. He's recently been made a cardinal and holds some senior post at the Vatican. He and I were roommates and have remained friends ever since. He's here now. I trust him. I suggest you do the same."

Brian handed over the page. He then walked around the desk and hugged her. Hard. "God has drawn you out of your comfort zone. Get used to it. I doubt it will be the last time."

10

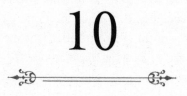

Elena arrived at her office a few minutes before nine. The Mercedes limo was not idling on the curb outside her office. Instead, a trio of police vans were parked catty-cornered in front of her building and the one to her left. As she rose from her car, a policeman walked over and demanded, "Do you have business here, madam?"

"This is my office."

"May I see some ID, please?"

As she reached into her purse, they were joined by a man in a rumpled tan suit. The policeman said, "This lady claims to work here."

"I'm Detective Mehan." He inspected her license. "You are a counselor, Ms. Burroughs?"

"Clinical psychologist. And it's Doctor Burroughs. Can I ask what's the matter?"

"The building next to yours was broken into last night. Are you aware what goes on in there?"

"Of course." Neighboring Balliol College had purchased the building and turned it into a library for their rare manuscripts. "What did they take?"

"Thankfully, the college has installed a very adequate security system. The burglars did not get close to the most valuable items." The detective had a voice that reminded Elena of pounded tin. "Might I inquire as to your own security?"

"We don't have any. But other than one painting and a few computers, there's nothing in our office worth stealing."

"Break-ins are a growing problem in the city center. You can't assume that the burglars will be well informed." He handed back her ID. "I would urge you to rectify the situation. Immediately."

Fiona greeted her by waving a pamphlet from Strand Securities and said, "This was slipped through our box. Remarkable timing. I don't suppose they had a hand in the break-in."

Elena fashioned a smile and said, "At least they've shown some initiative. The detective said we needed to get something in place immediately. Why don't you give them a call."

The ambassador's wife chose that moment to enter. One of her bodyguards held open the outer door, while the other remained in conversation with the police. "Is everything all right?"

"Fine. The break-in was next door."

"I'm so relieved to hear it."

Her bodyguard said, "Even so, ma'am, perhaps we should get out of the public areas."

"Of course." Elena felt Fiona's eyes upon her as she led the ambassador's wife up the stairs. The bodyguard held open the door, followed them across the outer office, and slid the double doors shut.

Before she settled into the chair, Sandra Harwood announced, "My husband refused to join me."

Elena walked around her desk. "I'm sorry to hear that."

"He accepts that there are . . . needs. But he . . ." Sandra Harwood spoke with the woodenness of an actress reading from an unfamiliar script. "I'm sorry. This is not easy."

"Would you like coffee?"

"No thank you." Her gaze was a silent warning. "I love my husband very much."

Elena remained silent as Sandra made a stilted list of her husband's good qualities. She knew the ambassador's wife was speaking for the unseen listeners. Elena loathed how her counseling session had become party to a lie. Her office was intended as a haven for secrets and healing. What was happening went against everything she and her profession stood for.

Abruptly she broke in: "I'm sorry. This is an extremely difficult day for me, and I'm not certain I can give you the attention you deserve."

Sandra Harwood was taken aback. She tasted several responses and settled upon "Is there something wrong?"

"Tomorrow is the anniversary of my husband's death."

"I didn't know."

"How could you. I started to call and suggest we meet at another time. But I know how busy you are. Now I wish I had done so."

"No, no. It's fine. Really." The ambassador's wife tasted a smile. "Actually, it's rather nice to know you have a human edge."

"Such confessions from the clinician are not part of the equation. We are trained to hold a professional distance. It is vital to most successful therapies."

"But not in my case."

Elena nodded slowly. That was exactly what she had been thinking.

"Would you like to tell me about him?"

"Jason was born to an American scientist working for Roche in Switzerland. He studied biochemistry first in Geneva, and then at Duke." Elena remained aware of the other ears, and yet didn't care nearly so much. "He spoke English with an accent that I always found delicious. He was very American in his tastes, but in his deepest recesses there lurked an extremely European soul. That was one of the things I loved about him."

"What do you mean by having a European soul?"

"So many things." Because of her conversation with the vicar, her mind settled on a particular point: "Jason used to talk about how the country of his birth had been riven by wars between various Christian factions. He refused to take sides, or argue, or even remain in the same room whenever discussions turned to religious issues. In private, he used to tell me that he could not find it in himself to condemn anyone. He questioned the purity of all their motives. He said this was one of the things that drew him to Jesus. How he needed the one who had risen above all the human imperfections. How he needed the Messiah to remind him of where he should maintain his focus. And how vital it was to forgive . . ."

Elena found herself unable to continue. Her throat had suddenly constricted to the point where her breathing rasped in her own ears.

Sandra Harwood rose from her chair. She walked to the corner cupboard where Elena always kept a bottle of Evian and plastic glasses. Sandra poured a cup and brought it back to Elena. She nodded her thanks and drank. She set down the cup and tried to recall if a patient had ever done that for her before.

When she could trust her voice again, Elena said, "We should be speaking about your issues."

"Do you know, I believe we are." Sandra Harwood glanced at her watch. "I have to close things off a bit early today."

"I understand."

She rose from her chair and crossed the room. When she reached for the doors, she stopped and turned back to say, "I would like to think that you and I are destined to become the very best of friends."

The slender gentleman with the military bearing appeared just as the staff were leaving for lunch. The director of Elena's office had a previous engagement, so when she offered to take care of the security issue, he accepted gratefully. Nigel Harries introduced himself as though they had not met at the ambassador's reception. He then gave a brief but polished presentation on his firm, Strand Securities. Elena agreed for them to install a new system. Nigel Harries pocketed her signed contract with grave British politeness and said, "If you like, Dr. Burroughs, my man can do a sweep of your offices."

"A sweep for what?"

"Improper monitoring systems of one kind or another. Listening devices, usually."

"We're a university clinic, Mr. Harries. Hardly the sort of place that someone would want to bug."

"You would be surprised, ma'am."

"I don't want to be any bother."

"Not at all. My man has been working in the area on another assignment. He is waiting downstairs."

"How much will—"

"No charge, Dr. Burroughs. Our way of thanking you for your business."

The technician was a younger version of his boss—well dressed, discreet, thorough. And fast. Elena had scarcely enough time to unwrap her sandwich before he announced, "Your offices are bugged, ma'am."

"What?"

He walked to the door. "Nigel?"

The pair found another three microphones in her office, two more downstairs in the waiting room, and five others stationed throughout the building. Elena did not need to pretend at shock and outrage. Especially not when Nigel Harries slipped next door and returned with the detective. By then the technician had located the central monitoring device.

Nigel explained for both Elena's and the detective's sake, "This is actually a rather sophisticated system. The microphones are quite low-powered, they only transmit a distance of about thirty feet." He held up a palm-size box of black plastic. "This is a high-frequency burst transmitter. It collects the incoming data, and then once every twelve hours it will fire off a condensed broadcast."

The detective accepted the box and the plastic bag holding the microphones. "Pity you and your man had to handle everything."

"Oh, I very much doubt whoever put this in place neglected to wear gloves, Detective." He pointed at the transmitter. "This is not something generally available on the open market."

"But you happen to know all about it, do you."

"That is correct, Detective. I do."

He grunted and turned to Elena. "Any idea who might be behind such an attack?"

She shivered at the casual manner in which he used that word. Attack. "No. But I have an idea who was their target."

"I'm listening."

"This puts me in a very serious quandary. The patient is most concerned about her privacy."

The detective held up the devices. "We have evidence of a serious crime, Dr. Burroughs. It would take me less than half an hour to obtain a writ from the Crown Court."

"Would you gentlemen give me a minute? I need to make a call." Elena slipped into the empty office next door and phoned Sandra Harwood's personal cell phone.

The ambassador's wife listened to Elena's report, then said, "Can we be certain that the information will go no further?"

"I have no idea."

She sighed. "My husband warned me this would happen."

"I'm so very, very sorry, Sandra."

"For what? You accepted a stranger as a patient. You helped me when no one else could."

Only then did Elena realize what she had failed to ask that morning: "You didn't have a nightmare last night?"

"For the first time in a month, I slept through the night." Sandra was silent, then said, "I will clear this with Lawrence. Go ahead and tell the detective who I am."

Elena went back next door and announced, "I have a new patient. Her name is Sandra Harwood. Her husband is the United States ambassador to the Court of Saint James."

"Oh, my sweet stars above," the detective groaned.

Nigel Harries said, "The intelligence services must be notified immediately."

The detective groaned once more.

"I can take care of that little chore, if you like."

"That was your former bailiwick, was it?"

Nigel Harries did not respond.

"Oh, all right. Just give me a moment to phone this in." The detective headed for the door. "Is there—"

"The office next door is free."

"And here I was thinking I'd been called out to a nice simple burglary." As he left her office, the detective muttered, "Why did this have to happen on my watch?"

11

FRIDAY

Before her first patient Friday morning, Elena took a moment to phone the name her pastor had supplied. The cardinal had a slightly accented and honeyed voice. "Brian Farringdon spoke ever so highly of you, Dr. Burroughs. When can you stop by?"

Elena hesitated. After sleeping poorly all that week, she was desperately tired. But she had no real interest in going home. The anniversary of Jason's passage was not a time she wished to spend alone. But with everything else going on, she had made no plans. "My last appointment is over at five this afternoon."

"Splendid. I will be waiting for you. Have the bursar explain how to find me."

New College was for Elena a truly splendid place. She had attended several events there, most recently a banquet in the Founder's Library, a peaked chamber in the college's oldest building. The grounds included portions of the original Roman wall, which curved and weaved with an utter disregard for logic. As a result, no college passage ran straight, nor any path or quadrangle. The bursar was accustomed to guiding those easily lost, and used a photocopied map and a highlighter to show how Elena could reach the professor.

Cardinal Brindisi resembled a bricklayer far more than a Vatican official. He was big in a very solid manner, with a massive girth and arms like knobby tree limbs. He appeared to be aged somewhere north of sixty, and he was dressed in dark trousers and an open-necked shirt and frayed jacket. His overlarge hands were surprisingly gentle. They took hold of her own and blanketed them with warmth. "Dr. Burroughs, it is seldom that my friend the vicar speaks so highly of someone as he has of you. Will you take tea?"

The priest's offices dated from the era when professors could not marry until they gave up tenure. They lived in quarters behind their offices, only moving off campus once they retired. The stone-walled double chamber was high-ceilinged and rimmed by stained-glass windows that were open to the night breeze. She sighed contentedly.

"A tiring day, Dr. Burroughs?"

"No. Well, yes. But that's not . . . I was just thinking how good it is to be alive."

"What a delightful thing to say. May that sentiment mark every hour we spend in each other's company. Do you take sugar?"

"No thank you." She watched the priest settle into his chair. "Did Brian tell you why he suggested I see you?"

"Only that you sought wisdom." He tasted his tea, but Elena had the impression he had poured his cup out of politeness. "The ancients tell us that the beginning of wisdom is a good question asked by a listening heart and directed to the proper source."

Elena sketched out the events much as she had for the vicar, then finished with "I want to know what God's purpose is in all this, and how I can be certain this is God at all."

Brindisi's nod required a motion of his entire upper body. "That," he said, "is a very good question indeed."

His desk was planted on the side wall, facing the open window and the darkening sky. Footfalls and young voices drifted into the rose-tinted sunset. The priest said, "There are three Hebrew terms used in the Bible for sin. The first is *chet*, which refers to missing the mark. A believer knows the right action, but goes off on a wrong tangent, usually from selfish motives. The solution to *chet* begins with repentance, or acknowledgment that a wrong action has taken place. This grows naturally into turning away and improving, and thus making the mistake a part of progress."

The priest set his cup on the edge of his desk and went on, "The second term is *avon*, from the root verb *ava*, which means to take a crooked path. These sins refer to habitual error. Again, the answer begins with repentance, but here it is far harder because the desire is to explain, justify, excuse, and keep going. Smoking and drinking to excess are examples of *avon*."

Elena sipped from her cup. She heard a choir practicing in the chapel across the quad. The breeze through the open window carried the fragrance of blooming roses. Elena was suddenly filled with the sensation that her husband was in the room with them. Listening. And approving.

"The third term is *pesha*, or rebellion. The sinner knows his actions are wrong. But he does it anyway. Here again, the answer begins with repentance, recognizing there is a genuine wrongness and seeking to turn away. But with *pesha*, this turning is very hard indeed."

Elena watched the professor rise and cross the room to his overcrammed bookshelves. The sensation of having a third person in the room left her scarcely able to breathe. And yet, there was a deep sense of rightness. As though some major event was about to take place. One that required her to remain just where she was. Listening. Aware.

The priest resumed his seat and shifted his cup so that he could settle the worn book on the desk between their two chairs. His fingers turned the pages, which Elena saw were written in Hebrew. She saw how his fingers touched only the edges of each page, such that they did not handle the written letters. She saw how his lips pursed as he turned, as though mentally speaking certain words he found upon each page.

"Here we are. Do you speak Hebrew, Dr. Burroughs?"

She licked her lips but found herself unable to reply. For at that moment the room's other guest moved closer still. And settled a hand upon her shoulder. She was certain of it. As though he was leaning over to examine the page with her.

"No. Of course not. Perhaps you will allow me to translate, yes? Here in the thirty-fourth chapter of Exodus, verses six and seven, we see that all three types of sin are mentioned. 'And the Lord passed before him and proclaimed, "The Lord, the Lord God, merciful and gracious, longsuffering and abounding in goodness and truth, keeping mercy for thousands, forgiving *chet* and *avon* and *pesha,* but by no means clearing the guilty, visiting the iniquity of the fathers upon the children's children to the third and fourth generation."'"

The professor was so absorbed in what he read that his voice took on a chanting cadence, as though he was speaking Hebrew in his mind. As though he spoke in prayer.

"Much more than these three names for sin are lost in most translations. You see here, the verses chop up a sentence. This is very rare, especially when quoting God. But in Hebrew the reason is very clear. Because the first two words of verse seven, which is usually translated in English as keeping mercy, in Hebrew reads *chanun v'rachum.* This means literally 'the grace of the womb.' In other words, the Lord shows to the faithful believer the compassion of a mother for her unborn child."

Elena wanted to reach out and touch her shoulder. Take hold of the invisible hand resting there and never let go. Even if it meant following this guest away from the physical realm entirely. Just let go of her body and her life and all the impossibilities of her daily existence. Leave it all. Now.

"The priests have spoken long and hard about why the Lord first says he is so compassionate, and then he is visiting the sins of the fathers on four generations. How can this be?"

The priest was silent almost too long. Elena felt a need in her to cry out. To call to her husband. To beg him to take her with him. To end this lonely quest. No matter what she might be called into by the Lord they both adored. Her heart chanted loudly in the silence, filled with a longing for all that was no more.

"There can be no confusion here. This is God speaking. He does not create confusion. He *clarifies*. So what does this mean?"

The priest grew silent again. Only this time, Elena understood. Not the priest's purpose, but rather the answer that lay within the silence. The Lord *clarifies*. And here was indeed an illumination.

"Remember what I said when you entered, about the true pursuit of wisdom. It requires the proper question, asked from a listening heart, toward the true source of all answers."

Elena was nodding now, rocking cadence to the priest. She knew the answer, though she could not shape it consciously. And this certainty left her able to accept the experience with a new totality. The very air vibrated with a power she could not name, nor did she need to.

"The teachers say the answer lies in this question: How many generations are alive at any one time? Three, perhaps four of any family. So what does God mean here? That if man sins, it is not just that man who suffers. The sinner burdens his family with the *results* of his sin. They *all* suffer because one man has failed. Because one man has sinned."

The priest ceased his motions in gradual stages, as though finding it difficult to draw his attention away from the text. Finally he turned toward her, blinking slowly, focusing upon her once again. "Now what do you think God would want of you?"

Only then did Elena realize she still held the cup. She gently set it on the desk next to the Bible and replied, "To help people avoid sin, and where they do sin, to help them see the need to repent."

His gaze rested upon her. She realized there were tiny dark flecks in his gray eyes. She had the impression that the same ink that was there upon the page had somehow been transferred to his gaze. As though his study were so intent, so constant, that the words had become inscribed upon his eyes.

The priest asked, "So how might you know that God is using you here, that it is God who speaks?"

It was Elena's turn to pause. But not because she needed to search for the answer.

The room's other guest was leaving.

She met the priest's gaze, but her attention was focused upon the departing visitor. He moved to the door. Then he turned. And smiled at her. And in that smile, Elena knew.

Jason was gone from her.

This realization was the real purpose behind this sense of a third guest to the evening's discussion. Elena had needed to accept that not merely her time with Jason had ended. But so had her time of mourning.

The priest and his discussion were not merely a clarification of a Bible passage. They were a revelation.

Elena leaned over the open Book. It did not matter that the words were written in a language she could not read. She knew this passage. It sprang vividly to her mind. The Lord was passing before Moses. He was *presenting* himself.

Elena had the impression that the same thing was happening here. And for a very real purpose.

She was being called.

The priest's words formed a portal. The door to a future without Jason and, more important, beyond her loss.

In truth, the transition had already taken place. She was moving from all that had once been, into . . . what?

She realized the priest was still waiting for her reply.

Elena felt herself draw a trembling breath. The tremors touched the words that emerged: "I must further God's desire to draw man near to him. To clarify God's direction. And to shield and comfort his followers here on earth."

The priest had a smile as gentle as the spirit that filled his chamber. He rose from his chair. "Such a pleasure to meet another who searches after eternal wisdom."

She rose with him. "May we speak again?"

He enfolded her hand in both of hers. "My dear doctor, I would count it an honor."

12

SATURDAY

Saturday morning, Elena stood outside her front door and watched a pair of robins quarrel over her feeder. English robins were smaller than their American cousins, scarcely larger than sparrows. Their brilliant coloring was heightened by flashes of gold on either the male or the female, she could not remember which. The kitchen breakfast alcove had two windows, facing north and west. She had fastened a total of six feeders on the closest trees, so that she would be greeted each morning by the sound of feathered company.

At precisely seven thirty, the limo pulled up in front of her house. The black Mercedes looked no more inviting now than it had when she last rode it from her office to the hospital. The bodyguard-driver settled her into the rear seat, then returned to his position behind the wheel. He pulled away from the curb and asked, "Would you like some music?"

"No thank you." Elena pulled her minilaptop from her purse. "How long will it take?"

"Ninety minutes, perhaps a little less." He powered the overweight car down the winding road with a pro's smooth skill. "Depends upon traffic."

Elena had intended to use the time on her administrivia. She had become an expert at using paperwork to hide herself from silent hours. But today she could not focus. When she lifted her eyes from the computer screen, the bulletproof glass constricted the size of the window and left her feeling as though she were viewing the outside world through the wrong end of a telescope. The car was so silent that she could hear the dashboard's ticking clock. The protective metal plate resulted in a boatlike ride, spongy and rocking. She heard herself puffing softly, as though she could not draw a decent breath.

The ambassador's wife had phoned as Elena was preparing for bed, inviting her to join them for lunch. Afterward Elena knew she would not sleep easy. So she returned to her desk and, after a long moment's hesitation, opened the ancient tome. And felt nothing.

She had studied the image for almost half an hour. Praying occasionally. Waiting. The night had remained silent.

Elena had then pulled her digital camera from the drawer and taken several photographs. She had selected the best, one where the plate filled the entire screen, and downloaded it to her computer. As she settled back into bed, she wondered if perhaps she had done something improper, extracting the image from between the book's protective covers and drawing it into the modern age. Now, as she sat in the limo's rear seat and pulled the glowing image onto her laptop, she wondered the same again.

Elena scarcely saw the image at all. Instead, she recalled sitting in the priest's chambers at New College and heard again his gentle instruction. Once more she found herself filled with the sense of her husband's love and his departure from the room.

At the time, the two experiences had been so deeply intertwined as to be one and the same. Yet now, in the limousine's rear seat, she could only recall one at a time. It was, she decided, like studying a dual image, at one moment a face and the next a pair of vases. As she reflected upon one memory and then the other, she suddenly realized why the two had come together. The message was the same as she had sensed when seated with the priest. Either she could remain with the past, with the mournful loss of her husband, or she could move on.

She already knew the answer. It was as vivid now as it had been when she was seated beside the priest. The question now was, move on toward what?

When she looked up, Elena found they were driving beside a shoulder-high stone wall. The wall was fashioned in the ancient drystone manner, set in place without cement, and covered with centuries of lichen. Sandra Harwood had explained that a British industrialist had offered them the use of his Cotswold estate. This was only the second time they had managed to go there since arriving in England two years earlier.

The limo turned into an entrance flanked by matching gate-houses and passed beneath an archway crowned with a gleaming coat of arms. They entered a vast arboretum, a garden of trees. Elena spotted a quartet of redwoods, the tallest of which stood well over two hundred feet high. As slow as those trees grew, it suggested the seedlings had been brought back by one of the earliest explorers of the California coast.

The house was simply massive. The cars parked in the graveled forecourt looked like metallic minnows hovering beside a beached stone whale. Elena knew enough to name the style as Regency, a short-lived period between the Georgian and Victorian epochs. All four floors were framed by Corinthian columns, carved in bas-relief from the exterior stone. The windows were tall and peaked and rimmed by stained glass. As the limo halted before the entrance, a butler in striped trousers and a long formal cutaway jacket paraded down the front stairs. He opened the car's rear door and pronounced, "Welcome to Berkeley Park, Dr. Burroughs."

"Thank you." She rose from the car and gave the house an astonished moment.

"The ambassador and Mrs. Harwood await you in the library."

A white-gloved attendant in a liveried jacket of maroon and gold ushered her inside. Elena passed through an atrium with a floor of polished marble and a domed ceiling. She climbed a grand curving staircase behind the servant and was ushered through two gilded doors.

The library spanned the entire front of the house, perhaps a hundred feet long. One wall was flanked by a half dozen windows, each ten feet wide and twenty high. The other walls held three floors of bookshelves, with iron balustrades and curving staircases. Brass and crystal chandeliers marched down the gilded ceiling. Several dozen people were sprinkled around the room. The ambassador glanced her way, a single heated glare, then turned back to his conversation. Sandra Harwood waved from her seat beside her husband and motioned that she would be just a moment.

But before the ambassador's wife could join her, the butler entered, rang a crystal bell, and announced, "Lunch is served."

They were thirty-eight for lunch. They were seated in a formal hall with walls of golden wood and lit by the three largest chandeliers Elena had ever seen. Eight liveried servants waited on them. The refectory table could have comfortably held another dozen. Elena was seated midway down the table, between an elderly gentleman who was clearly hard of hearing and a striking woman of perhaps fifty. Elena did not catch the woman's name when they were introduced, but heard the man on the woman's other side refer to her as Comtessa.

The conversation was vapid, the lunch endless. Finally dessert was served, a gold-rimmed plate of fresh fruit and sherbet, topped by a wing of woven sugar. Elena discovered that the elderly gentleman seated to her right had fallen asleep. As she toyed with her dessert, Elena felt eyes upon her. She lifted her gaze to discover the ambassador's wife watching her. Sandra Harwood nodded once. Then turned away.

The ambassador rose to his feet, and in the ensuing tumult Sandra Harwood motioned for Elena to remain where she was. With practiced smoothness the ambassador's wife disengaged from an overbearing gentleman and moved around the table without appearing to hurry. She slipped into the chair the comtessa had vacated. "We don't have much time. Give me the other message for my husband."

Elena heard a booming laughter at the table's head. "I'm not certain that would be—"

"There are issues at work here that you do not need to concern yourself with. Just know that Lawrence has refused the President's offer. Now he wants to know the remainder of your message."

Elena turned in her seat. Perhaps a dozen people clustered around the ambassador. He stabbed Elena with a look just as Sandra touched her arm and said, "Lawrence remains in the room so we can speak and not be overheard."

Elena turned back and asked, "We are being monitored?"

"Always and everywhere. It is a price one pays for power in this day and age." She waved that away, the gesture more impatient this time. "Give me the message. Please."

"Three words," Elena said. "Feed my sheep."

The news pushed Sandra back hard in her chair. "There is nothing more?"

"I had the impression that the ambassador has already been asked to take on another job. He had to choose between that and the vice presidency."

Sandra Harwood was clearly rocked hard by the words. "My husband receives many offers."

"This one was very special. Something he was uniquely qualified for. Something he was called to do. The only other word I received was *mission*. As in, God was calling him to take this on." A shadow fell over Elena. She realized a servant was holding her chair, waiting for her to rise. Elena leaned in closer and said, "I had the impression your enemy nominated Lawrence for the vice president position so that he would be drawn away from accepting this other job."

The ambassador's wife rose with her, her face set in grimly determined lines. She repeated softly, "Mission."

13

───────────

Midway through the limo ride back to Oxford, Elena's phone rang. She had not even realized it was on. She checked the readout but did not recognize the incoming number. "Hello?"

"Carlo Brindisi here, Dr. Burroughs. I hope I'm not disturbing you."

"Cardinal, hello. Not at all."

"I am most grateful for our time together yesterday, Dr. Burroughs."

"Please call me Elena."

"Most grateful, both to you and Brian and to God. For I saw God's hand at work in our meeting."

"I did as well."

"I'm so glad to hear you say that. You see, I am phoning now because I was wondering if I might ask you to do me a very great favor."

"If I can."

"Wonderful. Wonderful." The priest's accent seemed much stronger today than it had while they were seated together in his office. Elena had the impression the priest was nervous, and the strain was affecting his command of English.

Brindisi asked, "Will you travel to Rome?"

"Will I . . . what?"

"Monday. The day after tomorrow." The priest's nerves were far more evident now. "Say you will. Please. I beg you."

Elena's protest sounded strangled to her own ears. "It would be very difficult."

Brindisi appeared not even to have heard. "A very dear friend and ally. A man who truly holds a heart for God. He is in need of your help."

"I'm sorry, I—"

"My friend, his name is Antonio d'Alba. He has been having dreams."

14

As soon as she arrived home, Elena called her pastor. Brian agreed to meet with her that evening, though clearly he would have preferred otherwise. She exercised for a half hour, showered and changed clothes, and set off again.

Oxford's medieval heritage was largely lost to the sprawl of industry and commerce. But tiny pockets still remained of its more rural beginnings. One such area was Wolvercote. The place was remarkably easy to miss, even by seasoned locals. The only road leading to the village began in the middle of a wretched sixties-era housing development. To anyone who did not know better, the narrow lane looked like just another driveway. But beyond the development's perimeter stretched a meadow, and then a forest, both of which were protected by royal treaty. The River Thames cut a narrow swath through the woods, and was crossed by a bridge whose foundations were set in place by the Romans. Standing next to this bridge was Elena's favorite restaurant in Oxford, the Trout Inn.

The inn's heritage was so ancient as to be inextricably bound up with lore and fable. Certainly the current structure had been in place for well over seven hundred years. But if legends were to be believed, Roman soldiers had once rested in the very same place, watching river trout feed in the sun-dappled waters. When Elena rose from her car, the faint rumble of traffic could be heard from the city's ring road. Other than this trace of metallic thunder, however, the present day was not allowed to intrude.

As soon as the pastor stepped from his car, Elena understood why he had been reluctant to meet.

Brian was accompanied by a woman Elena's age, tall with russet hair and an air of nervousness to match the pastor's. She wore a checked skirt of forest green. Over this was a long belted sweater. A brilliant silk scarf was tied about her neck. Elena watched as Brian reached for her hand, then dropped it with a teenager's uncertainty. Elena pretended not to have noticed and greeted them both with her warmest smile.

The inn was built in the early medieval style, when ship's timbers were used as support columns for upper floors. The walls were fashioned from the local honey-colored stone. Fires burned at both ends of the main room. Candles flickered upon every oaken table. The patrons' faces were painted with ruddy tones from another, softer era. Elena held her peace through the ordeal of menus and waiters and the arrival of their drinks. Then Brian excused himself to take a call, as she knew he would. Elena leaned across the table and said, "You don't have any reason to worry about me."

The woman tried for a haughty British air, but her nerves gave her away. "I'm quite sure I don't—"

Elena interrupted, "Let's not start what I hope will be a deep and abiding friendship with falsehoods."

Janine Featheringham possessed angular features and a direct gaze and strong hands that played nervously across the tabletop. "I-I've been terrified of meeting."

"I understand."

"He speaks of you with such affection. It's, well, I hope you'll forgive me . . ."

"There's never been anything between us, and there never

will be. Brian and I have seen each other at our absolute worst."

"And yet you still care for each other."

"Very deeply. But not in a romantic way." She sought some way to explain how she felt. "Shared hardships have cast us in the role of brother and sister."

Janine blinked fiercely. "I can't tell you how much it means to hear you say this."

"I think I know."

"He's very special to me, you see."

"Where did you two meet?"

"He spoke at my village church one Sunday as a favor to our vicar, who was ailing. It was, well, I know this sounds utterly foppish for a woman of my years . . ."

"Love at first sight," Elena finished for her. "For him as well?"

"He says so." Janine squared her shoulders. "And I believe him."

Elena reached across the table. "I can't tell you how thrilled I am for you both."

Which was when Brian reentered the restaurant. He stowed his phone in his pocket, looked down at the clasped hands in the center of the table, and took a long breath. "Well. How utterly splendid."

Janine smiled across the table. "I couldn't agree more."

Through dinner, Elena was content to sit across from the couple and listen as they shared the breathless delight of new love. She found herself making mental notes. This was how a pair of mature people could reknit the fabric of their worlds.

Janine revealed how her father had been addicted to unfaithfulness. Janine had always assumed the endless arguments between her parents had scarred her for life. She had put marriage down as something that happened to others. She had focused her life and energies on her role as senior child care supervisor for all of Oxfordshire.

Only now there was this sapling of young love taking root, and everything must be redefined. There was joy to the moment, and considerable fear. Janine and Brian looked to Elena, the professional, for advice, but she gave none. How could she, when another portion of her mind and heart were filled with what this couple represented. All the avenues Elena had willfully avoided. The chances never noticed. Because she had refused to lift her head from the sands of loss.

Finally over coffee, Elena said, "I need to speak with you about something."

Janine said, "Perhaps I should leave."

"No. Please stay."

Elena recounted the phone call and the limo and the manor. "I'm sorry to dispel your happy mood."

"You've done nothing of the sort," Janine said, though her tone was grave.

"I can't tell you who my patient is without breaking confidentiality."

"I wouldn't expect you to."

"But you need to understand that the people involved hold considerable political power." Elena then described the lunch. And then the phone call from Brian's friend. She said, "I have no idea what to do."

"Have you prayed about it?"

"All afternoon."

"You want my advice?"

"Desperately."

"Go to Rome."

"I must agree," Janine said. "This request was not offered lightly."

Brian went on, "Carlo Brindisi might present himself here as a bumbling professor, lost in his research and ancient texts. But he is a chameleon. The power he holds in Rome is quite considerable. He would only ask you to do this if it was very important. Even vital."

"I have patients," Elena protested weakly. "Responsibilities."

"And what if God is calling you?"

"Then why doesn't he say something?"

Brian directed a tender smile to the woman seated beside him. "Perhaps that is precisely what he is doing at this moment."

Elena hesitated, but the sensation of compressed need would not be denied. "There's more."

The couple showed surprise for the first time. Brian said, "More?"

Elena told them about the book. She wondered all the while if she was doing the right thing. When she was done, there was a long silence, then Brian asked, "Miriam has given you a book that is four hundred years old."

"Several books," Janine corrected. "Isn't that right?"

"Five in total. Yes."

"All identical copies of the same text. And the oldest . . ."

"According to legend," Elena said. "It's fashioned from scrolls two thousand years old."

"And each page holds a verse from the Lord's Prayer."

"In Aramaic. Yes."

"Should you be telling us this?"

"I have no idea."

"I'm honored that you chose to trust us," Janine said. "And touched. Deeply."

"This," Brian said, "I have got to see."

15

The night had grown chilly, which was nice, because it gave Elena an excuse to light a fire. She turned on a pair of lamps in the living room's far corners. She offered the couple coffee, then excused herself and went into her bedroom. She lifted the book from her desk drawer and felt the now-familiar tingle, as though the energy had grown while awaiting her return. She carried the book into the living room and set it on the coffee table. She pulled a cushion off the sofa and settled on the floor opposite her friends.

Brian's face appeared elongated by the room's shadows and the firelight. "I still wonder if we should be doing this."

Now that they were here and the book in its silk cover lay between them, Elena was filled with an air of certainty. "Miriam said distinctly that there were no rules. And if there once had been, she did not know them."

"A friend guides you into studying clinical psychology. She suggests you overcome tragedy by studying dreams. She waits for half a lifetime, hoping in silence for such a moment." Brian shook his head. "I've known Miriam for years and now wonder if I ever saw the woman at all."

Elena unwound the cords and slid the book from its cover. Brian and Janine both greeted the book with a long breath. Elena opened the cover and turned the book so the image was directed their way. Janine whispered, "What does it say?"

"*Abba.*"

"It's so beautiful."

Brian traced a pair of fingers along the base of the page, creasing his way along the track shaded by centuries of hands before his own. "The earliest alphabet known to mankind is the North Semitic, which dates from around 3000 BC. A thousand years later, Aramaic was developed from these Semitic roots."

Janine watched him. "How do you know this?"

Elena answered, "After his wife died, Brian taught himself to read Hebrew."

"Elena worked on her book about dreams," Brian said. "I had my studies."

"Tell me what I'm seeing."

"Modern Hebrew comes from the same Semitic roots as Aramaic. Arabic is also a direct descendant of Aramaic and still uses the Aramaic names for letters. These oldest languages— Aramaic, Hebrew, and Arabic—only wrote down the consonants. These slash marks, what in English would be accents, are known as diacritics. They represent the vowel sounds. Around the year 1000 BC, the Greeks took the Phoenician language, which also came from these same Semitic roots, and added actual letters for vowels. This became the base for the letters of the Roman alphabet, which is what we use today."

Brian traced his hand around the flowing script. "What you see here, this artistic drawing of letters, is called calligraphy. No one really knows when it began. In the Hebrew faith there were strict edicts against the usage of images, as these were used by idolatrous peoples as a focal point for worship. So calligraphy, turning script into a form of artistic image, was seen as an acceptable compromise." Brian leaned over until his face was inches from the page. "Which makes this page all the more astonishing."

Elena asked, "Why is that?"

"Because the Judeans were not permitted to speak the name of God. And then here came Jesus, who not only addressed his Father in heaven openly, but used the most intimate of terms. *Abba* quite literally is the way a young child would address a beloved father, but only in the privacy of a home. It is the most endearing way to address a parent. Cozy, intimate, cherished."

Elena waited until Brian settled back in his seat to say, "I've been waiting for days and I haven't heard a single thing more."

Brian kept his gaze upon the page. "You are called to Rome in the service of your Lord. You are going."

Elena reached over and shut the book. "I feel like everything is spinning out of my control."

Brian nodded slowly, his gaze still fastened upon what he no longer needed to see. "Isn't it wonderful."

"That is the *last* word I would use to describe this situation."

"Wonderful I said, and wonderful I meant." He looked at her then, his gaze burning more fiercely than the fire. "You are being gently forced beyond your comfort zone. You are being called to rely solely upon your Lord. Go, Elena. Go and serve."

16

SUNDAY

Saint Aldates's first Sunday service began at eight and held to the formal Anglican tradition. The choir and clergy wore robes, the liturgy was read from the official prayer book, and the vicar climbed the stone stairs to preach from the crowned alcove. The other two services were modern and informal and raucous. Young families packed the hall, children were everywhere, and music was led by a rock band.

Elena stood with the congregation as the choir and clergy entered, bearing the sacraments and Bible and cross. This formal service was half-empty, whereas the later services were standing-room only. Elena looked out over the hall and saw a sea of gray heads. She enjoyed the formality from time to time. Today, however, she was here for a different reason.

At the conclusion of the service, Elena waited at the back of the main aisle. The man she had come to meet walked slowly toward her. Jeremy Yates was the head of the university's counseling service. His height and well-cut suits partially masked his extra poundage. He was bald save for two strips of frothy white hair by either temple. He was a tutor at Lincoln College, a specialist in teenage emotional afflictions, and spoke all over the world. He was impatient with all meetings and heartily disliked any interruption to his weekends. Elena normally went silent in his presence.

Today, however, she greeted the gentleman and said, "I need a minute of your time."

"What, here?" His gesture took in the church, his wife chatting with three other ladies, and the day. "What could possibly require such an interruption?"

She was saved from responding by the vicar's approach. Brian's robes were of shimmering white satin, with brilliantly embroidered sleeves and frontice. He asked Elena, "Is this regarding what we spoke about last night?"

"Yes."

"Excellent." He gestured to the back of the church. "Use my office. Let me get out of these robes and I'll join you."

Elena said, "This is very important, Jeremy. Five minutes. Please."

When they arrived at Brian's office, the pastor was back in his normal street clothes, but the air of stern authority still surrounded him. Jeremy Yates waited until the door was shut, then demanded, "Now what's this all about?"

"I have to make a trip tomorrow," Elena said. "Very unexpectedly."

"Might I inquire where you intend on going?"

"Rome."

"Don't you have patients?"

"I'm booked solid all week."

"How long were you intending to be away?"

"I don't know, Jeremy. Hopefully just a couple of days."

"Out of the question. You'll simply need to reschedule your journey."

"Jeremy," Brian said. "Elena is going. And you are going to help her."

Jeremy swiveled back and forth between the pair. "I detect a faint whiff of conspiracy here."

"I wanted to be a part of this meeting so I could lend my voice to hers," Brian replied.

"I say. This is all rather unorthodox."

"You have no idea," Elena said.

"Elena will stay as long as is required, and not a moment longer." Brian leaned across the desk. "It is vital that Elena make this trip. Without delay."

The chief counselor blew out his cheeks. "I suppose we can make some adjustments. At least for a day or so."

"If Elena can't make it back by Wednesday, she will phone you. Won't you, Elena."

"I'll call every day."

"Does this have anything to do with that new patient of yours, the rather striking American lady and her hulking body-guards?"

Elena looked down at her hands.

Jeremy rose ponderously, straightened the lapels of his jacket, then said, "Well, if the pair of you are quite done, I'll go share this utter lack of clarity with my wife."

When the door closed behind him, Brian said, "Jeremy Yates can be an overbearing pachyderm. I didn't want him trampling on this mission of yours."

Elena said, "I wish I was half as confident about all this as you sounded."

"As I was preparing for bed last night, I had the most vivid impression that God addressed me. I've never doubted the Spirit's potency for communication. But it has rarely occurred to me." Brian fastened his gaze upon her. "Spiritual gifts are not intended for the recipient. Do you understand what I am saying?"

"I-I'm not sure."

"Sitting in this chair over the years, I've learned to tolerate just about anything. But the one thing that still raises my hackles is when a parishioner comes in here spouting off about receiving some gift of the Spirit or another, like they'd just been crowned on High Street. God bestows moments of higher awareness for a *divine reason.* Your job is to remain humble before the throne, and accept whatever direction he points you in."

"You're not suggesting I'm proud of all this."

"Of course not." His gaze was filled with an authority that could not be denied. "I'm saying you're comfortable. You loathe the spotlight. You like your carefully defined little existence. This is about a mission God seeks to place upon your life. This is about something far larger than we can imagine. Your job is to be ready and open for whatever comes."

"You're frightening me."

"I know I am." Brian reached across the desk. "Now take my hand and let's pray we both have the strength and the determination to see this through to the eternal end."

17

MONDAY

The morning flight to Rome was not full. Elena sat by the window and stared over the cloud-draped vista and recalled the morning's events. She had risen with the dawn and eaten her breakfast with Miriam's book opened on the table before her. Elena did not know why she had done it, and she still had no idea why she was making this journey at all. Then it had happened, a sweeping intensity so commanding that the outer world faded to an almost dreamlike appearance. She had the impression that the image had lasted only a moment, a few heartbeats at most. And yet it seemed as though she had remained within the amberlike force for eons.

As the plane started its descent into Rome, Elena's mind tracked back to her one other trip to Italy. Jason had spent his last winter working on a series of articles, running the department, and teaching. For months he had slept poorly. In February he had caught a cold, and the cough had lingered for months. Elena could find him by listening for his next raspy bark. Finally in late March she had booked them a week at a seaside resort in Sicily. Jason of course had not wanted to go. He spent the entire flight complaining about what needed doing. Upon their arrival, he went to bed and slept for almost two days. The remainder of their holiday had been perfect. They took long walks and talked for hours and dined on the hotel's veranda, overlooking the Mediterranean. Jason had lost both his pallor and his cough, and regained his smile. On the return flight, they had made plans to spend two weeks exploring the Amalfi coast that autumn. Seven weeks later, he was gone.

The plane shook violently from turbulence, followed by the chime signaling the seat-belt light and the flight attendant's hasty announcement. Elena continued to stare out the window, her interior world shaken far more than the plane. Following her husband's death, Italy had become just another place to avoid. Yet here she was, traveling there for reasons she could not explain even to herself. Her pastor's words rang softly in her ears. *Mission.* Odd how easily she could say it to someone else. How different it sounded when applied to herself.

The taxi ride into Rome gave her the sensation of having stepped through a mysterious door and entered a new realm. One where the sun burned more fiercely, where light etched everything with a crystal beauty, where even the most mundane sight held a singular aura. Elena rolled down her window and let the hot wind rush in, peeling away the airplane odors and the fatigue she always felt after a flight. The taxi driver caught her eye in the rearview mirror and grinned. Elena feared the elderly driver with his bad teeth and three-day growth was coming on to her. Then he raised three fingers to his mouth, kissed them, and opened them to the breeze. "Ah, Roma!"

Elena laughed out loud.

On the city's outskirts the traffic congealed. It took longer to arrive in the city center than it had to fly from England. The taxi finally halted before a marble-clad building of imposing dimensions. Elena rose slowly from the taxi. This might be her first visit to Rome, but she knew where she was. The dome of Saint Peter's cathedral peeked over the neighboring roofs. She said, "There must be some mistake."

The taxi driver shrugged his incomprehension. Elena pointed at the handwritten address. He nodded and pointed at the broad marble stairs leading up to a pair of massive bronze doors.

Elena paid the driver, hefted her case, and climbed the stairs to where a uniformed officer now waited. "Excuse me, is this the office—"

"Your name?"

"Elena Burroughs."

"Yes, Dr. Burroughs. You are expected." The young officer spoke heavily accented but clear English. "Please, you are to leave your valise here with me, yes? Security. You understand?"

"Of course." She followed him inside. The foyer was even grander than the exterior, a vast chamber of marble and gilded cherubs and columns and chandeliers. She passed through the metal detector while a second guard went through her purse and then her suitcase. He wore latex gloves and a professionally detached air, and did an extremely thorough job.

The first guard said, "You are please to leave transcripting here."

"Excuse me?"

"I say this wrong? Any device for taping."

"A recorder. No, I don't—"

"And your phone. It will all be here when you finish."

By the time the second guard had finished replacing everything but her phone back into her shoulder bag, a woman had descended the stairs and was waiting for her beyond the security station. "Dr. Burroughs?"

"Yes."

"Signor d'Alba is ready for you." The woman was impossibly elegant, her clothes as impeccable as her hair. She crossed the vast lobby, her heels clicking upon the marble.

Elena hurried to catch up. They climbed a sweeping marble staircase, each banister carved from what appeared to be onyx. The distant ceiling was painted with a vast angelic sunrise. Elena felt wrinkled and frumpy and utterly out of place. "I'm sorry, but I wasn't able to stop by my hotel and freshen up. The drive into Rome took forever."

The woman did not respond. She maintained a model's walk, back and head rigidly erect. She led Elena down a long corridor and knocked on a pair of polished doors. At a voice from within, she pushed open the large brass handle, cast Elena a single frosty glance, then said, "*La vostra visitatrice da Londre, Dottore.*"

"Ah. Very well. I suppose you might as well come in." The man was seated at a long refectory table. A younger man was seated beside him, tapping furiously into a laptop. A woman perhaps Elena's age stood to his left, sorting through what appeared to be graphs and sheets of statistics. The gentleman spoke a few soft words. Immediately the young man closed his laptop and the pair departed. The young woman glanced at Elena as they passed. Her expression was as rigidly cold as the receptionist's.

"So. My friend the cardinal has insisted that I see you." The man seemed reluctant to face her. He waved her forward without actually lifting his gaze from the pages spread across his table. "Please come in. Will you take coffee?"

"No thank you."

Elena walked stiffly across the largest office she had ever seen. The room had to be seventy or eighty feet long and half as wide. The ceiling was domed and frescoed like the entrance hall. The French doors behind his massive desk were open. The view was over the square and the tourists. He waved vaguely at a leather-upholstered chair on the desk's opposite side. "Perhaps you would care to make yourself comfortable."

Elena crossed the room and settled into the seat. She did not speak. There was nothing for her to say.

He still had not looked at her. His manner was as stiff as his voice. "My friend was wrong to ask you to come."

Elena felt distanced enough from his irritation to study him openly. Antonio d'Alba was a spare man, perhaps three inches taller than herself. She guessed his age at somewhere around forty, but she could not be certain. He had a timeless face and what she assumed was prematurely graying hair. His eyes were dark and intelligent, his manner somewhat professorial.

"Carlo has always been hard to refuse, however. Since he became cardinal he has grown even worse, if that is possible." He raised his hands in a gesture of Italian defeat. "And so we are here. On an extremely busy day. I am sorry you were forced to make this journey, Dr. Burroughs. I can only give you a very few minutes."

Elena remained silent.

Her stillness clearly irritated him. Antonio d'Alba finally looked at her directly. "Do you not have anything to say, madam?"

Elena did not speak.

"This is rather odd, wouldn't you agree? Traveling all this way, only to sit and stare at me?"

Even with his tie loosened and his shirtsleeves rolled up, he remained formal in an extremely Italian manner. The tie was woven silk and shimmered as he moved in and out of the sunlight. His shirt was starched and looked tailored to his slender form, gray striped but with white collar and cuffs. His gray hair was fashionably cut and long enough to touch his ears. He had sensitive lips for such a strong chin, and eyes that were filled with the only emotion he had revealed so far, which was impatient irritation. Antonio d'Alba rose to his feet and began striding back and forth between his desk and the French doors. Elena watched him pace and wondered if he expressed other emotions as vividly. She thought he might have a very attractive smile. But she doubted he smiled very often. His eyes seemed shadowed by more than just the dream they now shared.

She realized where her thoughts had taken her and felt her face go hot.

"Am I reduced to an amoeba on your personal petri dish? How long before you render an observation, Doctor? All day?

Well, I don't have the time to dedicate to your professional curiosity. Nor to my friend the cardinal's petty whims."

Elena knew it was time for her to speak. "I have seen your dream," she said quietly.

Antonio d'Alba glared at her. "What you say is more than impossible. It is offensive."

"I have seen your dream," Elena said. "And I have felt your pain."

The office's French doors were open to the afternoon light and the sound of tourists bustling about the square. A bus trundled by, its brakes squeaking. A cloud of pigeons rose from the square, their flapping wings a quiet applause. Antonio d'Alba stood where the shadows began, his pacing halted now. He stared at her.

Elena said, "I have no idea who you are. I can only assume you hold some immense power. You are obviously accustomed to people coming in here with one thing on their minds. How they can obtain something from you."

It was Antonio d'Alba's turn to remain silent. He crossed his arms and backed farther into the shadows. Only his eyes remained clearly visible, burning with a dark and slanted fire.

"I don't know anything about you. I only met your friend the cardinal on Friday. I did not come here seeking anything except to help. This is all so new to me, I'm still trying to find my own way."

"What precisely is new?"

"The interpretation of dreams."

"And yet you are called a world authority on the subject. That is what Carlo claims."

"This is very different. And we both know it."

"Different how?"

"I did not come here to speak of your dreams in any clinical sense. Your friend did not approach me on this basis. I am here because . . ."

He waited with her. The cathedral bells chimed softly. A group of tourists began singing in a language Elena did not recognize. Elena realized Antonio d'Alba was going to force her to finish the sentence without his pressing.

She said, "I am here because I felt God calling me to come."

Antonio d'Alba turned and shut the French doors. Instantly the noise was reduced to a soft murmur. He pulled on a cord, drawing the drapes. The afternoon light filtered through, softened and transformed into a rainbow pastel. The noise was muted now to the point that Elena heard a telephone ring in some adjoining room.

He seated himself and said, "So how do you wish to proceed?"

"The Bible is very clear about this. I know because I've gone back and studied the relevant passages. Divinely directed dreams come at a time of great need, and normally result in considerable distress. Even so, interpretations are only offered when they have been requested."

She waited.

Antonio d'Alba nodded slowly. Again. He opened his mouth. Shut it. Tried again. "Very well, Dr. Burroughs. I am asking. Tell me of my dream."

18

━━━━━━━━━━━━━━━━━━━━━━

Antonio d'Alba requested that Elena cancel her hotel reservation. He then had his secretary book her into a hotel just down the road from his home. The secretary stared at Elena in utter confusion as she returned to confirm the reservation. The two staffers Elena had seen leaving Antonio's office did the same.

When she arrived at the hotel, Elena showered, then dressed in the hotel robe, and lay down on the bed. She did not bother to pull back the covers. She was not interested in falling asleep. She needed to be at Antonio's home for dinner in less than an hour. What she wanted was a chance to sort through the day. She had found this very helpful after a particularly stressful series of sessions. Her mind would rebel against the idea of slowing down. But if she could force herself to stop, even for a moment, the perspective to any problem or issue was clarified. Elena shut her eyes and concentrated on her breathing. In and out. Steadying herself. Feeling the little jolts of rarefied energy shoot through her. Flashes of images. The instant of realization that came over breakfast. The taxi to Heathrow. The security check-in. The flight, the Rome airport, the traffic, the office, the man.

Gradually Elena's breathing eased and her mind slowed its frantic wrestling against issues that no longer surrounded her. The hotel room had French doors, not unlike those in d'Alba's office. Only these overlooked a hotel garden and a pair of pencil-thin trees that were filled with chirping birds. The sun was setting, Elena could see the light softening through her closed eyelids. She drifted now, breathing easily. She had intended to look again at the moment when she had related her experience of the dream. Instead, her mind drifted back further, settling upon the moment in the cardinal's office.

This often happened in such times of forced repose. Her mind would sift through various sessions with the same patient, revealing a pattern that she had missed until then. Only this time it was Elena's own experiences that were being woven together. She recalled sitting in Brian's office the previous morning and hearing him describe his revelation. Elena's entire body trembled slightly, as though Brian's words were a hammer and she a bell. She hovered there until she knew she was going to be late for dinner. When she rose from the bed, the light outside her window had dimmed to a purplish glow. Elena dressed hurriedly and left the room.

Downstairs, she showed Antonio's handwritten note to the concierge. He walked outside with her and pointed her up the road. He offered to get her a taxi, but her destination was less than five hundred yards away. Elena thanked the man and said she would walk.

Elena wore charcoal-gray slacks and a white silk top with a high collar and oriental-style cloth buttons. Her only jewelry was a string of pearls worn over the blouse. The night was cooling rapidly, and she was glad for the sweater she had knotted about her shoulders. The street sloped upward and curved around the hillside. Elena could see nothing except high stone walls and metal gates. Trees fronting the road were carefully trimmed, so that their limbs could not be used as a passage over the walls. Streetlights cast everything in a harsh glare.

Even the trees' springtime blossoms were tainted yellow. All the gates she passed, both for pedestrians and cars, were flanked by more yellow lights. The tops of the walls were lined with broken glass embedded in the concrete. As she approached her destination, a blue sedan slowed so that two uniformed officers could inspect her.

The house number was painted on a ceramic tile set in the wall beside a tall whitewashed metal gate. She pressed the buzzer and watched a security camera swivel over to study her. The blue sedan did not pull away until the gate clicked and pulled back on electronic hinges. The camera followed her inside. The gate swung shut.

The villa was three stories and gray and not particularly impressive, at least from the outside. A woman as gray as the house stood in the open doorway, waiting for Elena to climb the stairs. She nodded a silent greeting, let Elena into the house, then shut and double-locked the door. She said in fractured English, "*Il dottore,* Signor d'Alba, he have phone."

"I understand."

"Please, you to wait, yes?"

"Of course."

"He no be long." The woman scarcely came up to the base of Elena's rib cage. She was dressed in a simple dark sweater, black ankle-length skirt, and lace-up shoes. Her hair was drawn back into a tight bun. She led Elena through a second pair of doors. "You like veranda?"

"Wherever you want me to wait will be fine." Elena followed the servant down a long hall. The doors to her right were shut, and she thought she heard a man's muffled voice. To her left were another set of tall mahogany doors, open to reveal a high-ceilinged parlor. The hallway's white marble tiles were veined in rose and purple. Recessed alcoves lining the hallway held inlaid tables and alabaster vases. Four alcoves, four tables, four ancient vases. Their golden rims had been partially worn away with the centuries. Above the vases hung dark oil paintings. The paintings

to her left were of pastoral scenes, those to her right were por-
traits. Everything she saw, the rooms and the hallway and the
furniture, was immaculate.

The older woman led Elena out the rear doors and onto a
broad veranda. Elena walked over to the railing and sighed,
"Oh, my."

The view was a breathtaking swoop over night-clad Rome.
The dome of Saint Peter's glowed like a polished diadem. The
river was an inky line snaking through streets and buildings and
monuments to lost ages. Traffic noise drifted upon a breeze that
carried the flavors of eucalyptus and wood smoke.

"Signora, please."

She walked over to a covered canopy holding a table set for
two. As Elena took her seat, the servant released woven cords
and shut the windward cloth wall. Now that the breeze was
blocked, the old woman went about lighting candles set in tall
glass globes.

The servant clasped her hands beneath her rib cage and
asked, "You are liking drink?"

"I'll wait for Signor d'Alba, thank you."

The woman remained where she was. "Please, you are helping *il dottore*?"

"I will do what I can," Elena replied. "You must care for him
very much."

Now that she was seated, the old woman's face was almost
level with her own. She showed Elena an inscrutable mask. "I am
with family since before he is born. When *la signora* die, he is so
sad. Then he is better. Now the dreams."

"I'm sorry, who died?"

"*La sposa*. His, how you say, wife."

"He lost his wife?"

"Since three years. You are not knowing this?"

"I'm sorry. No." When the woman started to turn away,
Elena asked, "Do they have children?"

The servant inspected her for a long moment, clearly uncertain whether to respond. Finally she said, "A daughter. She study in New York. Here too is much sadness."

The old woman turned and walked away. She might have sighed as she left the veranda. Or perhaps it was merely the wind.

Elena relaxed on the padded metal chair and enjoyed the night. The veranda was tiled in ancient marble that had been repeatedly cracked and repaired. The outdoor table was covered by layers of fine damask cloth, but the whitewashed metal legs were blistered where rust was seeping through. The padding to her chair was mended in several places, as was the veranda's covering. Elena could understand now what she had seen inside the house and here on the veranda. The house was frozen in time, everything held as it had been when laughter had filled the rooms. And song. Elena saw a dozen more chairs lined up against the veranda's far wall, shadowy reminders of old friends and long dinners and nights that ended far too soon. She turned back to the view. She knew everything there was to know about futile efforts to freeze the passage of time.

"I'm so very, very sorry." Antonio d'Alba rushed out onto the veranda. He waved his hand vaguely back toward the villa. "Some days the world refuses to let go of me."

"It's fine."

"No, no, this is not right. I invite you into my home, and leave you here . . ." He glanced at his watch, then at her. Antonio looked genuinely harried. "You have been out here for an hour?"

The length of time surprised her, but on a very superficial level. "I didn't mind."

"Did they not offer you something to drink?"

"Of course she did." When he started to rise from his chair, Elena said, "Antonio."

"Eh, yes?"

She realized it was the first time she had used his first name. "Sit down. Relax. Everything is fine."

Slowly he lowered himself back into the chair. "First I am

rude to you in my office. Now this. What you must think of me I cannot imagine."

"What I think is that I would like to know more about you. Such as, what do you do?"

"Carlo did not tell you this?"

"The cardinal told me nothing. Except that you were having dreams."

"Until recently, I was chairman of a bank. Now I serve as adviser to the Vatican on the church's investments."

"When did you resign from the bank?"

"Three years ago. A bit less. Why do you ask?"

"Your servant told me about losing your wife. I'm so sorry."

"You obtain such information from Angelica? I am astonished. She will not tell most guests the time of day. In this she is very Sicilian."

"Angelica cares for you very much."

"She was my nanny when I was young. After my mother died, she raised me. I have offered to give her a house in the Sicilian countryside, where she is from. But she stays. Ah, excellent, food. Are you hungry?"

They were served by a slender young man named Gino. The table swiftly filled with an assortment of antipasti. Thinly sliced prosciutto draped over melon, flaky pastries filled with goat cheese, *melanzane* served with olive oil and fresh basil, delicately grilled aubergine and asparagus with flakes of parmesan cheese. On and on the plates came. Elena had eaten nothing since a hurried croissant at Heathrow. There followed shallow bowls holding pasta blankets filled with ground veal and spices, swimming in a meat broth.

The conversation started out at a casual level. Antonio explained that his villa stood upon the crest of the Cavalieri Hill, north of Vatican City. It was not one of the original seven hills of Rome, as those were all on the river's other side. His family had settled in this area during the medieval era. They had served as merchants to the Vatican, bakers and candle makers and then importers of fabric. This was the seventh villa that had been erected on the same spot, completed in the waning days of the eighteenth century. Over a third course of roast lamb, Antonio pointed out various sites within the streetlights far below. Elena listened and nodded and ate in silence. She knew Antonio had not invited her here to discuss the view.

Coffee was served by the same old woman who had led Elena onto the veranda. She accepted their thanks for the meal in unblinking silence. After Elena refused the offers of dessert and a digestif, the servant turned and padded away, leaving them alone with the night birds.

Antonio stirred sugar into his coffee and said, "You are very quiet."

Elena sat and sipped her coffee and waited.

They shared another moment staring out over the veranda railing. Finally he said the words she had been waiting for. "Will you tell me again about my dream?"

"Of course."

"I do not mean to suggest that you left something out. I am simply trying to digest the fact that someone else knows what I have been experiencing."

"I understand." Elena took a long breath and related again what she had told him in his office that afternoon.

In the image that had transfixed her over breakfast, she had stood in the road. In the gutter, actually. Water flowed over her shoes. She was dressed in a man's fancy suit. In the illogical pattern of a vivid dream, she knew the shoes were handmade. The shoes were ruined.

She also knew that this was not her own dream. She was looking through the eyes of another person. Seeing his dream. As her own.

The sun had blazed in an empty sky. Even so, the gutter was filled with savage floodwaters. She wanted to step out of the way, but she could not move. In front of her was a line without beginning or end. Men and women and children.

They were homeless and bankrupt and destitute and broken. As she studied the endless line, she realized two things. First, it was not water that flooded over the curb and ruined her clothes. It was a flood of shattered lives and hopes. And second, it was her fault that these people were here. She could have done something to stop this from happening. And she had done nothing.

When she finished, Antonio d'Alba stared into the darkness for a time, then spoke in a voice that was scarcely stronger than the night breeze. "I have never told anyone about what my dream contains, you see. And yet here you are. Arriving in my office, where I am the authority. Even the pope listens to me when I speak about financial matters. And you tell me the dark mysteries that have ravaged my nights."

"For how long have you experienced this dream?"

"At times it feels like all my life. In truth, perhaps two years now. It comes and then goes, and I am sometimes able to pretend that it is over and done. That I am free. And then it comes again. It attacks me." He addressed the city and the night beyond his home. "Last week it attacked every night. Which is why I mentioned it to Carlo. I never spoke of it before. To anyone. Now I wonder if perhaps the dream came more frequently to make sure I would pay attention when you arrived."

"Or so that you would mention it to your friend, the cardinal."

"Just so." He looked at her. "In the office, you said something else. You said you felt my pain."

Elena shuddered. "Yes."

"I'm sorry, are you cold?"

"No. It's not that." She took a very hard breath and related what had happened next. When the image had ended, Elena had started sobbing so hard that she could neither draw breath nor rise from her chair. Instead, she had rolled onto the floor and crawled to the bathroom. She had lain on the cold tiles until the weeping finally came under control. She had cried for the people, and she had cried for how her life was being taken from her control by this, this thing. And yet try as she might, she could not turn from the invitation. Because no matter how hard she wept then, she could feel the gentle presence of God. There. With her.

He watched her solemnly. His features were made craven by the flickering candles. He said softly, "Invitation."

"That was the word that came to me then, and how it feels now."

"For you or for me?"

Elena searched for a response. It was a good question, one she should have asked herself long before now. "This awareness of another's dream has happened only once before. That other time, the revelation carried a clear sense of a message. One intended for the dreamer. I shared the dream, as though it was a sign from God that I had the right to speak the message. This time . . ."

"Yes, this time was different?"

She carefully tasted the words. "Perhaps the message is intended for us both."

He studied her. "Two invitations."

"Perhaps. I have spent years hiding away. Mourning the loss of my husband. Remaining within my comfort zone. Everything about these experiences challenges me."

"You lost your husband?"

"Five years ago."

Antonio d'Alba gave a visible shudder. He pushed back his chair and rose to his feet. "It is late. Gino will drive you to your hotel."

"That's all right, I can—"

"No, no, I must insist." He led her back into the house, where he addressed the young man who had served them dinner in rapid-fire Italian. He then turned to her and said, "Please, will you join me for breakfast?"

"If you like."

"It would give me great pleasure to speak with you again. As for now, I have much to think about." He bowed over her hand, not quite drawing it to her lips. "Carlo was right to bring us together. *Buona notte.*"

19

TUESDAY

When the phone rang early the next morning, Elena needed a moment to remember where she was. She fumbled for the receiver and thanked the operator for the wake-up call. She took a quick shower, then dressed in the same slacks she had worn the previous evening and added to that a different blouse and a navy jacket. She checked her reflection in the mirror and was halted by a sudden memory.

When Jason had still been alive, Elena would travel back to the States at least twice each year for professional conferences and meetings. She had carried this navy jacket as a fallback, because it went well with most outfits and added a trace of formality. She had not put it on since then, mostly because she had refused to travel. Now as she checked her reflection, she heard once more Brian's final words: *Be ready and open for whatever comes.*

Elena stopped in the hotel coffee shop for a cappuccino, then walked the same street up to Antonio's house. The street glowed in the morning sunlight. The trees she passed were heavy with blooms. The cloying fragrance reminded her of honeysuckle. A few cars trundled by. Otherwise she shared the road only with the sun and the birds.

The servant woman buzzed the gate open as soon as Elena touched the button. Angelica stood by the doorway again, showing Elena the same inscrutable face. To Elena, the name Angelica suggested a delicate lady, fragile and ephemeral, only partly connected to the earth. Certainly not this stodgy woman dressed in black with her tight bun and dark, unblinking gaze.

Once again Angelica led her down the hall. The first set of double doors were shut, just like the previous night, and again Elena heard a man's voice inside. She followed the servant back to the veranda. The table was set under the covered alcove with fresh damask and places for two. A crystal vase holding lilies and tulips sat at the table's center. The alcove's cloth walls were all open now. The view was out over rooftops and gardens to the city below. Elena caught the faint hint of roses upon the morning wind.

"How you like coffee?"

"With milk. Please."

"*Con spremuta*? Juice?"

"Yes, thank you."

Angelica turned away. Then she stopped and said, "*Il dottore*, he sleep. All night. No dream."

Elena started to ask how the servant knew this, then decided it didn't matter. "This is a good start."

"Yes. Very good." The woman hesitated, then reached out and touched Elena's arm with one wizened hand. "You can stay?"

"I'm afraid not. I have a practice in Oxford. Patients. I must . . ." Elena stopped because the woman turned abruptly away, dismissing her answer as a feeble excuse.

Antonio was dressed in a fashionable suit and appeared both polished and disheveled. Elena decided he could be a very attractive man, if only he would make an effort. Instead, he seemed not merely distant but removed. He was there in body and mind, but his heart was elsewhere. Elena understood perfectly. He followed Angelica across the veranda, gave Elena a brisk smile, and asked, "How did you sleep?"

"Fine. Wonderfully, in fact."

"I also. A big surprise." He thanked Angelica as she poured them both coffee and then juice from a large crystal pitcher. Then he toasted Elena with his cup. "I am very glad you came."

The words warmed her. The old woman must have seen something in Elena's expression, for she sniffed softly and muttered something Elena did not need to understand. Elena felt her face redden.

Antonio asked, "Do you mind if we continue our discussion?"

"Of course not."

"I found myself resonating with that word you used last night. *Invitation.* Did I say that correctly, resonate?"

"Your English is excellent."

"Thank you. Yes. I find it very interesting that the divine message might have been intended for both of us."

Elena took a moment to respond. She found herself captured by a variety of thoughts. First, that he had simply moved beyond the previous day's rejection, as though his initial response no longer mattered. To either of them. It was the sign of a highly intelligent and very stable mind. Second, that he was a man of strong enough beliefs that the issue of divine guidance was not something he felt any need to question.

She asked, "Are you aware of the concept, perceptual illusion?"

"The words only, not their significance."

"A perceptual illusion is an image that can be seen one of two ways. But if the illusion is complete, the two images can never be seen simultaneously. The most common is a drawing of two women facing each other or, seen another way, of two vases. A series of images have been designed to suggest particular mind-sets. The image that dominates indicates certain emotional and mental predispositions."

"You are suggesting that the message is such an image?"

"I can't be certain. For a perceptual illusion to work, there needs to be some parallel pattern to the two images that can be used to fit them together. In this case, it is the fact that we have both lost the person closest to us. And as a result, we have both retreated from the world. You left your bank. I . . ."

Only when the servant returned with a breakfast tray did Elena realize the impact her words were having upon Antonio. He had taken on a wounded expression. Angelica set the tray down with a clatter and spoke to him in Italian. He responded with a hoarseness she had not heard before. Angelica spoke more sharply. Antonio drew the world into focus and addressed her at length. The old woman cast Elena a very hard look, then walked away.

Antonio waited until they were alone. He said, "Forgive me."

"No. It's my fault." Elena searched for a way to explain. "I've spent five years avoiding any discussion of my loss. But ever since this thing began, it seems like I've talked about nothing else. It's impossible that I've forgotten how hard it was for me every time Jason's name was brought up. But here I am, just tossing out the issue of our wounds with the same casual manner I might discuss the weather."

Antonio said to the napkin in his lap, "I have forbidden the family to even speak Francesca's name in my presence."

Elena reached over and took his hand. "I'm so very, very sorry."

He studied her hand for a moment, then said, "And yet they are here with us. The memories, I mean. All the time. Everywhere."

Elena thought of her meeting with the priest and swallowed hard. "Yes."

"Then we should acknowledge this and make these memories welcome, yes? It is the least we can do on such a fine morning."

Antonio rose and crossed the veranda to where the empty chairs were stacked. He picked up one and carried it back. He set it at the table's other end and carefully positioned it so that it looked out over the railing to the city beyond. He then selected a second chair, which he carried over and set beside the first.

Through the veil of tears she saw him return to his chair, then reach over and take up her hand again. He said, "There. That is much better, don't you agree?"

Antonio insisted upon driving her to the airport. They returned to the hotel, where she packed and checked out. Once they were back in his car, Antonio went silent. He descended the winding road, passed through a jumble of city streets, and joined with the main artery around Rome. There the traffic trapped them. Still he did not speak. Several times Elena started to inject a few words. She had a number of subtle hints she could use, things she had developed to help a patient open up and reveal the internal conflict. But Antonio was not a patient, and this was not a clinical appointment. Elena held back and waited with him.

The silence lasted over half an hour. When he spoke, it was to say, "I need to ask you what I should do."

"That puts me in a very difficult position, Antonio. I'm not sure I can respond."

"Explain, please."

"I feel it is best only to tell you what I have received. Clearly and fully. Beyond that, it is just my opinion."

"But you are a psychologist, yes? You counsel people as a profession."

"Actually, my primary role is to help patients clarify their own internal situation. Normally I do not supply answers. I help them find their own."

His accent was stronger now, the only hint he gave of internal conflict. "Yes. Of course. I understand that. But in this case, I have no clarity."

"Would you like to explain?"

"You said it yourself. I have built a safe little existence here. I am very good at my job. I analyze possible investments, not just for profit but also for any underlying links to something that might taint the church. This is very important to my superiors. They trust my judgment. My work has merit."

"But you do not feel you are living up to your full potential."

"The week before Francesca died, I was asked to head up a new Europe-wide commission. I was what is called a compromise candidate. The Germans wanted a German, the French wanted the French, the English and the Danes wanted someone who was neither German nor French. So they chose me. A very European-style decision."

"Then your wife died," Elena said.

He tapped the steering wheel with his fingertips. "It is ironic to be sitting here with you, Elena. Discussing these events. My wife had her heart attack on this very road. Caught in traffic. Just like us."

"I'm so sorry."

"Perhaps if I had been given some sort of warning. Francesca was in perfect health, you see. Or so we thought. Then she goes off to a meeting, and . . ." He gave a very Italian sort of gesture, part shrug, part dismissal. "It was all so long ago."

"But very much a part of the here and now."

A car horn sounded to their right. Then another. Abruptly the air was filled with an orchestra of blaring honks and angry voices. Antonio's only response was to roll up his window and turn on the air-conditioning. With the outside din somewhat muted, Antonio went on, "The commission was designed to investigate the banking industry. Their aim was to avoid any threat of another financial collapse. To see what risks they were taking and design a legal framework that would prevent a repeat of this recent disaster."

Elena struggled to keep her professional mask firmly in

place. But something must have emerged, because Antonio turned to her and said, "You are surprised by this?"

"No, well, yes. I mean, the other individual I . . ."

"The other person you met with regarding dreams," Antonio supplied. When she remained silent, he added, "This other person was also in the banking industry?"

"I really can't say. They came to me as a patient." It sounded weak to her own ears. "I'm sorry."

"But their work was related to the world's current financial crisis?"

Despite herself, she nodded. "Yes."

He let out a long breath. The blaring horns and shouting people might have belonged to a different universe. Antonio said, "Last Friday, three days before you arrived, I received a phone call from Brussels. The woman who had agreed to become the commission's chairperson had withdrawn her name due to health issues. I was again asked if I would accept the position."

"I can't help you with this, Antonio."

"But I need guidance."

"I'm sorry. Even if that's true, it is not *my* guidance you need. Do you understand? I came to deliver a very specific message. I have been given nothing else. To suggest otherwise would shift things away from God, and toward me. I may be new at all this, but I know that would be very wrong."

A man with a huge paunch emerged from the car ahead of theirs and shook his fist at the road. Antonio gave no sign he saw the man at all. "This commission, it has the potential to do important work. For any financial watchdog to be successful, it must coordinate with other regions of the world. We must show the banks a unified front, otherwise they will merely shift their high-risk operations from one region to another. Such transactions are international by their very nature."

"We're moving, Antonio."

"Excuse me?"

"The traffic."

"Oh. Thank you." He started forward. "The United States is establishing a similar oversight commission. Or perhaps you already know this."

Elena did not respond.

He accepted her silence with a nod. "Japan and Singapore and Australia are also in serious discussions. There are problems, of course. The international financial community is fighting this ferociously. They claim there is already oversight in place."

"Is there?"

"In theory. But in the high-risk areas, derivatives and hedge operations, the banks police themselves." He gave her a very sad smile. "Look where that got us."

The traffic sped up as they joined the main highway leading to the airport. Antonio did not speak again until he pulled into the short-term parking garage. He cut the motor, hesitated a moment, then asked, "Would you be willing to pray with me?"

Her professionalism rebelled at the thought of sitting here, parked in such a public place, and praying with a man she hardly knew. Prayer was for her a private matter. And yet this entire journey was all about moving outside her comfort zone. So all she said was, "I would be honored. Here, give me your hand."

Elena shut her eyes to the passing throngs. She prayed for guidance, and protection, and wisdom, and strength. For both of them. She prayed for answers, for the ability to carry through whatever divine purpose might be at work. She hesitated, then thanked God for bringing her to Rome. She thanked God for the chance to meet this fine man. She found herself wanting to pray that they might somehow have another chance to meet again. When she finished praying, she discovered that her face was hot. Antonio refused to release her hand, and her face grew hotter still.

20

Antonio's presence lingered during the two-hour flight from Rome back to London. Elena could hear his melodious accent more clearly now than when they had been together. The man seated next to her was broad-shouldered and kept brushing up against her. Elena shut her eyes and tried to block out the uncomfortable seat and the cramped flight. Then she landed and exited the airport into a cold rain, and felt the soft Italian sunshine shoved aside by the blustering wind.

She took the bus from Heathrow to Oxford's central station. The highway was a long concrete ribbon through a wet and colorless world. Elena took a taxi to her home. She unlocked the door, turned on the lights, and coded off the alarm.

Then she froze in the process of shutting her front door.

Someone had been here. Or perhaps still was.

How she could be so sure, Elena had no idea. But she was certain her home had been broken into.

Elena stepped back onto the front porch and waved to the taxi, but the driver was focused upon the rain-swept road ahead. Elena turned back and searched through the front door. From her position she could see part of the living room and kitchen.

She detected nothing out of place. Yet the sense of foreboding could not be denied.

She reached through the doorway, picked up her case, and set it on the narrow front porch beside her. Then she shut and re-locked the door. She searched through her shoulder bag and came up with a card she never thought she would need. She called the number and said, "Detective Mehan, please."

"It's probably nothing at all."

"Describe for me precisely what happened."

"I opened my front door. I felt something was terribly wrong. That's all."

"Did you see anything in particular that might have alarmed you?"

"No. Nothing."

The detective was dressed in the same tan suit he had worn when they had last met, only now he also wore a rain-spackled overcoat. His hair was cropped in an impatient way that matched the rest of him. His manner was brusque without being rude. He studied her in a detached manner. Elena knew he was thinking this was probably a waste of time. Elena said, "I shouldn't have bothered you. I'm sorry."

"Your office was recently discovered to hold a number of highly sensitive monitoring devices. You have a senior diplomatic official as a client."

"Patient," Elena corrected, glancing at the uniformed police-woman standing behind the detective. "And that is highly confidential information."

"Her Majesty's constabulary are quite experienced at holding secrets." He turned to the young policewoman standing on the front walk. "Isn't that so, Officer."

"Quite correct, sir."

He asked the policewoman, "Did you bring the equipment I requested?"

"In the boot."

"Be so good as to fetch it."

"Sir."

Detective Mehan went on, "I'm not asking because I doubt you, Dr. Burroughs. I am simply being thorough. Now I want you to describe precisely what you found upon entering your home."

"That's just it. I didn't really enter at all. The taxi dropped me off and—"

He held up his hand. "You are returning from a trip."

"To Rome."

"How long were you away?"

"Two days."

"All right. So you unlocked your door."

"I stepped inside. Turned on the light. Coded off the alarm."

"You're certain the alarm was set?"

"It pinged when I opened the door. And pinged again when I entered the code."

"Fine. Then something triggered such a sense of apprehension that you did not remain inside." He gave her a moment, then said, "Describe for me the instant you sensed something was wrong."

"I . . ." Elena stopped. She had been on the point of saying she had no idea what she had noticed. Then she realized that was not true. She watched the constable return up the walk, carrying a black plastic case. "I just thought of something."

"Do share it with me."

"There was a smell. And the kitchen table wasn't like I had left it. The chairs were out of place. And the light . . ."

Detective Mehan accepted a black plastic case from the young officer. "You were saying."

"The kitchen has a Tiffany lamp over the table. The shade was tilted."

"Like someone had checked it," Detective Mehan said. "Or perhaps inserted a listening device."

Elena shivered. "Yes."

"All right. Now the smell. Describe it, please."

She could taste it on the air now. The detective's intensity sparked her own memories. "Smoke. Old. Not fresh. Like from a used ashtray. But it wasn't a tobacco type of smell."

"Very good, Dr. Burroughs. Does your home have a rear entrance?"

"Off the kitchen."

The detective said to the constable, "Have a look around back." He opened the door. "Is the alarm still off?"

"Yes."

"Perhaps you would be so good as to wait here." The detective left the plastic case on the porch beside her own suitcase and stepped inside. He hugged the side wall as he walked the hall and then disappeared into the living room. A few minutes later he reappeared and entered the kitchen, where he unlocked the rear door. The constable spoke too softly for Elena to catch the words. The detective stepped outside and studied something at his feet. He then reentered the kitchen and called to her, "Have you had visitors around back recently, Dr. Burroughs?"

"No."

"What about a gardener. A cleaner or repairman, perhaps."

"No. Nobody."

"Stay where you are, please."

After calling the detective, Elena had unlocked her car and waited inside, out of the cold and rain. She had felt increasingly foolish at the time. Now she stood as far under the small front alcove as she could manage, feeling the wind blow rain fine as mist over her, shivering from far more than the chill.

"All right, Dr. Burroughs. You can come in now." Detective Mehan reentered the front hall. He gave the house's alarm controls a careful examination, then turned and said to the constable, "Get your fingerprint kit and give this a brush."

"Sir."

"Doubt we'll find anything of use, but you never know." He pointed to the controls. "See here, the paint around the screw heads has been broken. And we found what appears to be two sets of footprints in the mud by your rear door. One looks to be smaller than your own foot, hard to be certain with all this rain. But the other definitely belonged to a man."

Elena felt the chill bite deeper. "Someone was really here."

"Your powers of observation would do credit to an experienced officer of the law," Detective Mehan said. "Have a careful look around, Dr. Burroughs. Try not to touch anything more than absolutely necessary. Tell me what has been disturbed. See if anything is missing."

Elena headed straight for the chest of drawers in the living room. It was Victorian oak and fronted in ebony and rosewood, forming a series of interlinked hearts. Elena had found it in a junk shop soon after she and Jason had arrived in England. She had spent two months sanding off the old varnish and making it shine once more. Even before she opened the drawer, she knew. The left handle was tilted upward, out of sync. It was something she would never do, particularly since it had become the repository of her newest prize.

Her heart sinking, she pulled open the drawer. Elena stared at the empty space.

Detective Mehan stepped up beside her. "Something is missing."

She nodded, her entire body numb.

"Describe it, please."

She swallowed. "A book. In a pouch. Of silk. Very old."

He photographed the empty drawer, then drew a pad and pen from his pocket. "Details would be helpful."

Elena described the book and its cover. The detective paused several times in his writing to stare at her. When she was done, he said, "Am I right in assuming the book is valuable?"

To her surprise, Elena discovered she was weeping. "Price-less."

He stepped away from her, pulled out his cell phone, punched in a number, then said, "Mehan here. I need you to send up a serious-crimes squad."

Detective Mehan urged her to make a pot of coffee. He and the constable had a cup with her.

Another police car arrived, sliding almost apologetically through the rain and slipping into her driveway. A police techni-cian erected a minitent over the mud by her back step and began taking clay molds from the footprints. Darkness fell. The rain turned heavy as the wind died.

Detective Mehan retrieved the plastic case from her front hall. He opened it on her kitchen table. "I don't have much call for this. Hope I still remember the instructions."

She watched him extend a pair of antennae and fiddle with controls, then begin drifting through one room after another. Four times he stopped and searched and came up with listening devices the size of metal spiders. One from her kitchen lamp. Another from her bedroom phone. He used a pocket camera to photograph each before removing them.

It was after ten before the detective and his team finally de-parted. A police car sat in her driveway, and would remain on duty all night. Elena's first call was to Miriam. She started weep-ing once more as she passed on the news.

"My dear, don't trouble yourself. You have other books, re-member?"

"But this is the *book*."

"No, my dear, sweet Elena. I'm sorry, but you are wrong. It is *only* a book."

Elena wiped her face. The constable had dusted for finger-prints everywhere the detective found a device. From her place at the kitchen table, she could see a half dozen places on the walls and on her Tiffany lamp that were smudged with gray dust. "I thought you'd be furious."

Miriam sounded genuinely surprised. "Whatever for?"

"You've kept that book safe all your life. I've had it for less than a week." Her voice cracked. "And I lost it."

"I'm sorry, dear one, but you are wrong. You had the book for less than a week and you *used* it. Now listen carefully. The book is not important. What you do with it, how it helps you be used by God, this is *vital*. Was anything else stolen?"

"Not that I've found."

"There. You see? Someone considers this mission of yours so important that they would break into your house and steal a book. What have they accomplished?"

"They scared me."

Miriam sniffed. "That will pass. It must. You have important work to accomplish, and you can't let fear stand in your way. Now go to bed and sleep. Will you do that for me?"

Elena hung up the phone, then was filled with a sudden desire to call her oldest friend again and tell her to take back the books that had not been stolen. She did not want to be used. She did not want a bigger life or a deeper meaning or a chance for greater service. She wanted her comfortable existence, her safe little world. She wanted a home where she felt secure, where there was no need to have police cars parked in her driveway. Twice she reached for the phone, then stopped. Even if she dialed Miriam's number, Elena knew she could not shape the words.

Elena carried her valise into the bedroom and left it un-opened beside her closet. She left lights on all through the house. She walked to the front window and stood looking at the police car in the driveway. Her house was bordered on three sides by a yew hedge that blocked it from most of her neighbors and the street. Before, she had treasured her privacy. Now she was glad for the police presence and wondered what she would do when they left.

Elena showered, put on her nightgown, and sat on the side of the bed. She stared at the phone for a long time before finally searching through her shoulder bag and taking the card Antonio had given her before kissing her cheek and sending her into the Rome airport. Just holding the card and looking at the handwritten number he had inscribed on the back drew him closer and gave her the courage to phone.

When he answered with a sleepy hello, she said, "I woke you. I knew I would. I'm sorry."

"No, no, Elena, this is wonderful. You're home?"

She listened to the comforting sound of his soft breath. "Yes. Your accent is stronger when you're sleepy."

"Is it?"

"Yes. It's nice."

He asked, "How was your trip?"

"The flight was fine. But my home was broken into."

"Elena, no. Was anything taken?"

"Yes." She felt her smile fracture. "Maybe I should call tomorrow."

He was fully awake now. "No. Wait. Let me turn on the light. All right."

"It's late. You're a very busy man. You have—"

"I am your friend. Is that not so, Elena?"

For some reason the question caused the tears to come again. "Yes."

"*Bene.* This is what friends do. They are here for one another in the middle of the night. When the light is gone and the need is greatest. They are here. Now tell me what has happened."

The comfort she felt in hearing Antonio's voice lasted until she climbed into bed. Then the fear returned. Faint tremors raced through her. Perhaps she was only releasing the latent fear now, or perhaps she had simply been able to ignore it until now. She climbed out of bed and opened her bedroom drapes. She sat on the edge and stared at the police car, willing herself to accept that she was safe. Then from the kitchen came the sound of the refrigerator cutting on. The soft hum had never sounded dangerous before. A floor creaked. The rain lashed her window. Elena lay in the dark and wished she could even name what she wanted.

21

WEDNESDAY

It was still raining when Elena rose from her bed. The clock had read one in the morning the last time she had sat up and checked to make sure the police car was still parked in her driveway. She had eventually fallen into a sleep so deep that when the alarm went off, Elena had felt like she rose from a dark well. She drank three cups of coffee, two more than normal, and still felt disoriented as she drove into the city center. It seemed as though she had been gone for years, rather than just a night and two days.

Elena arrived at the office a little before eight. She was pleased to discover the office door was still locked. She wanted a few moments alone, just to make the space her own again.

But inside, her sense of disorientation remained. Elena felt as though she had entered another of those perception puzzles. One moment she stared around the reception area, a welcoming place full of comforting hues. But when she blinked her eyes, she saw something else. A place subtly designed to weld her inside a prison of her own making, while keeping the illusion of freedom alive.

She went upstairs to her office and forced herself to launch into paperwork. At a quarter to nine, Elena was startled by a knock on her door, and was even more surprised when Jeremy Yates entered her office. "How was your trip?"

"Fine, thank you, Jeremy. Again, I'm sorry to have disturbed your Sunday."

He harrumphed something she was not intended to hear and slid her doors shut. Jeremy wore his standard dark suit with broad chalk stripes. His height and girth seemed to shrink the dimensions of her office. "I received a phone call this morning. From a Detective Mehan."

Elena didn't know what to say.

Jeremy reached toward the patient's chair in front of her desk, then thought better of it. "The detective felt I should know about your break-in, since it may be tied to the listening devices found in our offices."

She had a sudden terrible fear that he was about to fire her. She mouthed a reply she did not bother to hear.

"Is there a connection between these events?"

She started to deny it. Which left her ashamed. "I think so. Probably."

"Really, Elena. This simply won't do. Our goal here is to offer troubled individuals a haven." Jeremy loomed over her desk. "A place where they can come and safely divulge their innermost secrets. Am I making myself clear?"

"Yes, Jeremy. Of course."

"I do so hope there will be no further need for such discussions."

As he turned and left her office, Elena's entire being shrieked with a single shrill thought. She had nowhere else to go.

The morning went slowly. Elena tried hard to pay attention. But her first two patients had been with her for months, and there was a guarded repetition to the sessions. They came for comfort, but not if it meant letting down their internal barriers.

After her second appointment, Fiona buzzed through to say

that a Detective Mehan had called. When Elena called him back, the detective reported that the police had completed their investigation. His superiors felt that as there had been no threat of bodily harm, there was no way they could continue to maintain a police presence. Elena thanked him, buzzed for her next patient, and pretended not to feel hollowed by the prospect of returning to her empty home.

The third appointment followed the pattern of the first two. Toward the end of that hour, Elena broke in: "Are you certain you want to keep seeing me?"

Her patient was a very attractive young woman with a streak of electric blue in her long, brown hair. She had been describing a recent argument with her boyfriend and looked startled by the interruption. "Of course."

"I am only asking because we don't seem to be making progress."

"I thought I was doing what you wanted. Telling you about my problems."

"What I want, Melanie, is for you to arrive at a point where you can handle life on your own. How long have you been coming in?"

"A while."

Elena looked at her schedule. "Eight months, to be precise. And during that time, you have been through a series of how many boyfriends? I believe it is seven. And each follows a clear pattern. You begin by describing the current flame as the love you have spent your entire life looking for. Then I don't hear anything for a few weeks. And then one day you arrive, disillusioned and bitter. Even the arguments are the same. He has done something that leaves you certain he cannot be trusted."

The woman tied her hands in a knot. "I don't know what you want me to say."

"What I want is for you to *heal*. And I'm suggesting that perhaps your young man is not the problem at all."

Her eyes welled up. "But he *hurt* me."

"Yes. I understand that. And I am here to tell you that it happens. If you open yourself up to love, you must accept that from time to time there will be misunderstandings and hurt feelings. Life is not perfect. Neither is the young man."

"I know that."

"Do you? Because what I hear you saying suggests that there is something at work here. Not in him. In you. An internal issue that is revealed when the man you are currently with does something that hurts. It also uncovers whatever it is you have tried to seal away inside. Your responses suggest that you have an unresolved—"

The young woman jerked to her feet and punched her shoulder bag into place. "I don't have to sit here and listen to this."

"Naturally not. Perhaps you might want to consider talking to another—"

The woman flounced across the room, rammed the sliding door open, spun about, and said, "I thought you were my friend."

"You were absolutely correct to speak as you did," Miriam said.

Elena was seated at her office desk with both the outer and inner doors closed. She could hear the other therapists gathered in the off-duty room. It held a pair of low refrigerators, a hot plate, a microwave, and two coffeemakers. The room was directly above Elena's office. She rarely used it for more than a cup of coffee. But today the murmur of voices and scrape of chairs left her feeling excluded.

Miriam went on, "You are their therapist. Not a crutch. And this means sometimes you must deliver the verbal shock to get them to hear what is going on inside themselves. Perhaps you should refer her to another therapist within your practice."

"I'll see her once more," Elena decided. "If it's back to business as usual, I will make that suggestion."

"As you wish."

"I had no idea where my words came from. I'm normally the

soul of patience." Elena toyed with a bowl of yogurt and fruit she had no interest in finishing. "But now I'm wondering if my staying power with such patients is fueled by my own inability to heal."

"On the contrary," Miriam replied. "I would suggest that you are healing rather well."

Elena continued to play with her spoon. Above her she heard a sonorous drone followed by a burst of laughter. Jeremy plying the others with one of his after-dinner jokes.

Miriam said, "You and your late husband were especially close. Soul mates is a term that is absurdly overused, but in your case I find no other words apply. Yet here you are, four years on, doing quite well for yourself."

"Five," Elena corrected softly. "It's been five years."

"You have an international bestselling book to your credit. You have patients who adore you. And now you are off on some mysterious quest. Your life has become filled with powerful people and bodyguards and exciting destinations and detectives and break-ins and listening devices and spies and who knows, maybe even a touch of—"

"You're making fun of me."

"Am I?" Miriam's voice carried the lilt of suppressed humor. "Well, perhaps a little."

The afternoon dragged on. Elena counseled two more patients, doing her job, doing it well. And inspecting herself at the same time. She felt as though a corner had been turned, and yet something was missing. Something she should be seeing. Between patients her mind rained a scattering of images upon her closed eyelids. The priest, Brian, the vicar's new love interest, the missing book, Miriam, Antonio, the ambassador, Sandra Harwood. So much hitting her at once. Yet Elena could not shake the feeling that she lived inside a perceptual illusion of her own making.

Her next appointment was a new patient. Elena's computer

schedule showed the details in red, signifying that the patient had been referred by a local doctor. They took such referrals in rotation. Elena dry-scrubbed her face as she waited for the clock on the opposite wall to click the hour. She could not remember the last time she had felt so thoroughly drained. She swiveled her chair around and stared at the rain-streaked window. She struggled to draw up an image of a veranda at sunset, and a city of lights far below, and the faint hint of roses on a warm breeze, and a man with an impossibly gentle smile.

Behind her was a knock. Then the doors slid open. "Dr. Burroughs?"

The instant she turned her chair back around, any sensation of fatigue utterly vanished.

Her room was filled with the smell of smoke. Old and cold and vaguely sulfuric.

The patient who entered through the sliding doors was a lovely young woman with raven-dark hair and a bounce to her walk. Her overly short skirt flounced about her thighs. Her stockings held a faint shimmer, as though she took pleasure in having men stare at her legs. Her eyes were guileless and very wide, almost perfectly round, and the palest gray.

At the same time, Elena recognized a *different* reality. Elena felt threatened without clearly understanding the reason. All she knew for certain was, the closer the woman came to her desk, the greater was Elena's sense of dread.

"Stay where you are!"

The sound of her voice, one notch below a scream, shocked them both. The young woman faltered, but just for a moment. "Why, Dr. Burroughs, is that any way to greet a new—"

Elena reached into the box on her desk and hit the red button. Pressing the button ignited a flashing red light in every office and downstairs in the reception area. Each office had one. In the nine years she had been here, the alarm had sounded only four times.

The young woman was almost at Elena's desk when the stairs

outside her office and the ceiling overhead thundered with what sounded like a herd of rampaging elephants.

"Elena!"

"Here!"

So many people were struggling to enter her door at the same time that they jammed up. Finally Jeremy used his quite substantial bulk to break free. He rushed over. "What is the matter?"

"This woman needs to be reassigned."

"Most certainly." Jeremy inserted his bulk between the woman and Elena. "This way, please."

"But I want—"

"We will discuss what you want downstairs, madam." Jeremy took hold of her arm.

The woman shocked them all in the way she broke his grip. She clipped the inside of Jeremy's forearm, twisted her body in a blur of motion, and was free. As shocking as the move was the ice that entered her voice. "Don't touch me."

Fiona had entered the office without Elena seeing. But Elena saw her now, as the unassuming receptionist raced over and blocked the woman from slipping around Elena's desk. In a voice that matched the woman's in icy fury, she said, "Get out. Now."

The woman backed away, her posture that of a cat arched for combat. "What is *wrong* with you people?"

Elena said quietly, "Nothing at all."

Jeremy asked, "Are you quite all right?"

"A bit shaken, but yes. Thank you so much for coming."

"Did she attack you?"

Elena tested the words. "She made a threatening move."

"Yes, I can well understand, given how she responded to my touch. Is she tied into yesterday's break-in?"

"I . . . can't say."

Now that the woman was gone and the crisis over, Jeremy's gaze had gone cold as his tone. "Should we call the police?"

"That won't be necessary."

"Are you certain?"

"Very." She said to the others, "Thank you all for coming. So much."

Jeremy waited for the room to clear, then said, "You and I must have a chat. But now is not the time. I have a patient in a rather serious state up in my office, and having observed my panic-stricken disappearance will not help things one whit."

She swallowed. "I understand."

He started to say something more, then nodded abruptly and left the room.

22

Elena went through the motions with her next appointment. Yet each time she slipped into her professional mode, listening and gauging and becoming deeply involved, the image of that woman jerked her back. The only way she could hide her turmoil was to remain completely immobile. When she rose to her feet at the session's end, her entire body felt stiff and cramped. She had a half-hour break, then a makeup appointment from Monday. She was tired but was not looking forward to finishing up. The prospect of returning to her house and not finding the police car filled her with dread.

Fiona buzzed her phone. "You have a visitor."

"I'm supposed to be on break."

"This is definitely not a patient." Fiona sounded remarkably cheerful. "Shall I send him up?"

"No, no. I'll be right down."

As she exited her office, Elena saw a man standing at the reception desk with his back to the stairway. Fiona was smiling at him, her face illuminated with what appeared to be genuine pleasure. Elena was midway down the stairs when the man turned around.

The sight of Antonio standing there froze her on the spot.

"Hello, Elena."

"What are you doing here?"

"You needed me. I came."

Fiona sighed. "What I wouldn't give to hear a handsome gentleman say those words to me."

Antonio smiled at the receptionist, then again at Elena. "I hope it was right, my coming like this."

Elena found her eyes burning again. "It's better than right. It's wonderful."

Elena led him back upstairs and into her office. She smiled uncertainly over his compliments about the room. She felt shy now that they were alone but did not know why. She wanted to hold him and was ashamed of herself for thinking that. What would friends do in a time such as this? She stood as close to him as she could, hoping he would reach across the impossible distance between them. She could smell the stale fragrance of travel on him, airplanes and terminals and taxis. He was perhaps four inches taller than her own five-eight, which meant she would need to lift herself up slightly on her toes to fit her face in snug beside his. She saw how Antonio bore dark stains in his gaze. She realized that he was not going to reach for her, and the knowledge left her sad.

He said, "May I ask you something?"

"Of course."

"It is a professional question. You as a counselor might be able to help me understand."

"You can ask me anything you like."

"Perhaps we should sit, yes?" When they were settled on the sofa, he went on, "For years I have felt as though I carried two hearts. One for the outside world. Another for myself. Even my daughter was so affected by my sorrow that I hid from her as well. Or tried to. But it finally was too much for her. So she ran away. Of course she does not call it that. She claims to be studying music in New York. She plays the cello. I did not point out that the finest professors of cello were in Europe. We maintain a certain peace, even though we both know I drove my own daughter away. It is perhaps too Italian a compromise for most people to accept. But I believe you will understand when I say this is far better than her remaining close and being forced to avoid me and make excuses for why she cannot come home."

"I understand perfectly," Elena said. "Your daughter sounds very wise."

"She is, yes. In this and much else she takes after her mother." He studied her with a gaze that left Elena feeling as though the years of protective barriers were gradually evaporating. "Ever since you first appeared in my office, I feel as though my two hearts are in conflict inside my chest. One still grieves for Francesca. The other whispers things to me that I almost wish I do not hear."

Elena wondered if he noticed her flutter of nerves, or how they turned her heartbeat to that of a hummingbird.

"You understand this, yes? Of course. I am wondering, is such a thing possible? Can I truly hold two hearts? Two directions? Two different courses for the same life?"

Elena replied slowly, "Before I left for Rome, my pastor told me that I faced very great changes and even greater opportunities. If only I would be willing to . . ."

"To what?" When she did not respond, he pressed, "Perhaps this message was as important for me as for you, Elena."

"To open myself to change. I thought he meant, accept the danger and the responsibilities. Not . . ."

"This."

Elena nodded slowly. Whatever it was. This.

They had a quick meal at a Lebanese deli off High Street, a place Miriam had first taken her to years ago. The food was authentic and the atmosphere vibrant. Antonio listened as she described her confrontation with the young woman, then urged her not to return home that night. Elena found herself grateful for an excuse not to drive back to her lonely house in the dark.

They returned to the office. Antonio waited downstairs in the empty reception area while Elena saw to her final appointment. They then walked together to the Randolph Hotel, a stone bastion facing the newly renovated museum. As they climbed the hotel's central stairs, he asked, "Are you sorry I came?"

"No, Antonio. I'm very grateful."

"You haven't spoken a word to me since dinner."

She forced out the words: "I'm afraid my director will order me to leave the practice."

He showed no surprise whatsoever. "Last week your offices were bugged, is that not what you told me? Then Monday you fly to Rome on some mysterious errand. Last night your home was broken into. Today someone entered your office and threatened you. Your director must be thinking about what happens tomorrow."

Elena leaned her head upon the doorsill. Having her fears discussed in such calm tones only made them worse.

Antonio went on, "You have become involved in some project that goes far beyond merely treating a patient. Your director must fear it will escalate even further. He will worry if this might become a threat to others." Antonio waited for a couple to pass them, then said softly, "I feel responsible for your troubles."

"You? How?"

"Perhaps if you had not gone to Rome, if Carlo had not—"

"Antonio, you're not to blame for anything."

He was clearly not convinced. "Rest well, Elena. We can talk more tomorrow."

Elena went inside, washed her face, and used the toothbrush supplied by the receptionist. She lay on the bed, cut off the lights, and stared at the ceiling. The prospect of losing her position left her insides frozen.

She heard movement in the room next to hers. The floor

creaked as someone moved about. She heard the murmur of a man's voice and knew Antonio was on the telephone. She wondered who he might be calling at this time of night. She was certain the conversation had to do with her. The sound of his voice, and the knowledge that someone was concerned for her, gave her the ability to push her worries and fears aside. Elena reached behind her and touched the wall. She fell asleep that way, her fingers resting upon the space between them.

23

THURSDAY

Elena rose early, so she would have time to drive out to her home, change clothes, and apply fresh makeup before going to the office. She sipped a cup of room-service coffee and watched the dawn light strengthen. She was wondering if she'd dare call Antonio's room when there was a knock on her door. "Yes?"

"It's me, Elena."

When she opened the door, she found him dressed in a tailored navy suit. "I heard the room-service waiter and was hoping I wouldn't be disturbing."

"I was just going out to the house."

"*Bene.* Excellent. Let me make a quick call and then I will join you, if that is all right. There are things we need to discuss."

She followed him downstairs, where he urged her not to check out. Elena complained, "This place is too expensive to be a long-term solution."

"Leave that for the moment, please."

Elena found herself somewhat disconcerted by his brisk manner. "What's going on?"

He motioned toward the front door. "Please. We must hurry."

"I don't see what . . ." She exited the hotel to find a gray-suited man holding the door to a dark Mercedes sedan. "Is that yours?"

"It is for both of us." He gestured impatiently. "Please, Elena. The clock is running with or without us."

When they were settled and the car pulled smoothly away, Antonio said carefully, "Last night I phoned a friend within the international financial community. He was hosting a visiting official from Washington, so I spoke with his wife. Her name is Sandra Harwood."

Elena stared at him.

"I did not ask her anything. I simply told her what had happened. The dreams. Your visit. And then the break-in at your home." Antonio glanced at the driver, then back at her. "Of course I was taking a risk. But the little you said in Rome suggested your other experience had to do with someone within the international financial industry. Someone in a position that perhaps was related to the commission I have been asked to chair. Sandra then told me of her own experiences, and I knew I had been right to make that call."

"I'm not certain I feel comfortable with that, Antonio."

"Please, there is time for all this later. Right now I ask you to listen carefully. Will you do this?"

"All right."

"I then spoke with her husband. We are more than friends. Lawrence and I share many of the same concerns. We also, the three of us, feel responsible for the dangers you have been placed under. And for the threat that you may face in possibly losing your position."

"You shouldn't."

"Lawrence and Sandra have both agreed that we should work together on this. And that you are a vital part of whatever happens next. They are coming to Oxford this morning."

"Antonio, it's very kind of them to want to help. But a meeting would actually be counterproductive. If Jeremy hears a patient has discussed clinical issues with other people I know, and with my seeming approval, he would dismiss me outright."

"We understand this. And we are not gathering to meet with your director. This has gone far beyond that point."

"What is going on, Antonio?"

"One of two things." He glanced again at the driver. "If you wish, we will simply ensure that your position here is secure. Or, if you prefer, we will take the first steps toward a new future."

A sudden surge of fear gripped her chest. "If *I* want."

"Yes, Elena. Of course. This is all about you. We have made our decisions. We are moving forward. Lawrence is accepting the chairmanship of the American commission. I am doing the same in Europe. The question now is, do you want to be a part of what is about to happen? If not, we will be disappointed, but we understand."

She felt as though the final threads connecting her to her comfortable existence were being plucked away. She licked her dry lips and tasted the sudden coating of fear. "Would you really? Understand, I mean."

"How could we not? Perhaps your work with us is done. If we publicly step away and are seen to do this by the watchers we have drawn into your universe, then hopefully you will be able to return to your life and work. And do so in safety."

Elena started to ask what the next stage would entail. But she could see the answer there in his eyes. If she did not accept to be a part of it, what difference did it make? For her own safety, it was better she did not even know.

The word lingered in her mind. *Safety.* She had known a safe and comfortable existence for so long, she took it for granted. It formed a simple pattern to her days. It would define the rest of her life, if she chose.

Suddenly she wanted nothing else.

Elena closed her eyes. She could not make this choice. The

lure of safety was too great. Her prayer was a very few words. *Show me, Father. Give me the wisdom and the strength to see beyond myself.*

She remained as she was. Silent. Eyes shut. The car rocked and slowed and started forward again. Accelerating around one curve after another. Traffic whooshed by. She waited.

And suddenly realized that God was waiting with her.

The silence was as complete a response as she had ever known. The choice was hers.

When she opened her eyes, the car was on the final approach to her house. "All right."

"You are with us?"

"I don't know what good I can do, but yes."

Antonio sighed and released a tension she had not noticed until then. "I am glad, Elena. Very glad indeed. We are soon going to come under attack."

"From where?"

"I have no idea."

A sudden desire to retract her offer left her clenching the seat between them. "Then how can you be so certain?"

He faced her then. Somber, determined, focused. And frightening. "Because I know our enemy."

Two other cars were pulled up in front of Elena's home. She would have recognized the black Mercedes bulletproof limo even if Sandra Harwood had not been leaning against the front fender and there weren't two bodyguards stationed by the car. The rear door was open. The ambassador spoke into his phone, papers spread across the seat and a little fold-down table. Lawrence Harwood watched her emerge from the car, spoke into the phone, slapped it shut, and pushed the table up so he could slide from the car. He walked toward them, his wife stepping up alongside him.

Lawrence Harwood said, "Good morning, Dr. Burroughs."

"Mr. Ambassador." She gave the woman at his side a tentative smile. "Hello, Sandra."

Lawrence looked at Antonio. "Did you ask her?"

"I told you I would, and I did."

The ambassador looked back at Elena. "Have you reached a decision?"

The day matched the man. The sky above was iron-hard and forbidding, the wind cold. The new leaves on the maples framing her front lawn flickered in minty defiance. Lawrence Harwood was every inch a man accustomed to wielding power. Elena struggled to keep the fear and tension from her voice. "I will try to help you. But I have no idea what further assistance I can give. If any."

"None of us are certain of anything," Antonio said.

"You understand there may be danger," Harwood said. "We can offer you all the safety in the world. But history shows that a determined opponent can breach virtually any security."

"Lawrence," Sandra protested. "You are frightening her."

"I intend to. This is serious business."

"I am already frightened," Elena replied. "But I can't just walk away from what feels like God's will."

He studied her a long moment, then gave an abrupt nod. "Very well."

Antonio said, "Perhaps we should continue this inside."

As they walked toward her front door, a figure stepped from behind her house. Elena recognized the security agent, Nigel Harries. He gave her a friendly enough smile as he said, "Everything looks fine, Dr. Burroughs."

"Thank you." Elena remained unsettled by his presence as she unlocked her front door and ushered them inside. "Would anyone like coffee?"

The ambassador barked, "No time."

Sandra chided, "Lawrence."

"My dear, you know perfectly well—"

"Our schedule is more than adequately laid out." She turned to Elena. "Why don't you go change and let me play hostess."

"Yes. All right." She waved vaguely at the kitchen. "Everything should be easy to find."

Sandra Harwood revealed a very warm side to her nature. "I'm so glad you agreed to help us."

Elena changed clothes, brushed her hair, and applied fresh makeup, hurried along by the unfamiliar rumble of voices in her living room. She reentered the hallway to find Nigel Harries inspecting her security alarm with a magnifying glass. He asked, "Did you change the codes since the break-in, Dr. Burroughs?"

"No."

"Might bear thinking about." He cast her another brisk smile. "Sooner rather than later, if you don't mind my saying."

"Very well." It was one thing to discuss such issues in her office. But standing here in her foyer, the walls still smudged with fingerprint powder, left her feeling somewhat violated.

"I'd also like to wire your alarm system into the local police station, if you don't mind." He slipped the magnifying glass into his pocket and used the screwdriver implement on a pocketknife to attach the plastic face. "This lot knew what they were doing, right enough."

Antonio appeared in the doorway leading to the living room. "What makes you say that?"

"They broke in using either previously obtained keys or in the company of a master lock-breaker. There's not a scratch I can find on any of the doors. I'd say their aim was to get in and out unnoticed." He used his screwdriver to point at wires. "There are scratch marks on the appropriate wirings where they attached the alligator clips. They were hurrying at this point. Keyed in a scanner, ID'd your code, turned off the alarm, then put it back on again before leaving. Very crafty, your fellows."

Sandra Harwood appeared behind Antonio. "Coffee's ready."

"Take a seat here at the table, if you would, Dr. Burroughs."
Nigel Harries seated himself beside her, opened his briefcase,
and pulled out a manila file. "Now, I understand the individual
who raised your alarm at the office was female."

"That's right. In her late twenties or early thirties."

His file contained a selection of photographs taken at a very
odd angle. "See if you can recognize her among any of this lot."

"What are these?"

"All the females who entered your office yesterday. Don't
worry. We positioned the camera on the side of the next building, the one that was broken into, with their written consent. So
there's no need to inform your director of our little surveillance."

Actually, Elena felt certain she should inform Jeremy. Yet
every such additional issue raised the prospect of losing her position.

Many of the women were not identifiable, as their heads
were down, or they wore hats, or had turned away to speak with
someone. Elena was about to say as much when she turned over
the next photo and said, "That's her."

"You're certain, are you."

"Positive." She felt the same chilling impact as the first time
she saw her. Elena turned the photo over. "Without the slightest
doubt."

"Excellent." He stowed away the folder and set the photo on
top, then shut his case. "Mind telling me what precisely alerted
you?"

Elena said slowly, "There was something dangerous in her
manner."

"Threatened you, did she."

"In a way. I'm sorry, I can't be more specific than that."

He looked first at Harwood, then at Antonio. Clearly the security chief found what he was looking for, because he said, "Not
to worry, Doctor. I have more than enough to go on here."

Elena rose and followed him to the front door. Her gaze was
captured by every point upon the walls still stained with the fin-

gerprint dust. Nigel Harries must have understood, for he said, "My job is to make certain you are able to once again feel safe and happy in your lovely home. And I am very good at my job."

Elena asked, "How much will all this cost?"

Antonio called from the other room, "I suggest you leave that for a moment, please."

Elena started to argue, but the presence of unexpected guests and the pressure of the day ahead left her mute. When she entered the living room, the ambassador met her with the same steely glare as he had outside. His features looked ready for Mount Rushmore, stern and powerful and slightly forbidding. As though he had been genetically formed to carry the weight of political office. He said, "I want to know what impact the loss of that book is going to have on your ability to function."

His wife sighed but did not speak.

Elena settled on the sofa next to Antonio. "None whatsoever."

He blinked, clearly having expected a different response. "Explain."

"To begin with, there are other books."

Sandra Harwood said, "I'm sorry. I had the impression this was a unique and historic text."

"It is." Elena explained about the other duplicates.

When she finished, Lawrence Harwood said, "So you have four others."

"Three duplicates plus the original."

Antonio asked, "Should you be telling us this?"

"I have no idea. The person who entrusted me with the books said that any rules governing this process have been forgotten. If there were any to begin with."

"Let's get back to the matter at hand." Lawrence Harwood imposed himself once more. "What is important here is that this connection has not been lost."

"I'm sorry, but you don't understand. Having another copy does not guarantee that I will have anything else to offer."

The ambassador said, "Nothing in this world is guaranteed."

Antonio glanced at his watch. "Forgive me. But the time."

Harwood said, "Dr. Burroughs, we want to know if you will agree to join with us in a semiofficial capacity."

"Her name," Sandra Harwood corrected, "is Elena."

The ambassador went on, "Antonio and I have agreed to chair the financial oversight committees. We face serious opposition. We want you in our corner."

She replied, "It is not me you need."

"We are aware of that." The ambassador's voice was one notch away from a bark. "But you have proven yourself to be a vital conduit."

"It was Antonio's idea to include you," Sandra said.

"And Elena has already said she will help," Antonio said, rising to his feet. "It's almost time for our meeting. I will explain what we have in mind on the way back into town."

Antonio's explanation continued through the return journey. Elena tried hard to pay attention. But everything seemed to carry a subtle sense of disconnect. She was seated next to a handsome Italian with tragic features. She traveled in the rear seat of a new Mercedes, driven by a man who did not speak. She watched their car skirt the ring road and enter the heavy morning traffic. She had done this twice a day for years. Yet nothing looked the same. A new reality was becoming overlaid upon her comfortable existence. Things were spinning out of her control. She tried to pray, but the words would not take form.

Just ahead of them, the ambassador's limo entered the city center and drummed across the cobblestones. The region behind the Sheldonian, the medieval rotunda where the university held its official gatherings, was largely off-limits to cars. But the guards standing duty before the Bodleian forecourt were expecting them, for they swung open the large iron gates and waved them into the ancient courtyard. The few tourists braving the early-morning rain gawked a moment, then walked on.

Oxford's chancellor kept his offices in a sixties-era block-house off Wellington Square. But today the chancellor hosted them in chambers resembling a royal audience hall. The chancellor himself was a rotund individual with a studied demeanor and a frown to match the ambassador's. He used it to great effect as Antonio began explaining what they intended. Elena listened as he described their joint commissions, the need for a point at which they might meet and coordinate and speak outside the boundaries of their work. How they wanted to establish an independent center. How they wanted Elena appointed as its director.

She had never met the chancellor before. But the gentleman had clearly been prepped, for he respectfully pointed out that Elena was a psychologist, with no experience in finance or banking. Lawrence Harwood gave a tight nod and an even tighter look her way. At which point his wife reached over and took his hand.

Antonio explained, "Our goal at the center is not to monitor the financial aspects. We will all have teams in place. Highly trained, very skilled. Lawyers and financial analysts and politicians. What we will not have is a moral compass."

The chancellor's previous position had been the chief of staff in the prime minister's cabinet. He steepled his hands and nodded ponderously. Elena watched the mental cogs grind and knew what the chancellor was thinking. Having the fulcrum between the oversight committees located here could prove an enormous boon to the university.

Antonio continued with his description of a center to which they might retreat. Speak in safety. Beyond the public eye. Unknown to the outside world.

"Yet critical to your work," the chancellor intoned. "A joint task force that serves as your own oversight committee."

"Precisely."

"Very well. The university is most definitely honored to be the focal point for such a worthy cause."

With the chancellor's backing, things moved at a pace that Elena could only call blistering. By the time she left for her morning's first appointment, the transformation was under way. The ambassador and the chancellor remained together in the audience chamber, while Antonio fielded calls and e-mails in the hallway. Elena was not the least bit sorry to leave the administrative whirlwind behind.

But the same sensation of her world being swept from her control followed her back to the office. Fiona greeted her with the news: "The chancellor just phoned. Not his secretary. The man himself. I thought it was a prank at first. You could have knocked me over with a feather."

Elena nodded. "Any messages?"

"You already know about this, do you?"

"I've just come from there."

"Ah, Elena. Excellent. Might I have a word?" The director lumbered down the stairs. "I have just spoken with the chancellor. About you."

Elena nodded.

"It appears you are to be seconded to a new institute. One that will be housed next door. You are aware of all this?"

After the break-in, New College decided they should keep their sensitive manuscripts inside the college itself, where there was constant security. Elena replied, "The building is empty. They are letting us use it."

"Us."

"Yes."

"I'm still not clear about who precisely this 'us' is meant to be."

"It's a new institute."

"Pertaining to our work?"

"Not exactly." Elena was acutely aware of Fiona's interest. "It's related to the financial industry."

"Ah. Your patient. With the bodyguards. And the trip to Rome."

"Yes."

"Really, Elena, don't you think you might have informed me about this before I received a call from the chancellor himself?"

"I only heard about it this morning."

Fiona demanded, "You're leaving us?"

Elena kept her eyes on the director. "This institute work will be part-time, at least in the beginning. I'd like to continue to see as many patients as I can."

"You can route them through me," Fiona announced.

The director frowned. "Fiona, really. I would appreciate being the one to make any such decisions—"

"There's no decision to make. Her patients still come here. I send them next door. End of story." Fiona smiled sweetly. "Unless, of course, you prefer for me to shift my office fifty feet?"

24

We need to determine why we are here."

Elena sat in an almost empty room and stared at the three people seated around her. The four folding chairs were the room's only furniture. Her voice echoed back at her. She wanted nothing more than to go home and take a long, hot bath, curl up on the sofa, and watch the rain wash away the threat of change.

"I know what we look like to the outside world," Elena went on. "An institute designed to give an ethical perspective to the new financial oversight committees. But right now, this is just words."

Lawrence Harwood demanded, "Shouldn't we have already moved beyond the business of definitions?"

His wife said, "Lawrence."

"I'm not allowed to ask a question?"

"Elena is simply doing what we all asked her to do."

"Look at how we're sitting here in a circle. It looks to me like we're being fashioned into some kind of encounter group."

Elena said, "If you don't feel comfortable, we should change things now."

Lawrence glared about the room. When no one else spoke, he crossed his arms and shook his head.

Elena pressed, "You are questioning our structure. If that's the case, what would you prefer?"

"Don't turn this on me. I'm not your patient."

"But you've raised a valid question. What is to be the point of our gathering together?" Elena addressed them all. "Lawrence is correct. This is not meant to be an encounter group. I have adopted this pose because I am comfortable with it. If it does not work for you, we need to change things. Now. Before we become entrenched in habits that are not productive."

Antonio said, "We are here because of you."

"I'm sorry. But you're wrong."

Sandra Harwood nodded slowly. "We are here because of God."

Lawrence said, "You're the contact point."

"I was," Elena agreed. "But what happens next time?"

The room dominated the building's second floor and swallowed the four of them. The walls were painted a dingy cream, one shade off yellow, and the ceiling was about eighteen feet high. Once, this had been the formal parlor of a grand city home, probably belonging to a senior don. Now the stained grayish-brown carpet was crimped into three long ribs under the front windows. The walls were dotted with screw holes. One of the ceiling's strip lights buzzed quietly.

Elena went on, "I feel uncomfortable giving my view, because that is all it is. My words are merely the opinion of a woman who has no place in your world. When I related what I thought was a message from God, it was very different."

Sandra Harwood' said, "I want to hear your opinion."

Antonio said, "We all do."

"All right. I think we should ready ourselves for the next time that God speaks. All of us."

The three of them remained silent. Watchful.

"You've said you want a haven that is isolated from the

pressures you will face. All right, fine. But now that we're here, what is our purpose? I suggest that you came expecting me to tell you what to do. But what if God has a different purpose in mind?"

Lawrence opened his mouth, glanced at the others, and subsided.

Elena went on, "I suggest that this become a place where we turn away from the world and toward God. I propose that we commit to meeting here and praying for one another. Our time together will be aimed at supporting and caring and holding each other accountable."

Rain spackled the windows behind her. Somewhere beyond the building a car horn sounded. A bus rushed through the rain-swept street. Otherwise the room was silent.

"Part of our task here would also be to examine any issues that hold us back from being fully open to God's will. Naturally, no one would be required to speak. But it may prove helpful if we hold to this encounter-style gathering, at least initially, because it is a form that has proven successful in the past."

She gave that a long beat, then took their silence as the only assent she would receive. Elena knew that if she had not been so tired, she would have dreaded what came next—what she had been preparing for all day, ever since Antonio had described what they intended on the way to the chancellor's office that morning.

Elena said, "I will go first."

She had always been a private person. In the years since Jason's death, the walls keeping the world out had only grown higher. Elena took a very hard breath and said, "I almost wish God had not used me."

Lawrence Harwood huffed softly, like he had taken a punch to his heart. But he did not speak.

Elena said, "I feel so conflicted right now. I know this is the right step. But it does not make it any easier. I miss my life. I'm afraid of what comes next. When all this started, and I received my first impressions, I had no idea how far this was going to go. Now my entire world has shifted on its axis."

"You feel threatened," Antonio said softly. "As do I. Until you arrived in Rome . . ."

When he stopped, Elena found herself frightened by what he had left unsaid. As though she suddenly yearned for something she could not name, and which Antonio was about to turn away from. Even so, she urged softly, "Finish your thought, please."

"No, no. It was wrong to think that way. This sense of being drawn away from my safe little existence did not begin with your arrival. It started with the dreams. It started even before then. Because in truth I have wanted for some time to step out of my comfort zone. And yet . . ."

"You're afraid," Elena said.

"That and more," Antonio agreed, his voice a husky murmur. "I feel guilty because I want things back the way they were."

Elena found the strength to reach her hand toward the side wall. "My former office is right over there. But the director of the counseling service doesn't want me back. He is increasingly concerned that I may endanger other patients and staff. I'm afraid he may try to find a way to cut me out of the group. I know I should be open to whatever God wants. But I don't. I feel . . ."

Cars swished through a wet world beyond the front windows. The silence held for a long moment, then Lawrence said, "You feel threatened."

Elena wiped her face. "I tell my patients all the time that it is vital to be honest about your feelings. But nothing about this feels right."

"Personally, I never did like the idea of encounter groups. Spending time sitting in circles like this, blathering on about feelings. I've never been one to talk about how I feel. I'm a doer. If I don't like something, I want to get out there and change it." Lawrence inspected his hands. "But I can't change this. And the result is, I've never been so angry in my entire life."

Sandra touched her husband's shoulder. The soft, comforting

gesture of a woman in love. "I think it's very good of you to speak your mind. Very good and very brave."

Lawrence kept his gaze focused on his hands. "I could have been the next vice president of the United States."

"I know." Sandra chanted the words. "I know."

"I wanted that. So much." He bunched his fists. "Maybe my heart would have been strong enough."

"You would have risked everything on that chance? You would have risked us? Our future together?"

"God has done all these great things. He gave you dreams. He told Elena what they meant. Why couldn't he just heal my heart?"

"You know the answer to that," Antonio said.

"You are called to important work," Sandra said. "This cause of ours is vital. You've spent your entire life getting ready for this moment."

Lawrence looked at his wife. "How can you be so sure of this?"

"Because I know you," Sandra replied. "And I know God has chosen the best man for this job."

Elena waited until she was certain they had finished, then said, "Why don't we join together in prayer."

25

FRIDAY

Antonio was in the hotel lobby when Elena emerged the
next morning. His greeting seemed very subdued. She
did not have a chance to ask if something was wrong. Antonio
fielded three calls as they left the hotel and walked to her office.
Two were in French, the other in German. Elena wanted to ask
him about this gift for languages, but his grim expression held
her back. As she unlocked the office doors, he said simply that he
had to fly to Brussels.

Their second gathering started precisely at seven. A night of
tossing and turning had granted Elena no better course to take,
so she began again by asking what issues might be holding
anyone back from a closer walk with God.

They were joined by a young woman from the ambassador's
staff. Angie Cassels was a political analyst who was following her
boss. Angie expressed her fear over leaving the security of the
Foreign Service for a committee position that might fizzle and
burn when the next administration was sworn in. The ambassador scowled at this, which frightened the woman so much that
she froze in midsentence. The prayers that followed seemed a
feeble attempt to fill the empty air.

At Lawrence's request, they agreed to meet at lunchtime Monday at the embassy. Antonio said he would try to return from Brussels in time to join them. The others departed swiftly, leaving Elena to face the rain-swept day.

When she came downstairs, Elena found a gray-suited man standing in the empty reception area. "May I help you?"

"I'm Gerald, ma'am."

"Yes?"

"Your day man."

"My what?"

"Bodyguard, driver, I understand you may be needing a receptionist." He had a thin smile that matched his almost toneless voice. "I've been used as a butler. And a repairman. I draw the line at gardening. Never did have much time for flowers and such. The only green things I'm interested in are the ones on my plate."

The front door opened. Sandra Harwood shut her phone and said, "I see you've met."

Elena said, "Could you step into my office, please?"

The front entrance led into a smallish parlor. The narrow hallway led to a kitchenette, a secretary's office, and a larger room overlooking the rear garden. The view through the curtainless windows was dismal. Bare stems of dead vines climbed a crumbling brick wall. A cracked fountain rose from a carpet of dead weeds. Overhead, clouds formed a ceiling the color of slate. Elena asked, "What is he doing here?"

"You already know the answer to this. Nigel's group will do what is necessary to keep us safe."

"Do I have to go in that Mercedes?"

"That is the car they've been trained in." Sandra responded in the same calm tone she had used when speaking with her husband. "Nigel's men log hundreds of hours of defensive driving."

"Who is paying for all this?"

"The same interests who will finance the new institute." Sandra stood there in the empty room, waiting. When Elena did not speak, the ambassador's wife prodded gently, "But that is not the real issue, is it."

Elena's voice was scarcely above a whisper. "I'm sacrificing everything I've built up. I don't have anything left. No life, no privacy, nothing."

Sandra's gaze tracked her around the room. Cracks ran up the side walls from floor to ceiling. In the place where a chandelier had once hung was a gaping hole. The carpet was the same dingy brown as upstairs. The room's only furniture was a phone set on the windowsill. Sandra Harwood said, "It's almost as bad as the deal handed someone who could have been the President's right-hand man."

"You two chose this life. I didn't."

Sandra went on, "Or a banker from Rome who is still suffering from the loss of his wife, torn from his comfortable position and sent to Brussels. A city where he knows no one."

Elena opened her mouth, but no sound emerged.

"Or a wife who was dragged to the point of insanity by forces over which she had no control. Or a young woman—"

"All right. I understand."

"Do you?" This close, Sandra Harwood's perfectly coiffured appearance revealed tight crow's-feet by her eyes and mouth. Tiny wrinkles around her ears and neck, evidence of the strain that could not be painted over, not even by a professional's hand. "Simply because the sacrifices you've been asked to make are different, do you truly fathom the pressure and risk faced by others?"

Elena did not respond.

"Do you feel it in your heart? Are you able to reach beyond where you are and what you feel and how frightened you are about your own state, and share with others their needs and fears?"

Elena remained silent.

"For the first time since the nightmares began, I feel a sense of being exactly where I should be. Doing precisely what I need to be doing."

Elena said, "You should be leading this group. Not me."

The edges of her eyes and mouth tightened slightly. "I'm quite satisfied with the person God has set in place, thank you very much."

Elena had five appointments that day. Between patients, she went through her records with Fiona. Those patients whose progress was firmly wedded to their time together, she placed in one pile. Added to these were patients who risked stalling or even regressing if shifted to another therapist. Everyone else was to be reassigned. Elena moved through the files in a coldly analytical frame of mind. She began making the calls over her lunch hour. Her detached firmness remained a subtle undertone, like a hidden shield against all the uncertainties and unknowns. She held to the same manner when she met with Jeremy that afternoon. She did not ask his permission. She just laid it out, the move next door and the new institute and the proposed leave of absence. Then she waited.

Jeremy protested, "This is all rather sudden."

"What you mean is, you dislike having control of the situation taken away."

"Hardly a surprise, wouldn't you agree? I've only spoken with the chancellor twice in my life. The first was when I received an award that he bestowed. The second was when he phoned yesterday and ordered me, *ordered* me, to do whatever you requested."

"You were going to fire me."

He lifted an aristocratic eyebrow. "Whatever gave you that idea?"

"Fire, dismiss, order me to take a sabbatical. It's all the same thing."

At least he had the decency not to deny it. "What else was I to do with you? The risks just kept growing. They threatened our safety, and that of our patients."

"This is the best solution for everyone. Tomorrow I'll arrange movers to shift my office next door. Fiona has agreed to schedule all appointments related to patients. You will be kept apprised of any further changes."

"I see." He fumbled with his watch chain. The gold spun back and forth between his fingers, flickering hypnotically in the light. "Will you be coming back?"

She felt her entire body clench with the sudden urge to cast it all away. Throw herself on his mercy, beg him to forget she had spoken at all. But all she said was, "The very instant this is over and done."

Jeremy turned to the rain-streaked window. "All I can say is, I hope you know what you're doing."

26

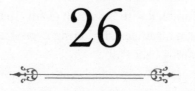

MONDAY

The entire weekend remained gray, windswept, and wet. Gerald, the daytime bodyguard, made a little place for himself in the garage. He emerged at regular intervals to patrol her yard. He refused to come indoors, he declined offers of food and coffee, he seemed utterly indifferent to the weather, and he spoke hardly at all. The night man, Charles, was even quieter. Elena remained firmly planted at home, emerging only for church on Sunday. As she left the house she caught sight of herself in the hall mirror. She saw the strain around her mouth, the tense muscles in her neck, the almost frantic light to her eyes. Gerald drove her into town in her car, which she found both silly and somehow comforting. She went to the late service and sat with Janine, Brian's fiancée, and refused an invitation to join them for lunch. The rest of her weekend was spent reading before the fire and resting and pretending that she was okay with the great sweep of changes.

Monday morning Elena went into Oxford and saw to her three morning appointments. By the time she left for London, the rain had passed. Miriam was standing inside the bank's entrance when Elena arrived. They embraced and walked downstairs and entered the vault. Elena waited until the guard had opened the safety deposit box and returned to his position by the security desk to ask, "What happens if I lose another one?"

"You have more," Miriam replied. "The book is not the issue, and you know it."

"I feel like I've let your great-grandmother down."

"How, by fulfilling the invitation she passed through me to you?"

"You know exactly what I mean."

"I know you are concerned about nothing."

"Losing a priceless artifact is not nothing."

"You worry too much. It is not healthy."

Elena lifted out the remaining duplicate books, not touching the original. She set them on the padded top of the wheeled metal table. All three books were wrapped in coverlets that had gone black with age, and were vacuum-sealed inside plastic cases.

Elena asked, "Which one do I take?"

"I numbered them when I sealed them inside those bags. That was what, thirty years ago." Miriam lifted her spectacles and inspected the little orange slip of paper inside the plastic casing. She shook her head and turned to the next one. "This is the one you want."

Elena returned the two older books to the box and slid the box back inside the vault. "How old is this one?"

"The missing book was three hundred and fifty-nine years old when my great-grandmother passed it on. I was nine. That makes it, let me see, four hundred and thirty-one years old. This one was two hundred and sixty years older."

"Six hundred and ninety-one years old."

Miriam smiled. "Something like that."

"And the others?"

She shook her head. "Legends told to a child. I forget."

"I can't get over how casual you're treating this."

"You will understand," Miriam said calmly. "In time."

Elena carried the book out of the bank, where the bodyguard sprang from the car and opened the rear door. Miriam said, "Is this yours?"

"Sort of. Gerald, this is Miriam."

"Ma'am."

"You certainly do look the professional."

"Thank you, ma'am."

When they were settled in the rear seat, Elena said, "The embassy, please."

"Certainly, Dr. Burroughs."

Elena lowered her voice. "I hope I'm doing the right thing."

Miriam's voice retained the same confident calm. "You feel led to these actions?"

"Vividly."

"To question a divine invitation borders on the unseemly." She patted Elena's hand. "Come. Let us enjoy being chauffeured by this fine young gentleman."

"Miriam—"

"Shah, my dear one." She turned glittering dark eyes to the side window. "Isn't it a lovely day."

The embassy of the United States of America occupied one side of Grosvenor Square, two blocks off Hyde Park. The square was rimmed mostly by redbrick buildings dating from the Georgian era. The embassy, however, was a steel and concrete behemoth that had offended three generations of gentrified city dwellers. There were so many mistakes embedded in the design that most Londoners pretended the building did not exist at all. The street fronting the embassy was closed to traffic and rimmed by concrete triangles known as tank-busters. All visitors were required to enter a new bulletproof hut, one of two that now squatted in the middle of the street. Police in full riot gear and armed with submachine guns patrolled the perimeter. Elena submitted to the inspection and the registration and the metal detector and the x-ray of her belongings.

But she drew the line when the guards wanted to unseal the plastic case.

The guard said, "I can't let you in until this has been inspected."

"Call the ambassador."

"Ma'am, you need—"

"Tell him Dr. Burroughs is downstairs. She has a package that is for his eyes only. Otherwise I am leaving."

The guard did not like it. But he did as she instructed.

Five minutes later, Sandra Harwood hurried down the embassy's front stairs. Sandra entered the hut and pointed at the case, now resting in a tray beside the x-ray machine. "Is that it?"

"Ms. Harwood, I can't—"

"Have you x-rayed it?"

"There are shadows I can't identify."

Elena said, "It contains a book that is seven hundred years old. The writing is done in gold leaf and perhaps other metals. That's probably what you picked up."

The ambassador's wife gaped at her. "You brought it? Here?"

Elena sorted through several possible answers and settled on "It is important."

Sandra turned to the guard and said, "I'll sign for it."

"Ma'am, my orders—"

"If the ambassador has to personally come downstairs and deal with this, he will. But this book is coming with us. And you're not opening it."

The older man running the machine said, "Let them pass."

"You know as well as I do—"

"Did you hear the lady? The ambassador is waiting. That package is going up. The question is, are you keeping your job or not." He gave the other guard a chance to respond, then slid the tray over. "You're good to go, Ms. Harwood."

"Thank you. Come on, Elena."

27

The ambassador's office was located on the embassy's seventh floor, just below the infamous rooftop eagle, which the British had mistakenly built facing the wrong direction. The outer office was flanked by three desks. One belonged to Angie Cassels, his chief aide. The others were staffed by secretaries. The atmosphere was both august and slightly seedy. The wood paneling gleamed, but the royal-blue carpet was worn down to gray nubs in places. The chairs and desks were battered. One window by the senior secretary's station was cracked. In two years the embassy was scheduled to move into a new structure on the opposite bank of the River Thames. Very little was being spent on repairs.

The ambassador's office was suitably large, but the shabbiness was still evident. Everything Elena saw, from the drapes to the desk to the corner sofas, was well beyond its sell-by date. As they entered, Lawrence Harwood and Antonio d'Alba were deep in a heated discussion. Both men looked drawn and fierce and very tired. As they rose to their feet, Elena had the impression that both men were reluctant to let go of their conversation. Antonio was accompanied by two aides whom Elena had last seen in his Rome office. He greeted her with a smile that did not touch his red-rimmed eyes.

The ambassador pointed to Elena's package and said in greeting, "What is this?"

His wife said, "She's brought us the book."

Antonio's gaze focused sharply. "*The* book? Here?"

Lawrence said, "I thought you told us it was stolen."

"I went by the bank and retrieved another one."

Both men stepped forward. But no one made a move to touch it. Antonio asked, "How old is this one?"

"About seven hundred years." Elena gestured to Miriam. "This is my friend Miriam Al-Quais."

It took a moment for the name to register. "The lady who . . ."

"Yes."

Lawrence asked, "You agree with her letting us see this?"

"I do."

"I thought, well—"

Antonio finished, "This is a sacred secret."

"There is nothing and no one who deserves the term *sacred*, except our Lord," Miriam replied.

Antonio smiled. "Well, well."

Sandra asked her husband, "Do you have scissors?"

"I brought some." Elena set the package on the coffee table and knelt on the carpet. The others stood around her. No one sat down. She carefully cut away one side of the plastic cover. The air became full of the scent of crushed flowers.

Miriam said quietly, "It was springtime when I did this. I pressed roses from my garden inside the cover."

The coverlet was as frail as an old lady's skin. Elena slowly untied the catch and slipped her hand through the opening. She drew out the book and brushed away the faded petals. The petrified olive-wood cover had different swirls, but there was a sense of bone-deep familiarity. For some reason, Elena felt her eyes fill with tears.

Miriam must have noticed, for she reached into her purse and came out with a tissue. "Here you are."

"Thank you." Elena cleared her vision, then opened the cover. The page was yellow and darkened and the bottom right corner had become frayed by generations of fingers. But the initial image was precisely the same. "This is the Aramaic word *Abba,* or Father."

She turned the page and recited, "Our Father, who art in heaven."

Elena kept her gaze fastened upon the page. The ability to focus was becoming easier. She had not noticed it before now. Probably because the change had come in subtle measures. But the swirl of conversation did not touch her. She studied the now-familiar image and felt only calm. Only a rightness.

As she reached for the page, Miriam huffed a single quiet sob and fumbled in her purse for a second tissue.

Antonio asked, "Do you feel this is wrong?"

"What?" Miriam blew her nose. "Oh my, no. Not at all."

"It's just, well . . ."

"I am so very happy." Miriam needed another tissue. "I have not seen this next image."

Lawrence barked, "What? Never? Why on earth not?"

"It's a long story." Miriam cleared her throat. "Another time."

Elena turned the page.

"The people asked the Savior, how are we to pray?" Elena touched the page. "He answered with these words."

The vellum was soft beneath her fingertips. The image glowed with a fire undimmed by time. Her own heart felt ignited by the sight. The image was a mixture of gold and silver. Up close, it was possible to see brushstrokes in the drawing.

"Jesus did not declare this to be a mystery. He did not say it was only for a certain few. He started with the most intimate of terms for Father and went on from there." She tapped the page. "This was meant for all of us."

Beyond the ambassador's closed door, the embassy hummed

with activity. Phones rang. Feet beat a constant rhythm in the neighboring corridors and offices. Inside the wood-lined chamber, however, all was hushed. Intent. Sandra Harwood's voice was scarcely above a whisper. "But you told me this was a secret."

Miriam replied, "It might have been. But who knows? Certainly there were others who knew of its existence. A wealthy patron of my great-grandmother gave her a quilted book cover with gemstones for buttons."

Antonio said, "The Lord promises that everything will work to the good of those who love him and seek to do his will. Who knows. Perhaps there is a reason why any former rules have been lost."

Elena took that as an invitation to ask him, "Will you tell me what has made you so upset?"

Antonio replied, "I am facing opposition. The moment I accepted the appointment, they attacked."

"They have gone after the commission?"

"The concept, the group. Me personally. They question my ability. They suggest the loss of my wife has left me unable to take on such a strain." His smile carried no humor. "The cynics suggest I am perfect for the job. An emotional cripple leading a group doomed to failure from the outset."

Lawrence murmured, "So it begins."

Elena said, "This is precisely why I want the book to be open for us all. We are united in a single purpose. One to which we have been called by God. We do not understand a lot of what is happening. We have far more questions than answers. But each of us needs to be intimately connected to God's will."

Sandra asked, "What do we do?"

Miriam replied, "I was nine when my great-grandmother gave me responsibility for these books. She died the following year. So her instructions were meant for a little girl. What she told me was this. Look at the image. Empty your mind. Wait for God to fill it with his presence. Wait as long as you must. I have waited seventy-two years."

The ambassador demanded, "Why didn't she write out more instructions for when you grew up?"

"My great-grandmother was the product of a different culture and a different age," Miriam replied. "She could neither read nor write. I was the first woman in my family to attend school. I might never have fulfilled my great-grandmother's intent. But I have done what I can. I have dedicated my scholarship and my practice to her memory."

"Your grandmother is so proud of you," Elena replied. "Of that I am completely and utterly certain."

Miriam's only response was to look back down at the image and dab at the corners of her eyes.

Elena gave the image a ten-minute silence, long enough for them all to grow somewhat uncomfortable and for the noises from beyond the closed doors to invade their thoughts. Then Elena suggested they hold hands and that all who felt guided should pray.

As they joined hands to pray, Antonio said, "I am scheduled to make an appearance on BBC television tonight. I forget the program's name."

His aide murmured, *"Newsnight."*

"Of course." Antonio glanced at Elena. "It will be a declaration of war."

Elena asked, "Would you like me to be there with you?"

"If it is not too much trouble."

Lawrence interrupted, "We should all attend."

Antonio was as surprised as the rest of them. "It is too much to ask."

"You didn't. I volunteered. What time are you slated for?"

"Seven."

The ambassador glanced at his wife, who said, "We are not due at the reception until eight thirty."

Lawrence said, "I suggest we meet in the television studio's lobby at six forty-five. And we will need to meet early tomorrow morning. My replacement arrives this evening. Tomorrow I begin the process of formal introductions."

Elena studied the group. Antonio sat between his two aides. Sandra Harwood sat to their left, then Angie Cassels, then the ambassador. Miriam and Elena made eight. All of them shared a sense of somber intent. Elena recalled studying her reflection that morning and felt somehow ashamed.

Antonio spoke first, asking for calm and wisdom and strength. He then prayed for Lawrence with the same softly accented conviction. Miriam followed, thanking God for the sense that her task was well and truly fulfilled, and that the empty chambers of her life had been filled with promise. Sandra prayed for her husband and for Antonio and their teams. Elena did not speak at all.

They exited the office to find Nigel Harries standing by the window. The ambassador's secretary said, "I'm sorry, sir. But this gentleman insists that he must speak to you immediately. He doesn't have an appointment."

"It's all right."

"I don't understand how he was permitted up here in the first place."

"Friends in high places," the security agent said. He was dressed as usual in a charcoal-gray suit and carried a thin leather satchel tucked under his left arm. "I apologize for interrupting your morning, sir."

"I assume it's important."

"Very." He said to Elena, "Perhaps you would care to stay as well, Dr. Burroughs."

The ambassador's secretary said, "You're expected at the meeting with the Greek finance minister in fifteen minutes."

"Have the car ready." He waved them back toward his door. "Let's do this in private."

Miriam remained where she was. "Perhaps I should say my farewells."

"Either you are part of this team or you are not." Lawrence held the door. "Join us. Please."

They all trooped back into his office, where Nigel Harries removed a file from his leather satchel and set an eight-by-ten photograph on the corner of Harwood's desk. "Dr. Burroughs, could I ask you to confirm this was the woman who accosted you?"

One glance was enough. "That's her. But she did not exactly accost me."

"Let's leave such details aside for the moment. What is important now is that you are certain this woman and the individual in your office are one and the same."

Elena forced herself to look more closely at the photograph. The stench of cold smoke tainted the air. "No question."

"Might I ask the others to have a look?" They did so, but no one showed any recognition. Nigel Harries read from his notes: "Her name is Jessica Ravel. Five years ago, she resigned after just thirty-one months with the CIA. Since then we have no record of her being employed anywhere in the developed world. No tax records, no driver's license, bank accounts, charge cards. A check of computer records at the Home Office shows no documentation related to a UK entry. The name she used in making her appointment with Dr. Burroughs, Kimmie Kirkland, also showed up nowhere."

"Some of my patients will initially use a false name."

"Quite." Nigel Harries glanced at the ambassador. "Her CIA records indicated no hint of misdeed behind her departure. Her name came up clean. Immaculate, in fact."

Lawrence smirked. "You're saying the records are whitewashed."

"There is certainly nothing to suggest anything underhanded. But in the past the agency has been known to layer over a decidedly messy situation by supplying the individual in question with an impossibly flawless record."

Lawrence explained to the others, "She either did something

or knows something that could cause senior officials major embarrassment. They gave her a clean out, in exchange for her silence. It works better than any vow."

Nigel Harries went on, "My allies within the security services are most perturbed about this bugging incident at Dr. Burrough's clinic. The idea that someone monitored confidential conversations involving the ambassador's wife has them positively livid. They have scoured their files and come up with one item that might be of interest."

They were gathered in tight around the table. Elena felt bodies touch her on either side. She could hear someone breathing behind her. She suspected it was Miriam, who seldom moved to the forefront even when invited.

Nigel Harries set a photograph on top of the image of Ravel or Kirkland or whatever her name was. "Might I ask you all to give this your most careful attention."

Instantly Sandra Harwood exclaimed, "That's him!"

Lawrence demanded, "Who?"

She stabbed the individual standing next to the woman. "The man in my dream!"

"You're certain?"

"Do you think I could possibly mistake him? He woke me up screaming for weeks!"

"Pardon me, ma'am," Nigel Harries said. "Which dream would that be?"

"It does not concern you," Lawrence snapped.

Elena corrected, "Actually, it might."

Lawrence gave Elena a tight look before saying to his wife, "You told me you never got a clear look at his face."

"And I am telling you now there's no question. This is the enemy. The one who wants you dead."

Elena heard the person to her left take a hard swallow. She glanced over. The ambassador's aide looked ill. Elena took hold of the younger woman's hand.

Lawrence said, "I know that man."

Nigel Harries said, "His name is—"

"Cyril Price," Lawrence said, his voice rough as gunfire.

Nigel Harries nodded approval. "He is employed by the Treasury Department, where his title is deputy secretary. His precise role has been hard to pin down."

"The title is unimportant," Lawrence said. "Cyril is a fixer."

Sandra had gone the color of sun-bleached bone. "A fixer? You're certain?"

"Absolutely." Lawrence glared at the photograph. "Every administration has a trusted shadow whose sole duty is to make problems disappear. I know of three fixers for the current team. Which is very rare. Johnson was the last president to employ three fixers."

Antonio said, "Why would there be three?"

Lawrence glanced over. "Factions."

"Ah."

"You understand?"

Antonio's smile was ancient. "I am Italian."

Lawrence explained, "Our party is splintered by factions. They fight one another almost as vehemently as they do the opposition party." Lawrence stabbed the photograph. "This man works for the segment of my party that I truly loathe. Their only aim is to strengthen their hold on power. Whoever backs them is a friend. Any opposition is an enemy to be destroyed."

Antonio said, "All this would make them the banks' natural ally."

Sandra asked, "What does this mean?"

Lawrence said, "I have no idea."

Nigel Harries gathered up his images. "Rest assured I and my former colleagues are determined to find that out. In the meantime, I was wondering if I might join your little band."

The request caught them all by surprise. Lawrence asked, "You know our intentions?"

"I know enough. You are gathered under the banner of shared convictions to pray your way through a battle for the hearts and minds of everyone concerned. You seek to carry one another's burdens while fighting the good fight." As he spoke, Nigel Harries came to rigid attention. "I would consider it an honor to be counted among the chosen few."

28

Elena's return to Oxford was a fifty-mile journey straight up the M40, with bad traffic at either end. Elena spent the journey working by phone with Fiona, going through records and administrative matters. The staff secretary seemed to enjoy her role as official mediator. When they finally arrived, Elena cast her former office a wistful glance and entered the neighboring building. Her office furniture had been shifted over. The books, shelves, desk, sofa, and chairs only seemed to make the rear ground-floor office appear emptier and shabbier.

Elena saw the day's three patients. If any of them found it odd, how she had moved one building over and now had a silent gentleman staffing the front foyer, they did not mention it. As she departed, Elena resisted the urge to go over and speak with Fiona. Instead she walked down the front stairs and entered the waiting car. She touched the glass as they drove away, tracing the design of her former office's front portal, and mouthed the same words the ambassador had said that morning. *So it begins.*

Elena stopped by her house and packed an overnight bag. She was driven back to London by Charles, her nighttime bodyguard. Whereas Gerald was slender, Charles was built like a human fireplug, squat and so solid that he might as well have been cast from iron. But he held to the same bland voice and expression as Gerald, and possessed the same ability to vanish in plain sight.

Elena spent the drive south making notes on the day's patients. As they approached London, the highway's opposite lanes became jammed with traffic going nowhere. But entering the city proved both smooth and swift. They arrived at the BBC Television Center twenty minutes early. Charles sat behind the wheel, motionless. Inert. He had less interest in small talk than Gerald, who could go all day without saying a word.

The clouds had vanished and the afternoon sunlight was strong enough to bake the car. Elena sat with the windows down. She had completed her file entries but left the laptop open. A small anchor to the life that was slipping away.

"Elena!" Antonio was midway across the broad sidewalk fronting the BBC when he spotted her. He veered over, and when his two aides started to follow, he halted them with a word. Antonio did not say anything to the two bodyguards who shadowed him. Elena watched how Antonio ignored the guards and wondered if she might ever grow that accustomed to being handled.

He spoke through her open window. "May I join you?"

She moved over so he could slip into the rear seat. The two Italian bodyguards exchanged a word with Charles, brief and too soft for her to hear. They then moved to flank the car.

Elena said, "They scare me."

Antonio did not need to ask what she was talking about. "It is not them. It is what they represent."

The sunlight illuminated his weariness. "Are you all right?"

"I feel as though I have been under attack ever since I agreed to take this on."

"I understand."

He studied her a long moment, then reached over and took her hand. "You do, don't you."

They remained seated there together, sharing a look deep as the sky overhead, until one of Antonio's bodyguards stepped over and rapped on the car's roof. "The ambassador has arrived, *capo*."

"I am ready." Antonio leaned toward her and spoke softly, "I am glad you are here, Elena. Very glad indeed."

The BBC Television Center looked like a glass barrel with two brick arms embracing the front plaza. When it opened in the early sixties it was the world's first structure designed specifically for television programming. The young staffer sent to meet them was surprised in a discreet British manner at the sight of them all—Antonio, his two bodyguards, Elena, Lawrence and Sandra Harwood, another pair of guards, two Italian staffers, Nigel Harries, Miriam, and Lawrence's aide. Elena had ordered Charles to remain in the car. Lawrence ordered his own guards to remain at the entrance. They did not like it any more than Charles had.

The staffer led them through the central block, known within the BBC as the glass doughnut. The news center was structured around a circular control room, with studios extending like arms of a high-tech octopus. Antonio was taken to makeup while folding chairs were stationed behind the cameras for his guests. The atmosphere was tight, focused, electric. Large clocks beat the seconds in exact strokes. Voices were muted, footsteps always one pace off a full run.

A news presenter whose face Elena had observed for years walked by, a white makeup napkin tucked into his shirt collar. He was already past them when he realized what he had just seen. He retraced his steps. "I say, you wouldn't be the United States ambassador."

"I am," Lawrence replied. "Until tomorrow."

"Andrew Kerr. I interviewed you last year."

"I remember."

"Are you involved with this commission?"

"The American version. Assuming we succeed in moving the required legislation through Congress."

"Could I persuade you to join us on camera?"

"I am not permitted to speak publicly until I relinquish my current post."

"And that restriction holds until tomorrow, did you say? What if we were to tape the segment and air it later?"

Lawrence hesitated, then said, "That might be construed as a breach of the formal rules."

The newscaster accepted the decision with bad grace. "Could I convince you to come back in two days?"

"I have to travel back to Washington. But my plan is to return to the UK for further consultations with my colleagues on the European front. When that happens, I suppose—"

"I would be most grateful if you would please confirm this at your earliest possible convenience. I don't mind telling you, Ambassador . . ."

"Lawrence Harwood."

"Of course. This has the makings of an international coup." He whirled about, searched, and called, "Agnes! See to this gentlemen's details, make an appointment to connect with him day after tomorrow. Now if you'll excuse me, I must dash."

The ambassador stared at the empty air where the newscaster had stood until Sandra walked over and said, "Lawrence."

"Eh. Yes?"

"We are here to pray for one of our own."

Antonio responded to the newscaster's first question with, "The definition of an oligarchy is political power based upon economic power. This dual force is then held by a limited number of people or institutions. That is precisely the situation we face today."

Elena studied him from the safety of her position behind the cameras. Antonio held an almost overwhelming intensity. He was also grimly irate.

The newscaster said, "Would you care to explain?"

"In the United States, the assets of just six banks equal sixty percent of the nation's annual economic output. In Europe, nine banks control assets worth three-quarters of the European Union's total GDP. In Asia, the same. Also in South America. In each case, a few financial institutions hold the power of economic life and death." Antonio spread his hands. "Four oligarchies spread around the globe. Seats on their boards are exchanged. Shares are owned and traded. They do business with one another. They assure their mutual safety and profitability. They fight, but they also cooperate. And one perspective they all share is this: they care nothing for the common man."

The newscaster was a young man turned old by life beneath the glare of publicity. Andrew Kerr was lean and taut and intelligent. His voice was both melodious and raspy, like a professional runner who smoked cigars on his off days. "And the result?"

"Put simply, these banks have the power to change the rules of the game. Now when there is a problem, they can order their respective governments to rescue them. Even when the banks caused the crisis in the first place."

The newscaster turned to the camera and said, "For those of you just tuning in, my guest tonight is Antonio d'Alba, chairman of the EU's new financial commission." The newscaster turned back to Antonio and lifted a collection of broadsheets. "In anticipation of your appointment and this conversation, articles are appearing tomorrow in the world's financial dailies. The banks' spokespeople have treated you rather harshly."

"I can imagine."

"Shall I share some of what they have to say?" He slipped on a pair of reading glasses. "This from the Frankfurter *Allgemeine*, and I quote: 'D'Alba has become utterly disconnected from the pressures of modern financial trading. He has hidden himself away for over three years, using his appointment to the Vatican

as a monastic retreat. He is out of touch, and as a result, dangerous to our still-fragile economic recovery." The *Corriere della
Sera* claims that you are a menace to the European banking industry in a time of great risk and devastating losses. The Paris
Figaro suggests you have been made mentally unstable by the
loss of your wife. Our own *Financial Times* claims that you are
driven by a personal vendetta and intend nothing less than the
dismantlement of our vital financial institutions." He lowered the
sheaf of newsprint. "Do you have any response to these accusations?"

"The gloves have come off," Antonio replied. If he was fazed
by the attacks, he did not show it. "They are fighting with all the
power at their disposal to halt reform."

"What are your plans?"

For the first time, Antonio faced the camera. To Elena, it
looked as though he stared straight at her. The power of his gaze
was a physical pressure.

"That is simple enough," Antonio replied. "I intend to hold
these financial institutions accountable for the damage they have
wreaked, and make sure it never happens again."

"Even if that means the breakup of the largest banks?"

Antonio continued to grip her with an energy directed at the
camera. "I have answered your question."

Their farewells after the interview carried an undercurrent of
emotions Elena could not name, much less isolate. Angie Cassels, the ambassador's aide, revealed an infectious smile. Elena
watched as the young woman embraced Antonio and said how
his words had made the fear vanish. Whatever happened, she
said, she knew her decision to join the ambassador had been the
right one. She was glad she had faced down her fears this time.
After Angie left with the ambassador and his wife, Elena said, "I
wish I had said that."

"*Anch'io,*" Antonio's aide murmured. "I as well."

Elena went on, "You did a marvelous job."

Antonio did not share their elation. "I hope you feel as positive when you see what our opponents do with my remarks."

"I will feel the same way for the rest of my life."

Antonio said to his aides, "Excuse us a moment."

"*Certamente.*" His senior aide was named Leonardo and was not a handsome man. But his smile held a transformative force. His accent was strong enough to suggest he translated his words directly from the Italian. "I feel as Angie, signora. Thank you for the inclusion in your group. This work, it is vital."

Antonio drew her behind a trio of potted palms. The evening rush was in full swing. People flowed toward the exits in a steady current of footfalls and weary chatter. Antonio said, "I found you behind the cameras. I could not see anyone else but you."

There was no reason why such simple words should fill her with another wave of utterly conflicting sensations. No way she could feel her face burn and her body shiver at the same time. "You were magnificent."

"I will tell you what is magnificent. This ability of yours to draw me into focus. To push away all the things for which I have no answers. To help me not be afraid of tomorrow."

Elena started to say that it was not her at work. But the air felt trapped inside her chest again. His dark gaze was that strong.

Antonio said, "I must go back to Brussels. We are booked on the Eurostar. I do not know when I can return. Two days, perhaps three. The banks will try to stack the commission with cronies. They will do their utmost to neuter all of us who seek to do our job. I must do all I can to stop this."

She had so much she wanted to say. But all she could manage was, "I will miss you."

His dark eyes opened far enough for her to fall into and never come out. "Such beautiful words, ones I never thought I would hear again." He leaned close and kissed her cheek. She smelled his scent and shivered again. "I will call you."

Elena walked over and joined Miriam by the glass doors leading to the gathering night. Her oldest friend was smiling slightly. But all she said was, "Well, well."

29

They walked back to where Charles waited by the car. Elena tried to make light of the introduction. "Charles is my night man. Charles, this is my friend Miriam."

"Ma'am."

Miriam allowed herself to be helped into the rear seat. "I could grow used to this."

Elena waited until the door was closed and Charles was walking to the driver's side. "I wish I could say the same."

"A bit hard to take in, I suppose."

"I've never even had a maid."

"You always were one for your privacy." Miriam reached over and took hold of Elena's hand. "Just remember there is a difference between your life and your role in these events. This is a permanent change only if you choose to make it so."

They stopped at the market for a selection of ready-made salads and a whole roast chicken. When they pulled up in front of Miriam's home, the old woman leaned forward and said, "Charles, you are welcome to join us for dinner."

"Thank you, ma'am, but I'm obliged to remain on patrol."

"What, all night?"

"Comes with the profession, ma'am." He waited while Elena retrieved the book of dreams from the car's trunk, then carried their parcels up to the front door. When Miriam unlocked the door, he gave the interior a swift check, deposited the bags in the kitchen, and returned to the front hall. "You ladies have a pleasant evening."

When the door was shut and locked, Miriam asked, "What happens if it rains?"

"I have no idea. That was the longest conversation Charles and I have ever had."

Over dinner they talked in the easy manner of old friends. The only interruption came when Charles tapped on the kitchen door and returned his empty plate. They moved to the rear sunroom and turned off all the lights, so as to watch London capture another night. Now and then Charles walked around the back garden, a silent silhouette that vanished as swiftly as he emerged. Miriam spoke of her granddaughter's visit that summer, and Elena volunteered to show her around Oxford for a day. Miriam's daughter was married for the third time, to an industrialist in Philadelphia. She and Miriam did not get along. The granddaughter had worshipped Miriam as a child, but now at eighteen she tended to paint all adults with the same cynical brush.

They were silent as Charles cut another shadow through the blanket of city lights. Then Miriam asked, "How do you feel?"

"Conflicted. But less so than yesterday." Elena listened to a nightjar's mournful tune, up and down a three-note scale. "They are trying to accomplish something important. But I worry that I have nothing else to give this team. I am afraid my job is done, and this whole thing is a mistake."

"You play a vital role. Of that I have no doubt. None whatsoever."

Her calm certainty did much to lighten Elena's burden. "Thank you."

"Something came to me while we were praying in the ambassador's office. It was quite a remarkable experience, almost as though it had been planted in my heart by another's hand." Miriam searched the pocket of her jacket and offered Elena a slip of paper. "It was meant for you."

Elena read aloud, "Proverbs Twenty-Five, Verse Two. 'It is the glory of God to conceal a matter; to search out a matter is the glory of kings.'"

Miriam's features were painted in glowing strokes by the city's illumination. "Your team is about to be struck from all sides. They will soon become too busy to search for God's word. That is your task. To reach for the unseen. To read the hidden script. To speak to the heart of the matter. To remind them of the eternal quest."

Elena shivered.

"You will face great challenges of your own. The noise will grow almost impossibly loud. Hold your focus tightly upon the true north. You will find your passage home."

Elena wanted to say that she wished she shared Miriam's confidence. But the words belittled the message, and the giver. She did not speak and was glad for her silence. Elena shared the night with her dearest friend for a time, then said, "I'm very tired."

"Good night, my dear one. Sleep well."

"Are you coming up?"

"Not just yet."

Elena rose and leaned over to kiss Miriam's cheek. The skin was as frail and worn as the vellum page. "Thank you."

Elena was almost at the door when Miriam called to her. When she turned back, Miriam asked, "Do you regret my having given you the book of dreams?"

"Not for an instant." Of this, at least, she was certain. "Not even in the darkest of my hours."

Miriam's sigh was sweet and long. "If I had to wait seventy-two years for God to speak through me, I am glad it was today."

◆

Elena woke with dawn's first faint light. Afterward, it seemed to her that she sensed the change before her feet touched the carpet. The sensation was like a shift in the weather, a fragrance of coming change.

The door to Miriam's bedroom was open, the bed still made. Elena walked to the stairs and called down softly, "Miriam?"

A hush blanketed the house. Elena felt the silence gnaw at her. She walked down the stairs and started into the kitchen, then saw the profile silhouetted against the gray dawn.

Before she hurried down the hallway's creaking wooden floor, she knew. Before she passed through the doorway and came around the coffee table. She knew.

Miriam remained seated in her favorite chair. She gazed out over the city she had loved and would never see again.

30

TUESDAY

An ambulance arrived and declared Miriam gone. The medical technician put the cause down as heart attack. Charles remained after Gerald, her day man, arrived with Nigel Harries in tow. The three men handled everything with a steadying calm. Elena leaned against Nigel as they carried her dearest friend away.

She then went upstairs and showered and dressed. The tears returned and demolished her makeup. Elena had not realized she had put any on. She scrubbed her face and went downstairs. She refused to glance down the hall and through the doorway to the sunroom. She knew how it would look. The room was positioned so that it caught the morning sun. It would glow with an ethereal light, as though heaven itself shared mysteries with anyone fortunate enough to sit and cherish the day's softest hour. It was a room of joy and calm and revelation. It had suited Miriam perfectly.

Elena left the house with Nigel. Gerald would remain to deal with any authority that might stop by. During the drive, her cell phone rang. Elena checked the readout, then had to clear her eyes before she could read the number. She saw it was Antonio and turned the phone off. She would make it through this day by dealing with one thing at a time.

When she arrived at the embassy, Sandra Harwood was waiting for her at the bulletproof hut. The ambassador's wife hugged her and shepherded her upstairs. Sandra did not protest that Elena shouldn't have come. All she said was, "Nigel called each of us. Antonio phoned me when he could not reach you. He wants to have a word."

"I can't talk with him right now."

"I understand. I'll let him know you'll be in touch later." When they arrived upstairs, Sandra released her to the consolation of the others, took out her cell phone, and stepped away.

Elena set the book on the table and opened it to the same image as the previous day. She sat alongside the others. Nigel joined them on the speakerphone. As did Antonio and his aides. Thankfully, Antonio said nothing. Tears came and went. Elena did not care. Apparently nor did anyone else.

After a time, she said, "As Miriam told you yesterday, she had never seen this image before. A nine-year-old child accepted responsibility from her beloved great-grandmother, who was dying. The books carried a tradition and a duty that stretched back into the shadowed recesses of time. But if there were any instructions that came with the task, Miriam did not receive them. Perhaps her great-grandmother intended to give them later, after Miriam had grown up. Perhaps there were none to begin with. We shall never know."

Elena turned the page back to the first image. "Miriam studied this image for seventy-two years, as long as she had the book. She never turned the page. If it had been me, I would have gone through the entire book and started over. But that was not her way. She assumed if God wanted to speak with her, he would have used this first image. Her entire life, she has looked at these books as a sign of her own failure. She did not ever receive a message from God, not until . . ."

Elena extracted a damp handkerchief from her pocket. She

carefully wiped her eyes so as to see the image. "In Miriam's mind, she failed to live up to the duty laid upon her by her great-grandmother. As a result, Miriam never truly valued the gifts she did possess. Her faculty to heal troubled hearts and minds. Her wisdom as a counselor. Her gift as a teacher. Her ability to inspire others. The deep and abiding love she held for her departed husband and her child and her granddaughter. Her insight and astuteness and understanding."

She stopped then. Elena knew there was more she needed to say. But the words simply would not come.

"I understand what you are saying," Angie, the ambassador's assistant, said. "We all have gifts."

Sandra Harwood said, "We do not see the world with God's eyes."

"We must lift our gazes beyond the obstacles," Lawrence softly agreed.

Nigel Harries added, "And focus our attention beyond the human horizon."

Sandra said, "We must give thanks for the task and the challenge set before us."

Lawrence said, "Hold fast to the course."

Antonio's voice emerged from the speakerphone. "Do what is set before us, and accept that God is leading us."

Angie Cassels said, "Trust that his wisdom and guidance will always see us through."

There was a silence then, until Elena said, "Let's join hands and pray."

During the journey to Oxford, Elena made two quick calls, first to Miriam's daughter and then the granddaughter. Elena wanted them both to hear the news directly from her. As expected, Miriam's daughter was only too glad to leave all the arrangements to Elena.

Elena then called her mother. It was a longer call, and much harder. As soon as she was done, Elena turned her phone back off. She had collected another three calls from Antonio. But Elena was afraid she would start weeping and not be able to stop. Antonio would just have to wait.

She told Fiona what had happened only after she had finished with the day's four patients. Fiona promised to spread the word. They all knew Miriam. The director had considered her a friend as well as a colleague. Elena stopped by the market for food she had no interest in eating. She went home and forced herself to down a few bites of salad. She then walked out to the garden bench. The sun was setting over Oxford. Rain clouds paraded in from the south, casting wet ribbons over the countryside. Elena took a long look and spent a few moments thinking of departed loved ones.

Then she turned on her phone and called Antonio.

31

WEDNESDAY, THURSDAY, FRIDAY

"Things are threatening to unravel."

Lawrence Harwood's words echoed around the empty office. Elena's speakerphone sat on a small coffee table in the middle of the room. She was as alone as she had ever been in her entire life.

Lawrence went on, "The Senate Finance Committee will vote on the legislation next week. We're certain of passage. The public demands that Congress do something about the banks and their freewheeling methods. The law has support from both sides of the aisle. So the banks are using their allies in Congress to push for appointments who will neuter the commission."

Wednesday morning, Elena had returned to the embassy for their dawn meeting, then accompanied Lawrence and his wife to the airport. On the way, Sandra had spoken about a mutual friend, Shirley Wainwright, whose husband had been appointed to the position Lawrence now held. Teddy Wainwright had suffered a heart attack while traveling to meet with the same Washington power brokers who had now summoned Lawrence. Sandra Harwood's voice had trembled slightly as she said that Shirley wanted to get in touch with Elena.

Thursday morning Elena completed arrangements for Miriam's funeral, then walked to High Street and purchased a speakerphone. With Fiona's help she arranged for a daily conference connection and had everything in place when the group called at one. Lawrence and Sandra were in their Washington hotel, Nigel was off somewhere doing security things, Angie Cassels was prepping for Lawrence's first meeting with the Senate Finance Committee, Antonio and his aides were in a Brussels limo en route to their lunch meeting. Everyone was frantically busy except Elena. The phone sat on a card table in the middle of the upstairs room. Beside it rested the open book. The image remained dormant. Miriam's absence was everywhere she looked.

Friday morning Elena met with Brian Farringdon, supposedly to discuss the funeral, which he had agreed to lead. But in truth it was mainly so she could grieve. He listened as only a pastor could, prayed with her, hugged her, and sent her out feeling genuinely prepared for the day ahead. Elena had then returned to her new office and welcomed the others as they came online. Elena had opened with a passage from First Corinthians, then read the brief message she had prepared the previous evening. In the silence that followed, tension radiated from her speakerphone.

Finally, Sandra Harwood said, "Yesterday Lawrence and I met with allies. Everyone is very worried."

Antonio sounded impossibly tired. "The bankers are trying to work the same underhanded maneuvers here in Brussels."

"Of course they are," Lawrence said. His voice grated from the smoke of battles still to come. "If their tactics work in Washington, they will work anywhere."

Antonio asked, "Lawrence, how many allies can you expect to have on your commission?"

Lawrence pondered a moment. "Three, maybe four."

"How many will serve on the commission?"

"They're still arguing over that. My guess is somewhere around fourteen."

"So you will be a tiny minority."

"Looks that way. What about you?"

"I am one ally away from a fifty-fifty split."

"I ought to have you come help out over here."

"Thank you, my friend." Antonio tried for humor. "But I am a little busy at the moment."

As they said their farewells, Lawrence offered, "Larry King is taping a segment with me this afternoon. Sandra, when will it air in Europe?"

"Saturday evening. Nine o'clock in England, ten in Brussels."

Antonio demanded, "Why didn't you say something before now? We need to pray for this as well."

After they prayed a second time, Elena hung up the phone and sat in the empty room. Wind rattled a window's loose pane. Clouds and sunlight sent shadows scuttling across the stained carpet. She had no idea how long she sat there. The sigh she emitted as she rose and crossed the room could have come from her own grandmother.

When she opened the office door, she found a gray-haired woman she did not recognize seated in the foyer. "May I help you?"

"Your man said it would be all right if I waited inside." The woman rose and swayed dangerously. "Oh my."

Elena reached out and gripped her arm. "Are you all right?"

"I've never been much of a flier. I feel like I've been trapped in a can of bad air for eight hours."

The woman was angular in a manner that was both intelligent and severe. She was also very tall, standing close to six feet. Elena asked, "Do I know you?"

"I'm Shirley Wainwright."

"Of course. The woman who lost her husband."

"I didn't *lose* him. And despite what you've heard, Teddy did *not* just have a heart attack and die in the back of that limo." She had a voice that sounded permanently cracked, perhaps from crying herself hoarse once too often. "Teddy gave himself up to God's cause."

"I needed to make this trip. I had to. Soon as Sandra told me what you were doing, leading them in prayer every day, helping them focus on God's will, I knew I had to be a part of this."

Shirley Wainwright wore a dove-gray suit that looked both expensive and travel-worn. She allowed herself to be guided into Elena's office. If she noticed the building's hollow vacancy, she gave no sign. "Teddy was one of the architects of the Wall Street bank failure and the recession that followed. What do you know about derivatives?"

Elena guided her into the chair, went back around her desk, and seated herself. "Almost nothing."

"Derivatives traders manipulate risk. They hunt out danger points and they magnify the swings. They don't care whether the market is going up or down. What they want, what they thrive on, is movement. The greater the movement, the faster the swings, the more money they can make." She settled a large black purse in her lap, opened the gold clasp, and began rummaging. "Teddy's first day on the job, the chief of derivatives came to him and said they needed more capital. Teddy already knew this man. They weren't friends. Most derivatives traders have the social skills of a cougar. But Teddy knew what the board was hiding from almost everyone, including their own shareholders. The derivatives department was responsible for more than two-thirds of the bank's total profit."

Elena watched the woman across from her dig impatiently in her purse. Shirley Wainwright's movements were almost manic. Her words carried a repetitive quality, as though they had been said so often that she no longer had to give them any notice.

"The derivatives chief told Teddy his department had become extended on several huge bets and were desperately

short of cash. He didn't care where it came from. But the bank's
funds were used up. The derivatives chief said they were onto a
sure thing. A fire sale, was what the man told Teddy. They had
the chance to double the bank's capital. Teddy asked him what he
had in mind. The derivatives chief asked Teddy to supply him
with as many new mortgages as Teddy could arrange." She
started pulling items from her purse and slapping them on Elena's desk. "I'm positive I put it in here."

"Perhaps it would be best if you first told me—"

"Teddy identified a California bank that specialized in subprime mortgages and bought a controlling interest. He then ordered the bank's loan officers to ignore standard procedure.
Approve every loan they could get their hands on. The first year
of operation, Teddy's plan netted the bank eight hundred million
dollars. The second, three *billion*. The next year, the subprime
market collapsed, dragging the world economy down with it.
The federal government bailed Teddy's bank out. The traders and
the bank's directors all got their bonuses. Everybody was happy
but Teddy."

Shirley Wainwright drew a crumpled envelope from her
purse and waved it at Elena. "I've been a believer since the year
our second daughter was born. Teddy used to scoff at it. But this
tragedy brought Teddy to Jesus. I weep for all the families who
have suffered. But I thank God that Teddy finally saw the light."

Elena reached over and took the letter. Keeping her motions
easy. Calm. Like her voice. "Why are you telling me this?"

"I've tried and tried to talk about this with Lawrence. But he
treats me like an addled old woman. Which I suppose I am." The
woman's hand trembled slightly as she pointed at the letter.
"Read what Teddy says. It's all there."

Antonio did not return her call until that evening. He listened to
her describe the conversation with Shirley Wainwright, then
said, "Wait just one minute, Elena." He muffled his phone, but

she could still hear Antonio's voice and someone else in response. Then he came back on and said, "All right. I'm listening.
Tell me what the letter said."

"Where are you?"

"At EU headquarters."

"But it's eight o'clock at night."

"I needed to speak privately with one of the leaders here.
We've both been tied up in meetings all day."

"Should I call you back?"

"He has been delayed. I am sitting in an outer office. His aide
is off fetching me a coffee I don't want."

"You sound tired."

"I am more worried than tired. And I am very tired indeed.
Now tell me about the letter."

"Most of it was very personal. He was grateful for how faith
had healed his relationships with Shirley and his daughters. He
was grateful for salvation. He wished he had come to know and
understand these things years ago. He wished he had a chance to
do his life over again. Then at the end of the letter, Teddy Wainwright said that the banks were planning to do the whole thing
again."

Antonio's voice hardened. "He suspected this, or he was certain?"

"His letter states it as fact. Teddy said the only real profit
generators in the Wall Street banks these days are the derivatives
departments. The banks' standard operations are all down. New
laws have stifled the banks' predatory credit card practices. Sav-
ings are down because of the low interest rates. And the finance
officers are too frightened of another downturn to generate new
loans."

"We have suspected this. Banks are careful to hide their derivatives operations, even from other divisions. All we can say
for certain is, banks are not loaning money. Their credit operations are run with savage brutality. Small businesses are going
bankrupt because of the lack of capital. And yet the banks are

generating profit. We are fairly certain this income is spawned by derivatives. But until our committees are up and running, the derivatives markets still remain uncontrolled. And the banks' shareholders are making money. They do not ask because they prefer not to know." Antonio was silent a moment, then asked, "Where is Teddy's widow?"

"I booked her into the Randolph. Antonio, the letter said something else that—"

Antonio's voice underwent a sharp change. "I must go, Elena. The minister has arrived. We will speak tomorrow morning."

"I'm sorry to have bothered you."

"What bother? This is important news. Until tomorrow."

32

SATURDAY

Antonio did not call.

Elena kept the phone beside her as she packed a bag and prepared for the day. She rode into Oxford with her cell phone open on the seat beside her. Charles parked in front of her new office and Elena walked over to the Randolph, the phone in her hand. Shirley Wainwright was waiting for her in the lobby. Elena sank into the chair beside her and set the phone on the table between them. "How did you sleep?"

"Fine. Well, not fine. I haven't had a fine night since Teddy left me. I slept enough."

The woman certainly looked better than she had the previous day, though her calm facade still showed cracks and her voice still refused to settle on any one octave. Elena said, "I shared the information in Teddy's letter with Antonio."

"The gentleman you told me about in Brussels, is that right?" She shrugged. "Anyone in finance already knows about it. Or at least they suspect. I showed you the letter because I didn't want you to think I was crazy."

"I didn't—"

"I know how I look, and I know how I sound. Borderline,

isn't that the correct word? I've heard my daughters use it enough. 'Mama is borderline frantic.'"

"Clinical psychologists tend not to use words like *crazy* or *borderline* anything. But thank you for showing me the letter."

"Why do you keep looking at your phone?"

"Antonio was supposed to call me this morning. He hasn't. I'm trying not to worry." Elena shut her cell phone and slipped it into her pocket. "I have a very busy two days coming up. A friend passed away. Her memorial service is tomorrow."

"How can I help?"

Elena said what she had decided on during the drive into town. "You've had your own share of loss. Maybe it would be best if you took the weekend to rest."

"Oh, piffle. A weekend isn't going to make any difference. Teddy was the center of my world. He's gone. God is just going to have to fill the void." Shirley Wainwright rose to her feet. "Right now, the nicest gift you could give me is something useful to do."

When the day's meeting began, Antonio did not join them. Instead, one of his aides came on the line and breathlessly apologized, Antonio was in another meeting with the minister. Elena swallowed her disappointment and introduced Shirley. Sandra Harwood was clearly surprised by the woman's presence. Lawrence sounded too preoccupied to care. After the opening prayer, Sandra praised her husband's performance on Larry King. Lawrence simply muttered the word, *performance.* Otherwise he did not speak.

Shirley Wainwright proved the right companion for the day. She did not speak once during the journey from Oxford to Heathrow Airport. When they had parked, Elena checked the phone once more, just to be sure she had not missed the call. Shirley asked, "Why don't you call him?"

"I can't."

"Okay."

"No. I mean, Antonio must be busy with something extremely important, if it caused him to miss our meeting. That's never happened before."

"Antonio is a banker?"

"Most recently he's been a financial adviser to the Vatican. Now he's Lawrence's counterpart in Brussels."

Shirley watched a man pass through the customs gate and embrace a young woman who awaited him. "I know my being here is an imposition."

"Not at all, you're—"

"I had to come, you see. I couldn't stay in New York another minute. My daughters think I'm going crazy with grief. That's not it at all. I feel like I've stepped into a vacuum. Teddy gave his life for something very important. I need to help. I've *got* to help." She turned to Elena. "Can you understand that?"

"Yes."

"My days have become so futile. I feel like I'm failing God. There must be something I can do, some way to make this loss and this sadness all feel worthwhile."

Elena reached across and touched the woman's hand. "I'm glad you came."

Miriam's daughter was precisely as Elena recalled, pinch-faced and acquisitive. She kissed the air by Elena's cheek and expressed empty condolences, then returned to an argument with her daughter. Miriam's granddaughter was growing into a younger version of her mother, which was ironic, since the two women clearly did not get along. Elena was not the least bit sorry to hand them over to Shirley Wainwright, who bundled them into a taxi. An hour later, Elena's parents came through customs.

Elena's mother had taught high school biology for thirty-one years. Elena's father was a metallurgist. They had filled Elena's home and early years with much love and a fair share of good times. They still attended the same uptown church where they had met. The church had been one of the few bones of contention between Miriam and Elena's parents. Miriam had always referred to it as a country club where God was occasionally granted a visitor's pass. Elena's father had responded that the only religion he ever intended to give more time and attention to was golf. Elena was certain he only said it to goad Miriam.

Her mother was red-eyed and stumbling from fatigue and loss. She had not seen Miriam in several years, but the two women talked by phone at least once a week. For several years now, Elena's mother had shown growing signs of early-onset dementia. But her father had adapted, turning his love into a protective barrier between his wife and any need for change. Her father greeted Elena with an embrace and the same words that had started and ended their conversations for years. "Your mother is fine."

"Hello, Daddy. I'm sure you're right." She hugged her mother, then slipped the purse from her shoulder. "Let me take that, Mom."

Elena introduced Gerald simply as a driver. To say anything more would only cause unnecessary concern. Gerald drove them to the Courtyard by Marriott, the closest hotel to the church and where everyone involved in the remembrance service was staying. Two hours later, Elena and her parents walked to an Italian restaurant around the corner from the hotel. Charles maintained a discreet distance and went unnoticed by her parents. Her mother was most comfortable with memories and regaled them with stories from her and Miriam's school days. Candles softened the evening's ragged edges, and the shared recollections left them all able to smile. They walked back to the hotel through a soft spring rain.

As soon as Elena returned to her room, she called Antonio. Elena's heart clamored and her hands turned damp as she punched in the numbers. When his answering machine responded, she sketched out where she was. Then she cut the connection. She stood by the hotel window, staring out over the parking lot, and said the words she had not spoken on the phone. "Please come. I need you."

She then spent half an hour seated at the hotel desk, staring at a blank sheet of paper. Brian had wanted her to say something at Miriam's memorial service. But she had no idea how to compact a lifetime's friendship into a few sentences. When Shirley Wainwright knocked on her door, the page was still empty.

Elena turned on the television in time to hear Larry King introduce the evening's two guests. Lawrence Harwood had aged several years since leaving London. His expression reminded Elena of an eighteenth-century etching that had occupied one wall of her father's office. It had shown America's founding fathers at the Constitutional Congress, debating the structure of their new country's first laws. She had been fascinated by the picture as a child, though some of their expressions had frightened her. They had looked like fierce birds of prey, the strength so profoundly severe, she knew they were capable of the unthinkable. Her father had often said such conviction was necessary to accomplish the impossible. They had faced established interests and entrenched powers. Elena had not understood much of what her father said. But she had loved the way he had held her and studied the image with her. As though the picture's deep and abiding mystery joined them. She had not thought of that picture in years.

Lawrence Harwood responded to Larry King's first question with "The collapse of Lehman Brothers proved that the nation's top banks had become too big to be allowed to fail. But since the bailout, these same financial institutions have only become larger."

Larry King said, "But your opponents are swift to point out that this is not a monopoly. This is just healthy business. There are over a dozen major players on Wall Street, and the competition between them is fierce."

Lawrence Harwood's craven features made a mockery of the presenter's easy manner. "At one level, this is true. But at another level, they are allied. They do not merely work together. They collude. They do so in secret. They hide their tracks well."

Larry King's other guest was Easton Grey, a former secretary of the Treasury. The secretary's on-camera presence was very polished, his responses smoothly glib. Easton Grey smiled easily as he countered Lawrence's comments, pointing out that Lawrence had himself worked for these very same institutions.

"I worked for several of them and sat on the boards of others. I have resigned from all these positions," Lawrence replied. Compared to the former Treasury official, Lawrence looked like an aging boxer, off his prime, unable to defend himself against the opponent's blows. "How many of these banks are paying your bills tonight, Mr. Secretary?"

Easton Grey shrugged easily. "I am employed by one of the banks that has helped make America great. My loyalties are to my employer, and to this great nation. Unlike you."

Shirley Wainwright said, "The banks will hire a high-powered television presenter to grill their man before he goes on air. They go over and over every conceivable question. He is coached to smile and gesture smoothly and respond with warmth. A team of PR types sit in a circle and feed their man the most damaging possible responses. Terry got prepped like this a couple of times a year."

Elena did not respond. Her attention remained tightly focused on the screen. The former secretary's eyes were colored a clear washed gray and held nothing. Every time the camera shifted from Lawrence back to this man, Elena felt enveloped by old smoke. It coated her nostrils and her tongue. She felt it seep down the back of her throat until she feared she might gag.

Lawrence Harwood said, "Today the major US banks spend one million dollars *per day* to lobby and influence Congress. Foreign banks together spend another million dollars per day. In

Washington. That is collusion. That is how important they consider this legislation. That is how worried they are about my commission."

"I'm sorry, Lawrence, but you're wrong on that point as well." Easton Grey dismissed his opponent with a smile. "Our system already has sufficient oversight in place. And far too many laws, as everyone watching this program knows firsthand. Another commission will only add further strain to an already overburdened financial system."

Larry King asked a question Elena did not bother hearing. Her attention remained fastened on Lawrence Harwood. He wore the grim expression of a man who already knew he had lost, but fought on because he had to.

Lawrence Harwood said, "One hundred and twenty-five former members of Congress and White House cabinets are now employed by the banking industry and their lobbying affiliates. This revolving-door policy has been copied from the military-industrial complex. And we all know how much that has cost the American public. Decades of cost overruns, lax oversights, boondoggling, it's all part of the banks' plans. Their version of the five-thousand-dollar hammer is just around the corner."

The former Treasury secretary laughed out loud. "This is just too rich. There is no secret collusion going on here. I sacrificed five years of my career and over three million dollars in lost salary in order to serve my country. The President called, and I went. The President chose me because where else would the administration find the talent to run the nation's finances than inside a successful financial institution? The last time I checked, this was still a free country. Run on sound business principles."

Larry King thanked each of his guests and the program switched to a commercial. Elena cut off the set as Shirley rose slowly to her feet. "I've been filled with sorrow and helpless anger since Teddy died. I keep hoping . . ."

Elena nodded slowly, her eyes on the empty screen.

"Lawrence didn't land a single blow," Shirley said, and opened the door. "I wish I hadn't seen this. I wish . . ."

Long after Shirley departed, Elena remained where she was.

Elena lay in bed staring at the ceiling. The drapes did not close fully. Every passing car sent a ribbon of light flickering across the ceiling. Her cell phone vibrated on the bedside table. She rolled over and checked the readout, wishing her heart did not race with anticipation that Antonio might call. Even this late. As though she were a teenager again. But the phone showed a US number she did not recognize. Elena assumed it was a friend of Miriam's family and was tempted not to answer. But with the memorial service the next afternoon, she knew she had no choice. "Hello?"

Sandra Harwood asked, "Did I wake you?"

"No."

"Really?"

"I can't sleep."

"I'm not surprised, with what you're facing. I'm so sorry I'm not there for you."

"You're where you need to be."

"Can we talk? I know this is a terrible time. But I'm so worried."

Elena rose from her bed and pulled open the drapes. The street beyond the motel parking lot had emptied. The night was slick with rain. Water dappled the window. "About Lawrence?"

"He is devastated. He feels like whatever he does, they are ready for him. He spends his days pounding on locked doors and losing every battle. Those are his words."

Elena angled the chair so she could watch the night and the rain. She hugged her knees to her chest, slipped her nightgown over her legs, then tucked it around the edges of her toes, like a tent. It was a habit from childhood and still brought a measure of comfort.

Sandra went on, "He's been through tough times before. My role has always been the same. I play the wise woman. He comes to me with his problems. I'm able to see what he can't. The opposition's weakness, the offer that will turn things around, the unspoken desire, the one point that no one has addressed."

"It's your gift," Elena said.

The city night sounded very different from her home. A London taxi trundled along the wet road, its motor making an unmistakable sound, like a metallic bullfrog. A car trunk lid slammed shut. Footsteps and voices drifted up from the parking lot. Elena saw a shadow flicker past the motel's front entrance. She assumed it was Charles, off on another nightly patrol.

Sandra was saying, "I spend my days sitting inside a Washington hotel room. I watch Lawrence get ready for another meeting. He feels he's lost before he leaves. Nothing I say makes any difference. I feel . . ."

Elena turned and stared at the empty sheet of paper lying on the desk beside the television. The words she was supposed to speak at the memorial service still had not come. "I understand."

Sandra asked, "Is it possible to feel something so intense you can't either name or describe it?"

Elena replied, "You feel as though your days are wasted. You feel as though you have lost your center of gravity. You know you should be doing something, but you don't know what. You feel guilty that you don't feel closer to God. You know he is in control but you don't understand what role you're supposed to play. All you feel is lost and alone, and you're too honest with yourself to pretend otherwise. You are afraid that you're not getting anything right. That maybe God has spoken to you, and you missed it. And that leaves you feeling even guiltier than before."

The only sign Sandra Harwood gave that she was crying was the lingering silence. Finally she asked, "What am I supposed to do?"

"Let's pray together," Elena replied. "Maybe God will answer us both."

33

SUNDAY

Elena spent Sunday morning with her parents. Over a late breakfast, her father announced they were taking the evening flight back. Elena glanced at her mother's wan features and knew it was a bad idea. But she also knew her father was ready for what would be another futile argument. She could already hear the reasoning, how her mother had not slept well, how she was better off in familiar surroundings. The truth was, her father felt unable to control things here. Elena simply said she was certain he would do what he thought was best.

The weather cleared around noon. Antonio never called. As she checked out of the hotel, Elena wished there was some special formula she could use to make herself not care.

The memorial service took place where Miriam had worshipped. The parish church stood inside a waist-high stone wall that bordered Hampstead Heath. The meadows and the springtime trees glowed with a promise of new beginnings. The church was Norman and dated from the very earliest days of the twelfth century. The doors leading to the squat tower were open, and Elena watched the bell ringers toll a timeless welcome. The nave's ancient stone and stained-glass windows glowed with a honeyed warmth in the afternoon sun.

If Brian Farringdon found anything unusual in Elena's decision not to say anything, he gave no sign. He spoke eloquently about their departed friend, spent a few minutes at the reception afterward at Miriam's home, then rushed back to Oxford for the evening service.

Charles drove Elena and her parents to Heathrow. Shirley Wainwright remained a silent presence in the front seat. At the terminal, Elena hugged her parents and waved them through the security line, wishing she could put more heart into her farewells.

On the return journey to Oxford, Shirley said, "Gerald received a call from Nigel Harries. He wants to talk with me tomorrow afternoon."

"How does he know about you?"

"I have no idea. I suppose Sandra must have said something."

"Nigel is part of our group. And a very good man. Isn't that right, Gerald."

"The best there is in this game, ma'am."

Shirley said to her side window, "I've had my fill of police who repeat their questions a hundred times and don't listen to a word I say. They think I'm crazy to even suggest Teddy had anything other than just a normal heart attack."

"Nigel isn't like that. If he says it's important, I think you should talk with him." When Shirley did not respond, Elena continued, "I want you to come stay with me."

"That's very kind. But to be frank, I'm beginning to think my daughter may have been right. That I came for all the wrong reasons."

"I can't say anything about that. But as long as you do stay, I want you to be my guest."

Shirley turned from her surveying of the side window. "Why?"

"We are all in this together," Elena replied. "Maybe all that connects us is a lack of clarity and our fears. But we still need to rely on one another."

Shirley nodded slowly. "I see why Sandra speaks of you as she does."

Elena had turned her home's two extra bedrooms into an exercise room and study. As she made up the sofa with sheets and a blanket, she felt the home's currents move in odd directions. She wished her guest a good night and retreated to her own room. As Elena settled into bed, she decided inviting Shirley Wainwright to stay with her had been the right decision. She had been alone long enough.

Elena felt as though she had just managed to fall asleep when the phone rang. She fumbled around the bedside table before she managed to snag the receiver. "Hello?"

Antonio said, "I'm sorry to bother you. But I had no one else to call."

"What is it?"

"I've had another dream."

Elena rose from the bed and padded into the bathroom. She washed her face and slipped on her robe, then returned and picked up the phone. The bedside clock read one in the morning. "All right. I'm back."

"I haven't contacted you for days. I was not able to join you for the memorial service. Now I wake you. Only when I need you do I call."

It was precisely what Elena had been thinking. But she replied, "I'm glad you did."

"It is just, when I woke up, I was filled with an utter certainty that phoning you was very important."

"It is."

"I've missed you, Elena."

She drew her robe more tightly against the sudden tremors. "Why haven't you called me?"

"Things are not good. In fact, they're terrible."

"Where are you?"

"Brussels. A hotel room. As alone and worried as I have been since I lost Francesca."

Elena had an impression of the man sitting up in a strange bed, a pile of pillows plumped behind his back. His tousled hair, his worried gaze, his drawn and weary expression, it was suddenly so vivid that she felt as though she were seated beside him.

Antonio went on, "After our meetings and prayer times, I have felt so certain of everything. But the opposition I face, you can't imagine how hard they are attacking. I have given a number of interviews. At the time, what I said felt right. But afterward, I have doubted . . ."

"Everything."

"Yes."

"Even me," she said. "And what I represent."

"I'm so sorry, Elena."

"Do you want to tell me about your dream?"

"It came and went in a flash. That was what I thought when I woke up. That I had been struck by lightning. Twice."

"The dream has come two times?"

"Once just after I went to sleep. Another time just before I phoned. Both times I felt I had to call you. As though the need to call you was the last portion of the dream. Is that normal? I mean, feeling this way."

"We are all in new terrain here. If we were discussing dreams from your own subconscious, I would tell you that each framework is new and derived from a specific emotional issue."

"I'm so glad we're talking, Elena."

"Describe what you saw."

"I am standing in a formal chamber, like so many I have visited over the past days. People swirl around me. I stand before a man whose face I cannot see. He raises a gun and I stare down the barrel. The opening grows as big as a cannon." Antonio's accent strengthened with the tension. "He shoots me. In the mouth. I fall to the ground. I leave my body and rise up. I look down but I cannot see myself. The man whose face I cannot see leans over me. Other men and women without faces come forward and crowd around him. They look down at me and pat the shooter's back. Finally they draw back and I see myself. Then the dream starts over again."

Elena felt a hum circulate through her, an energy vibrating far above the range of normal senses. It grew with each word Antonio spoke, as if they were both hooked into a high-voltage charge. "The exact same dream repeats itself?"

"The same but not the same." Antonio's breathing became harsh, rasping. "It is the same man and the same gun. I am shot. I rise up. The faceless people gather. Only this time, when I am able to see the body lying on the ground, it is not me. It is Lawrence."

Elena fought against a force that now locked her chest up tight. "Something is happening."

"Elena?"

"They are gunning for you both. They are going to silence you."

"You sound . . . different."

"Call Lawrence. Tell him the dream. Tell him I said . . ."

"Yes?"

She gritted her teeth and shook with the effort required to say "They're coming."

"What do we do?" he said.

"Nothing."

"But we stand to lose everything."

She clenched her eyes shut so tightly that she saw stars. And something more. "This is not your battle."

Elena sat for a time staring out the rain-streaked window. Twice she saw Charles's shadow pass from left to right, walking her home's perimeter. But she remained too captured by the power filling her room to concentrate on anything else.

Eventually she shifted to the desk and opened her laptop. Elena drew up the image from the book of dreams, then opened her Bible to the passage of First Corinthians she had been studying. The power she had felt during her conversation with Antonio had not so much faded as leveled off. The burning intensity remained with her still.

Elena read a passage that appeared rimmed by fire. "For the Kingdom of God is not a matter of words, but of power."

For the first time, Elena saw everything she had been enduring as a period of preparation. The hollow days and futile hours, even her doubt and false cravings, all had played a vital role. She saw that clearly now.

It was all part of God's plan.

She lowered herself to her knees and spoke the tersest prayer in years.

"I'm ready."

34

MONDAY

I want to help. I need to."

Elena sat across the desk from Brian Farringdon. The vicar of Saint Aldates sipped his first cup of coffee. He glanced at his watch, clearly drawn to whatever Elena's unexpected arrival had pulled him from. She found herself vaguely jealous of the man and his busy schedule. Other than the five-minute gathering at noon, she had one patient that day. One.

Brian picked up his phone, dialed, and said, "Ask Janine to join us, please." He listened a moment and said, "I'll be a while yet. Why don't you start . . ." He listened, then said more sharply, "What has come up is important too. I'll be there when I can."

Elena winced at the force he used to replace the phone. "I'm so sorry—"

"Stop right there." He sipped from his cup. "I'm the one who needs to be apologizing here."

"What are you talking about?"

There was a knock at his door. He raised a finger to Elena. Wait. "Come in."

Janine opened the door. "You wanted to see me?" She sounded very cross.

"Join us. Please."

She slipped into the chair beside Elena. She glared at Brian.

Brian said, "On the way back from the memorial service yesterday, Janine and I had our first true quarrel."

Jane interrupted, "Really, Brian. Could that possibly be of any interest to her?"

"Actually, yes."

"I hardly think now is the time for us to bring in a relationship counselor."

"I did not call Elena. She came on her own."

Janine crossed her arms. Waited.

Brian nodded at Elena. "Be so good as to repeat what you were telling me. Start at the beginning."

Elena hesitated.

"This is important, Elena. For all of us. Please."

"I feel as though I had another message from God last night. I know Brian says I should set doubt aside at these times, but I can't. I'm afraid of a lot of things right now, most especially getting a divine message wrong, or hearing the wrong voice. I have my own desires, and they are so fierce that I often want to claim they are God's desires for me as well as my own."

Janine glanced across the desk. She uncrossed her arms.

Elena said, "I have watched one bit after another of my former life peel away. And I hate it. It's painful. I feel like I'm living inside a vacuum. What's more, I don't feel that there's any role for me in this new work. It's not enough for me to lead these brief daily meetings and occasionally pass on a divine message. I spend hours and hours doing nothing at all. I hate it. Maybe I shouldn't use that word. But I do. I loathe this feeling of wasted days."

Brian gave his fiancée a tight smile. Janine's expression had undergone a remarkable transformation. She stared at Elena in openmouthed surprise.

Elena went on, "I saw last night how I need to look beyond myself. How families and lives and relationships are being shredded by this crisis. This is not just about people losing jobs and homes. This is about the crushing of hope and the destruction of lifelong dreams. I am a trained counselor. I have an empty office building and an empty schedule. I want to help knit families back together."

There was a long silence. Finally Brian said to his fiancée, "You were right and I was wrong."

Janine shivered, as though forcing herself awake. When she spoke, her voice was an octave lower than normal. "I find the idea of being a vicar's wife utterly repellent. Taking tea with old ladies, being a sounding board for people who want to complain and are afraid to approach Brian. I want a purpose that is all my own. Yesterday I told Brian I wanted to help with the families who are being wrecked by this foreclosure crisis."

"And I told her there are two problems with her suggestion," Brian said, smiling openly now. "The first is, she's already working too hard. The social services are being cut back by the current budget crisis. At the same moment when people's needs are greatest. Janine is already working twelve-hour days and coming home so exhausted she stumbles. And she wants to do more? I know firsthand the danger of compassion driving a servant beyond the brink."

"I can restructure my schedule," Janine said. "I took today off to show you just how possible that is."

"I doubted your resolve last night. And I was wrong to do so." Brian turned back to Elena and went on, "The second problem is space here at Saint Aldates. Our own counseling services are stretched to the breaking point. The shelter we started has been overwhelmed. And now Janine wants to bring in more people."

"I have the space," Elena said. "And the time."

"Not for long," Brian said.

Janine said, "I have identified families who are truly willing to accept help, and not just use counseling service as another opportunity to complain." Her voice sparkled now.

Elena was now the one who shivered. "How long do you need to set this up?"

"Hours," Janine said. "How much free space can you offer us?"

Elena was already on her feet. "Come and see for yourself."

Elena's day filled at a very rapid rate. By the time she stopped for the noon teleconference, Janine had signed up nineteen families who had been struck by the economic crisis and were desperate for counseling. Another seven couples were booked into an encounter group slated to begin the next evening.

When the others came on the line, Elena described what was going on and explained how this was a new area for her. She said she would appreciate their prayers, as she had never worked on family counseling issues before. She then introduced Janine and said she had urged her to join their group.

The only comment came from Lawrence, who demanded, "What is that racket?"

"My afternoon appointments," Elena said.

Janine said, "They are used to waiting hours for appointments. Days. They're afraid if they don't show up early, they won't get in at all."

Janine had filled the front rooms with battered but usable furniture. She had repeatedly come and gone, quick flashes of movement and bursts of conversation, then off again. Janine remained breathless with the thrill of her work. Her elation was so infectious that she managed to draw smiles from the people waiting in Elena's front room.

Without being asked, Shirley Wainwright had taken up station at the reception desk. Gerald remained a silent guardian on the periphery of their world. The families let their children play on the floor and did not seem to care that the sofa was lumpy or the carpet stained. On one visit, Janine had arrived with a bundle of church posters, which she and Shirley taped to the walls. The posters shouted messages of hope and light and new beginnings. At midmorning Shirley went out and bought a box of children's toys. The next time Janine returned, the two of them had tacked soft blankets to the kitchen walls and floors and turned it into a crèche.

Elena read a passage from her Bible, then asked if there were any specific prayer requests. Lawrence spoke first. "Antonio was right. They're gunning for me."

Nigel Harries, the security chief, had slipped in just before Elena had placed the call. He leaned forward in his chair and frowned at the phone but did not speak.

Lawrence went on, "I'm still not clear on whether this dream of his was a foretelling, or just his subconscious at work."

"Let's set that aside for the moment," Elena said. "We may not know the answer to that for days, weeks, or perhaps not at all in this life. What is important here is that the dream resonated with you both."

Antonio said, "My meetings this morning could not have gone worse."

Lawrence's voice sounded metallic, as though all human emotion had been pounded down to a steel-hard core. "Where are you now?"

"In the backseat of my car, parked outside the EU finance ministry."

"Are your aides with you?"

"Yes."

"How long do you have?"

Antonio did not hesitate. "A few days at most."

"That's more than me."

Sandra's voice broke in softly. "Lawrence."

"I'm not quitting. I'm just speaking realistically. I have a meeting this afternoon with the head of the Senate Finance Committee. My guess is, he's going to hand me my walking papers."

"I may follow you," Antonio replied. "As soon as tonight."

Elena thought she heard someone cry softly and wondered if it was Sandra Harwood. Elena found it wrenching to think that such a strong and capable woman had been brought so low. But all she said was, "Does anyone else have something they wish to share with the group?"

When no one spoke, Elena reached into her purse and withdrew a folded sheet of paper. "Yesterday at Miriam's service I could not speak. I had a hundred things I wanted to say. A thousand. But none of them felt right. Last night, after Antonio called to tell me about his dream, I finally realized what it was I needed to say."

She unfolded her notes but found it unnecessary to look at her words. "Even those of us who only knew Miriam for a brief moment came to care very deeply for her. I imagine that each of us also learned from her. I certainly did. Her wisdom and gift of instruction carried me through some of the most difficult and most important periods of my life.

"Miriam's last lesson is the one I feel needs to be stated here today. In such moments as this, when we are hollowed and confused by loss, we might be tempted to view our course and our causes and our actions as failures. But if we can look beyond our sorrow, if we can hold fast to the gift of faith, we can feel the unique wholeness of eternity. We can realize more clearly than at any other time that God is near. At such times as this, the world's grip upon us has been shaken and the dross falls away. We see our need to heed the eternal call. We can know the peace and hope and joy that defies the world. I can hear Miriam reminding me of this right now. And I intend to go forward honoring her example."

Elena set the page on the table by the Bible and said, "Let us pray."

The security chief waited until Janine had departed, then asked if he might have a word. As usual, Nigel Harries was dressed in a well-tailored gray suit. The gold watch chain strung across his vest glittered in the afternoon light as he slipped a manila file from his briefcase. He said to Shirley, "Sandra Harwood informs me that you disagree with the official version of your husband's demise."

"Do we have to go through this again?"

"Not if you don't wish. But it might aid us—"

"I've spent hours and hours with various officials. They all thought I was wasting their time to even suggest such a thing."

"I can assure you, madam, that I consider this anything but a waste of time." When Shirley did not object again, Nigel asked, "Do you have any evidence that might suggest your husband did not in fact have a heart attack?"

"Teddy had a full physical three weeks before this happened. He passed with flying colors."

"Had Teddy any history of a heart complaint?"

Shirley sighed. "For the ten thousandth time. No."

"Be so good as to indulge me a moment longer." Nigel slipped a photograph from his folder. "Do you by any chance recognize this individual?"

Elena found herself staring at the photograph she had last seen in the ambassador's office. Of a young woman with dark hair and a pixie's face slipping up the outer stairs to Elena's former office.

Shirley Wainwright must have noticed the change to the room's atmosphere. She asked Elena, "What is it?"

"The picture," Nigel pressed gently. "Do you recognize the woman?"

She gave Elena another glance, then leaned over the picture. "Sorry. No."

"This could be most important, Mrs. Wainwright."

"Shirley."

"Please be so good as to give the individual another look. What about the name, Jessica Ravel?"

Shirley leaned in closer. Elena caught the faint whiff of old smoke filtering into the room. Shirley said, "Nothing."

"Thank you." Nigel slipped a second photograph from his file and set it on top of the first. "What about this gentleman."

The stench of old smoke heightened as Elena looked down at the grim visage of the man Lawrence Harwood had called a fixer. The photograph caught him as he rose from a table. The young woman was a vague blur to his left. Elena could not see the woman's face. But she knew it was her.

"I don't recognize either of them."

"That's rather interesting. As they clearly know you. Or at least, have found you both of interest."

"I don't understand."

"No. Quite." He reached into his briefcase for another file, this one tied by a blue ribbon and stamped with the British seal. "My colleagues at MI6 remain most perturbed by the illegal bugging of an Oxford counseling service. Particularly since confidential conversations involving a senior member of Her Majesty's ambassadorial corps took place there. They offered to apply their face recognition software to their visual records. I believe we may have identified something of use."

He untied the ribbon and withdrew three photographs. He shifted the speakerphone and laid them on the table in careful sequence.

Shirley Wainwright touched the first photograph. "I remember the night these were taken."

"Describe the event, if you would."

"It was a little over a month before Teddy died. Five weeks and a day. I remember exactly, because on the flight Teddy told me that God had spoken to him. You can't imagine how that made me feel, how long I'd waited and prayed." She traced a fingertip over her husband's face. "I wept. The flight attendant thought we were arguing."

"The event," Nigel prodded.

"We were part of a delegation of global financiers. We met with officials from the Bank of England. These were taken at a reception the first night. It was at . . ."

"The Ritz," Nigel said.

"Yes. That's right. Three days before, Teddy had been asked

to chair the new regulatory commission. He had asked for time to think things over. He had prayed about it. We both had. Teddy had been planning to retire. Goodness knows we didn't need any more money. He detested his work and the attitude the bankers had been showing since the bailout. Like they had won the lottery, and they could turn their backs on the devastation they'd caused and go back to making money—"

"The reception," Nigel gently pressed.

"That morning, when we arrived in London, Teddy called the White House and accepted the appointment. By the time we showed up at the reception, everybody knew. They all treated him differently. Like they weren't certain who he was anymore. Or if he could be trusted."

Nigel leaned back in his seat. He studied something only he could see on the far wall. "And then this gentleman shows up."

"I told you. I don't remember him at all."

But there he was. Elena inspected the three photographs. Teddy Wainwright and his wife stood in a receiving line, waiting to shake the hand of the chairman of the Bank of England. Two people behind Teddy was the man Lawrence had called the fixer, Cyril Price. He was chubby in the manner of a man who still carried his childhood fat, his features slightly underformed. A little dimple of a chin, a small mouth, smallish ears set tight against his head, thinning hair that was more transparent than blond. In the first photograph, he glared at Teddy.

In the second photograph, he gestured to someone out of sight.

In the third picture, the fixer was joined by a dark-haired woman with a pixie's face. She joined the fixer in staring at Teddy. She did not glare. Her expression was vaguely erotic. Like she was enjoying a secret spectacle. Elena could see the tip of her tongue touching her upper lip as she smiled.

"I don't understand," Shirley said.

Nigel reached into the embossed folder. "There is something else I think you should see. This sequence was taken by a closed-circuit camera mounted on a side street about thirty yards from where your husband's limo reportedly broke down."

"Reportedly," Shirley repeated.

"Quite so." Nigel slipped the reception photos to one side. "Now in this first, you can see the limo driver walking away."

"It's blurry."

"Stills taken from a video camera can only be enhanced so far."

"Even so, I never met the man."

"What is important is that the limo driver claimed he walked around the corner to find a signal for his cell phone."

Shirley leaned in closer. "His hands are empty."

"Precisely. There are any number of perfectly innocent reasons for this. But I find it interesting nonetheless." He set down the second photograph. "Now here we see the man exiting from the camera's upper perimeter. Just as he does so, we see another figure walking in the opposite direction."

"You don't see a face."

"I offer this photograph just to establish the sequence of events. The limo driver departs, minus his phone. A second figure appears, walking toward the place where Teddy waits."

He set down a third photograph.

Shirley breathed. "It's her."

"It would appear so."

A dark-haired woman in a navy trench coat walked beneath the camera. The camera's angle did not reveal a clear view of her face. But Elena nodded silent agreement. The woman who had appeared in her former office was shown stalking the street toward Teddy Wainwright and his empty limo.

Shirley Wainwright said, "Where else could she be going?"

"There is nothing down that street but a bus stop and the Teterboro highway. No shops. A pair of run-down tenements used mostly by immigrants."

"That woman doesn't live in a tenement and she doesn't ride buses."

Nigel Harries made a process of gathering up his photographs.

"She was going to murder my husband."

"Perhaps. Quite possibly, in fact." Nigel revealed a cold edge to his character, a stern, unwavering force as solid and permanent as gunfire. "Rest assured, madam, that is precisely what I intend to determine."

35

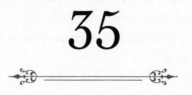

The telephone calls arrived within three minutes of each other. Sandra's came first. As soon as Elena answered, Sandra declared, "Lawrence has been fired."

"Where is he?"

"On his way back from Capitol Hill. He phoned me from the car." Sandra sounded broken. "I don't understand what's happening."

"You need to come here."

Sandra did not seem capable of taking in Elena's words. "Just a few days ago, this all seemed so *right*."

"Sandra. Listen to me." Elena used the same tone she took with trauma patients. Talking them down off whatever emotional wall they were trying to claw their way up. A calm metronome, commanding them to come back to earth and focus. "You and Lawrence need to get on the next plane to England."

"We can't just leave."

"You most certainly can. You must."

"We can't be seen to give up."

"Nobody said anything about defeat." The energy that had continued to course through her all afternoon made it difficult to hold to the calm monotone. "Bring Angie Cassels with you."

"If we leave, they will know they've won."

"It doesn't mean a thing, what they think they know."

"Lawrence will insist on staying to fight."

"Tell him I said he can't. He has to come. Today."

"But—"

"Sandra, listen carefully. Tell Lawrence this isn't his fight. Do you understand what I'm saying?"

She was silent a long moment, then said, "Are you sure?"

"Yes."

Sandra breathed once, twice. Then she cut the connection. No farewell, nothing. Elena shut her phone and cradled it to her stomach. She stood in her office, listening to the clamor from the front room. Now that the conversation was done, Elena half expected for the power and the certainty to vanish, leaving her wrestling with doubt and remorse. How could she order such important people to do anything. Like that. But the sense of being guided by another's hand remained powerfully present.

She was still standing there, cradling her phone, when it rang a second time. She checked the readout and answered with "Antonio?"

"I've been fired."

This time, the power was a palpable presence, so intense that she could not keep the tremors from her voice. "You need to come here. To Oxford."

"Everything's gone. I've failed us. I pushed too hard. I insisted on a majority on the commission. The politicians resisted. I went public. They used my statements to the press to fire me."

"You haven't failed anyone."

"Did you hear what I just said? They've won. Everything we might have accomplished is over. The commission will be formed with the banks' puppets in control. There will be no governance. The public will assume they are protected, and it will be a lie." He sighed. "I'm so tired."

"Antonio."

"I'm so sorry, Elena."

"Listen to me. Get out of there. You and your team." The silence between them was charged with all that could not ever be put in words. "When can you leave?"

36

⸙─────────⸙

"Perhaps it would be best if Shirley and I moved into a hotel."

"Don't you dare."

Janine was clearly having difficulty finding the right words. "But shouldn't you like to have some time alone with your young man?"

They worked at the kitchen counter, preparing salads. Elena had no idea what Antonio might want to eat, if anything. A trio of salads seemed suitable. There were sliced tomatoes and fresh mozzarella from the Italian deli in the Covered Market. Endive with blue cheese and walnuts and tangerines. Fresh bread. Elena fried bacon for a spinach salad. "My young man? You make me sound like a teenager."

"You know exactly what I am saying."

"You can't leave. First of all, it's late. Second, Antonio is not my anything."

Janine lay out Parma ham alongside a selection of cheeses. "Then why is it you flush every time you speak his name?"

"Don't make this any more difficult for me than it already is."

"I'm just saying."

Elena pulled the bacon from the pan and lay the strips on a paper towel. "The only way this works is if you two are here also." She glanced at the wall clock. The train took just over two hours from Brussels to London. Another hour to cross London. Trains ran from Paddington Station to Oxford every twenty minutes. Which meant he could be here at any—

The front doorbell rang.

Elena cut off the stove, wiped her hands on a towel, and asked, "How do I look?"

Janine had the sort of face that lost both cares and years when she smiled. "Like the teenager you claim not to be."

Elena's rush carried her past Shirley, who had stopped midway through setting the table and was seated in one of the dining room's chairs, staring at the side wall. Her expression was as blank as her gaze. She had drifted away like this several times since Nigel had shown her the photographs. As though learning that her suspicions were real proved too much for her to take in. Elena slowed long enough to step over and give the woman a one-armed hug. Then she checked her reflection in the hall mirror, took a long breath, touched her hair, took another breath, and turned to open the door. "You came."

Exhaustion stained Antonio's features as deeply as a tattoo. Even so, he gave his smile as much as he possibly could. "How could I go anywhere else?"

The words were perfect. Why, she had no idea. But any reserve she might have still felt was gone now. There was no reason not to do what she had longed to do for what seemed like years.

Elena stepped across the threshold and embraced him. His arms were strong and welcoming. She had always envisioned Italian men as being short. But Antonio was tall enough that she had to go up on her tiptoes to fit her chin into the space between his shoulder and his neck. She breathed away the tension and the lack. Her senses became filled with starch from his shirt and stale fragrances from the trains and something else, perhaps his aftershave, a faint fragrance of cloves and mystery. She shivered.

"Are you cold?"

"Not at all." She could not say what the outside temperature was just then. Nor did she care.

"How is it possible," Antonio murmured in her ear, "that your arms can knit my world back together?"

She released him, not because she wanted to, but because it was time. She looked into his sad and weary face and put all she had into her smile, holding nothing back. Then she drew him inside. "Welcome home, Antonio."

They dined by candlelight. Antonio sat at the head of the table, his back to the curtained window and the night. Janine sat opposite Elena. Shirley was seated in the chair closest to the kitchen doorway. She stared at her plate and toyed with her food. No one was particularly hungry. Antonio's features had turned craven by the strain he carried. Even so, every time he glanced her way, the shivers returned.

She cleared the table with Janine's help and made tea. When she returned to the table, Antonio asked, "What are we to do now?"

"I don't know."

"You are comfortable with this absence of direction?"

"More today than yesterday."

He nodded slowly. "I have spent the trip today thinking about my father. My father was an *avvocato*, a lawyer in a village near Milan. As a boy, Papa always thought he would enter the priesthood. But when he was fifteen he met my mother. They fell in love. Her father was a doctor from the next village. When I was young, the two of them meeting and falling in love was the family's favorite story. Everyone would laugh, except my father, who always turned very quiet as the story was told, very sad. My mother would always reach over and take his hand. And the love between them was strong enough to draw him back from the halls of regret."

Elena poured him a cup of tea. She did so because she wanted an excuse to draw closer. His voice had taken on the rich accent again, as though he held a special Mediterranean talent, one that granted him the ability to turn English into song. Antonio said, "I know he wanted me to enter the priesthood for him. But I was fascinated with numbers from an early age. Numbers and statistics and the ability to measure things like risk and buying patterns and economics. I read Adam Smith's famous treatise on free-market economics for the first time when I was nine."

In the candlelight his eyes gleamed like opals at the bottom of a dark river. Antonio went on, "My faith has always come easily. Even in the darkest moments after Francesca's death, I never found a need to question God. Italian society went one way, I went another. Faith was my deepest connection to my father's memory, my way of honoring the finest man I have ever known."

Only when Elena was certain he would not say more on his own did she speak. "And now everything has changed."

His nodding became a subtle shift of his head, the grave gesture of a prince of the realm. "No longer am I able to lose myself in the soft comfort of ritual and memory. I am being challenged to—"

"To grow," Elena said, aching in a manner that redefined her interior world. "To trust. To walk into the unknown. To reach out for a hand that might not be there."

There came a terrible wrenching of his features and his voice. "Have I failed God?"

"No, Antonio. Of this I am certain."

"He sent me to do a thing. I have been cast out. Even my own assistants have left me. When we said farewell today in Brussels, they treated me as they would a corpse."

"They were wrong to do so."

"I'm so tired, Elena."

"I know."

"I just wish . . ." Antonio rubbed his face with one hand. "I wish I knew what to do."

"All I can give you is the next step." She rose from her chair and offered her hand. "It's time you went to bed."

Elena settled Antonio into the extra bedroom that had its own private bath. She had been using it as an exercise room because the ceiling was a foot higher and she could stand comfortably on the stair machine. Before starting dinner the three women had slid her equipment to the side wall and fashioned a pallet of blankets on the floor. Elena had hesitated, then taken a quilt from her hope chest and used it as the cover. The quilt had been sewn by members of her Durham church as a wedding gift. It smelled slightly of age and dust, which was hardly a surprise, as it had not seen the light of day for five years. Elena sat at her desk and listened to Antonio settling into the next room, glad she had been able to make that small and secret step.

There was a knock on Elena's door. "Yes?"

"Can I come in?" Janine entered wearing a robe sewn from multicolored strips, draping her in a terry-cloth rainbow. Then she noticed the two open books on Elena's desk and said, "Perhaps I'm interrupting."

"No, you're not."

"I just wanted to thank you."

"Stay. Please." Elena rose, walked to the side wall, and lifted her clothes off the bedroom's other chair. She dumped them on the bed and pulled the chair over beside her own. "I'm not getting anywhere."

"You do this every night?"

"And morning. I—"

Another knock and Shirley Wainwright asked, "Mind if I join you?"

"You should be asleep."

"Tell my mind that." Plum-colored stains rimmed her eyes. "I shut my eyes and see Terry and that woman."

Elena walked down the hall, past Antonio's closed door, and brought back a chair from the dining room. "Join us."

"What are you doing?"

"Not a lot." She included the image and the Bible in one motion. "I study a little each morning and evening. I find a passage to begin the next gathering."

Shirley squinted at the image. "Does the book speak to you?"

"Does God," Janine corrected.

"Of course. That's what I meant." Her nose was inches from the vellum page. "I just can't get over the age of this book."

"And the legacy," Janine agreed. "Were they all women, the people who studied it before you?"

"I have no idea. I can't see any reason why they should be," Elena said.

Janine said, "Tell me what we're supposed to do."

"There are no instructions. I treat these times like prayer. Sometimes I feel a remarkable closeness to God. Rarely."

Shirley asked, "Which verse is this again?"

" 'Holy is thy name.' "

"Why do you suppose the letters are bunched up around the top of the page like that?"

"*Holy* means separate. Isolated. Inviolate. I'm assuming it means God remains apart from the world he created, giving us the power and liberty of free will."

Janine nodded distractedly. "Why don't you turn the page?"

"I don't know. Maybe I should. I just keep waiting for a sense that I've done what I've supposed to here. That God is ready for me to move on."

They sat in silence for a time. In the distance, a motorcycle raced up Boars Hill. Then the night closed in once more.

Shirley murmured, "I miss Teddy so."

"I cannot imagine," Janine said, "what you must be feeling."

"Friends from church keep saying how glorious it was that Teddy accepted Christ before he died. Like that's supposed to make his absence better. Like I should be able to dismiss the sorrow as easily as they do." She gave her cheeks two impatient swipes. "I was glad for a reason to get away."

Another silence, then Janine said, "Sitting here like this reminds me of church when I was a child."

Shirley cleared her cheeks a second time. "Where was that?"

"A farming village to the west of here. My family raised sheep. And they fought. Continuously. Sunday mornings were the only real peace I knew." She addressed her words to the page. "Everyone dressed up in their best clothes. Our church was over a thousand years old, with very thick walls and narrow windows. Even in the height of summer it was like entering a cool, dark cave."

"A safe place," Shirley murmured.

"Our community followed the old tradition of arriving early and sitting in silence. I loved those times. The scent of old incense, the candles, the quiet. This was God's gift to a frightened little girl. Allowing me to escape from the world one morning each week. And sit in his house and imagine a different life."

Elena rose to her feet. "What a brilliant idea."

Janine looked up in surprise. "What did I say?"

"I'll be right back." Elena went into the front of the house and returned with the candlesticks from the dining table. She lit them and placed them around the room, then turned off the lights and set the last candle beside the book. "There."

"That is indeed lovely," Janine said.

The silence fashioned a haven for secrets and shared mysteries. Elena's mind flitted about like a winged night creature. Small sounds crept through her closed window. An owl cried in the distance. Shirley said, "Antonio seems like a very nice gentleman."

"And handsome," Janine added. "Let's not be forgetting that little item. Not for one second."

Elena shifted over the book. "I've spent years in one-way arguments with Jason. Angry with him for leaving and with God for taking him away. Now when I think of him, there's a sense of him watching me with approval. But from a new distance. Not like he's moved farther away. He's where he's always been. Like I'm finally accepting his absence."

Shirley lifted her gaze from the book. "You love Antonio."

"We've only met a few times. It's too early to use the word *love*."

Janine smiled at her. "I wouldn't know anything about that. I was in love with Brian the instant I set eyes on him."

Afterward, it seemed as though they all saw it at the same moment. Janine said, "Is that a crease?"

"It's too broad." Elena leaned closer still. "Look, it doesn't continue to the edges like it would if the page had been folded."

Shirley reached over and switched on the desk lamp. Instantly the crease disappeared. She turned the light off. The line was there, a faint gray shadow perhaps an inch wide. It cut across the page, just below the cloud of golden script. "Someone did this on purpose."

"It's part of the page," Elena agreed. "And the message."

Janine squinted over the page. "What do you think it might mean?"

Elena touched the cloud of golden script. "Our Father in heaven. Holy is your name." She slid her fingers down to the lower third of the page, an empty space cut off from the golden script by the invisible wall. "Here we are. On earth." Elena then touched the line. "Separated from our Father by the invisible barrier of sin."

Janine looked at Elena, then back at the image. She touched her lips with her tongue. She might have spoken. But it was at that moment that Elena lost the capacity to hear.

Quite simply, the image came alive. Elena ran her finger

along the invisible barrier. The wall that most of the world did its best to ignore, to claim it did not even exist. Freeing them to do whatever they wanted, as often and as harshly as they wished. Without restraint. Without any remorse or need to change direction. Without heroes or purpose or beacons of hope. A world without the promise of eternity.

Elena felt a trace of eternal sorrow then. Just a trace. And it seemed as though everything she had known since Jason's death, all the anguish and the loss and the empty hours, were merely a faint scent of the truth. That man would never know what God suffered because of the invisible barrier, separated from his most precious creation by sin. Because man did not know the true and full meaning of love.

Elena traced a finger along the line and saw a wall that remained invisible unless a person sought with a questing heart. A heart searching for wisdom. A heart open to the message the world sought to destroy. That God had so loved the world that he released man from the barrier, erased it from vision, so long as man took the steps to repent and believe.

Then she smelled it. The eroding odor of old smoke. Cold and sulfuric. The stench grew until it threatened to cut off her air. The reek of ancient wrong. Timeless and vicious. And now. Here. In the room with them.

Elena rose from her chair and shut the book. She said, "We have to get out of here. Now."

37

The two women did not want to go with her. Elena saw the doubt and confusion in their expressions. Particularly after she had woken Antonio and insisted that he had to come with them *now*.

Elena rushed them into the kitchen in the dark. She opened the rear door, then stood listening for what felt like hours. Long enough for the two women to share another worried glance. When Shirley started to say something, Elena hissed at her. Quiet and sharp. Both women drew back another step. Clearly regretting their decision to overnight with this strange woman.

Antonio, however, showed no such hesitation. His hair was tousled and his face creased with heavy sleep. He wore a shapeless T-shirt, the trousers to his suit, and his dress shoes without socks. But he was fully alert. And close enough for Elena to feel his warmth. He breathed, "Anything?"

"No."

"Then we should move. Waiting does not help."

"I was hoping to find Charles."

"Your guard, yes? Elena, you say the threat is real and now. What does that tell you about Charles?"

He was right, of course. Elena breathed the question she should have asked hours earlier. "Where are your guards?"

"They came with the job," Antonio replied. "I am unemployed."

These three friends were Elena's responsibility now. She did not need to consciously work through this. It was embedded in her bones. She had to get them to safety. Which meant entering the dark.

Janine lifted her cell phone and whispered, "Shouldn't we call the police?"

"When we're safe," Elena said. She held the book of dreams in both arms. It was wrapped in the sheet off her bed. The bundle formed a comforting solidity across her chest, like a shield against everything that waited to pounce.

Janine protested, "But they could help us."

"They can do nothing until they arrive," Antonio said.

Elena gestured the women in tight. Her words were a faint shift in the air, softer than the ticks of the kitchen clock. "The rear garden has a hedge. The section closest to the rear ledge has a gully washed out by rain. That's our goal."

The two women shared another glance, very frightened. Both clearly wanted to tell Elena she was overreacting. But Antonio's gaze was steady and unblinking. One hand rested on her arm, ready to propel her forward. His confidence silenced the women.

Elena hugged the book of dreams more tightly to her chest. "Don't stray to the right, the ledge is very steep and there's a rusted fence. Stay close."

Shirley started, "Is this really necessary—"

Antonio turned and silenced her with a millisecond glare.

"On three," Elena said. "One, two, three, *run*."

Elena went first, then the two women. Antonio's heels clicked on the stone stairs as he followed them. Elena flew across the lawn. The grass smelled freshly mowed. Flowers she could not see filled the still air with perfume. A night bird trilled to her left, urging her to go faster. She wore the first shoes she had pulled from her closet, an old pair of running shoes whose laces came undone as she fled. Elena was tempted to kick them off. Then the ledge came into view. To her right loomed the swooping drop into the flatlands below Boars Hill, festooned with a hundred thousand flickering lights. The hedge rose into a solid wall between her and any possible help. She dropped to her knees and crawled forward, feeling for the gulley with her hands.

Elena's husband had planted the yew hedge the summer after they bought their home. Yew was a fast-growing shrub that if left unchecked would climb to towering heights. The branches were thick and clinging and started growing at ground level. But over the years, rain had fashioned a gulley beneath the two shrubs closest to the ledge. Elena knew about the space because last summer her neighbors' cat had birthed a litter of kittens there. The cat was a tabby with a gentle soul who sometimes allowed the neighbors' twin daughters to dress it up in doll clothes. Elena had brought the cat food and water until the kittens were weaned. Her mind was racing fast enough to speed through this as she crawled and hunted in the dark. The hedge formed a solid wall to her hands, the interlaced branches tight as woven cord. She was beginning to question her own memory when the ground dipped under her hand and the space opened up.

She whispered, "In here."

Shirley Wainwright was still on her feet. "I can't possibly—"

Antonio hissed, gripped the back of her neck, and pushed downward.

Shirley whined, "This robe is shantung silk."

"Quiet," Elena said. "For your life."

Janine backed into the space on her belly, then Shirley, still huffing soft protests. Antonio slipped in beside Elena. The space was about six feet wide and less than a foot high. There was room for them only if they layered in tight as sardines. She could feel Antonio's chest breathing in and out, in and out. Janine was crammed up next to her other side.

Elena's lungs filled with the scent of night-damp earth. Streetlights played through the trees separating her house from the road. They dappled the front lawn with surreal shades of ocher and orange. A shape flitted across her vision, probably the neighbors' cat. There and gone in a flash, like it was chasing something. Or being chased.

Then a second shadow flicked in and out of sight, moving even faster than the cat. On two legs. Small as a child. Or a woman with elfin features and taunting eyes.

Janine opened her mouth, perhaps just to breathe. But Elena could not take that risk. She reached over and clamped a hand to Janine's mouth. In the vague light, Janine's eyes turned to pale moons.

Elena breathed, "They're here."

As though in emphasis to her words, there was the faint tinkle of broken glass. They all stopped breathing.

The alarm whooped once, then cut off so swiftly that it might as well have been strangled.

Then nothing. The night held its breath with them.

A sound came from the house, harsh as a bark. Elena imagined it was a curse from finding the place empty.

From the bedroom window came two quick flashes. No noise. Just blinks of light, faster than heat lightning.

To her right, Shirley moaned softly. Elena felt Janine's body jerk in time to the pistol shots.

Another shadow flickered about her garden. A man this time. Hulking and very fast. He was joined by the woman. Flashlights came on. Elena did not need to urge them farther back into the gulley, to push under the hedge's far end with their feet. Elena felt the branches dig into her bare ankles. She knew it should hurt. But just then the lights sweeping her rear garden left her utterly numb to all but terror.

Then the woman returned inside the house. A few moments later, the night gave off a quiet whump. A light started in her kitchen, bright and unsteady. It spread in lazy smoothness to the window of her dining room and the guest room. The man was clearly silhouetted now. Elena saw the gun in the hand not holding the flashlight.

The woman appeared around the front of the burning house and whistled softly. The man joined her. They cut off the flashlights and sprinted away.

The fire grew and grew, vicious fingers rising from her bedroom window, reaching up and gripping the roof. Elena moaned with the others. It did not matter what sound she made. The fire was burning so fiercely that the house groaned with her.

38

J anine called the police and the fire department on her cell phone. They remained where they were, fearful that the flames might mask a lingering attacker. They emerged only when the police arrived.

By the time the first fire truck pulled up, the house was smoldering and fuming. Shirley stood next to a cluster of neighbors, her eyes glazed, her grimy features slack. Janine wept for the loss, which Elena found very touching. She felt nothing at all. Perhaps the numbness would eventually subside. Maybe she would then be swamped by regret. But she did not think so. What she really felt, hugging the book to her chest and staring at the wreck of her home, was affirmation.

Detective Mehan arrived just as the fire chief completed his preliminary inspection. The fireman told the detective the house stank from incendiary charges. The detective asked them questions while the fire chief and the two officers who had arrived first on the scene stood and listened. The neighbors huddled farther back, all but the mother of the twins, who brought over a thermos of sweetened tea and plastic cups. Elena stood sheltered within a blanket someone had placed around her shoulders without her even seeing who it was. She drank the tea and let Janine describe what had happened. The prayer time. The sense of danger.

The fire chief said, "Describe precisely what made you feel threatened."

"I can't," Elena replied.

The fire chief frowned his dissatisfaction with her reaction. But Detective Mehan asked, "Was it similar to what you felt after the break-in?"

The fire chief was an older man whose face was streaked by soot from the house and by a thousand previous fires. "What break-in was that?"

Detective Mehan lifted a hand. The fire chief's frown deepened, but he did not speak.

Elena said, "Something very similar."

"Is there anything that might help us with our search?"

"One man hunted for us while a woman set the fires."

"This was the same woman who accosted you in your office?"

"I never saw her face. But the shape was identical. Deceptively small. Almost childlike. Very fast."

"And the man?"

Antonio replied, "Tall. Over six feet. Very big. Well over two hundred pounds. All muscle. And fast as well."

Janine said, "They both carried guns."

"You saw weapons but you did not see their faces?"

Elena replied, "The silhouettes were vividly clear. They had pistols. With silencers." Then it hit her.

Mehan noticed the change. "What is it?"

"Charles."

"Who?"

"My night man."

Mehan turned to the listening officers. "Check the perimeter."

Shirley Wainwright spoke for the first time since emerging from the shrub. "This same woman also murdered my husband."

Elena said, "We don't know that."

"I do. And so does your Nigel."

"He's not—"

A shout turned them around. Together they rushed across the front lawn. Beyond Elena's house, the road tightened in close to the ledge and curved around a bend in the hillside. The empty lot was rimmed by ancient chestnuts and wild thornberry bushes. Charles lay sprawled below the branches of a dead oak beside the road, illuminated by the police officer's flashlight. A black pool glistened beneath his head. The officer was on her knees, the fingers of one hand pressed to his neck. "We've got a pulse, sir."

Mehan was already lifting his radio from where it was clipped to the collar of his overcoat. "We need an ambulance. Sound and lights, please. Code green."

Detective Mehan was against it, of course. As were the two women. But the impression had come to Elena while she knelt by Charles and prayed over him. She had asked for his recovery and her own forgiveness for putting a good man in danger's path. By the time the ambulance took him away, she knew what they needed to do next. Even though it was the last thing she wanted. Her own desires meant nothing. Not that night.

Mehan had one of the officers call around the hotels, trying to find them rooms. But it was after midnight in early June, and the tourist hordes were in control. A pair of neighbors offered beds, but Mehan didn't want to split them up.

Which was when Elena said, "We need to go to the church shelter."

Mehan showed genuine astonishment. "Pardon me?"

"The waiting list is a year long," Janine replied. "I should

know. I've been pressing them to add more rooms in the basement."

"Call them," Elena said. "They have an opening."

Janine stared at her.

"Please. Call."

Janine opened her cell phone and punched in the number
from memory. She spoke softly, her eyes never leaving Elena's
face. She shut the phone, stared at Elena, said nothing.

"Well?"

"They kicked out a family for drug use. About an hour ago."

"Let's go."

Mehan said, "Out of the question."

"You can protect us there as well as anywhere."

"It's not very nice," Janine said. "Rather wretched, actually."

Antonio said, "If Elena is telling us we must do this thing, we
should agree and go."

Mehan must have seen something in their expressions, for
he shrugged and said to the waiting officer, "Call for a taxi.
Follow them in. I'll arrange for the duty officer to relieve you."

"Thank you." Elena handed the detective her book, still
wrapped in the filthy sheet. "Put this somewhere safe, please."

The shelter was three blocks from Saint Aldates Church, in a
former department store that had anchored the smaller of Oxford's two center-city malls. The shopping plaza was cramped by
American standards, fewer than two dozen stores. The department store's closure had hit the mall very hard. There was talk
that it might still go under.

The church rented the space from the bankruptcy auditors.
They had papered over the display windows and used cheap fiberboard to section off the two floors. The structure now held
twenty-seven studio apartments, each sixteen feet square.
Communal kitchens and washrooms anchored each end of
both floors. Initially the church had opened the shelter to any

family who had lost their home. Immediately they were swamped. So they limited it to single mothers with children under six. Even so, the waiting list held a hundred and three names.

All this Janine told them on the ride into town. She explained that men were allowed in two hours each morning and evening. The men could shower and eat with the families. "Of course it also means some of the mothers aren't single, just desperate enough to live apart from their men. But we don't have the luxury of aiming for perfect. Only fair."

The taxi driver glanced back several times as Janine spoke. He was Indian or Pakistani and clearly wondering at the three women and man in his car, filthy and mud-streaked, dressed in odd clothing and talking about a homeless shelter. He had taken them because the police had been standing by and watching. But when he stopped at a light he finally turned all the way around and said, "Please, you are being able to pay for this ride?"

Antonio said, "We are."

"I am asking this because it will be twelve pounds. Perhaps fourteen, yes? That is of course without the tip."

Antonio reached into his pocket and inserted a twenty-pound note through the Plexiglas slot. He then turned back to Janine and said, "Go on."

But it was Shirley Wainwright who declared, "I've had about all of this I can stand."

No one responded.

"I've just been through the longest day since Teddy's funeral. Not to mention that security man showing me those photographs. Then we're trapped in the bushes by bad men, and the fire . . ." She looked down at her ruined silk robe. "I've lost all my things."

Janine said, "The church has a goodwill hamper—"

"I don't want castoffs. I want a *bath*. I want a *clean bed*. In a *hotel*."

"Shirley . . ."

"I'm tired, and I want it *now*."

"We're all tired." Antonio spoke in the quiet monotone of a man who had left mere exhaustion far behind. "We are alive because of Elena. She says doing this is important. I for one do not need to hear anything more."

39

TUESDAY

The first sound Elena heard upon awakening was the same that had carried her into sleep. Somewhere down the line, a baby cried.

The dividers did not reach all the way to the ceiling. The walls merely suggested a private space. The air was packed with the smells of frying grease and baby powder and wet laundry and too many people. Elena rose to a seated position and rubbed her face. She had slept on a thin foam mattress that she had pulled off a pile and carried into their cubicle. She wore the sweatpants and T-shirt she had obtained from the goodwill hamper. The previous night she had showered and washed her hair twice. But she could still smell the smoke.

Janine and Shirley were already awake and seated at a table with foldout legs. The cubicle contained two folding chairs. Elena stared around their little chamber and wondered what families did if they needed more seats. She rose slowly to her feet. Antonio snored softly, his face turned toward the side wall. The night supervisor had not wanted to let Antonio enter. But Janine had mentioned Brian, and the police had firmly insisted. The night supervisor had promised they would be kicked out the next day, like any rule breaker. Shirley had begged her to be sure that happened.

Janine asked softly, "Shall I make you a coffee?"

"I'll do it."

As she turned for the door, Shirley said, "You were right to bring us here."

Elena did not understand what she meant. But was glad just the same.

Their cubicle was the closest to the outside door. Nearby were the laundry and showers. Elena walked the long central hallway, past a dozen or so doors, most of which were open. She saw many children, some asleep, others playing with toys on the floor. Others were crammed around the scarred table, seated on packing crates and rickety stools, eating off paper plates with plastic spoons and forks. Some of the children watched her pass with solemn gazes. Elena had felt eyes on her since their arrival. Shutting and locking the flimsy door had not changed anything.

When they had arrived the previous night, a number of men had clustered outside the shelter's doorway. They had given Elena and the others the same wary inspection as the children did now. Then the men had spotted the police car pulling up behind the taxi. They all vanished, silent and swift as smoke. Like they had never been there at all.

Sunlight struck the brown paper covering the building's east-facing windows. The light inside was muted and tinted like an old photograph. Fluorescent strips glowed far overhead, but many did not work. Elena boiled water in one of the kettles and made herself a cup of instant coffee. A sign on the fridge said the fresh milk was for children under four, two cups per child per day. She spooned in sugar and powdered milk. She grimaced over the taste, but she drank it anyway, standing with her back to the kitchen and observing the scene that surrounded her—and wondering what these families must have been through to bring them to a point where they would call this place a refuge.

At the stroke of ten the rear doors opened, introducing

brighter sunlight and a silent tide of men. Elena made another cup of coffee and took it back to the cubicle. Antonio stood in the doorway, watching everything with an expression that probably mirrored her own. He accepted the cup with a tight smile but did not speak.

Elena joined him in the doorway, observing the people and relishing the small comfort of being near this good man. When he finished the cup, she turned and said, "It's time for us to go."

Shirley asked, "Will we be coming back here?"

"No."

"Are you sure?"

"My sense is, this particular lesson is over and done."

Both women shut their eyes. Shirley whispered, "Thank you, God."

They went by the hospital first, where the station nurse would not permit them to enter Charles's room. But Nigel Harries was there and informed them that Charles was resting comfortably. He had woken twice in the night and spoken with the police but could not give any description of his assailants. The doctors had found a hole in his neck that corresponded to a needle fired by a high-compression air pistol. A mixture of several sedatives was found in his bloodstream. The man had gone down hard and evidently banged his head on a root. He was concussed and required stitches for the cut to his forehead. But otherwise he was recovering well. Nigel Harries delivered the news in very concerned tones.

"I can't tell you how sorry I am about your lovely home."

"Thank you."

"My team and I have failed you. It won't happen again. You need to move into secured accommodation until we identify and locate—"

"That is not happening."

"I can't guarantee your safety otherwise."

"We are not being secreted away. We have work to do." Elena turned to the others. "Coming?"

"With all due respect, Dr. Burroughs—"

She said over her shoulder, "Today's meeting will take place at noon. As usual."

A chalk-blue Ford was parked in front of Elena's office building when their taxi pulled up. Elena had wanted to walk over but the police had nixed that idea. The Ford had an Enterprise sticker in the rear window. The passenger door yawned open, as though the car were unable to contain Lawrence Harwood's wrath. He sat and glared through the front window as they approached.

Sandra, however, rushed over and hugged Elena hard. "Nigel called. I'm so sorry to hear about your house."

"It's good to see you."

She glanced worriedly back at her husband. "I wish I could say it was good to be here."

Elena nodded. There was no room in the day for false sentiment or empty words.

Antonio walked over to Lawrence's open door, leaned over, and said, "Come inside, friend."

"There's nothing for me here. I shouldn't have come."

"I'm sorry. But you're wrong."

Elena felt as though they had all become spectators of something both tragic and wonderful. She watched Antonio take hold of the former ambassador's arm and pull him from the car. Lawrence swatted futilely at the other man's hand. "Let go of me."

"This is important, Lawrence. Vital."

"I don't even know what I'm doing here. All this is finished."

"I'm sorry. But you could not be more wrong."

"I'm tired. I want a bath and a bed. *My* bed."

From behind her, Elena heard Shirley Wainwright murmur, "I know that tune."

Lawrence said, "I came because she said we had to. Do you

know how this looks? Like I *ran*. I've never run from a fight in my entire life."

Antonio said, "You are precisely where you need to be."

Lawrence glared at the group clustered around Elena's locked front door. "Who are all these people?"

"The reason why we are gathered here."

"Are you deaf? There's nothing we can do no matter where we are. It's *over*. I've lost *everything*."

"Like Elena lost her home? Like Shirley lost her husband? Like I was fired?" Antonio waited long enough to be certain Lawrence was taking this in. "My friend, it has only just begun. Isn't that right, Elena."

She took that as her cue and fished in her purse for her keys. "Let's all go inside."

The families filed in behind them. Shirley set up the coffee-maker on the reception desk. The children raced into the former kitchen and pulled their toys from the cupboards. The families settled down on the sofas and chairs. Some of the men leaned against the side walls. They picked over the crates of books and old magazines.

Lawrence stood in the doorway to Elena's office. "What are they doing here?"

"They have nowhere else to go," Antonio said. "Come. It's almost noon."

"But there's no reason for us—"

"You cannot imagine what has happened over the past twenty-four hours." Antonio's smile was enough to silence the former ambassador. "I have witnessed *miracles*."

In the space of time it took for them to gather in Elena's office, the skies over Oxford turned the color of asphalt. Elena opened the rear windows. Her garden was filled with birdsong and the gentle patter of rain upon new leaves. The air was sweet. She turned off the overhead lights and let the shadows envelop the room. Noise filtered faintly up through the floor from the crèche below.

Only when she was seated in the little circle did Elena realize this was the first time she had passed her former office and not stared at it in yearning. But she did not have time for that today.

Nigel Harries entered three minutes before noon. He took a folding chair from the side wall and inserted himself into the group, silent and stiffly formal. They were then joined by Lawrence's aide, still in Washington. Elena was very relieved to hear from them. She felt a burning need for them all to be a part of whatever was coming next.

The book was still with the police. Her laptop had been lost to the fire. So there was no image for them to focus on. It did not matter. At all. When the others came on the line, Elena read the Bible passage she had landed upon the night before, from First Chronicles. " 'He answered their prayers because they trusted in him . . . The battle was God's.' "

Then she waited.

It was Antonio who said, "God spoke to me this morning. I have never known such a communication. It was silent, yet as loud as anything I have ever heard with my ears. It was also unmistakable. And for the first time, I understand. This is not about the banks. Or finance. Or the economy. Those are all just man-made concepts. This is about his people."

Elena sat and surveyed the group. In the front rooms there must have been two dozen adults and twice as many children. The din was enormous. The building's high ceiling and hard walls and absence of drapes turned the space into echo chambers.

Antonio said, "Those people out there are why God brought us to this place. This is why we have failed, or at least thought we did. Why we have been forced to give up everything. Why we have been brought low. So we can *understand*. So we can *feel*."

Elena felt as tired as she had ever been in her entire life. Yet she was also more satisfied and fulfilled than she had been since Jason's death. Here before her was the true reason for it all. She felt as though she surveyed the scene with both her own and heaven's eyes. The needs and noise and love and healing grace, the ability to serve the one over all, the chance to fill their vacuum, just as hers was filled. Elena felt overwhelmed with the wonder of it all.

Antonio said, "God has not called us just to lead a commission. He has given us a holy duty, a divine task. We must do what we can to heal these lives and hopes and dreams and families. That is why we are here. To serve."

Elena waited long enough to be certain Antonio was finished. Then she said, "A transformation is taking place in us. We do not understand a great deal of what is happening. Even so, it is vital that we remain steadfast. Our eyes and hearts are becoming open. We see what we have successfully avoided. How vast the repercussions are. The toll this tragedy is taking on relationships and families and hope. We see the battlefield. We see the enemy."

Lawrence said, "I have not succeeded."

"You don't need to."

"I don't know about you. But I didn't start down this road to fail."

"You set the groundwork in place. You have readied yourself. Now God will give us . . ."

Elena stopped. She had no choice. The ability to speak was suddenly stripped away.

She felt as though every one of her senses was heightened to the point where every sensation arrived in exquisite precision. She heard the children's laughter and a phone ringing and a rumble of male voices. She smelled the rain and the earth and what seemed like the fragrances of individual wildflowers. She heard the creak of a chair, the quiet intake of breath. But what was most intense about that moment was the sense of moving *beyond*.

Elena felt as though the room became utterly removed from the rain and the birds and the children's faint din. A wind swept in and through them, one that did not enter through the open window.

Elena's heart blazed in her chest, a great molten surge of force and love and peace. It was impossible that peace could carry the power to strip away her ability even to think. But this peace came and dominated. This love. This certainty.

There was a gasp from one of the others there with her. And perhaps a sob from another. Elena could not be sure. Perhaps the sound had come from herself. Otherwise the room was silent. And yet, at some level far beyond mere sound, the rushing wind continued. Elena did not need to hear this to know it was with her, a cleansing flame, a surging rush of power so great it could remain silent, yet dominate everything.

40

Throughout her day's appointments, Elena continuously returned to the moment of revelation. The certainty that she had experienced the divine presence only grew stronger with the passing hours.

Elena compressed her schedule so there was time to see all the patients she had missed earlier. Each time she ushered one family out and called to the next, she observed an office being transformed.

Lawrence Harwood was, put simply, a new man. Gone was the latent rage, the regret, the frustration over the choices he had made and those he'd turned away from. All of it so totally vanished that they might as well have never existed. In their place was a leader.

He and Antonio operated like a pair of generals. They sketched out new duties in terse bullets. They interviewed the families before and after Elena's sessions. Together they helped the couples more clearly define the problems they faced. They cut through the regret and blame with sparse words and no volume. Lawrence remained quiet and precise and powerful enough to have even the most resentful visitors willing to follow their lead.

Janine and Sandra set up files and worked the phones, bringing in others required to work through the tangled morass holding the families down—bankers, lawyers, accountants, tax authorities, parole officers, social services. Shirley Wainwright took over the front desk. Nigel Harries hovered on the periphery, patrolling with Gerald and fielding calls of his own. Elena found great comfort in this combined strength. As though her team was forming an entirely new unit of force. A measurable power with the capacity to withstand whatever struck them. Even an eviction notice. Which came at midafternoon.

Detective Mehan arrived two minutes after the bailiff, who brought four police officers of his own. Mehan had the decency to look ashamed. He explained, "The bailiff's office received an urgent request via the university, who hold the building's lease. My office has your name and this address flagged for obvious reasons. Soon as we heard, my chief lodged an official objection, both to the manner and the timing."

Lawrence said, "It's all right, Detective."

Antonio said, "There was nothing you could have done."

Mehan said, "Our objections were overruled. By whom precisely, we have no idea. All we know is, strings are being pulled in London."

Lawrence said, "We've been expecting this."

"Not this exactly," Antonio said. "But an obstruction of some form. It was inevitable."

Mehan's head swiveled from one man to the other. They stood just outside the doorway, on a rain-spackled front walk. "Sorry. I'm not following you."

"They have to shut us down," Lawrence said. "And fast."

"It's as much about how this appears as the act itself," Antonio said.

"Brutal and sharp," Lawrence said. "That's what they're after."

"It sends a message," Antonio said.

"Go against them and they'll crush you," Lawrence said.

Elena and Sandra and Shirley and Janine stood crammed together in the doorway. The families clustered behind them. Still more hovered behind Mehan and the bailiff, or farther out where Nigel watched and spoke on his phone. At least, the adults were there. Most of the children had vanished. For them, the bailiff was the boogeyman. Even the littlest ones squirmed in their mothers' arms and hid their faces.

The bailiff was a stodgy gentleman in a three-piece suit and steel-framed spectacles. His pudgy cheeks were masked by a walrus mustache that almost met his sideburns. He stamped his feet on the pavement. "I'm not used to being kept waiting, Detective."

Fiona chose that moment to step through the next doorway and demand, "What's going on here?"

"None of your concern, madam."

Elena took one step through the doorway. "It's all right, Fiona."

"I just heard about your house. It's terrible. Where are you staying?"

"Kindly go back inside where you belong." The bailiff had the sonorous drone of a man who enjoyed the sound of his own voice. He turned to Elena and demanded, "Would you be Dr. Elena Burroughs?"

"I am."

"By the powers invested in me through the Oxford Crown Court, I hereby serve you—"

Fiona protested, "You can't be evicting her!"

"Madam, I told you to return—"

"But her house burned down! Last *night!*"

The bailiff motioned to one of the police officers who had accompanied him. "Show her inside. If she resists, detain her."

"You are *insane.* I've had loads of experience with your kind. You're the one needing to be detained! And I know just the place!" The door slammed so hard that it rattled the bailiff's spectacles.

At that moment a van weaved through slower-moving traffic halted by the police cars. The van was white and had no rear windows. The BBC News logo was painted in fluorescent shades on the sides and rear door. A radar dish with motor drive lay folded flat against the roof.

Mehan sighed. "How do those clowns manage to hear so fast?"

"It's to be expected," Lawrence said.

"They need our humiliation to be as public as possible," Antonio said.

"Maximum exposure for maximum effect," Lawrence said.

"Otherwise the warning lacks bite," Antonio said.

The same newscaster who had interviewed Antonio at the station's London headquarters emerged from the front passenger seat. Nigel drifted over and inserted himself between the newsman and the bailiff. "That's quite far enough."

"It's all right," Lawrence called over. "Let him come."

"Most kind," the newsman said. "I'm Andrew Kerr. We met recently. Might I have a word?"

"I've had just about enough of this." The bailiff tugged his vest tight over his bulging middle and used the folded papers as he might a sword. "Dr. Burroughs, consider yourself served."

The lanky newscaster with the young-old face did quick stand-up interviews with both Antonio and Lawrence while the bailiff cleared the building of families. Kerr's producer was a tightly wound young woman who hovered around the periphery near Gerald. She flitted forward to whisper instructions to the cameraman, then retreated to the trees and vanished in plain sight. She tried to speak with Sandra, then Elena and Shirley, wanting to know if Andrew Kerr could interview them in hopes of adding background to the story. All three women refused point-blank. The producer slipped back out of range. Clearly she had a lifetime's experience of being rebuffed.

Janine spent the entire period on the phone. The only time she paused was when Fiona returned for another blistering exchange with the bailiff, which the cameraman caught on tape. Then Janine walked over and announced, "Everything is arranged. We're moving our offices into the shelter's top floor. And Brian says we can all lodge in the vicarage."

Sandra Harwood said, "I suppose I should be astonished."

"Not today," Elena said. "Please thank Brian for us all."

Elena and Shirley sat on the news van's rear fold-down seat and followed the others in a taxi. Brian was waiting for them when they pulled up in front of the shelter. He glanced once at the news crew, then ignored them. The defunct store had a full third floor that had been turned into offices and storage. He led them upstairs, introduced them around, got them settled, and stood and observed for a time. Then he had a quiet word with Janine and returned to his office. Whatever he had said left his fiancée glowing.

Elena caught the late afternoon in ninety-second snatches. Every one of her appointments had transited over from the building on Saint Giles to the derelict store. No one complained about the move, just as none had commented on their hour-long appointments being shortened to twenty minutes. Eighteen and a half, actually, with ninety seconds of downtime between sessions.

The store's creditors had stripped the former offices, kitchen, staff room, and conference areas. Elena could see where wall panels had formerly been bolted into the floor. The creditors had taken the carpet but left the underlay. The gray felt material served as a decent sound baffle. Elena was tucked into a cubby near the storerooms at the back of the vast open chamber. Her space was rimmed by shoulder-high fiberboard panels. The front was open, forming a human stable. Across from her, Antonio occupied another stable. When she finished with her last appointment, she watched him hold a young woman who wept in his arms while an infant bounced a rattle by her feet. Antonio stared over the woman's shoulder at Elena, his dark eyes glittering. Elena thought the man had never looked more handsome.

They stopped at half-past six. Brian and Janine and the producer arrived bearing crates of sandwiches and soup and drinks. They ate around a trestle table used for sorting donations. The news crew joined them. As did Gerald, who had lost his jacket and tie and pulled out his shirttail to mask the equipment strapped to his belt. Elena knew she should be exhausted. But her sense of peaceful resolve remained strong enough to defy even this long day.

When they were done, the newscaster asked if he could do another round with Lawrence. Elena could see the man was about to refuse, and that Sandra wanted to object. But the newscaster cut in with "Here's the thing, Mr. Ambassador."

"Don't call me that."

"We're still in need of one brief hook to draw all this together. A short sentence that people will carry away with them. Something they will talk about for days to come. Because I must tell you, sir. This afternoon has affected me like few things have."

Lawrence bowed his head. Elena found herself swallowing against a constricted throat. It had been such a natural response. Eventually Lawrence lifted his gaze. "All right."

They positioned him down by the cubicles and the storeroom. The bare upper floor stretched out behind them. At the far end, Brian and Janine and several helpers from the church began to set out folding chairs and put a white tablecloth on a table by the windows. Brian had decided to hold the evening service in the shelter instead of the church. Between them and the makeshift chapel, a dozen or so people still worked at forms and sorted donations. A male nurse in hospital blues spoke to a mother while her child whimpered on a padded examination table. The rain had cleared, at least momentarily. Late-afternoon sun illuminated the west-facing windows and their paper covers.

Andrew Kerr was seated on a folding chair at a sixty-degree angle to Lawrence. They had decided to shoot with just natural lighting. Janine, the producer, Elena, and Shirley all held reflectors. They were given terse instructions by the cameraman as he adjusted angles. A growing number of shelter occupants and churchgoers came up the stairs and gathered along the side wall. Antonio and Gerald stationed themselves by the stairwell entrance and kept silent order.

When they were ready, Andrew Kerr asked, "How should I refer to you?"

"Lawrence has worked well enough all my life."

"As you wish, sir." He said to the cameraman, "Ready?"

"We're rolling."

"Lawrence, less than a week ago you were the United States ambassador to the Court of Saint James. Reportedly the President had tapped you to become his running mate. Then you gave this up in order to become the first chairman of a commission intended to rein in the banks. But the bankers disliked your brutally frank accusations of misdeeds within the financial industry. Their lobbyists pressured allies in Congress until you were fired. And the same fate has awaited your friend and associate, Antonio d'Alba, who also yesterday was dismissed from his position as chairman of the European commission."

Andrew Kerr turned to the camera and said, "Cut. Where is Mr. d'Alba?"

"Over here." Antonio waved from his place by the stairs.

"Pan over and get a shot. No, no, if you people would remain exactly as you are now. Yes, with the children. That's splendid. Thank you." To the cameraman. "Did you get it?"

"In the can."

"Back to me." Kerr said to Lawrence, "Now here you are, reduced to volunteering in a shelter for families left homeless by the crisis. Surely you must feel considerable resentment and frustration over watching all your ambitions and aspirations being ground into the dust."

Lawrence replied, "I am exactly where I am meant to be."

"I find that very hard to believe, sir. In fact, if you will excuse me for saying, it sounds like you're trying to sell sour grapes as vintage champagne."

Lawrence's face was turned to stonelike severity by the sunset shadows. "I accepted the finance committee chairmanship because nobody is looking out for the common man. I saw it as my duty to protect the American family and the American dream. My aim was to shield them from the selfish and morally perverse actions of our banking system."

He turned and stared at the people clustered by the side wall. "If I cannot work for the commission, then my place is here. My duties remain exactly the same."

41

For the evening service, Elena settled into the rear row along with her friends. The makeshift chapel was encased by sunset hues. The light through the covered windows was gentle enough to complement the candles that rimmed the gathering. Eleven tall candelabra had been stationed at each corner, along the central aisle, and at either end of the altar table. Brian was joined at the front by two assistant pastors and Janine. The four of them were dressed now in formal robes of white, adding an august mystery to the moment.

Andrew Kerr was seated next to Antonio. Sandra sat to Antonio's left, then Lawrence. She held the hands of both men. The cameraman drifted in and out of Elena's vision. She found it increasingly easy to ignore him entirely.

When Brian gave the formal invitation to join in the Communion, her entire being seemed to resonate with the vicar's words. "Come to this table, not because you must but because you may. Not because you are strong, but because you are weak. Come, not because any goodness of your own gives you a right to come, but because you need mercy and help. Come, because you love the Lord a little and would like to love him more."

As they gathered at the end of the service, Janine walked over, still in her robes. "The families were wondering if we were still planning to hold the encounter group tonight."

Elena had forgotten about it entirely, but could think of no reason to say anything other than "Of course."

"I could tell them to come back tomorrow."

"No. Lawrence was right." Elena felt as though she were slowly coming back to earth. "Show them back to my cubicle. We need to set chairs in a circle."

"My name is Janine Featheringham. Welcome to our gathering of hope."

Elena was one of twenty-six people seated in the circle of folding chairs. A second semicircle was gathered back along the walls. Antonio, Lawrence, Andrew Kerr, Shirley, Sandra, and Brian. All of them had wanted to be a part of this. The cameraman, sound technician, and producer stood on the partition's other side. Janine had started by introducing the others and asking if the group minded being observed and filmed. She said it was entirely their choice. If anyone objected, they would return to the standard approach of privacy and confidentiality. Elena was as surprised as anyone when the group nodded in unison.

Janine continued, "Dr. Elena Burroughs is our leader. She is a clinical psychologist. I am a social services professional. You may think of me as the group's sergeant at arms. There are several ground rules that you need to be made aware of. First of all, no whining."

Janine showed both Elena and the group a new face. She had only told Elena that she wanted to start the evening with a wake-up call. Elena had been too caught up with everything that had happened that day to disagree. The best word to describe herself that evening was *detached*. The force that had carried Elena through the day remained with her still. The events connected to the fire and the eviction were hazy now, as though they had happened to another person.

Janine went on, "Some of you may be expecting to use this as another opportunity to complain. You are angry, which is understandable. But you have become so accustomed to your anger that it defines you. In selecting this group, I have tried to weed such people out. But if this is the way you have come to see the world, and if you are not willing to leave that attitude behind, you are not welcome here. Please leave."

Shirley Wainwright was seated on the outer perimeter, in the corner where the partition met the storeroom wall. She sat very erect, her hands folded in her lap. Whatever she thought of the gathering was hidden behind a visage of stern weariness. Nigel Harries was seated beside her. For the first time that Elena could recall, the man's features were stained by all that the day had held.

Janine continued, "Some of you do not believe in God. That is not the issue here. What is important is that you are willing to accept that your attitude toward our Lord may be wrong. That if God shows himself to you, you will acknowledge your need of him. If this is unacceptable, you need to leave the group now."

Elena inspected the group. None of them seemed surprised by Janine's confrontational tone. Many seemed pleased. Antonio caught her eye from his place by the rear wall. His look was so deep, his expression so caring, she felt it in her bones.

Janine turned to her and said, "Elena?"

She forced herself to ignore Antonio and focus on the group. "Most of you are surrounded by confusion and helplessness. You feel that your life has spun out of your control. You played by the rules. You did your best to fashion a home and a future for your family. Yet you find yourselves caught in a crisis that is not of your making. You don't understand what is happening, or why. Of course you are angry. It is natural."

Several of the women reached into their purses and came out with tissues, which they crumpled and pinched to the sides of their eyes. The actions were so habitual that none of the rest of the group gave them any notice. Elena went on, "Most of you also recognize that this undirected rage has become a destructive issue within your own lives. Your frustration and your helpless anger is a poison. The slightest thing can set you off. Your families carry wounds that you have caused. Your own hearts are injured. And with each passing day, your sense of helplessness grows, because you can't control your interior rage any more than you can control your exterior lives."

The group was very mixed. There were two Jamaican couples, one Indian, and the rest extremely British. Several couples were well dressed and carried themselves with a refined, upper-class manner. All of the faces, however, were streaked with the same tragic brush.

Elena went on, "Our goal is to establish a haven where you are able to step outside your current situation and reexamine your lives. Find areas where you can retake control. And do so with God's help."

She had never before invoked God's presence within a group counseling session. But after the day's experiences, it felt utterly right. "Our goal is to help you rebuild hope. My friends and I have faced our own impossible moments. And our experiences have revealed to us that the way out, the path to a true healing, one where scars and past mistakes are miraculously mended, only comes with God's help.

"Our sessions will follow a standard course. We will open with a Bible passage and prayer. We will then ask if anyone has experienced a miracle that week, a point in their lives where a new seedling of hope has taken root. We will then go around the room and ask each of you to name one specific issue where you have lost control, and where you want God's help in regaining order and stability. It is important that you make note of this issue, and that you remind yourself daily that this is an area where you are seeking God's help. These sessions will be all about building a clear recognition of God working in your lives.

"In the run-up to this session, one thing has become very clear to me. This is a house of miracles. We invite you to be a part of this process. Open yourselves once again to the transformative power of our dear Lord. God is waiting to reveal himself. I urge you to *expect miracles*."

Elena gave that a moment, then quoted from memory the same passage she had used in that day's noontime gathering. She then led them in a brief prayer and asked, "Who would like to start us off by naming a specific issue where they want hope or relief or just a clear answer?"

In group therapy, this was a critical and defining moment. Most patients did not fit the requirements for joint counseling. They wanted to be coddled, to have someone else do the heavy lifting. And most people were afraid to reveal themselves to strangers. Group counseling only worked when everyone participated willingly, and did so in the public eye.

Group therapists were trained to begin with an innocuous question and lead up to personal revelations. Only after this happened would the leader state the real purposes for the group. Elena's method went totally against the grain. Not to mention the famous newscaster seated next to the former ambassador. Or the cameraman who drifted around their perimeter. Elena held her breath. And prayed.

The woman seated to her left said, "I want my husband to stop shouting at me and the kids."

Elena shook her head. "Your husband's actions are not under your control. Look at yourself. The issues you face internally. Name one that is of critical—"

"I want to remember how to smile." The woman choked on the last word.

"That's fine. Next?"

Her husband nodded slowly. "She's right. I'm shouting. At everything. Don't really need any reason to shoot off."

"State this as an objective. Something you want God to help you achieve."

His swallow was audible to the entire group. "Like Masie says. I want to laugh again. With my wife. And my kids."

"Good. Very good. Next?"

The next seat was occupied by a man with refined yet ravaged features. His voice came out at a reedy crawl. "I want to sleep through a night."

Several heads around the circle nodded. Another man said, "I'm with you there, mate."

A woman said, "Without the nightmares."

Elena felt a slight chill. Not in anticipation. At being brought full-circle. She licked her lips but did not speak.

They continued around the group until they came to Janine, who stared at the floor and said, "My problem isn't regaining control. It's giving control *up*. I'm getting married in seventeen days. For the first time. I'm forty-three. I am the product of a purely horrid upbringing. I never thought I would heal to the point where marriage was even conceivable. I am so scared."

Elena said softly, "State this as a goal. As something definable, a means by which God can reveal his purpose and his love."

Janine murmured, "I need something to show me that I'm right to hope. That I'm going to be a good wife. That I deserve a man like Brian."

Elena smiled beyond the circle to where Brian wiped his eyes. "Remember what I said at the beginning. Expect miracles."

Brian gave up his home to them. The Saint Aldates vicarage was a Victorian residence of honeyed Cotswold stone, situated on a quiet lane two blocks from the church. Brian could not stay with Janine sleeping over. The older church wags would have had a field day. He and his son moved in with the associate pastor responsible for the shelter. No one felt any need to ask how long this might go on. People in shelters managed by living day to day, hour to hour. Elena decided the sentiment was probably contagious.

She and Shirley Wainwright and Janine shared the top-floor loft, a large sloped-roof chamber Brian and his son had fashioned into a mini-apartment. Back during their counseling sessions, Elena had urged them to take on such a joint project to help them through the conflict period and reknit their lives. By the time the project was finished and the boy moved in, father and son had become friends again. Shirley took the narrow bed while Elena and Janine prepared pallets on the floor. As Elena pulled up the covers, she felt a quiet pride in helping two such fine men find a new peace.

Afterward it seemed as though the dream had been there waiting for her. One moment she was drifting into sleep. The next, she was back inside her darkest hour.

The week after Jason's funeral remained a very dim memory, as though the world's light had been papered over. In her dream Elena saw it clearly for the first time. She stood by the dining room window, staring at her front lawn and passing cars and a world to which she had lost all connection. She had stood like that for hours. In the dream, she felt only a trace of the old pain. What held her most was the expanse of time between that moment and this night. In her dream she asked aloud why she had been brought back here.

Then Antonio was there. Standing beside her. Observing the scene with her. And he spoke. Such simple words. Yet it felt as though she had waited five long years to hear them.

Antonio said, *If you don't want to see this anymore, then come with me.*

And she did.

She took his hand and she turned away. And it was gone. The image and the memories. Vanished.

As simple as that.

The dream ended. But Elena did not awaken. Instead, she found herself standing downstairs in the vicarage kitchen. The room held a thoroughly unkempt and masculine air. Elena knew Janine was itching to redo the place, strip out the cheap cabinets and linoleum counters and prehistoric stove. In her dream, Antonio and Lawrence and Sandra sat around the battered central table where Brian and his son ate every meal unless they had company. Janine hated that table most of all.

In her dream, Lawrence and Antonio held large sheets of paper, big as posters. She could not read the words. She did not need to. She knew they declared that the pair had been crushed into dust. Vanquished. Obliterated. Left to crawl on their bellies in shame.

She was drawn over to the kitchen's rear window. The walled garden was another project Brian and his son had always intended to take on but never did. But Elena did not see the garden. Instead, she stared over a field of battle. The house was no longer in Oxford at all, but rather stood alone and isolated upon a high hill. Arrayed against them was a vast army. It was raining and the vision was without color. The army stretched out to where it joined with the mist, a sea of fury and death. And it was coming. For them.

Then the rain ended and the clouds began to break up. The sun lanced through the clouds. More brilliant than anything Elena had ever seen before. So powerful it seared her heart.

Wherever the sun touched, the army melted away. The clouds dissolved. The enemy was gone.

A new light entered through the kitchen window, bathing Elena in joy and triumph. She felt herself flooded by peace, by victory. The emotions were so strong they lifted her up, out of the house, carrying her away into the sky.

She woke and lay on the pallet, listening to the rain patter against the roof overhead. She heard the other women's quiet breathing. The joy remained a living presence. She had no idea how long she lay there. Hours, perhaps. Breathing in the peaceful presence with each breath. Finally she closed her eyes and slept deeply.

◆

Dawn came gray and gradual. Elena awoke but lay where she was, drifting upon a beautiful calm. Another overfull day called to her. But she did not want to let the feeling go. She lay on her pallet and listened to the rain and the quiet shuffling footsteps as either Shirley or Janine padded to the bathroom. She felt filled with a languid disregard for the hour or the pressures soon to come. Then sleep returned, and with gentle fingers it tugged her away from the morning.

The dream was over almost before it started. Which was very good. If it had lasted any longer, Elena's heart might have exploded from her chest.

They were seated on a bench. Antonio was there beside her, to her right. Elena could not see him. But she could feel his arm and shoulder touching her. The heat between them was palpable, the energy. Elena felt her tummy tremble slightly, like she was a teenager again, on a date with the guy of her dreams.

Antonio was speaking to her. Elena could not make out the words, and in her dream she did not care. She heard the warmth and affection in Antonio's voice. The words were a gentle wash over her, like the sound of the ocean on a moonlit night.

Elena assumed they were in her back garden, though everything she saw was blurred, as though Antonio's presence affected her so powerfully that she could focus on nothing else. She turned her face upward. She watched as heavy clouds peeled back like sky-bound drapes. The sun turned the cloud's leading edge to fire. The sky was blue-black and pure and achingly empty. Antonio said something to her. She wanted to reply. She wanted to tell him how blessed she felt, how happy.

But she could not speak, because suddenly she was gasping for air. The stench of old smoke became so fierce that she could not breathe. She tasted the cold sulfur eat into her lungs. She was dying and there was nothing she could do about it.

Antonio leapt from the bench. He ran toward the danger. He was going to protect her. But the smoke opened like the maw of a gray beast, and it consumed him.

Elena gasped and shot up in bed, then opened her eyes. She rose from her pallet, greeted the two women, and padded into the bathroom. She stared into the mirror and told herself over and over that it was just a dream.

42

WEDNESDAY

The scene awaiting Elena in the kitchen was achingly similar to her second dream. Even so, it was not the same. Elena did not so much wonder what the differences meant as wish she could simply cast the dawn aside. All the goodness was gone. All the hope. All the divine assurance. In their place was only dread.

Lawrence stood by the kitchen window. His wife stood beside him and rubbed a spot between his shoulder blades. Soft circular strokes, a reassuring touch. Feeding a need that was evident on Lawrence's face. A folded newspaper dangled from Lawrence's hand. Elena recognized the masthead for the *Wall Street Journal.* Antonio was seated at the kitchen table. The *Financial Times* was spread out before him. Rumpled copies of *The Times* and *The Independent* and *The Guardian* were piled at the table's far end. Shirley Wainwright and Janine were both seated at the table as well. Brian stood in the corner. The vicar was the only person to acknowledge Elena's arrival. "Coffee?"

"Yes, thank you."

Brian poured her a mug. "Milk and sugar is on the counter there. How did you sleep?"

"All right. What's the matter?"

Lawrence Harwood walked over and seated himself across from Antonio. Sandra moved to where she could place one hand on his shoulder. Her eyes were softly tragic. She did not look Elena's way.

Antonio said, "They have named the commissions. Both of them."

Lawrence rubbed a hand across his mouth. The firm resolve he had shown the previous day was gone now. In its place was a hollow vacancy.

Antonio said, "All of our allies have been erased from the list. Every single one. They have been replaced by the banks' lackies."

Shirley Wainwright said, "That can't happen."

Lawrence looked at her but did not speak.

Antonio said, "People will think the commissions are there to protect them. But they are a sham. A mask. The banks will actually have more freedom than before."

Shirley Wainwright said, "We have to stop them."

"We don't even have an ally we can trust to pass on what is actually happening," Antonio said. His voice was flat as pounded tin. "They have won."

Shirley Wainwright's voice cracked softly. "My Teddy did *not* die in vain."

Elena walked to the kitchen window. The morning light was gray and dimmed by a heavy rain. But there was no army. Her view was of a garden that had been left fallow for three years. A few perennials pushed through the blanket of weeds, defiant splashes of color and hope. Elena watched Gerald make another silent pass around the rear of the house. The bodyguard's face was lost inside his hooded parka. Elena lowered her head until her forehead met the window. She prayed, or tried to. But the words felt as empty as the sound of rain striking the window's other side.

She hated the doubt as much as she hated the fear. She assumed she had moved beyond all that. Toward what, she had no idea. She figured she would know when the time came. The days were already too full. Elena opened her eyes and lifted her head. The rain still fell.

She turned around and said, "Last night I had a dream."

Even Lawrence turned around.

"Actually, I had two. Or three. I'm not . . ." As she raised her mug she realized her hand was trembling. "There is some confusion. And it's left me uncertain whether it really was the truth that I saw."

"Tell us," Lawrence said.

She related her dream about the army, then described the feeling that had accompanied it. She finished by saying, "But all around this was such confusion that now I'm just not sure I should even have told you."

"It was absolutely the truth." Shirley Wainwright did not quite shout the words. "This is from God. I *know* it."

"Shirley is right," Brian said. "The Scriptures are full of accounts where man is called to do his best, then stand aside. Which is precisely what is happening today."

Sandra Harwood asked, "What do we do now?"

"That's simple enough. Elena has brought to us the divine call to wait." Brian reached out his arms, motioning for the others to join hands. "And pray."

Whenever Elena opened her door on Boars Hill, she always breathed deeply enough to carry the country fragrances into the city. The action was so natural that she had not thought about it until this morning, when she opened the vicarage's front door and tasted a wet metallic tint. She wore a wool turtleneck with a cotton shirt underneath. The defunct store's top floor was stuffy and tended to get overheated. The air-conditioning worked in name only. The windows were papered over and would not open. She could not imagine what it would be like working there in July. Elena waited while Gerald flagged a passing taxi and she wondered where she would be in another month's time.

Antonio slipped into the taxi beside her. "Is everything all right?"

"I have no idea." When she had announced she was going to the hospital to check on Charles, the bodyguard who had been injured in the attack on her home, Antonio had said he very much wanted to go with her. Which was a surprise, since he had never even met the man. Elena disliked how looking his way brought up the nightmare images. She opened her mouth to tell him of her fears. But the air did not come. It felt as though an invisible fist had closed around her throat. Denying her access to her own words. She watched the gray world swish past, wondering where God had gone.

Antonio checked the controls above his door. These new black cabs were fitted with Plexiglas screens behind the driver's compartment. If passengers wanted to speak with the driver, they had to flip a switch by the reading lamp. A light burned green on the switch when the microphone was activated. The light was off now. Antonio asked, "Can I tell you something?"

"Of course."

"I had a dream last night."

Only when she swiveled in her seat did she realize he was nervous. "Why didn't you say something when we were all together?"

He gave her what she could only describe as a mechanical smile. His lips compressed and turned up at the edges. His features rearranged into familiar creases. But the nervous look of his gaze said it was all a mask. "Two reasons. First, it was not really a dream. I was awake. Or almost. I really don't know how to describe it. I woke in the middle of the night and lay there listening to the rain."

At that instant, Elena knew the other reason. The dream had been about them. She clenched the wool over her racing heart.

"I was drifting. I knew I was almost awake, and almost asleep. It was a wonderful feeling. I remembered how I used to do this when I was young. There was a meadow near my grandparents' home. Their village was on a hill in the region known as Umbria. The meadow was communal, an ancient right handed down for centuries. All the villagers could graze their animals. There were a few very old trees. My favorite was a truly massive chestnut, where we lads would climb for hours. One day it was a pirate vessel, the next a castle being attacked by dragons. When we grew tired I would lie on the soft grass and watch the clouds until I drifted away. Just another cloud in a beautiful blue sky. I had not thought of this in years."

Elena could not take her eyes off him. Antonio's features gradually refitted themselves into new lines. He stared at her, but his eyes saw something else entirely. The act of looking back opened his gaze to where she felt as though she could fall in and never come out again. It only caused her grip over her heart to tighten.

"I was drifting like I did as a boy. And then something entered the room. A man who was not a man. Perhaps I should have been frightened. But the feeling was beautiful. I do not use that word lightly. The man entered the room, and my heart was filled with wonder."

She watched his hand reach over and take hold of the one not gripping the sweater over her heart. She heard him say, "The man did not speak so much as share with me a message. I had an opportunity. One that was a gift from heaven."

Antonio focused on her now. The openness at the center of his gaze deepened. He said, "The impression was very intense and very vivid. It was of you sheltering me. But shelter is not the right word. You stretched your spirit out around me. And I felt as though I was lying there beneath angel's wings."

She released the hold on her heart. Not because it had eased its frantic beat. The worry was still there, the fear. More intense than before. She let go because she needed both hands now to hold on to this good and gentle man. She lowered her head so she could nestle Antonio's hand up close to her cheek. Wishing there was something she could do to make certain she could keep hold of this moment. And this man.

43

The taxi left them by the hospital's north entrance. The staffer monitoring the Accident and Emergency entrance checked the computer and announced that Charles had been moved to a ward on the sixth floor. As they walked the long interior hallway to the elevators, Elena explained to Antonio that the move was very good news. The sixth-floor wards held all A&E and surgical patients that were deemed noncritical.

They arrived to find Charles sitting up in bed, white bandages wrapped around his forehead and chest. He talked softly with Detective Mehan and a uniformed officer. Nigel hovered by the foot of the bed, dressed in tones to match the weather. Elena spoke a few words while Antonio waited in the hall. She did not need much time. She merely wanted to show her gratitude and concern.

Nigel and the detective followed her from the room. The security chief asked, "Are you holding a meeting today?"

"At noon."

"In the shelter?"

"I imagine so. Is there a problem?"

"The place is very exposed. I'd need a small army to do an adequate job of protection."

Antonio said, "There is the matter of cost."

Elena said, "Long-term security is not a part of our equation."

"We're not discussing the long term," Nigel said. "My aim is to keep you alive today."

Mehan said, "We can assign police protection for only so long."

"Your attackers are still at large," Nigel added. "And we still don't have a line on that woman. I can pare your expenses down to what it costs me, but—"

Antonio said, "Why not speak with people at the shelter?"

"Pass out that photo of the woman, ask them to keep an eye out," Elena agreed, then glanced at her watch. She had no intention of adding Nigel's fears to her own. "I have to go. My first appointment starts in twenty minutes."

"Actually, there is another matter I need to speak with you about." Nigel looked uncomfortable for the first time. "A few days back, I showed you a photo of Mrs. Wainwright and her husband. Do you recall what I said about face recognition software?"

"Of course."

"The authorities in this country have since done a more extensive check but turned up nothing more. On a hunch, I had my allies within the service pass on a request to Interpol. They've come up with something that might interest you." He unzipped his briefcase. "Have a look at this, if you would."

Elena stepped in close enough to smell the city rain on Nigel's clothes. The security agent hesitated, then revealed his image.

The photograph was of Antonio. Elena found herself staring down at a very different man. In the picture, Antonio smiled with his entire being. He was dashing and strong and vibrant and powerful. He stood in a very grand chamber, beneath a glittering chandelier. He held the arm of a woman with dark hair and expressive features. The woman so captivated Antonio's attention that he gave the grand hall and the sparkling people no notice whatsoever. The woman smiled up at the man who held her arm.

Antonio's hand trembled as he reached out. "I remember this. It was . . ."

Nigel's voice had become deeply apologetic. "The night before your wife passed away."

The photograph was brutally sharp. Behind the couple walked a lovely elfin figure with a refined oval face. She also gave the palace no mind. Her attention was tightly focused in a manner that turned her smile into a lie. She stared intently at the woman walking alongside Antonio.

Mehan demanded, "How did you know where to look?"

"I simply asked if they might scan whatever records they had of events within a week of Signora d'Alba's demise. And up this popped."

Elena could not take her eyes off the photograph. She knew she should be doing something to ease Antonio's shock. But the man in the picture held her captive. This was who he had once been, her mind said. Yet her heart whispered that this was the man he might once again become.

Mehan shifted his gaze from the photograph to Antonio and back, clearly uncertain how far to take it. Nigel appeared willing to wait all day.

Antonio said, "Why would they use the same assailant?"

Nigel's gaze tightened slightly. He gave an almost imperceptible nod.

Mehan said, "We don't know for certain that they have."

Elena said, "Oh, please. This woman just happens to repeatedly pop up?"

Nigel said, "Most people willing to commit murder have a criminal record. They leave a trail. They are notoriously unstable. They follow traceable patterns. This woman is . . . different. Remarkably so."

They were all watching him now. Mehan was the only one who spoke. "Just exactly what were you doing before you went into security?"

Nigel ignored the question. "This woman has the ability to vanish. She crosses borders with impunity. She shows up on no records. She is a ghost. Which makes her unique. And extremely effective."

Antonio returned his gaze to the photograph. "She has help."

Nigel's gaze tightened a second time. Elena realized the man was smiling. In approval.

Antonio said, "She has an organization who is sheltering her."

Nigel said, "That is my thinking."

Mehan said, "You mean, a government?"

"Doubtful," Nigel said.

Antonio said, "The largest banks employ a security force that numbers in the hundreds. They have to. They manage billions. Their reach extends to some of the world's most dangerous quarters."

"It would certainly be possible for an organization with that sort of international clout to hide such an asset." Nigel slipped the photograph back into his briefcase and zipped it shut.

Antonio stared at the empty space where before his wife had smiled at him. "What do we do now?"

"That's simple enough." Nigel's cold fury gave his speech an almost musical lilt. "We must find a way to shut this lot down."

By the time Elena finished with her morning appointments, the entire shelter knew about Antonio and Shirley Wainwright and the possible tie-in to the assault on Elena's home. Elena saw photographs of the female attacker everywhere.

When it came time for the noon gathering, Nigel broke off discussions with a group of the shelter's occupants and joined them. They brought folding chairs into Elena's cubicle and clustered close together, as if they had been going through the same routine for months. People working in neighboring cubicles glanced over, then away.

Elena started with verses she had selected from the fifteenth chapter of Exodus: " 'The Lord is my strong defender, he is the one who has saved me. He is my God, and I will praise him; my father's God, and I will sing about his greatness . . . In your steadfast love you led the people whom you redeemed; you guided them by your strength to your holy abode.' "

But when she shut her Bible, she had no idea where to go. There was no image for them to focus upon. The book of dreams remained locked inside the police evidence room, which according to Mehan was a safe that filled half the headquarters' basement and was manned around the clock. She could not draw up the photograph of that image because her laptop had been lost to the fire. She knew she should offer a brief homily. Something of spiritual significance. But the words would not come. All she wanted to talk about was Antonio. The final dream remained imprinted behind her eyes. It carried the force of a branding iron.

Antonio was seated next to her, silent and withdrawn. He stared at the floor by his feet. She knew he was seeing the photograph of that elfish woman studying his wife. She knew Antonio's words in the taxi, saying she would cover him with love strong as angel's wings, were gone now. She wished she could say something to return them to that moment. She felt powerless.

Lawrence said to Antonio, "We need to talk about what Nigel has turned up. The question is, can you handle it?"

Antonio straightened in his chair. "Why not? It's all I'm thinking about."

Sandra looked across at Elena. "But perhaps we shouldn't talk about such matters while we're gathered in our prayer group."

"I told you the first time we met," Elena said. "There are no rules except the ones we make for ourselves."

"Okay. Good. Who wants to start?"

Nigel surprised them all then. He rarely spoke at all during the sessions. "I have the distinct impression that we're missing something."

"Explain."

"Antonio, perhaps you would be so kind as to describe the events leading up to the night in question."

"I had just been named managing director of the Banca di Roma. Three days later, the president of Italy appointed me to a commission to look at possible misdeeds involving the major banks. The principal thrust was to be money laundering. That afternoon, I met with officials . . ."

"Yes?"

"The new chief of the ECB, the European Central Bank, had come down for his first meetings with the regime. We had lunch. He mentioned the ECB's interest in our work. They were wondering if a similar sort of commission might be put in place to oversee the European financial system. I told him . . ."

"Do go on, please."

"I confessed to him my fears for the banking system and the risks they were taking. Hedge funds and derivatives trading were hidden from view. Legally they operated as separate institutions, but they were wholly owned by the parent banks. These same banks also carried all the liabilities. The risks they were taking defied belief. I had spent the first days of my appointment trying to fathom the hidden structures within my own bank. These traders were setting up leveraged bets larger than the bank's entire asset base. Every *day*."

"What was this gentleman's name, please?"

Antonio waved that aside. "It doesn't matter. He retired soon after. But there was another man with him. The new assistant secretary of the Treasury had arrived the same day as the ECB chief. They were old friends. They met with me together."

Lawrence said softly, "It was Easton Grey, wasn't it. The man I debated on Larry King's show."

"How did you know?"

Lawrence glanced at his wife. "He and I go way back."

"After Francesca's death, I resigned. I could not possibly go on. It was over a year later that I accepted the Vatican's offer of a consultancy. I did it mainly to fill the hours." Antonio's face was plowed with sorrowful lines. "Did I murder my wife?"

"How *dare* you ask such a question!"

The vehemence in Shirley Wainwright's voice shocked them all. She continued, "Did I murder my husband by praying that God might open his heart and reveal himself? Did Miriam cause Elena to lose her home by giving her the book of dreams?"

"I didn't say anything—"

"No. Of course not. You only suggested that because you tried to take a moral stand, you had a role in your wife's death. You profane her memory with such thoughts."

Antonio nodded slowly. "You are, of course, correct. But to think that perhaps Francesca might still be . . ." He shook his head. "My heart has shouted the same thing ever since I saw the photo of us together. All day long, I have heard nothing else."

Elena said it for him. "You would do anything, give up anything, just to have her back with you again."

Antonio's gaze reminded her of fractured gemstones. "You are no doubt a remarkable analyst."

Shirley Wainwright said, "Can you hear her response to this, Antonio?"

His shattered gaze remained on Elena.

"Can you listen beyond your sorrow and the day's events, and listen to what she would say? What she *is* saying?" Shirley gave that a moment, then went on, "Wouldn't Francesca want you to go forward with this? Isn't she urging you to hold fast to your call?"

44

As soon as the meeting ended, Elena walked over to Antonio and said, "Why don't we go get a bite to eat."

Janine said, "They're about to serve a salad buffet for all the workers."

Shirley huffed a quiet laugh. "The lady wasn't talking just about food."

Janine reddened. "I do beg your pardon."

Antonio said, "I would like that. Very much."

Nigel was having a quiet word with Gerald and three men by the stairs. When Elena approached, Nigel said, "Something's come up on another job. I must leave. And a producer with ITV Television just rang. They want to film another interview."

Antonio said to Elena, "I can't. Not now."

"Ask Lawrence to handle it," Elena told Nigel. "I'm getting Antonio out of here. We both need a break."

Gerald said to his boss, "I can't be in two places at once."

Elena saw that Nigel wanted to order them to stay. She tightened her hold on Antonio's arm and said, "We are just going to the market for a bite."

Nigel said to Gerald, "Now's as good a time as any to test

our new helpers. You stay and monitor the incoming crew. Have a couple of these gentlemen accompany Elena and Antonio."

They left the shelter by the side door. Clouds brooded heavy and ominous, but at least the rain had stopped. The air was very warm, very close. They crossed the street and walked up a block. The road was shut to all but bus and taxi traffic. Where the street did a loop around the shopping mall, a space had been formed for the regional bus services. Behind the glass bus shelters was a small park.

The narrow expanse of green was filled with people Elena recognized from the shelter. In the past, when she met her patients in public, Elena had learned never to approach them or give any sign she saw them at all. Many patients were very embarrassed, as though they were sharing a deep and shameful act. But here today, almost everyone she passed met her with smiles. Even so, no one approached her. Elena realized it was probably because they thought *she* would be ashamed of *them*.

She said to Antonio, "I need a minute."

Elena then turned and spoke to the two men shadowing their footsteps. "I want to speak with those people over there. Please stay well back."

She walked around the park. Not stopping. Just making a point of greeting each of her patients, offering a few words. The pleasure they showed twisted her heart. As she walked, she realized they were using the tiny park as a back garden. Sitting crammed into the benches or resting on the damp grass, watching the kids play, having a quiet word, taking what ease they could find. Only one of those she passed slowed her passage, a man from the group session, who said, "I got what I asked for, Doc."

"Excuse me?"

"The miracle. I did like you said, wrote down the problem

and the need. I thought it was a bit of old rubbish, truth be told, writing down my hope. But I see it now, how I go straight on to the next thing, like I've got blinders on. All I want to see is the next problem. Got to stop and accept the answer to know there's been a miracle. Right, Doc?"

"This is very important. After I open tonight's session with the Bible reading, I want you to share with the group what you just told me. Will you do that?"

He puffed up measurably. "Sure thing, Doc."

"Thank you." She walked back to where Antonio waited and retook hold of his arm. "All right. I'm ready."

A street band played at the market's entrance, four Anglos, none of them young, all with tangled Rastafarian locks. There was a drummer on a lone battered snare, an alto sax, a percussionist playing oversize Indian hand drums, and a guitarist with a battery-powered amp. They hammered out a jazzy rendition of a Stones hit from the seventies. They were very good, and had attracted a crowd large enough to spill off the broad walk and into the bus lanes. Every time a bus from the outlying districts pulled up, the crowd pressed in good-naturedly.

The park's northern border was jammed with kids who screamed and shouted and danced to the music. Beyond the park, one of the neighboring shops sold CDs, probably pirated. A boom box blared Bob Marley from the doorway. Dogs barked and ran among the kids. Buses rumbled and brakes squealed. Elena took a deep breath of diesel, roasting meat, spices, and city life. Antonio spoke to her, but the surrounding din made it impossible to hear what he said. She looked into his eyes, shared a smile, and decided it did not matter. For the first time he seemed freed from the shadows he had carried since Nigel showed him the photographs.

They bought falafel and soft drinks from the Lebanese deli. As they returned to the park, a couple she had seen the previous afternoon as patients rose and insisted they take their spot.

Elena and Antonio sat on the bench and ate leaning over, so the yogurt dressing dripped off their fingers and onto the grass. When they were finished, Antonio gathered up their trash, then walked to the wall fountain and wet their remaining napkins. He returned to the bench and wiped her fingers like he might a little child's, one at a time, cleaning them thoroughly. Elena felt her smile twisted by a conflicted heart. She wanted to warn him about her dream. But something still held her back. As Antonio carried the dirty napkins over to the trash can, Elena was struck by the thought that perhaps her hesitation came from the fact that the dream was not real. After all, it had not arrived with the two others. Perhaps it was just her old self trying to break this new hold. The sudden hope granted her the ability to smile at his return. Smile with all her heart.

Antonio seated himself and slipped his arm around her shoulders. She slid down slightly on the bench, so that she could lean her head against his arm. She turned her face to the sky. Like they had been lovers for years and knew how to fit into each other's space.

The scene could not have been farther from her nightmare. Whereas she had dreamed of utter quiet and solitude, here they were swamped by the city's din. Whereas in her dream there had been an incredible sky, blue one side and gray the other, Elena now stared up at clouds drooping with their burden of more rain. Antonio did not speak now as he had in the dream; how could he, anything he said would have gone unheard. Elena sighed deeply and snuggled in closer to his shoulder.

She shut her eyes. A languid calm seeped into her bones. She could have stayed there for hours. Years. Antonio's closeness was a blanket draped over her heart and mind.

She lifted her arm so she could glance at her watch without lifting her head from his arm. Antonio responded by pushing her arm back down. She started to protest that her afternoon appointments would be waiting. But the moment was too sweet, the languid feeling too strong.

The sun managed to pierce through the clouds. The effect was so remarkable that the children between her and the street pointed and stared. A rim of gold formed, like the sky was being split in two. Then Elena realized she could no longer hear the din. It was as though she and Antonio had sealed themselves inside a shield of peace. They might as well have been utterly alone.

Then it hit her.

Even before the thought was fully formed, Elena shot from the bench.

She understood why she could not say anything before. To alert Antonio would have caused him to act. And if he acted, he would die. It was that simple.

Then Elena saw the woman.

The elfin attacker was dressed like the shelter's occupants, cheap dungarees and a hooded sweatshirt with camouflage print and a fake designer logo. Small as she was, she could easily have passed for a young boy. The sweatshirts—and some who wore them—were called hoodies and were favorites with the more violent teens, skinheads and yobs and local gangs. They fought over grimy bits of council estate and used the hoodie's wide front pouch to hide knives and other weapons. Hoodies generally walked with both hands tucked inside the front pouch, just as the woman was walking now. When they appeared in central Oxford, people did their best to ignore them. It was safer that way. Some hoodies used anything, even a sideways glance, as an excuse to fight.

The woman wore the hood up and pulled far forward to hide her face. But as she passed between two buses, the same lance of sunlight invaded the shadows. Elena saw the feral gleam in her eyes, the little smile, the tight focus upon Antonio.

The space between the woman and her target was packed.

Three long lines of people stretched out from the glass bus shelter, waiting for their afternoon rides. They stood jammed in together to stop line-breakers. Even so, they made space for the small person in the hoodie to slip through. The kids in the park were not so disposed. Two little girls tossed a Frisbee with a barking dog. The girls could not throw. The Frisbee almost hit the woman in the face. She ducked and weaved, and almost tripped over the dog. Which was probably why she did not notice Elena running in from the side.

Elena turned and shouted at her two minders. But the noise swallowed her terror as easily as it did her words. The minders were also not professional. They watched her with wide-eyed alarm but had no idea what to do. Elena ducked the Frisbee and leapt over the dog. It was all up to her.

She would never have imagined herself capable of such a deed. Running toward a killer. But the act sprang from a visceral need. She had to protect the man she loved. Her heart shouted those words so fiercely that her fear had no place to grow. A *man* she *loved.*

The woman spotted Elena's approach. She scowled, and the elfin features twisted into a mask that looked not just angry but old. As though the cute little mask had been tossed aside and the true person revealed. Ancient and perverse and warped as sin.

The woman lifted her arm from the hoodie's front pouch. The hand held a small gun. The motion was so fluid it almost seemed slow. Like the woman had done it a hundred thousand times.

When she aimed at Elena, the barrel of the gun looked huge. Big as a cannon. Large enough to swallow her whole.

Elena did not try to dodge. To do so would risk the children and Antonio and whoever else might be behind her. Instead, she leapt forward, into danger, arms outstretched. Like she wanted to fly away and carry this danger with her. Like she sought to shield her man with angel's wings.

There was a little pop, nothing more than a firecracker of sound. A fist slammed into her shoulder, spinning her helplessly around. There was no pain. The ground raced up and slammed into her, hard as the fist.

The pain hit her then. And the blackness.

45

THURSDAY

Elena drifted in and out. The first time was when they lifted her onto the gurney. A blue-jacketed medic looked down at her and said, "Can you hear me, miss? Nod if you can hear me. We're taking you to the hospital. Are you . . ."

She didn't bother listening to anything else. She saw Antonio hovering behind the ambulance medic. His eyes looked very frightened. She wanted to tell him everything was fine. Wonderful, really. But holding on to consciousness was like catching water from a stream.

The next sound she heard was of metal sliding against metal very close to her ear. She opened her eyes and saw a nurse cutting away her clothes. A voice said, "She's coming around."

"Can you hear me, Dr. Burroughs? Nod for me if you can, please. Good. Are you in any pain?"

There was a sharp burning sensation between her neck and her shoulder. Something there was very not right. She could not recall exactly what had happened. She wanted to ask if Antonio was there. She knew this was very important. The doctor said, "We've given you something for the pain. It should . . ."

Then the darkness swept up again, encasing her like a blanket.

When she came to the third time she knew everything had changed. The space by her shoulder still hurt, but it was a different pain altogether. Before, there had been a sharp wrongness she could feel even through the drugs. Now it felt clean. Right. Healing could begin. She remembered what had happened now, the woman and the gun. Elena breathed a faint sigh and drifted away. Antonio was alive and so was she.

When she returned, it seemed as though she had only been gone a few moments. Only now she heard voices. Men. Two of them talked softly. She felt no need to open her eyes.

Lawrence said something she could not catch, but she knew it was him, the deep bass carrying a force even when quiet. Then Antonio spoke, not as deep and much more fluid, as though he had been trained since birth to sing his speech.

The voices gradually crystallized to the point where Elena could make out the words. She could also place them in the room. Lawrence sat or stood somewhere beyond the foot of her bed. Antonio was nearer and to her right, perhaps even close enough to touch. She wanted to reach out, but she didn't because of what they were discussing.

She heard Lawrence say, "I always let Sandra carry the faith issue. I delegated it to her. I've always been good at delegating. Staffers fought to work for me. I gave them duties and the freedom to carry them out. And the credit for doing a good job. Sandra was so passionate about God. Fine. Let her handle it."

Antonio said, "Then she started having the dreams."

"I was so worried about her. And me. And us." Lawrence was quiet a moment. "I think at some deep level I knew from the start this meant the end of my ambition for the vice presidency."

"You have been in politics all your life?"

"Congress two terms, back into business, then the Senate for one term, then head of the party, then business, then the ambassadorial appointment. Always climbing the ladder. Until God struck."

"I'm so very sorry, my friend."

"I'm right where I should be. I know that now. But when I look back, all I can see is my anger. Rage at Elena. At Sandra. At you. At God. I feel so ashamed."

"We have all failed before God. We have all been searched and found wanting. You know those verses?"

"Yes."

"God called. You have answered. In your own imperfect and human way, you seek to serve him. Let the rest of it go."

Elena felt a single tear slide down her cheek, hot as lava. It was a delicious sensation, one sweet enough to carry her back away.

She had no idea how long she was gone. It seemed like just a moment, a single slip down the languid path, a few breaths, then she was back. Sunlight glinted rich and golden against her eyelids. When she opened her eyes, all she could see was the light. It struck the window to her left and filled the entire room.

"She's awake."

"Elena? How are you, my dear?"

She peeled apart her lips. All she tasted was dryness.

"Here." Hands inserted a straw into the side of her mouth. Antonio said, "Drink slowly."

Forms took human shape within the light-filled room. Nigel was there. As was Shirley and Sandra and Antonio and Lawrence. Mehan leaned against the door.

Antonio waited until she had stopped drinking to ask, "Shall I get the nurse?"

"Just hold my hand."

They all gave that a beat. Lawrence and Nigel smiled. Janine slipped quietly away. Antonio asked, "Are you in pain?"

She was, but in a way she liked how it helped anchor her to wakefulness. "I'm fine."

Janine returned with a doctor and nurse. The doctor asked

them all to leave. When they had filed out, he inspected her wound, asked a few questions, then described her as extremely fortunate, as the bullet had passed within millimeters of both bone and vital nerve centers, but had merely pierced the soft tissue above her collarbone. When he was done, the group filed back in, filling the room. Mehan said, "I need to ask you a few questions."

The detective had already heard the story from Antonio. Elena answered most of his queries with a simple nod. When he was done, Elena asked, "What happened to the woman?"

"Remarkable, that." Nigel did not so much smile as crinkle the edges of his features. "Several people in the park took umbrage at her shooting you."

"Umbrage," Lawrence said. "Interesting way to put it."

Antonio said, "The woman was mauled."

Nigel said, "Have you ever seen one of those nature programs where the bait hits the water and every fish within a hundred miles goes berserk? That woman shot you and instantly became bait."

Lawrence was grinning. "You weren't even there."

"I saw the end result. They bunged her up right smartly."

"No serious damage," Mehan said. "But I doubt she'll sleep comfortably for a while."

Antonio said, "Your friends from the shelter would have done much worse, but our guards managed to pull them off."

Mehan said, "Your assailant is currently incarcerated in the hospital wing of our local women's jail. Chained to her bed. Bars on her one small window. Bad lighting. Beastly smells. Worse food."

Nigel said, "It appears she is rather averse to enclosed spaces."

Mehan said, "She hasn't said anything yet. But I'm told it's like watching a kettle come to a boil."

"That's enough," Sandra said. "Talk like this can wait until she's better."

"Glad to know you're in one piece." Mehan patted the bed's metal railing. "We take shootings in public places quite seriously in this country. Your two gentlemen friends will be watched closely from now on, courtesy of Her Majesty's government."

"And there's a guard outside your door," Antonio said.

When the detective had left, Elena asked, "What time is it?"

"Four in the afternoon, the day after your attack," Antonio said. "You've been gone a while."

Elena murmured, "We missed today's meeting."

"We did no such thing," Shirley said.

"We held it in the lobby here on your floor," Antonio said.

"Shirley carried it," Nigel said. "Did quite a lovely job."

"Not as good as you," Shirley said.

"Janine had to leave for a meeting," Sandra said. "Brian sends his best. Along with everyone at the shelter."

Elena felt the fatigue slip up and over her, a lethargic warmth that spread through her bones and pulled down her eyelids. She slipped away with somnolent ease.

When she returned, Antonio was reading a newspaper in the chair beside her bed. He held the cup for her to drink, then asked, "Can I get you something?"

"I'm fine."

"The doctor wants you to eat. I'm supposed to ring downstairs for a meal."

"In a minute. Have you stayed here all this time?"

"Where else am I to go?" He refilled the cup, then snapped the lid back on tightly. "The nurse said I was to call if you needed something for the pain."

"It hurts, but in a good way. And I don't want to sleep anymore."

He studied her with an impossibly open gaze. "Shame on you, frightening me like that."

"You have the most amazing eyes."

"Don't change the subject. When you saw that woman, why didn't you warn me?"

"I couldn't. I didn't see her before I moved." Elena decided now was as good a time to tell him as she would ever have. "Besides which, if I had said something, you would die."

"You know this how, precisely?"

"A dream."

When he frowned, his forehead creased in rows shaped like a boat's prow, deep furrows that ran from his hairline to his eyebrows. "Elena. Why am I learning about this now?"

"I tried to tell you. Several times. But something held me back. And I wasn't sure that the dream was anything more than nighttime fears."

She described the night's sequence. The dream with him. The dream of the dissolving army. Then the one at dawn. She finished by saying, "I didn't understand until I ran toward that woman. The dream was meant for me, not you. It was both a warning and a choice. It was time for me to commit. Not just to loving you. To everything that love requires."

Antonio was silent a long moment, then said, "I cannot lose you, Elena. I cannot survive that a second time."

"Love comes with no guarantees, Antonio. Take my hand. Feel that? We are together now. I love you, my dearest. I would give everything to keep you safe. Sacrifice anything."

Antonio leaned forward and planted a kiss upon her temple. "Don't you dare."

An orderly arrived with two dinner trays and drew over a metal table on rollers so Antonio could eat beside her. When they were done, as the orderly cleared things away, there was a knock on her door. When it opened, Elena caught a glimpse of a woman in a police uniform seated outside her door. Then

Lawrence Harwood blocked her view. "Do you mind a little more company?"

"Come in."

Nigel slipped in behind Lawrence. "We're your nightly emissaries. The ladies are all busy at the shelter and send their regards. They'll return in the morning."

Antonio said, "Elena is feeling much better. I can tell. She's started giving me orders."

"Terrible sign, that." Nigel fitted himself onto the side wall. "I'd watch my step if I were you."

"I am," Antonio said, smiling at her. "Very closely indeed."

Lawrence asked, "Do you mind if I turn on your television?"

"Of course not."

"Andrew Kerr's producer called this afternoon. *Newsnight* is airing our segment."

"Detective Mehan phoned," Nigel reported. "The woman has started to talk. But so far she has said little of use save to confirm her name. Mehan remains confident that it is only a matter of time."

Elena shook her head slowly, sliding it back and forth on the pillow. "That's not how it's meant to be. Moving forward in dribs and drabs."

Lawrence turned around to watch her with the others. Elena went on, "The dream was very clear. We were to stand and watch God perform a miracle."

"Your assailant is in custody," Nigel pointed out.

"The miracle was not limited to just one woman. God's light erased an *army*." When the three men did not respond, she said, "Neither of you have your positions back. The people who manipulated you out of the vice presidency are still hiding in the shadows. The enemy remains in control of the commissions."

The three men studied her for a time; then Lawrence glanced at his watch and said, "It's almost time."

"Bring another couple of chairs from the waiting room," Antonio said.

The men settled just as the *Newsnight* logo appeared and the music trumpeted. Andrew Kerr came on, looking far more polished than when he had been with them at the shelter. He began, "This week I traveled to Oxford with the intention of interviewing two men I classed as failures. There was certainly an abundance of evidence to support my assumption."

On the screen to his left appeared a professional photograph exuding power and money. "Lawrence Harwood, formerly a United States senator and before that CEO of America's fourth-largest bank. He had been named as a front-runner for the American vice presidency, and until recently served as America's ambassador to the Court of Saint James. This week, just five days after his appointment, Harwood was dismissed as chairman of America's new financial oversight commission."

The photograph switched to one of Antonio, clearly taken at the height of his power. "Antonio d'Alba, former chairman of Italy's largest private bank, former adviser to the Vatican on financial matters. He also survived just five days before being fired from the European financial commission's chairmanship. Both men washed up at an Oxford institute that they helped establish. We caught up with them just as the bailiff arrived to evict them and close down the institute. As I said, total failures."

The photographs vanished and the camera tightened on Kerr's face. "What I found affected me as few stories ever have. The reason is quite simple. For the first time, this financial crisis has been given a human face."

The switch was intentionally abrupt. One moment they were safe inside the television studio. The next, the camera was tight on Fiona's face as she hurled angry invectives at the bailiff. There followed a three-second close-up of the bailiff's haughty chill; then it switched to Lawrence and Antonio in their rumpled and weary states.

Which only added to the force of Lawrence's words. He stood upon the institute's lowest step and spoke with a resonance that sent shivers up Elena's spine. Of being precisely where he needed to be. Serving the common man.

Then the cameraman found the children.

The ones hiding behind trees. The ones wailing in their mothers' arms. The ones clutching their fathers' trouser legs, watching with tragic expressions as their pasts were played out once more.

As Elena watched the camera follow them across town to the shelter, she felt an immense calm settle upon her. She recalled a late-August afternoon seated on the bench in her back garden. The sky overhead had been utterly clear, the air breathless and hot. Not a blade of grass moved. The light reflecting off the Radcliff dome had been so brilliant that it had hurt her eyes. But beyond this patch of calm, out over the plains north of Oxford, the sky had been purplish black. Thunderclouds had formed a massive wall. The rain beneath them had been so heavy that she could not tell where the clouds ended and the storm began. The entire tableau was lit by a forest of lightning, the strikes so frequent that all she heard was a constant rumble. Yet there she had sat, safe and shielded within her breathless calm.

The news segment ended with a back-and-forth sequence, binding together Lawrence's closing statement with images from the evening service. Lawrence spoke of his duty, and his words were illuminated by the papered-over windows and the candles and the faces.

The return to the studio's cold brilliance was intentionally harsh. Andrew Kerr was once again in his seat at the curved dais, with his makeup and his suit and his perfectly coiffed hair. "Joining me tonight is Easton Grey, newly appointed to replace Lawrence Harwood as chairman of the US financial oversight committee."

Antonio said, "Did you know he was here?"

"How could I?" Lawrence did not take his eyes off the screen. "All my sources have gone silent."

"Rather a coincidence that he would show up at our lowest moment," Antonio said.

Nigel shook his head. "Every investigator on earth shares a distinct loathing for coincidences."

Elena barely heard the exchange. For as the camera switched to Lawrence's replacement, her senses became filled with the stench of cold smoke. "Switch it off."

Lawrence kept his attention on the screen. "I need to hear this."

"No you don't."

Lawrence muted the sound. "What's the matter?"

Elena pointed at the screen. "That's him."

"What are you talking about."

"The man behind the attacks. The face of the enemy."

The three men turned in unison. Antonio said, "What are you saying?"

"I sensed it before. When he argued with you on *Larry King*. I thought the sensation was coming from the banks, the people behind him. I was wrong. It's him. This is the man."

Antonio said, "Are you certain, Elena?"

"Utterly."

The three men exchanged a long look. On the screen, Easton Grey gave what was no doubt a very polished performance. But with the sound turned off, it was possible to look beyond the words and the preparation. Underneath it all, deep in the man's gaze, was the unmistakable look of panic.

Antonio asked, "What do we do?"

Elena turned to Nigel. "Ask Detective Mehan to give you the book."

"I beg your pardon?"

"Mehan has the book in his evidence locker. We need it for tomorrow's session."

Newsnight ended. Lawrence fumbled with the controls and cut off the television. He continued to stare at the empty screen. "You have no idea the power behind Easton Grey."

"I think I do." A dark army stretched over a windswept plain.

"Dr. Burroughs." Nigel remained at attention. "You do me great honor. I will guard the book with my life."

Elena started to tell him it was just a book. But instead she reached out her hands and said, "Let's close with a moment of prayer."

46

FRIDAY

Elena slept deep and well. She woke only once in the night, when a nurse checked on her and the hall light spilled across her face. Elena saw the police officer on guard outside her door, a man this time. She lay in the stillness and felt the energy course through the night. Working at a level far beyond the ability of man to direct or even understand.

The dream came with the dawn. In it, she stood in the street before a vast stone structure. It looked like some sort of monument, gray and as imposing as a battleship. Broad steps led up to a portico fronted by stone columns. The building was crowned by thunderclouds, as though heaven itself brooded over whatever went on inside. Instantly she smelled the smoke, stale and cold and slightly sulfuric. A scent old and dead as an open grave.

A man stood before her. She could not see his face. She did not need to. The man said, "Teddy Wainwright left you a gift."

The final word, *gift,* propelled her up and out. Into daylight.

The doctor arrived a few moments after she opened her eyes. Elena remained detached from the inspection and changing of her bandages. She mouthed thanks at the news that she would be released that day. She was still mulling over the dream when

Sandra Harwood entered, carrying her breakfast tray. "How are you feeling?"

"I slept well."

"The doctor says you're ready to go home." Sandra rolled the tray over and raised the back of her bed. "That's great news."

Sandra did not look at all good. Elena doubted she had slept at all. "What's the matter?"

"Eat your breakfast. You need your strength."

"Sandra. Tell me what's wrong."

"Easton Grey." She slipped into the chair. "He and Lawrence go back a long way. They were both division VPs at one of the major banks. Both went for the CEO slot. Lawrence was the front-runner. Easton beat him out. Neither of us saw it coming."

Elena lifted the coffee cup and pushed the tray away.

"Lawrence left the bank to run for Congress; then afterward he took the top position at one of their competitors. When he became ambassador, he tapped his number two to take over. The head of investment banking—you know that is the name banks use for their derivatives units, right? The derivatives chief put Easton's name forward. Lawrence fought them and lost. His own man was sacked."

"And now Easton Grey has been named to chair the commission. I'm so sorry."

"Easton is sneaky, fast, ruthless. And utterly without scruples."

"You're frightened over what he might do next."

"There are a lot worse ways to destroy a man like Lawrence than just kill him. Lawrence has never been more vulnerable." She swiped at her face. "Last night we got a call from friends in the media. CNN and MSNBC are both carrying the *Newsnight* segment. Easton and his backers will be furious. They will try to find a way to crush Lawrence. Publicly."

Elena waited while this strong and loving woman reknitted her world, then asked, "Where are the others?"

"Downstairs with Antonio in the cafeteria."

"Would you ask them to come up?" When Sandra reached the door, Elena said, "And there's something else I need you to do."

Elena studied each face as they entered the room. Most carried a combination of fear and resolve. All looked very tired. Nigel Harries entered last, the book of dreams clasped to his chest.

Elena accepted the book and lay it on the bed. She led them in prayer, then opened the cover. She paused over the second image. She traced her finger over the line that was invisible now in the light of day.

Then she turned the page.

The image was almost welcoming, as though everything they had experienced had readied her. The insight did away with any need to read the words. After all, she knew what it said. *Thy Kingdom come.* She had spoken the words all her life. They resonated through her now.

A cloud of script hovered along the page's upper half. It sent a soft golden rain down. A second layer of script, down at the base of the page, sent up tiny shoots of hope and life. Elena understood with a sense of having left doubt behind. The acts of servants, filled with the power of God, lay the groundwork for the coming of God's will. To the ends of the earth and time.

She looked at the others and said, "Miriam's great-grandmother said nothing to the young girl who was to become her heir because there were no instructions to pass down. No *earthly* instructions."

They were all silent. Watching.

"The key is not what another person says. It never has been. The objective of this book, and of the prayer it holds, is communion with God. It was then. It is now. For everyone. This was the lesson Jesus gave us. The gift of this prayer. To unite us with the Father."

They stayed as they were. A human still life. No one spoke. Or moved.

"The farther I move down this road, the more I treasure the Holy Spirit's presence. So I sit and wait and hope. For insight. For wisdom. For guidance that truly deserves the term *eternal*. And for the strength to turn the wisdom into action."

Elena motioned to Sandra. "Did you bring it?"

Sandra lifted a simple metal pitcher used by the cafeteria for salad dressing. "It's not the fanciest vessel I've seen."

"It's fine." Elena said to them all, "The Scriptures are full of times when the Lord's servants prepare themselves through the act of anointing. That is what we are going to do now. Each of us will stand here by the bed so that I can join with others in laying hands upon them. Sandra will then anoint their heads with oil; then we will pray over them. And ask the Father for all that he and only he can grant us."

The group did not disperse after the final prayer. Elena understood their reluctance. In here was the safety of a sacred calm. Out there, beasts of the dark coiled and writhed and hunted. Elena was sorry to disturb their tranquillity. But it had to be done.

"Last night, I had a dream." Elena related her experience. Then she asked Shirley, "Do you have Teddy's letter?"

"I carry it with me everywhere."

"Would you read it to us, please?"

Elena had read the letter through several times. But hearing Shirley speak the words brought the man to life, him and the love they had shared and the sorrow his absence had created. Shirley's voice broke only once, not over his declaration of love, but rather when he makes his final prayer to God. Elena found that the most moving of all.

Lawrence stared across the bed at Antonio. He looked ready to launch himself out of the room. "Read that part over."

Shirley wiped her eyes. "Which part?"

Antonio said, "About the money."

Shirley did as they asked. Elena did not understand. She did not need to. The light in the two men's gazes was enough.

Sandra saw it too. "This is it. Isn't it."

Teddy's letter said his bank's derivatives traders had begun demanding more capital. Just like last time. And the banks had identified a major new source.

They planned to drain life insurance companies. Buy controlling interests through shell corporations, then redirect the insurance capital that backed the life insurance policies into the derivatives markets. And then bundle life insurance policies like they did subprime mortgages.

Lawrence said, "The mother lode."

"Teddy has come through for us," Antonio agreed.

Shirley said, "Explain, please."

"We suspected this," Lawrence said. "But we had no proof."

"They knew we were opposed to it," Antonio said. "So they hid it from us."

Sandra asked, "Can they hide such activities from their own people?"

"So long as the CEO and a majority of the board are on their side, they can do whatever they want," Lawrence replied.

"Remember, the derivatives and hedge funds are not regulated," Antonio said. "That is what the commissions were for. To protect the world's economies from the banks creating havoc all over again."

"Most bank directors don't *want* to know what's happening," Lawrence said. "These derivatives traders are bringing in a major portion of the banks' profits. The banks aren't making loans to the average consumer or small businesses. Credit has never been tighter. The flow of capital is still contracting and the banks' normal customer base is starved of funds. Why? Because the banks have redirected capital to their biggest profit center. The derivatives trading arm."

Antonio said, "But the money on hand is not enough. Derivatives *devour* money. The more they gorge, the more they need."

"Money and risk," Lawrence said. "If there isn't enough risk, they create it. They bundle risk and they calculate the odds and they sell it on before the risk becomes toxic. Fast trades and tiny margins. Done in such sizes, and with such lightning speed, that the profits continue to mount."

Shirley said, "We have to stop them."

Lawrence and Antonio stared at each other across the bed. Searching the air between them for the answer.

Nigel pointed out, "Easton Grey is here for a meeting with the Bank of England."

"The Bank of England is a regulatory body," Antonio said. "Like the Federal Reserve Bank. They can't know what he's doing."

"But Easton is the key," Lawrence said.

Antonio nodded slowly.

"You don't know him like I do. The official reason for Easton's visit may be some public announcement. But the real reason . . ." Lawrence drummed on the railing at the foot of the bed. "How do we capture him. That's the real issue."

Nigel said, "We must catch the beggar with his hand in the till."

Elena decided it was time. "I have an idea."

47

I told you before, this can't be the place."

Lawrence was adamant. "Whatever Easton Grey is up to, he won't do it here. If the Bank of England ever discovered he was intent upon wrongdoing, they would shut him down. He might as well set up shop in the lobby of the Federal Reserve."

Nigel said, "My sources were very clear. He's scheduled to sign the articles linking the US commission to the UK's oversight arm at four this afternoon."

Lawrence checked his watch. "It's just gone noon. He could be anywhere. We're surrounded by hedge funds and derivatives operations."

"The dream was very clear," Elena said. "This was where I met the man. Right where we are standing."

"That's sound enough for me," Nigel said.

"I'll gladly plant myself here for the duration," Janine agreed.

"I've got chills," Shirley said.

Lawrence merely sighed.

They stood on a narrow lane in the heart of the City, the financial district within London's original Roman walls. They were surrounded by bankers and their minions dressed by Savile

Row and armed with money. The Bank of England was directly in front of them. The Georgian edifice was surrounded by new steel-and-concrete monuments to financial clout. Even so, the Old Lady of Threadneedle Street, as the Bank of England was known, still had the power to impress.

The day was cloudless and still. The dense city buildings trapped the air and the heat. Their lane was crowded with noontime traffic. Elena reveled in the light and the freedom. She was tired, and the taxi ride had left her shoulder aching. She was glad for how Antonio's arm encircled her waist and the way he offered his support. She molded herself more tightly to him and wished they were alone so she could say how nice it was to let him be strong for her.

Farther down the lane's opposite side, a noisy crowd spilled from a pub. Drinks and food were handed out through the pub's door and open window. In her dream, Elena had been alone. Just her and the man whose face she could not see. She did not remember the sky, or if she had noticed it at all. None of this mattered. The sense of rightness, of *intention*, was so powerful that her entire body vibrated.

Antonio must have sensed her tremors, because he said, "Perhaps we should find a place for you to sit down."

"I'm fine. Really."

Their narrow lane angled slightly to the left from the bank's front entrance. Everyone had insisted on coming. They formed a tight cluster, shielded from the foot traffic by two uniformed officers. Oncoming pedestrians caught sight of the police and veered to the lane's opposite side. Detective Mehan stood just behind her, wedged between them and the pub's crowd. Elena had been waiting for him to ask questions to which she had no answer. But so far he had remained silent.

Sandra said, "Here they come."

The white van with the BBC logo threaded the pedestrian traffic and halted behind the police car. Lawrence said, "Big mistake, calling that man."

Sandra said, "I felt it was important that he came. I felt, I don't know, guided."

Elena said, "The Spirit is working in us all, Lawrence."

Andrew Kerr popped out of the side door before the van stopped rolling and rushed over. "What have I missed?"

Lawrence looked from his wife to Elena and did not speak.

"We are working on guesses and suppositions," Antonio warned the newscaster. "You might have come for nothing."

Sandra said, "But if it is what we think, it could be a major development."

Kerr rubbed his hands together. "From the fireworks display you have put on for me thus far, I'm more than willing to work on a hunch."

While the cameraman took lighting measurements and the sound technician fitted them with body mikes and battery packs, Antonio and Lawrence related what they knew. Andrew Kerr continued to rub his hands together, tight circular motions. When they were done, Kerr said into his mike, "Did you get all they just told me?"

The sound technician had returned to the van. He must have said something through Kerr's earpiece, because the newscaster said, "Are you absolutely certain?"

The sound technician stuck his head out of the van's panel door and glared at Kerr.

The newscaster said to Shirley, "You wouldn't happen to have your husband's letter with you."

"In my purse. Where is your producer?"

"Shadowing another crew who is covering the story I dropped in order to join you." Kerr's smile was as tight as his gaze. "You heard CNN and MSNBC have picked up my piece?"

"Yes."

"It appears the segment will also be aired by the major news networks in Paris and Berlin. This could well transport my career to a totally new level."

Lawrence warned, "It could also be nothing."

"I'll take that chance."

"I just wish we could be more certain."

"Your concern is duly noted. I am here of my own volition. Mrs. Wainwright, could I ask you to stand so the bank is visible behind you? Excellent. Now for the camera, let us run through what we know." Kerr summarized the details of Teddy Wainwright's demise and the security-camera photographs identifying the woman now in custody. He then distilled the connections between the woman and the attacks on Teddy Wainwright and Francesca d'Alba. "Do I have all that correct? Splendid. Now, would you be so kind as to read the appropriate segments of your husband's letter?"

When Shirley was done, Kerr thanked her, then said, "Mr. Ambassador, could I ask you for an opening statement? Another hook, similar to what you gave me in the shelter."

Lawrence said to Antonio, "You do it."

"Indeed, Mr. d'Alba, it would be marvelous if we could use you this time."

Nigel said, "I happen to have the photographs of the woman in custody shadowing Teddy Wainwright and Antonio d'Alba."

"You don't say. Might I use them?"

"I took the liberty of making electronic copies." He handed over a memory stick. "Just make sure the agencies responsible are not mentioned by name."

"Oh, this really is splendid. You must excuse me while I pop back to the van for a look-see. Won't be long." He started to turn away, then stopped and said, "Perhaps I should also do a quick shot with you, Dr. Burroughs."

"I will not be filmed," Elena said. "I am not the story."

"But you are the woman's latest victim—"

"Leave her alone."

Something in Shirley's voice turned them all around. Kerr said, "Yes. Quite. Well, back in a jiff."

When he returned, Andrew Kerr positioned Antonio so the

sunlight lanced across his face and the bank gleamed behind him. Antonio held a resolute calm as he said on camera, "The world of international finance has become little more than a giant casino. It has lost sight of its responsibilities to anchor economic growth. They treat the principles of sound finances as nothing more than advertising jingles. They manipulate the American Dream, while they sit in their towers and watch the common man be crushed by debt and despair. Their only concerns are rising quarterly profits and the bonuses they will take home. They do not foster growth. They destroy it.

"Over the past twenty years, banks have made a concerted effort to transform the legal structure in both the United States and Europe. This allowed the meltdown to happen. People blame the subprime crisis. This is wrong. If it had not been mortgages, it would have been something else. The root problem is still there. The crisis will happen again."

Kerr demanded, "What about the new financial oversight committees?"

"They are being manipulated. They will be as weak and powerless as the laws that were supposed to have protected our economies from this recession. The banks have identified their next source of ready capital. They are attacking. The next meltdown is brewing. It is only a matter of time."

Kerr was into his follow-up questions when Sandra suddenly said, "There he is."

The newscaster showed irritation at being interrupted. "Who?"

"Him. The fixer."

Lawrence jerked off his position by the wall. "Cyril Price? Here?"

Sandra Harwood pointed into the traffic separating them from the bank. "Right over there."

"I don't see . . ."

"The sidewalk to the right of the bank. Wait, he's blocked from view."

A pair of trucks trundled through the intersection fronting the bank. "Perhaps you were mistaken."

"Lawrence, I saw the enemy."

"All right. Don't get . . ." He tensed. "I see him."

Kerr demanded, "Would someone kindly tell me what I'm not seeing?"

"His name is Cyril Price," Lawrence said. "He's a deputy secretary of the Treasury. But the title is nothing. It's a means of giving him official access. He's a fixer. That's someone—"

"I know what a political fixer is. I've brought several of them down in my time." Kerr focused on Sandra Harwood. "You referred to him as the enemy."

Shirley Wainwright said, "He's in one of the photographs with the woman who murdered my husband."

No one had noticed Detective Mehan slipping in tight behind them until he said, "Allegedly murdered."

Cyril Price looked even more unassuming than in his photograph. He was a pudgy fellow whose height was masked by what to Elena looked like rancid baby fat. His cheeks were full enough to push his mouth into a permanent little bow. As he waited to cross the street, he slicked his hair down tight against his skull.

Kerr demanded, "You think he's tied to our Easton Grey?"

"He must be," Nigel said. "They couldn't possibly just happen to be on this side of the Atlantic at precisely the same moment."

"Price is probably part of the baggage train," Lawrence said. "That's the term used for hangers-on who accompany White House officials on an international junket."

Mehan said, "I might just know where that fellow is headed."

"So do I." Nigel turned and signaled. "Gerald."

The bodyguard who had been circling their outer perimeter drifted over. "Sir."

"Scoot around the bank's left, then jink down that alley. Make sure he doesn't slip away."

"Roger that, sir." Gerald did not so much leave as vanish.

"You lot stay here. Is your phone on, Detective?"

"Yes. But I can help—"

"You stay put and stand guard. Allow me to do my bit for the higher cause." Nigel revealed a wolfish hunger. "I was born for the hunt."

Nigel drifted away and became just another gentleman in his fine City suit. Andrew Kerr asked the cameraman, "Did you get that?"

"In the can."

48

The call came ten minutes later and directed them around the bank's other side and onto Fleet Street. Nigel met them outside a pair of fancy gilded doors, his nose twitching with anticipation. Another crowd of rowdy lunchgoers filled the sidewalk. Nigel reported, "The prey has gone to ground upstairs."

"Main hall?"

"That would be my guess."

"All right." Mehan turned to the two officers. "Watch for my signal."

"Should we radio this in, sir?"

"First let's see if there's anything to report." He nodded to Nigel. "Lead the way."

They entered a vast chamber that was far too ornate to be called just another pub. Which was hardly a surprise, as the room had originally contained the Bank of England's law courts. Directly beneath a massive brass and crystal chandelier stood the bar, fashioned from seasoned oak that had once formed the chamber's wainscoting. A huge clock dominated the fourth wall, a mockery of Big Ben. An iron-rimmed balcony ran around three walls. Elena's gaze drifted over the gilded Italianate ceiling and the frescoes and the velvet-draped windows.

Nigel said, "I tracked him upstairs."

"Let's move on then," Mehan said. "Your man is on the rear entrance?"

"Yes."

"Do we need to tell him to stop any who try and slip away?"

Nigel's smile carried a feral edge. "His mate was just released from the hospital yesterday. I doubt seriously any of this lot would care to meet him in an empty alley."

As they started for the stairs, Mehan explained, "The upstairs has several small rooms and one formal chamber that used to serve as the main court. There is a side entrance where prisoners would be brought in. It opens into the alley where Nigel's man is stationed. It has made this chamber a favorite for City types looking for a discreet neutral territory, one where they can come and go unseen."

The sight of uniformed officers and a BBC cameraman silenced the pub. Elena felt the weight of eyes follow them up the stairs and down the side hall. Outside a pair of gilded oak doors stood a pair of suited bodyguards. One of them raised his wrist to his mouth at their approach, but Nigel moved swiftly. He gripped the man's arm, twisted him about, and planted him against the wall.

Mehan cut off his protest by placing his badge next to the man's eyes. "You are not under arrest. Yet." He turned to the nearest police officer. "Restrain him."

"Sir."

Mehan turned to the other guard and said, "Open the doors."

The second guard fished a key from his pocket and turned the lock.

A voice from within said, "I expressly ordered you not to permit any . . ."

The familiar voice died away. Easton Grey rose slowly to his feet as they filed in. His gaze flickered back and forth, growing more astonished with each new discovery. Lawrence. Antonio. Sandra. Elena. A newscaster he had last seen at the BBC studios. Cameraman. Sound tech. Nigel. Shirley. Janine. And the police.

Easton said, "What on earth . . ."

Sandra glared at the man seated by the side wall. "We meet at last."

Cyril Price stared at them in utter horror.

When Detective Mehan started forward, Andrew Kerr planted a firm hand on his arm. "Forgive me, sir, but might I first have a moment?"

"Be swift about it." Mehan said to the nearest officer, "Bar that other door."

"Most kind." Kerr turned to the two men who had entered behind the detective. "Mr. Ambassador, Mr. d'Alba, could you tell me what you see here?"

"Get out of here," Easton demanded.

Lawrence said, "This is a gathering of the forces of doom."

Antonio said, "The people seated to either side of Easton Grey are none other than the chairmen of two of Britain's largest insurance companies. And that gentleman at the table's far end is the chief of derivatives of France's second largest bank."

"Are you certain?"

"Absolutely." Antonio smiled at the man. "I fired him five years ago."

Lawrence continued, "And these two gentlemen head up Luxembourg-based companies used to hide certain activities of major Wall Street banks. They are actually owned by board members. One of their major shareholders is the gentleman you see here at the head of the table."

"Easton Grey."

"None other."

Grey stormed, "This is a private meeting!"

Kerr smiled at the gentleman. He then asked Lawrence, "So what do you suppose is the basis for this meeting?"

Antonio said, "You heard Teddy Wainwright's warning. The

banks intend to siphon off cash from the world's insurance companies and feed it to their derivatives traders. They will also bundle the risk and use it to develop what are known as sophisticated debt instruments. What you see here is another global meltdown in the making."

Kerr said, "All this done with the approval and direct participation of the man supposedly responsible for overseeing America's banks."

"This is *outrageous*!" Easton Grey's voice shook as violently as his hands. "I will have you arrested for *slander*!"

"You are certainly free to level whatever charges you wish, sir."

Mehan took that as his cue. "In the meantime, Cyril Price, you are hereby rendered into custody on suspicion of colluding in the assault on Antonio d'Alba, Lawrence Harwood, and Dr. Elena Burroughs. Officer, you may search and cuff the gentleman."

49

THE FOLLOWING FRIDAY

They were unable to leave England for another week. The furor surrounding the events continued to mount. Confronted with the photographs linking him to the female assailant, Cyril Price cracked like a chubby nut. In exchange for leniency, he spilled and spilled and spilled some more.

Easton Grey's home office contained a safe. Despite his lawyer's most valiant efforts, a writ was served and the safe opened. In it was Elena's missing book of dreams.

As Elena walked through Heathrow's Terminal Five, headlines shouted at her from every newsstand they passed. Easton Grey had been fired from both his Washington position and his Wall Street boards. He was free on bail of fifty million dollars, while Brussels argued with London and Washington over who could try him first.

When they were settled into the BA flight for Rome, a flight attendant offered them a *Financial Times*. Lawrence and Sandra Harwood's photograph dominated the front page, as the President of the United States formally welcomed Lawrence back to the same post he had been fired from.

In exchange for accepting the appointment a second time,

Lawrence had insisted on veto power over every other member of the commission. In the newspaper interview, Lawrence stated that he was not after allies. Dissenting voices were essential to good governance. What he wanted was honesty and a focus on the people and the nation they had been appointed to serve.

Antonio said, "Thank you for making this trip with me."

"I'm the one who should be thanking you," Elena said.

The book of dreams had been too large to be treated as simple carry-on luggage, so Antonio had bought a third seat. The book was belted into the seat next to Elena, bound inside a blanket and this inside a wide valise of parachute silk. Because of the gold on the pages, they had been required to open it for the airport security detail. Elena touched the case as the plane powered down the runway. She shivered.

"Something wrong?"

"Everything's fine."

"Your shoulder is hurting?"

"No. It's not that." She hesitated, then confessed, "I feel like there's an energy pulsating from the book. Like I'm being drawn toward another event."

Antonio gave a genuine moan. "Please, not yet."

"I completely agree." She looked at the case. "Maybe we should have left this for another time."

"I asked, they said yes, they said now. It's best to move while they are interested, no?"

Antonio had spoken with allies within the Vatican, who had said they would be delighted to have their finest artists in calligraphy help to duplicate the book. Recovery of the stolen book did not change the need to have a newer version that could be used on a daily basis. The Vatican specialists had begged for a chance to see the book and meet the person into whose care the book had been given.

Antonio said, "Brussels called."

"When?"

"Last night. They have offered me the position of chairman. Again."

Elena started to ask why he had waited this long to tell her. But his forehead was creased in the manner that signaled genuine distress. "What's the matter?"

"I am afraid."

She reached over and took his hand.

"To believe we can actually defy such powerful and entrenched forces, I fear it is a triumph of optimism over reality."

Elena thought of all he had gone through. The murder of his beloved wife, so they could publicly cripple this good man. The pleasure they had taken from watching him retreat into obscurity. She said, "I know what Francesca would say."

Antonio's head turned slowly toward her.

"I know because I share her love for a truly wonderful man." Elena smiled. "She would say it is time to stand and defy them. It is time to bring them down."

A trio of dark-suited guards met them planeside and ushered them into a private chamber where a customs officer stamped their passports and officially welcomed them to Rome. They were taken directly to a sedan with little Vatican flags fluttering from the hood. When their luggage was stowed in the trunk, the car lumbered away, made heavy by its bulletproof shielding. Elena observed the Italian countryside through overthick glass and wondered if she would ever grow accustomed to the trappings of modern power.

The Vatican glowed in the sunset like an empire beyond the reach of time. They were ushered through a pair of massive gates manned by Swiss guards in full regalia. More guards snapped to attention as they were greeted by berobed officials. One of them, wearing the crimson robes of power, was Cardinal Carlo Brindisi. "My dear Dr. Burroughs, what a delight it is to meet with you again." He turned his benevolent smile on Antonio.

"And to find you in such wonderful company. I cannot tell you how happy this makes me."

"Hello, old friend," Antonio said.

"Come, come. My specialists are so excited that they have not slept or eaten for days."

Brindisi led them into a main audience hall. A cluster of seven monks, identified as Aramaic historians and calligraphers, oohed and aahed over the book. They asked questions until Antonio finally declared that the rest would have to wait until the next day.

But as they were readying to depart, Brindisi's phone rang. He turned away, murmured a few words, then turned back and said, "Dr. Burroughs, there is someone who would very much like to have a word."

"Can it wait?"

"Unfortunately, this official is scheduled to depart for South America tomorrow."

"I really am very tired."

Antonio said, "She is still recovering from a serious accident."

"I am well aware of the recent attack on Dr. Burroughs." Brindisi carried himself with calm authority. "I would not ask this of you if it were not rather important."

"Oh, all right."

"Thank you. This way." But when Antonio started to follow, the church official held up his hand. "I'm sorry, my friend. Only Dr. Burroughs. You may wait here with the book, if you please."

Brindisi led her up a flight of stairs and down an impossibly long hallway. She would have complained about the trek, but her attention was captured by the artwork and the ancient surroundings. She followed him across an interior courtyard filled with evening light and birdsong and blooming trees, then back into yet another chamber, this one peaked like a chapel and over a hundred paces long. Then down another hallway, which ended at a narrow oaken door of impossible age.

Brindisi smiled as he opened the door and said, "I shall await you here."

It was only when she passed through the doorway did she realize she was inside the Sistine Chapel.

She gawked at the ceiling she had before only seen in photographs. Directly overhead, the hand of God reached forward, offering the brilliant touch of life to Adam. The wings of angels holding Adam aloft seemed to beat softly in the flickering candlelight.

Then she saw that she was not alone.

Seated upon a bench midway down the chapel's side wall was a man. He was not so much old as cloaked in two thousand years of heritage and authority. He smiled at her approach, but he neither rose nor spoke until she settled into the seat beside him.

In softly accented English, the man said, "I am having the most terrible dreams."

ABOUT THE AUTHOR

Davis Bunn is the author of numerous national bestsellers in genres spanning historical sagas, contemporary thrillers, and inspirational gift books. He has received widespread critical acclaim, including three Christy Awards for excellence in fiction, and his books have sold more than six million copies in sixteen languages. He and his wife, Isabella, are affiliated with the University of Oxford, where Davis serves as writer in residence at Regent's Park College. He lectures internationally on the craft of writing.

READING GROUP GUIDE

Discussion Questions

1. Elena's experiences suggest that following God's lead takes her in a very different direction from what she had expected. Do you see God's lead as offering an easier road?

2. Do you hold certain assumptions about receiving a spiritual gift? Are these images based on a desire to do God's will, or your own desire to receive acclaim and ease?

3. Elena realizes that she may have had a hand in holding herself back from true healing. She comes to see that her present perspective, how she defines herself, is based in part on her sorrow. To give this up and accept full healing means losing a connection to her deceased husband. And yet, until she relinquishes this hold, she cannot accept a vision of what future God might have in store. Can you find a parallel in your own life, where holding on to some less than positive or healing perspective might be keeping you from what you say you want, or what God wants for you?

4. In this story, several characters experience what at the time appear to be monumental setbacks. And yet these same events prove to be great leaps forward, both for them personally and for their causes. Can you recall a time when what first seemed to be a defeat actually became a lifetime triumph? Can you look back now and see God's hand at work in these experiences?

5. In her encounter group, Elena urges the participants to write down the request they are asking of God. One member of the group confesses later that this proved vital. Otherwise he would have risked forgetting the problem and its solution by simply moving on to the next unresolved issue. Have you ever asked. God for aid, then neglected to recognize his hand at work in your life? Have you failed to thank him for a gift like this? Why do you think this happened? Do you find it hard to acknowledge God's power at work in your life?

6. The basis for Elena's gift is a series of meditations on the Lord's Prayer. Have you ever spent time examining this prayer? If not, do you feel this might be an enriching experience, one you should take on? If so, have you experienced any particular gift of the Spirit that you would like to share?

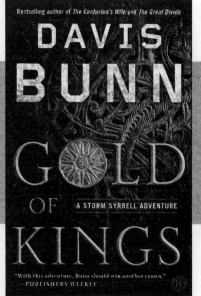

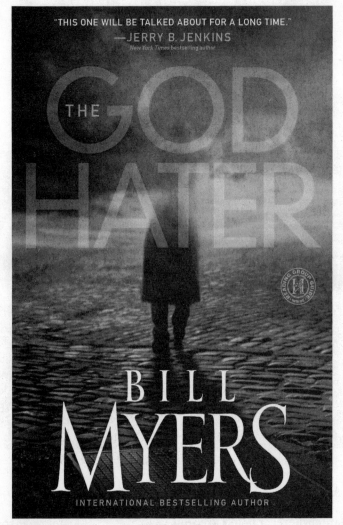

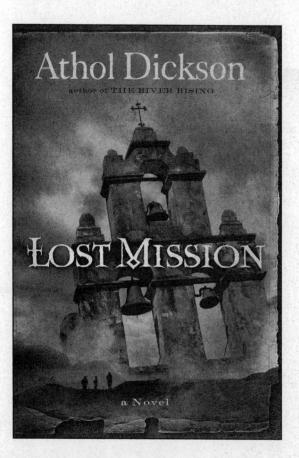